Praise for *Like a Bird*

"*Like a Bird* is a story about survival and healing. Like a melancholy song, this novel is both intimate and sincere."

—NPR

One of **BuzzFeed**'s New Books You Won't Want to Put Down: "Written with an undercurrent of anger, the novel offers a biting social commentary on wealthy, educated elites."

"With the lessons it holds on survival and strength, *Like a Bird* could be set anywhere; it could be a memoir, or it could be fiction; it could be about any person attempting to start anew. And that's where Róisín makes her mark as a writer, whether it's in *Like a Bird*, or in her book of poems *How to Cure a Ghost* released last year. She's able to communicate eternal, relatable truths through her characters that make you feel as if she's writing your life."

—Meghna Rao, Electric Literature

"Well-paced and hopeful, this stirring work will resonate with those interested in stories of young women breaking free of oppression and trauma."

—Publishers Weekly

"Fariha Róisín's novel sings of building joy within sorrow and spins a gossamer reverie that clings to the consciousness... With its profound testaments to the love of found families and the courage involved in daring to open a cracked heart, Like a Bird is an unforgettable novel."

—Foreword Reviews

"*Like A Bird* is such a generous text, teeming with layered and beautifully living characters. A flaw of so much book praise is the quest to make every book universal. This book sings, specifically, to a people, while leaving the door open wide enough for anyone else to walk through."

—Hanif Abdurraqib, bestselling author of *They Can't Kill Us Until They Kill Us* and *A Little Devil in America*

AN UNNAMED PRESS BOOK

www.unnamedpress.com

Unnamed Press, and the colophon, are registered trademarks of Unnamed
Media LLC.

Trade Paperback ISBN: 978-1-951213-44-2
Hardcover ISBN: 978-1-951213-09-1
eISBN: 978-1-951213-10-7

Library of Congress Control Number: 2020941728

Designed and Typeset by Jaya Nicely

Manufactured in the United States of America by Versa Press, inc.

Distributed by Publishers Group West

First Edition

Like a Bird

a novel

Fariha Róisín

The Unnamed Press
Los Angeles, CA

To every survivor. I wrote this for us.

The way of love is not
a subtle argument.

The door there
is devastation.

Birds make great sky-circles
of their freedom.
How do they learn it?

They fall, and falling,
they're given wings.
—Rumi

I don't imagine your death
but it is here, setting my hands on fire.
—Ilya Kaminsky

What I most regretted were my silences.
Of what had I *ever* been afraid?
—Audre Lorde

Like a Bird

1.

To be a person was a great mystery to me; even at a young age I felt heavy with the weight of dissatisfaction. Like a frog in warming water, I had spent much of my early years feeling as if I were slowly simmering toward my own demise. As if I were sedately, on a low setting, boiling to death. And yet, I was nothing if not quietly ambitious. I didn't know how to locate my compass, but I knew I had one; looking back, maybe that's what eventually saved me. My desperation to survive, even if I didn't know if I really could.

Because, since childhood, forlorn and fast-eyed, the most abstract of all emotions to me was happiness. How did one get it? I wanted to own it, to have it in my possession, beaming out, because I, Taylia (*Tay-lee-uh*) Chatterjee (*Cha-taar-gee*), had never been happy. It's something that I had never fully understood, either, as I had two parents who hated themselves and, together, passed down their own qualities of self-loathing on to me.

2.

Our building jutted out with perfectly aligned alabaster columns that stood like ivory trunks, recalling the miniature jewel-encrypted elephants Baba brought back from India once. The orange blossoms were arranged neatly in the yard, shaping the crisp exterior. The whiteness of our home, a beaming Taj Mahal on the Upper West Side, was gaudy. Like the way immigrants who desperately want to be white were all Gap-wearing and "Howdy," all Wonder bread and capitalism, incapable of knowing who they really were, like my father and his feelings of inadequacy, a constant lump in his throat. This is what it meant to assimilate.

Baba was a closeted law-abiding coconut. I always assumed that Indians, to Baba, were mosquito-ravaged infidels. But I'd see him sometimes miss the motherland. I would catch him lingering before the ghee at the supermarket, or taking a second glance at the DVD section dedicated to Bollywood films in a Blockbuster we used to frequent. I once overheard him telling Mama that he could still taste the faint sulfite burning in the back of his throat, the memory of his tonsils brushing against the arid heat of dry cinnamon. India was home—but the United States was the future, his star-spangled American dream. But it was complicated; I knew his feelings for America, for white people, were confused. I could see how he knew he was in a country of wolves, but I wondered if he believed in a real escape or just an imagined one.

Mama was an American Jew, Ivy League educated, and a woebegone liberal fighting for immigrant rights at dinner parties, where her faux-Marxist friends digested full-bodied côtes du rhônes and discussed the lack of American health care and Philip Roth. Her face was intoxicating, and her hair was either worn in twisted milkmaid braids or free-flowing and thick, bouncing silently as she sang. Her voice was rapturous and silky, rounding r's like a Canadian. My sister, Alyssa, was such a portrait of our mother, right down to the flushed cheeks, easily reddened to a perfect blush.

My parents met accidentally, inside a bodega. She was buying Tylenol for an impending cold; her face pale, a trickle of slime slowly oozing through her nasal cavity, she smiled at the handsome Indian as he slid past her to buy a soda. His voice had a transatlantic twang, the charm of a man who was begging to be taken seriously. "I love pop," he said, the incongruence of *pop* striking a strange subtlety, Mama recalled. He paid, gulping down his purchased goods. Perhaps fevered by the secret twenty-three flavors of Dr Pepper, they began talking. She explained her flu-like symptoms, and Baba commiserated, suggesting a concoction of lemon, honey, garlic, and ginger instead of pills. *A naturalist with a love for soda,* thought Mama, as she focused on the peach-fuzz beard Baba had managed to grow, paired with the Dr Pepper that dribbled at the corner of his lip. She decided right then and there that she liked him, and that was that.

They were both students at Columbia: Mama, an art history major; Baba, prelaw. In her mind, Mama had it figured out. The '80s, like the few decades before it, were about experimentation, and he, her soon-to-be husband, was the most exciting and masculine thing she had ever laid eyes on. Their blooming love was inevitable, their future impossibly quaint. They were smart, they were beautiful, and they were an aberration to tradition.

In the months before their marriage, she scoured his dorm for *Playboy*s and dirt. She found nothing, Baba was clean. Avoiding all things that could possibly distract him from his wholesome American future, he sublimated his desire for pussy by eating ice-cream sandwiches and slurping Popsicles, growing fond of encyclopedias, old almanacs, and the tattered pages of American classics. Naturally suspicious of narrative literature (but equally committed to safeguarding his pop-cultural knowledge), he resigned himself to mulling over the tomes of *Moby-Dick* and *The Adventures of Huckleberry Finn*—a preventative measure for the off chance he was ever quizzed on what it meant to be a true American, comme Melville, Hawthorne, and the rest.

Like many white girls, even Jewish ones, Mama wanted to cause her Ashkenazi parents deep distress. She watched *Guess Who's Coming to Dinner* with a sadistic reverie and preached to her friends that the racial divide was the true abomination in American society. Ignorant to the fact that her white-girl utopian idealism was a privilege in and of itself, she considered herself a savior and thought her protests were enough, an Angela Davis type wanting to be the target of police, not knowing that pretty white redheads were rarely seen in handcuffs. But she tried. And she fought. And she married Baba.

3.

Alyssa and I enjoyed competing against each other, just like any two sisters would. We constantly tried to best the other, usually in the form of proving to our father that we were something, *anything.* As a wannabe intellectual, my heart insisted on his approval, though it was hardly ever won. I related to him, I even looked more like him and felt Indian in a way Alyssa didn't. So, I guess you could say my love for him was more complex. Or maybe being Indian gave me a sense of purpose, in a way, that it didn't give Alyssa. For me, it became my very own lighthouse: a reflection of my being, or the possibility of who I could be and what I could become. It gave me a reference.

Warm nights always ignited conversation at the Chatterjee residence. Monomaniacal by nature, Baba was a militant grammarian, obsessively monitoring our usage and syntax, turning it into a game. His English had an archaic diligence birthed from a deep fascination with etymology. "What does *nadir* mean? And what is its direct antonym?"

Alyssa and I grew fond of dictionaries.

"It means 'the lowest point of any given thing,'" I would say, quickly looking at Alyssa as a buffer. "The antonym is *zenith.*"

I would usually stay focused on her, my hands sticky with perspiration, and as if through a chain reaction, she'd turn to watch our father. If we were right, he would sometimes nod, replying with "good." More often than not, he would simply say nothing. If we were wrong, he would clear his throat with a *hmm,* dismissing us entirely.

Baba wasn't cold, he was austere. He never learned the beauty or value of gesture, of kind words. Mama would say it was because men from India were socialized in such ways, but I disagreed. Baba was different. His austerity was rooted in a disinterest in small talk. He hated hyperbole and despised social niceties—he deemed them unnecessary. "There's nothing wrong with silence," he would say, muttering like a croaky parrot.

Through the years, his reluctance to show affection became manageable; it was accepted as one of his many idiosyncrasies. In some ways, I almost admired it. Still, I yearned to see a glimmer of familiarity shine through his face whenever I answered correctly. That look that would speak: *Good, I have taught them well.*

Alyssa, next to me, was a complete juxtaposition. People were drawn to her beauty and energy, and for that I was always jealous. In those days, I couldn't finish a glass of water without sighing. My mind, filled with deliberations, pulled at my interiors like a harness. There was a restlessness inside me, gnawing to be sated. I was no good at it. I wanted to be like her, and it crept through me like a disease. I sometimes felt like I was stalking her, obsessed with her languid, nymphlike mannerisms; with her face, the way her skin was pucker-free, not a pore in sight, dewy like dulce de leche. She was like Rani Mukerji in *Kuch Kuch Hota Hai*: divine, light eyed (almost), and brown haired. Every girl at every family gathering *ever* wanted to be like her, inching toward her like she was Mother Mary. Her tiny waist in her lehenga, the way she made it cute that she didn't hardly know any Bengali. All the girls fawned, and all the boys watched with wide eyes.

We sat at the dinner table, Alyssa groaning with despair about something school related, and our parents (especially Mama) gathered around her like lovers from commedia dell'arte. We were in our early teens, when Alyssa still had the verve, the steeped innocence, that she wielded so mysteriously. I remember the moon being swollen, like a wheel of cheese—*when the moon hits your eye like a big pizza pie*—a big hunk of brie, peering in and hitting us at the dining room table. The bones of the fish we ate glistened on our plates, and the mashed sweet potato that I abandoned still on mine, golden under the moon's hues.

"Ms. O'Neil is such a *bitch*, though, Ma!" She had grown cocky, swearing more to see how much she could get away with.

"Lyse, please..."

"It's true—Tay, back me up!"

Sometimes, I felt cuckolded by my sister. Drawn into her dance. I surrendered. "I mean... she's annoying, but she's all right."

"Tay. Don't... She's a goddamn paleolithic cr-creature."

"Lyse, don't talk about women like that."

"Maaaaa, you're not listening to me! I'm not talking about women any kinda way, I'm jus' saying that she's annoying as fu—!" She clicked her tongue to fill the sound of *fuck*.

Mama laughed, defusing Alyssa's strange current, the way, even when she was whining, she made you feel like she was revealing an important secret only *to you*. That was Lyse's strongest skill: her ability to feign intimacy. The two of them went about whispering, and I got up to clear the mood, returning to my own internal dance, where I was paid attention to.

Baba was prone to smoking a fat, dark cigar at the dining table after dinner, ashing into a beautiful crystal midcentury modern ashtray that Mama bought in an estate sale. He looked so out of place, a Brown, skinny Indian smoking a thick knob, resembling anything other than a Mob boss. Certainly not Tony Soprano, whom he was not-so-secretly emulating, given his recent and uncharacteristic obsession with *The Sopranos*. I returned to the table, sitting opposite him, lost in my thoughts about Ms. O'Neil, a pretty white woman who looked like a nun. She had introduced me to Toni Morrison, and I felt indebted to her for that. I related so much to Pecola, the protagonist of *The Bluest Eye*. As I watched Alyssa in full form, heady with confidence, I thought of how odd it was that two girls with the same parents, one white and the other Brown, could feel so differently about existing in this world. How that impacted their cellular constructs in such a way that navigating life was so distinctly dissimilar. I thought of how much I longed to be seen and how I could count the people who had made me feel special on one hand.

Alyssa was beautiful in a way I'd never been, fair skinned and rapturous, the way that girls you can't place are normally exotified. The light-eyed/light-skinned cocktail. I was darker skinned and darker eyed, which made all the difference. Baba would talk about Alyssa like a specimen of grand genetics—"An almost Kashmiri!" he'd say, slightly proud. A rare compliment from a Hindu Indian, and the absence of one directed at me hit like a flood. Today I was merely observing the grace that Alyssa exuded, Mama fully locked in to her story like an avid audience member, and I felt the darkness in my center of not being enough, even for my own family.

After her story about Ms. O'Neil, we sat still, lapsed into the night's quiet fortress. The silence beckoning us into our separate slumbers. Nobody said another word, as we all in unison stood to help Mama clean up. That night even Baba helped.

4.

I covered the sadness of being invisible to my family in many ways. I treated my ability to hide and remain unseen like a sport. Besides, I told myself, I hated that the glare of attention made my body convulse in shame and nervousness, which made it impossible to casually interact with people. So, to avoid such atrocities, I'd blanch myself with unappeal, never wearing makeup, allowing my figure to be subsumed by toting a massive JanSport backpack at all times. Longish loungewear that Mama bought me from Bloomingdale's was my preferred method of clothing. I liked the way a basic smock could stretch and sling over my body like a compact hammock, erasing my physicality that had become such a burden.

Mama had a friend named Zeina. She was Mama's closest friend—the isomorphic auntie, an Eastern beauty—who was obsessed with telling me that I *could* be beautiful if only I didn't crouch all the time, frown all the time—if only, *only*, I smiled more. But I was disgusted by my own presence, and I wasn't sure how to cope while being in somebody else's. I had been whipped into thinking a certain way, and I was forsaken into that loneliness for what felt like an eternity. The pain festered in volumes.

Herself Pakistani, Zeina had married an Ashkenazi doctor. She and Mama had met at Columbia, after Mama had admired her emerald-green peacoat. Zeina still wore it years later, the coat the color of fresh-packed succulents, with big floating arms and a hefty bow at the neck.

Mama was obsessed with Zeina's beauty: her cowlicked eyeliner, the pale peach lipstick she'd wear—Mama never missed an opportunity to make us acutely aware of the power such beauty possessed. Of how Zeina would always have the best velvet bell-bottoms, curving over her ass, flowering out after her calves. Or her strappy sandals, matched with tailored white blazers. She was like Bianca Jagger, making Mama exotic by mere association. Once, recalling with embarrassment, Mama confessed her reliance on Pond's Cold Cream, Elizabeth Arden, and tacky drugstore perfumes—until she met Zeina, "the cultured one."

"I made your mother cool, you know!" Zeina had once told Alyssa and me as she obliterated a hamburger in just a few bites (after dressing it with half a jar of Dijon mustard).

I watched Zeina laugh, her face youthful, eyes brightly amused. She had a voice that was sweet and faraway, the timbre of the notes carrying through the house like diffractions of a lighthouse. She drank her cosmopolitans without spilling a drop, a clove cigarette or a Camel lodged between her right index and forefinger as she held the glass by its stem. She'd suggest polo, sudoku parties, and wear pantsuits with deep bare backs. Her hair was short like Mia Farrow's in the summer, then long and black like Cher's in the '70s just in time for fall. She was as elegant as a flamingo and flamboyant in the way Pakistani aunties are, vivacious, lively, and rapturous.

She owned an eponymous boutique in the Lower East Side, consigning the coolest brands from Sweden and Denmark, imprinting her fashionable quirks on the fabric of American style. She encouraged Lyse and me to come down for a visit and to bring our friends. Lyse would sometimes go. She even worked for her one summer as an intern. I passed by but never went in. Everything looked magical, if heaven was furnished with ergonomic lounges and heavy, wall-sized art. Every edge of Zeina's body smelled fragrant, as if wrapped in a robe of smoke and coriander. When I walked past, I could smell her from the curb, too.

One afternoon Zeina was over for tea, and her and Mama's voices reverberated through the dining room and into the rest of the apartment. It was Mama's favorite place to sit, overlooking the vines of ivy that laced the old walls of our back fence, the daffodils abloom with tiny petals of yellow.

"How's Alyssa?"

"Oh, she's great." Mama's voice was bursting with pride. "Wait, did I tell you she has a boyfriend?"

"No, you didn't! I can't wait to meet him. I bet he's handsome, or I hope he is, because she's so beautiful!"

The way in which Zeina said "she's so beautiful" was a fact, a summation. I could sense my mother's face light up from the kitchen.

"Oh, he's great. Ryan. He goes to the Dwight School, too. Plus he's Black."

Mama loved telling people this.

"Have you met him yet?"

"I haven't met him! It's agonizing! But she's been telling me about him... He sounds kind of perfect for her," my mother almost screamed.

They both laughed. "Kathryn, please!"

"Ugh, you know they always say this, but it's true—kids really grow up so fast, *too* fast."

Zeina started humming and laughing, maybe to dissolve the momentary sadness that lingered in my mother's voice. I sat on the staircase, listening, feeling the sudden grief usurp me.

"God, I don't know what I'll do when she leaves."

Mama loved art. An art history major, she'd take us to exhibits or on day trips to MoMA. I enjoyed the great expanse of museums and art galleries. The way people, full with ideas, interacted in galleries was intoxicating, gathered in reverent luminosity over the Carrie Mae Weemses and Kerry James Marshalls. Their measured footsteps like sleepwalkers'.

One time at the Brooklyn Museum, Mama looked at a line portrait by Kiki Smith and stated with an insipid arrogance (classically snooty, a perfect New Yorker), "All portraits of people are just portraits of Mona Lisa." Alyssa and I stood behind her, snorting with the infiniteness you experience when you're young—a rampant sense of possibility, especially in those diurnal art settings where rogue thoughts were fostered and encouraged. Well, at least from snooty, of-a-certain-class white women.

Mama introduced us to artists like Ryan Trecartin and Ryan McGinley, proving to us teens that art could be created from angst. They felt like rare moments when she was directing us, providing Alyssa and me with the tools for creation. I loved McGinley and Trecartin because sin attracted me. The sin of being alive, with the gangly bodies of McGinley's world, ripe like fruit, nudes that were supple and grotesquely white; with Trecartin's combustive colors, the agonizing breadth of his Sodom-and-Gomorrah-like panels. I was consumed by these things that I never had access to—that's when I felt most alive. When I could see the possibility of what was outside of myself.

On a Saturday afternoon we went to Walter de Maria's *Earth Room*. It was a terrifying place, the darkness of the soil contrasting against the lightness of the white, the sterility of the walls stark against the hard-packed earth, 140 tons of it. It made me feel small, as if I were standing at the edge of the ocean. In the stillness of that moment I thought of death. I thought of my body, sunken into the soil, in the very depths of being *no more*. Mama turned to me, witnessing the color drain from my face. Soon after, we walked out.

"What did you think, T?"

I couldn't stop thinking about being underground, in a casket, locked beneath the soil with no hope of coming out. I wanted to tell her that I felt Dadi-ma, my father's dead mother, deep in my chest, giving me a sign—ghosts, ghosts, ghosts, swishing through me like carp, guileless in a shallow pond. But, instead, I murmured inaudibly, pushing those imaginations as far from myself as I could.

We stopped for lunch at Mama's favorite restaurant, Souen (she liked it because she heard Fran Lebowitz ate there, too), and as I began to emerge from the dark place I had been, something shifted. Suddenly, a spirit of the dead began to materialize right in front of me. Mama and Lyse sat across from me, chatting about nothing, and I just sat, dumbfounded, before turning to the figure who had appeared to my right. Her neck was wrinkled, and she was wearing a shadha saree. Dadi-ma was sitting at the table. I could see her body moving like a ripple of water, and I could feel her hazy warmth surround me as I stared at the empty chair next to mine. Mama, in an attempt to break me from my daze, reiterated her question regarding my thoughts on the exhibit.

I breathed: "It felt like death."

"Do you want to explain 'it felt like death'?" She said it with air quotes, exaggerating the last bit through her teeth.

I shook my head.

She scowled, immediately turning to Alyssa. "How about you?"

Alyssa went on a tangent, but at a distance of a thousand miles away. I sat transfixed on Dadi-ma. Her moon-shaped smile lingering for just a moment, and then she was gone. I felt calmer, and suddenly, words didn't matter so much.

Alyssa would often recite Austen—"I declare after all there is no enjoyment like reading! How much sooner one tires of anything than of a book!"—her favorite *Pride and Prejudice* bit to whip out at times of social lethargy. Her faux-English accent, liquid and charming, wooed our guests and her friends; waxing lyrical of nineteenth-century realism, she'd educate us on Austen's history. "She suffered from Addison's disease, just like JFK! Did you know?" I didn't know. "She never married. Can you imagine never marrying, T?" I definitely could.

When she was young, my sister's waking life was spent dreaming of the moors and green pastures, the idyll of bluish clouds and grand Gothic castles of Great Britain. I'd sometimes find her watching BBC renditions of Austen on her MacBook, paused on swathes of fine linen (or was it silk?) and Elizabeth Bennet pondering the caustic nature of Mr. Darcy.

Her book collection told a story in and of itself: a candy-cane-pink copy of Nabokov's *Lolita* sat perched on the middle shelf, where everyone could see. Every young neo-feminist needed to understand the complexities of infantile sexual desire and the phenomenology of disgraceful, horny old men. She collected the classics, from a 1958 edition of *1984* to a battered copy of *Brave New World*. Books excited her, because there in the pages—indelible in blue—would be her distinctive scrawl, paragraphs blotted with ink and peppered with annotations. I had once picked up a copy of *Wuthering Heights* and read her inscriptions:

> *To love is to hurt... to sacrifice... to persevere for the other and for your own happiness. Torment is desirable and often required in order to fully appreciate life and love.*

She was such a Scorpio.

5.

I met Simon for the first time at maybe nine or ten. He was a couple of years older than Alyssa and me. It was at a family gathering in the fall. I remember because the air in New York is different in the fall—there's a crispness to the pavement, the sun-bleached sidewalks are no longer glistening with wavy heat. We enter a new realm of the psyche in the fall, fatigue setting in for the impending winter.

Alyssa seemed overly familiar with Simon. They always happened to find themselves next to each other at parties, and when she was near him, she'd oscillate a fold of hair to one side of her head, massaging the tendrils with the tips of her fingers as she smiled at him. Constantly. I knew this because I watched them both. Not in a creepy way, but out of curiosity and, later, with envy. Most boys would leave the girls behind, playing video games, gossiping in some unsuspecting bedroom, but I always noticed that Simon lingered. He talked to the mothers, welcoming their tedious questions about school, life, and so on, thoroughly enjoying how they fawned over him. And then, after a certain point, he always found Alyssa.

I wondered what he was like in his locked room, when he wasn't focused on keeping up appearances. His mind seemed brilliant but dark. I always got the sense that Simon would have loved to watch a beautiful house burn down in a magical, haunting way. Even still, I felt myself be open with him. I wanted him to decide that I was worth looking at, like how I imagined some people look at wolvish dogs: boldly, without thinking it might eat you—or maybe, more accurately, in spite of the thought.

Simon's father, Rakesh, wore thick-framed black Ray-Bans—the same style I'd see the politicians on billboards back in India wear. He was a handsome Indian, like Baba. He seemed impatient, the veins at his temple pulsating like the lines of a Matisse. We would see him occasionally, the once-upon-a-time Marxist now head neurologist at the Mount Sinai Hospital in East Harlem. As an avid walker, every working day he would march with diligence through the rain and mud, under the caved arches of Central Park. Alyssa and I would sometimes watch him, gossiping freely, as he vigorously walked past the edge of our block with a navy umbrella in one hand, always decked in pin-striped pants and crisp white shirts treated with Reckitt's Crown Blue. I once overheard that he had experienced racism similar to Baba. Patients telling him (to his face!) that they wanted the "best guy for the job," when what they really meant was "Get me someone white, or get me outta here!" Even still, he desperately wanted to be accepted by white people.

"Adi, please." Rakesh rocked his head back and forth. "Not this again."

"You can't possibly believe there's any oil in Iraq, eh."

"I don't have to know. That's not my job—"

"You don't think it's a ploy?"

"Ploy for whom*st*, old friend?"

"Eesh." Baba sat back on his tanned leather recliner and took a puff of his cigar, disappointed.

I overheard them debating ideology one afternoon, their voices carrying through the house.

From time to time the whole family would come over, Simon sidling behind his parents. His mother, Marissa, was a white woman type from Georgia, fragile and southern. She was small and mousy, kind but strange, and always slightly removed from the conversation. She had none of the personality that Mama had, who wore her Eileen Fisher jumpsuits and Ralph Lauren all whites next to Marissa, always in dowdy, almost hideous Chanel.

Simon was an only child and wore it with pride, as if it were an achievement. Puckering like broody men do, a semi–"blue steel," he'd sit with his parents, scanning our home like a thief. Alyssa would sometimes lock eyes with him, giggling dramatically. What they'd discuss in those half glances I'd never know. But they could never be anything more than silly flirts, because by then Alyssa was dating Ryan.

Ryan was of the "right class" and of the "right privilege," and even though he was Black (both Mama and Baba would never be outwardly racist, but instead just make a lot of racist assumptions), he looked implacable, like Alyssa, and therefore was just right. I'd watch as Mama and Alyssa would talk in secret: their hushed tones as Alyssa dried the plates that Mama washed; the excited whispers as Mama watered her gardenias and Alyssa stood dramatically, her animated hands moving fast as she relayed life and love in drastic gyration. I liked how Ryan treated Alyssa, the way he'd linger like a puppy, smiling and chatting or listening with admiration. I wanted someone to look at me like that, like I was wanted.

Any night was a good time for Baba to whip out his tin of cigars and his amber bottle of single malt Scotch. I'd watch as he would sit in his leather beast of an armchair, a generous sliver of Laphroaig perched in his left hand. He liked Ryan, so he would engage with him. In many ways, Baba was a male cliché: he loved talking about politics and economics, but wouldn't readily discuss either with Alyssa and me. In his mind, they were gendered topics—I guess our pussies couldn't handle it. I resented him for his sometimes subaltern weaknesses—you know, where they exaggerated gender like the bubonic plague. I always felt as if Baba fancied a boy and was secretly upset when both of his children turned out to be girls, something he took out subconsciously on me. Alyssa could be overlooked because she was the firstborn. But me? I was the familial force majeure. I was an immediate failure.

Ryan was sweet but not as charming as Alyssa. He always came to our home bearing gifts. Sometimes it was a geographically bright bottle of sauvignon blanc that his father had brought back on a business trip; other times it was a bouquet from the flower shop Mama loved on Amsterdam Avenue. We had a great big dining room that housed a table Mama had spent countless hours searching for, heavy and glazed with promises. Mama would arrange our meal on one-of-a-kind plates from a ceramicist near our summer home in the Catskills. She had two sets of dinnerware, one for her fancy (rude) Waspy neighbors, the other for herself that she used with us and people like Zeina and her husband, Karl, who had taste.

One night we sat down and began eating, and as usual, Mama started asking questions. She was a self-proclaimed cool mom, despicably nosy but in the most well-meaning way. "So what do you know about Simon, Ryan?"

"Simon?" Ryan asked, a look of surprise flooding his face.

At that exact moment I could feel Alyssa's body decelerate, her heart beating palpably slower. My body suddenly mirrored hers, tense in its inquisitiveness.

"You know, Simon..." It was a statement, as if Simon were like Prince or Madonna.

"Oh, Simon Sharma?" Ryan laughed. He knew Simon through school, both Dwight School seniors. "Oh man, I hear..."

He stopped midsentence and looked at my mother, her face smiling, her red hair in a loose braid.

"...oh, I dunno." He shrugged.

Mama looked disappointed.

"Why do you ask?" This time it was Alyssa. There was often unsaid communication between the two of them, but tonight I watched her gape at Mama and find nothing.

"I don't know, he's such an interesting character."

Ryan seemed unconvinced. "Frankly, Simon is a little obnoxious."

Alyssa froze again. I could feel the energy between us shift, the force field I had attuned myself to. Her index finger slowly tapping on the side of her fork buzzed mine like a puppeteer's claw.

"Oh, I wouldn't say that, Ryan," Mama said. "He's just ambitious."

"No offense, Kathryn, I know guys like him—men who've had the world handed to them."

This was the first time Baba's ears perked up, suddenly he was out of his academic fog. "Who are you talking about?" he asked.

"Simon. Rakesh's son," Mama explained.

Baba took a second. "Oh."

That was his vote of confidence. Baba would watch cricket with Simon and Rakesh, rooting for different teams, but maybe it was because of this competitiveness with Rakesh, and how Baba saw Simon as an equal, a fellow adult, that Baba never considered Simon as a choice for Alyssa to date. Or maybe secretly Baba was scared of him, too.

Alyssa's nerves were dancing off of her now, the sleeves of her dress creasing at the elbows as she pushed the hair back up behind her ears, pulling and un-pulling a single piece back and forth, listening intently. She was so fucking beautiful.

"Anyway, it isn't important," Mama concluded. "He's just a boy."

And he was.

A week later, Mama took us downtown to shop. Generally we stayed just around the strip of Broadway-Lafayette, where we were allowed to fraternize with the loud, fat Americans, as she liked to think of them.

We were on Prince Street, near the bookstore on Mulberry, when we saw Simon, wearing a black baseball cap back-to-front, gray pin-striped pants, and a Black Flag T-shirt, ambling toward us. He stopped to talk but looked out of breath, his eyes sunken and hollow. I bypassed the conversation, lingering only on the redness of his lips. I ignored what was said, entranced by how stunning he was.

"This one doesn't talk too much, does she?" Simon jeered.

All eyes were on me. Alyssa looked amused, Mama concerned. Simon's eyes were gray and insipid, but I was floating in them.

"She's not as outgoing as *me*," I heard Alyssa say, my cheeks flushing over immediately. I hated being the center of attention. My breasts were blooming, and I hadn't yet figured out how to stand to obscure my nipples from perking outward like little meerkats in the sand. Nothing seemed as horrifying as my nipples being visible through my shirt.

Mama agreed with Alyssa, but I felt Simon's gaze lingering. In my mind, I was hoping it was because he thought I was unstoppably attractive, that he saw past the merging pimples on my T-zone and my baggy, ill-fitted denim. I hoped that he recognized that I was a person, that I was pretty, that I was *enough*. When I looked up at him again, seconds later, he was still staring at me, just as he had been before, but he didn't seem moved. Alyssa grabbed his attention again, activating her sweetness. In a strangely rushed, perfunctory way, he asked her if she'd like to go have dinner sometime. Radiant, I knew she was about to say yes, when Mama interrupted.

"Alyssa is dating Ryan. You know him, right, Simon?"

I watched Alyssa roll her eyes as Mama detailed how much she herself liked Ryan. She managed to insert that he was Black, as if to impress Simon, though of course he knew. It was entertaining in its shamelessness. As Simon walked away, turning around to smile back at us, his dimples uncharacteristically boyish, Mama beamed in the afterglow of a man's undivided attention and declared, "What a terrifyingly handsome young man."

6.

A few weeks later, it was Sunday, a supposed day of tranquil, but at home nothing ever felt like rest. I was both surveilled and forgotten by my parents, as if they caught me only in moments of clumsiness or stupidity, which had a chain effect: the torment of being met with perpetual eye rolls from them both. Mama's were more dramatic, always followed with a deep groan: "Taylia!" Then there was "Taaaaaaylia...," an exaggerated huff of boredom at my ineptitude. *"Taylia!"* was sharp, it was fast, the annoyance like a whip.

I had taken the morning to read by my bedroom window. The sun felt like a flood of nourishment, a vitamin D zing. Over time, I had learned how to like being alone. I trained myself to embrace it, to kiss the sun and let the big chunks of light baptize me. Each week, a new beginning. I spent a lot of time in my room; socializing felt like a burden. Baba also had weird expectations that he let Alyssa thwart, but I would be judged and questioned if I ever wanted to have fun. As if I wasn't deserving.

If I went out, it was rarely to meet friends, but more to walk in the city's blind spots. To find New York unfolding on the neighborhood streets. Kids who are raised in the city are just different, too. Unruly. Or at least, the proximity to strangeness is so ubiquitous, you become fearless. But at times, especially alone, it felt cold. Topsy-turvy. The city had dark parts, too. Sometimes it was hard to look away. After these walks, I'd return home. But I longed for sanctuary, for someone to cradle my head. So, my room became a cocoon. After time, I trained myself to accept that this was a kind of care. At least I had a home, as many in the streets didn't. I imagined myself in their place, using it to humble myself. I may not have had the love that I deeply craved from my parents, but at least I had my imagination. My dreams became a portal to my survival.

This Sunday, Mama, in a bid to not feel isolated from her husband's roots, was hosting a bunch of Indians for dinner. She didn't dare cook, but had the entire event catered by a chic young Indian chef, Shriya Rao, whom she had met downtown at a New Museum mixer. Mama wanted to show (desperately prove) that she had perspective, that she wasn't just another balmy white woman, incapable of showing depth. She knew she had it, and she relied on her faith, to a certain degree.

Like most young Jewish New Yorkers, she had a relatively positive experience with Judaism; she went to temple, had a Bat Mitzvah, and was raised with the teachings in an intellectual way. She didn't agree with everything (least of all her parents, whom she found stuffy and incongruently racist), but she found respite in the Torah, in her people, in the struggle for justice. She read Susan Sontag and Vivian Gornick avidly and looked to them as a certain class of intellectual mentorship she longed for. She wanted to show these Indians that she understood the violence of white supremacy. Because, on some level, she did.

Baba and she had a shared sense of winning. They saw their marriage as a component to strengthen themselves, separately and together. An Indian and a Jew unite to make a better future for each other and their children. It was romantic, we (as a family, a unit) became a political statement. Except neither of them had the verve to carry this on with much intentionality. It was easier to pretend than to become. I witnessed this, in the ways they held their friends accountable for standards they were too lazy to unlearn. They slid in and out of political radicality, but for the most part, they got lost in the fumes of a desire for a good life. Because, in more ways than one, they both wanted proximity to whiteness. Which is why their self-hating qualities were so egregious and strong. Besides, when wealth became palpable, both from an inheritance for my mother (which included, among a lot of money, a brownstone in the Upper West Side) and their joint income as tenured professors at Columbia University (Mama was also a curator), they became upper middle class in a stealth way. They hated the idea of the rich, without acknowledging they themselves had joined the ranks of the class they hated so much. It went against their principles—oh, how garish and pompous were the wealthy!

They loved each other, which is why they could put up with this farce together. Both each other's protectors, comrades, partners in an innocent crime. It didn't seem so bad to be fake, to not stand behind your values in a total way. They were human, they were allowed to have faults—everybody had a black hole of foibles. In order to keep up with the charade, it was important to have someone to rely on, someone who would reflect only the most shiny parts of yourself back to you. So they needed the other. It was a weird, mild obsession. I knew it was rare to witness this kind of love from parents, and in that regard, I was lucky.

But, still, I personally felt like an add-on. I began to understand the dissonance of my being in this family in my early teens. But at that point, what was I to do? I knew they shared a love and devotion with Alyssa, but not with me. Not for a lack of trying, but I just wasn't like her. I was made with more mistakes. She was Michelangelo's *David*, marble bodied and toned. I was an Uffizi's *David*, a mere replica. Without distinction of my own, I was doomed to a life of comparison. It sounds dramatic, and it was. In so many ways not being like Alyssa haunted me.

Mama had warned Alyssa and me ahead of time that we were responsible for cleaning up the house before the Sunday dinner. She said, "Don't test me!" with a grave look I suppose every mother had a variation of. To me, it felt a task both reasonable and valuable, two things I liked. So I agreed.

I came downstairs, out of my private sun-time read, to help. Alyssa was on the couch, her headphones sucking her ears in. Her legs across the leather or the headrest like a slope. I tried to get her attention, but she was in her own world, so I skulked around Mama, awaiting instruction. A little anxious, I hated not knowing where to stand. Mama, slightly caustic, sighed passed me and I stayed silent, waiting for a signal. When she had her head in the pantry, I made my move.

"Ma, I'm here." Sometimes, even English, or language itself, felt foreign to me.

"I can see that Taylia."

"What can I do?"

"Hang on a second." Her tone was already annoyed.

I looked toward Alyssa, legs still sprawled across the sofa like a fan, chewing gum. I bit the inside of my cheek, a rubbery sole. Inhaling shortly, to minimize crying, I exhaled fast. "Okay, Mama."

Eventually she told me diligently, as if I were applying for a job. I ended up doing everything (cleaning the downstairs family room and the guest bathroom, vacuuming all the floors), as Alyssa had helped for roughly only ten minutes, feigned an excuse, and left. When I eventually told Mama all had been done, she looked at me and said matter-of-factly, "Please don't wear anything tight today, you're looking a bit lumpy right now." In response I didn't say anything, maybe in shock, and walked away.

I always wondered what it was about me that felt so abstracted next to my sister. I understood I was pretty, to a certain degree, but maybe it felt blurry next to Alyssa's definitions. My parents didn't help in that regard, either. In many ways, I was voluptuous in a way Alyssa wasn't. I had tits and an ass, I had form. I knew that was seemingly attractive on others, but on me it felt like an excess. I didn't wear it well. Mama would add to this by watching my body with a glaring awareness that pivoted to perpetual critique. As if all I needed to do was embrace x, y, and z—and I would be beautiful. "Just lose a bit of the baby fat," or "Don't walk so heavily on the stairs," or "Eat less at night." Mama became a weight checker and reprimander. Alyssa seemed to have perfect form, the kind of metabolism models have. Thinness felt like another passport I didn't have.

In her own ways, Alyssa tried to confront this, using her tools of persuasion against our parents. She wasn't the type of person who enjoyed being put on a pedestal. It annoyed her, and in that shared frustration, we formed an alliance. Things changed in our relationship when she decided to protect me. It was subtle, but we both knew. Sisters can be the worst, but with a shared goal, we could be powerful.

Zeina, though not Indian, was a perfect pawn in Mama's night for hosting the Indians. I watched her as she elegantly entertained a crowd of captivated women. Simon's parents, Rakesh and Marissa, were in attendance, including a few others who had teen kids who didn't come. Unsurprisingly, Simon had. Since I had cried earlier from Mama's comments, my focus that night was a bit blurry, though I do remember Alyssa and Simon walking in from outside looking sedated, eyes glazed, a frightening strung-out look of glee stuck on their faces like clown paint. They looked suspicious, but that night I didn't really care. I watched Zeina with mild reverie, the way she walked around the house, a giraffe, head to toe in a perfect brown beige, hair sleek. Mama looked like she was having fun, talking to Shriya, her pixie-cut-having, boy-band-member-hot chef friend. Shriya had served modern-style French-Indian cooking like crab curry bouillabaisse and chicken tikka masala mousse. Everyone seemed to enjoy the pretentiousness, including me, and Mama loved collecting cool Brown tokens, proof that she was more evolved than her own parents, at the very least. Baba looked bored for most of the pleasantries, like he gave about no fucks to begin with. But then, in a quick second, he'd look mildly alive—fired up like a birthday sparkler—as he debated Rakesh, the way best friends who were bitter rivals did.

Later, everyone but Zeina had gone. Baba, a splendid brat as usual, had left the dishes to the women, and Mama acquiesced because she loved him. She found humor in his latent, and arguably lazy, misogyny. A habit, and advantage, of being the only son. It's not as if his mother, Dadi-ma, had spoiled him, but his culture definitely did. It propped up his intelligence above any woman's, and like many unspectacular men, he believed in the bullshit to save his ego.

Alyssa was eating ice cream, Ben and Jerry's Half Baked, right out of the tub. I could tell Zeina was enamored by Alyssa's elegance, as so many were. It was her eyes, but also her entire demeanor: slightly coquettish, yet composed, with wisdom. It was less seductive and more alluring.

"My God, honey, you really are a beauty," Zeina exclaimed, a New Jersey accent emerging from the depths.

Ma sighed, taken, suddenly, by her eldest daughter's beauty, a sincerely perfect combination of hers and Baba's. Alyssa looked uncomfortable, shuddering at the attention. She sucked on her last spoonful of ice cream.

"Honestly," she muttered after a few moments, gulping down the last slime of cream, "Tay's the most beautiful person I've ever seen."

Up until then I had been staring at Zeina's perfect moon-shaped cuticles, wondering why mine didn't look the same. Pulled out of this thought, I was launched into the center of attention. One I hadn't asked for and, yet, I was moved by. Both Mama and Zeina were staring at me, smiling in the fake indulgent way people smile at you sometimes. Alyssa repeated herself, but this time to me: "You're the most beautiful person I've ever seen." Thing is, I believed her. Maybe that's why I loved her, she saw me. She validated me, even knowing I had hair on my lower back and bumps on my legs and arms that I had recently found out was keratosis pilaris.

Mama and Zeina smiled and carried on, moving through the weirdness of conversation, but a little drunk. Alyssa was dancing, tapping her toes on the Persian runner in the hallway as Alice Coltrane's *Reflection on Creation and Space* played, and we all, in our ways, languidly cleaned up the mess of the night's unravelings.

7.

Baba had been acting more erratic these days. His anger—once a collected fire that had limits, that knew its own terrain—was now a thick bloom of smoke, billowing over. Months after the loss of Alyssa, he was forgetting words (which made him angrier), stumbling on details. Phone numbers he once could recall with an impressive fastness he now no longer remembered. Simultaneously he forgot the names of friends back in India, of the colleges he went to, and the stores he used to love to peruse. His memories were fading, maybe as a protective measure, for all the pain he couldn't quite grasp anymore. But it scared him, and it scared Mama, too.

I saw her begin to worry, to shiver with subservience. She had never been a subservient wife, just a loving one. Still, she had during our childhoods put up with his mood swings, the fresh spark of his sometimes megalomaniacal anger that would eventually cool with time. Now, it was a different, more reserved kind of anger, and she was visibly gaunt from the stress, from the pressures of sadness. I could see that her emotions tugged at the idea that she and her husband would get through this together. That they could reconstruct their past, that their home should not be a tomb. At times, I saw her be strong for the both of them, but it frustrated me that she didn't understand that Baba was a broken trolley with an inclination to steer only toward what he deemed right. He never liked asking for advice, especially not now.

Since taking a break from college, I'd been spending hours in my room alone, remembering, revisiting, thinking what else I could have done or seen in advance. Suddenly, my mother knocked at the door. She never knocked, never beckoned, never called my name anymore. It's as if knocking was acknowledging the absence of Alyssa. I cracked the door open, but only just.

"There's a phone call," she whispered. "It's Simon Sharma."

"For me?"

She nodded. There was a lightness to her I hadn't seen in months. I took the phone from her hand and cumbersomely brought it to my ear.

"Hello?"

I watched my mother as he said hello back. We were both frowning, wearing the same expression of nervousness. He asked if he could see me. I said yes. He asked when. I said any time: "I'm always free." I knew that it echoed desperation, but I had never had a man call me at home before and I was hungry for that kind of love, for Mama to see me receive it. But I also felt silly thinking Simon Sharma could love me. He wanted to get drinks, "possibly dinner. Tonight?" I said of course. Of course I said of course. He gave me a time and I said sure, then with determination he hung up. I still held the phone to my ear, listening to the sound of an empty line. I looked Mama in the eye and she smiled. It was the first smile I had seen in months.

After what happened to Alyssa, I knew I had to do something, *anything*. It wasn't like me to watch my mother deteriorate. I had so many memories of them together—her pride of Alyssa blazed through her like beams of light, and Alyssa's filial piety shone like its beacon. Through the two of them, I was able to conceptualize the real strength of maternal love.

Simon picked me up at eight o'clock sharp in an Uber. Mama loved a punctual man. He stood and charmed her outside as I leaned against the base of the stairs, entirely nervous. Lately everything had been stunted, dimmed. At last, despite the nerves, I felt the air around me sharpening, the colors changing into brighter hues. I could smell the liveliness and I became excited, having forgotten entirely that I had the ability to feel that still.

We careened through the Friday night traffic with nothing much to talk about. Music, curated by the Uber driver, played to fill in the gaps of conversation, but I didn't mind. I was always more fond of conversational silence than I was of actual conversing. The air inside the car was stale and climatized, and my legs were cold inside my clothes. Another chill rose as I felt his hand on my biceps. "How are you doing over there, Ms. Always in My Head?"

"Oh, I'm fine," I said, reacting fast, laughing it off. I was uncomfortable by the tease, but angry at my uneasiness. I brushed it off and didn't indulge him with more of an answer. Instead, I watched as the tiny bulbs of city light moved across and around me. I was so captivated by the rhythm of my surroundings that the sound of a car door opening startled me as I realized we had arrived. Bracing myself, I took a few moments to open my own side, but by the time I reached over he had already come and opened it for me. Again, I felt uncomfortable, but I let it go, not knowing how to dissect the feeling in real time. I imagined I was just being dramatic, or a wuss. We walked into a wood-fired pizza place and it was crowded. I felt myself recoiling from the eyes on us, but I also wanted to stop the mental gymnastics of anxiety, so focused on shutting my mind down. I wanted to enjoy this, I reminded myself. Shifting my focus to Simon, I immediately noticed the glances from women nearby and the waiters at his feet.

As we were finally ushered to a table, I sat down and looked around meekly, feeling, for the most part, undeserving of his time.

"You're wondering why I asked you here, aren't you?"

"I can't say I haven't thought about that..." My smile was crooked. Grateful for the chance to be transparent.

He smiled back, saying nothing. After a break in the conversation, he changed the tone, abruptly, intently: "I am sorry about your sister."

"Oh."

"I really liked her."

I stared down at the fork lingering in my hand.

"I did it for Alyssa."

"For Alyssa?"

Today marked the second anniversary of her death. Did he know? Did he remember? He didn't answer me, but smiled.

"You always act so embarrassed," Alyssa admonished me days after seeing Simon on the street downtown. I was baking, attempting to make a flourless chocolate cake. She sat opposite, slurping on a tart cherry Popsicle, chastising me.

"I do?" I asked, already embarrassed.

"Girl, you know you do."

"I'm sorry," I muttered, greasing the cake pan with butter.

She leaned over the counter and flicked me on the side of my left shoulder, right near the bone. "Stop apologizing for everything."

"Okay, first, ow. Second, what the fuck else am I supposed to do?" I didn't know all the answers like her, I didn't have all the answers like her.

"You act like you don't know shit."

I didn't know how to tell her that I didn't know shit. "I'm not like you, okay? I don't have fancy good taste. I'm not confident..."

I paused and looked up. I felt like I was lying, like I was playing a role that had been assigned to me; subconsciously I had deemed Alyssa superior to me, and I felt like I served her at times. It's as if I baited her to feel sorry for me, to take pity. But I also wanted her to feel powerful, and I was feeding her. I was feeding her ego. I almost apologized again, but before I could she stopped me. "Yes, maybe you're right. Maybe I do have it easier..."

"I mean, just a little." I didn't want to enumerate all the ways she really did have it easier. I also didn't want to burden her with all the ways in which she benefited from her access to whiteness. So instead I just made a cake, pouring the batter diligently into the circular tin. I passed her the blue speckled bowl that had all the leftover batter, to dip our fingers into like Dadi-ma when she cooked, edging her pointed, fat finger, using it as a spatula to taste. We shared the moment, with batter in between, staring into the divide of our beings, all the things that separated us. These were moments that stuck out to me, when she tried to understand me. Nobody had ever tried to do that before.

Simon was evocative in the strangest way. There was an unnerving quality to his handsomeness, like a shrill, penetrating hostility. His eyes were shrewd and discerning, and an inexplicable sensation lingered in my gut every time I saw him looking my way. They were so gray, and at moments near the light, I saw them flicker with an emotion I couldn't place.

"Is there something wrong with your food?" he asked doubtfully.

"No, no." I was mumbling, chewing on a slice of a Margherita.

"Good. Good."

He took a swig from his beer, watching me as he drank.

"You ever been on a date before?"

This was a date? I wanted to gag.

"Um, no," I said, and laughed. "Not really."

"Yeah, Alyssa was more of the dating type."

"Heh." And I was more of the loser type.

"So, you enjoying college?"

I was thankful for him trying to start a conversation, even though I could have just sat, glumly eating my food, feeling like an undatable loser. But maybe some part of me was trying to be bolder, and I felt like this was my ticket.

I lied—I hadn't been to school in months. "Yeah, it's great."

"What do you do again?"

"History and comparative English."

"Oh yeah, that's it, I remember."

I could tell that he couldn't remember.

"Where?"

"Columbia." He didn't need to know that I had almost failed and that my professors hated me.

"Ah, right, like Uncle. Good girl."

I wanted to tell him it was like Alyssa and Mama, too, both of whom had also went to Columbia. I hated the way he said it, arrogantly, as if to feign intimacy, but I still nodded, awkwardly smiling, wanting to cringe. I didn't want to offend, so I didn't.

"What do you want to do?"

I looked at him fully. I wasn't sure yet, and it seemed like such an impossible, gnawing question. "I want to be a lawyer." I paused dramatically. "I think."

"You think?"

My tongue felt like a big useless object in my mouth, so I shrugged. I hated how condescending he was, but I kept being polite.

"Do you think you'd enjoy it?"

"Law? Does anybody?"

He took another swig. I felt like I was annoying him. Maybe it was the fact that I wasn't more like Alyssa. I wasn't flirty or seductive; I wasn't even a good conversationalist.

"It's a big plan for somebody that's not sure."

I agreed, laughing again, not wanting to anger him, but immediately I saw him look away. At that moment I resented how boring I was, embarrassed that I was wasting his time. There was a long silence until he returned to my face, taking me in with a deep, guttural sigh.

"You know, you have a lot going for you. Honestly, you're really pretty."

I stared at some red shoes at the bar, looking past him. Unable to raise my head any higher, I felt weighed down by my simultaneous shock and excitement.

"It's true."

The stern tone of his voice resonated through the small bubble within which we were sitting in, like an oracle.

"Some of my friends have seen you around. They like the way you look."

I nodded my head, deflecting. "Hmm."

"You want another drink?"

"Sure," I replied, fiddling with my napkin.

I looked around briefly. The restaurant was even fuller than when we first entered it. From top to bottom, the ceilings, walls, and floor were wooden. It looked like an old, repurposed barn, the edges of the walls and bar gilded with a strange rusted patina. The furnishings were kitschy, with the characteristic Brooklyn aesthetic of steel, wood, and ferns perched on shelves that lined the entire interior. The pies were soft-crusted, the cheese perfectly stringy, and the drinks strong, the smell of whiskey and yeast leaking everywhere.

"I guess I've been interested in real estate for a while. They say Brooklyn is the new Manhattan, but Manhattan will always be fucking Manhattan, you know?"

He droned on and on. He was once so handsome, but now he looked lifeless. His cheeks were ruddy and red, like a toddler's.

"I could have played professional cricket. I have dual citizenship, which is quite uncommon, you know? I used to play when I was younger and I was really, really good. Then I started growing an interest in medicine and I thought it'd be more meaningful if I pursued that."

"Also like your dad?" I tried to relate. "Do you think that will make you happy?"

"Some people just can't be happy, and that's why there's money, Taylia."

I saw him clink his pint of IPA with someone nearby, and the foam oozed out like a volcano as they both laughed. I looked over at the person, a white face that looked oddly familiar, but before I could process, Simon turned back and smirked at me, slightly annoyed. It was as if my challenge of happiness angered him. For the first time, in that moment, I felt an honesty shine through. No pretense, just Simon. From the back, I suddenly saw another familiar face. It belonged to Vijay, whom I recognized. Simon was always loitering with these two boys, and the three of them looked like a pack of dogs. Vijay was a distant family friend, also Bengali. His face was forever lined with a mild frown, bored, chewing gum like he was fighting nicotine. He was at the bar, talking to the white guy, which I found odd. But I decided to look away and pretended not to see him. I didn't want to start anything; I wanted this night to be easy.

I was not used to "going out." I didn't have the verve for it. I rarely enjoyed meeting new people unless they shared my oddly specific taste in film ('80s cult classic *Manhunter*). At Columbia, it was hard to make friends for this very reason. I was a strange being,

I knew this. I'd never been able to mesh with a group or belong to a clique. Consumed, instead, by books. In the absence of Alyssa, home felt like a different kind of reprieve—one removed from the social obligations of adulthood that I wasn't ready to face. I had lost the friends I used to have, and now I didn't know where, or how, to begin to retrieve myself. As I sat opposite Simon, maybe I hoped to be absolved of this burden.

"You know that I went out with Alyssa, right?"

I felt my senses, which were being blurred and thinned by the alcohol, suddenly kick in. "She never told me that." That was the truth. She had never told me that. Looking back, one could assume. I guess I could've tried to look at what was right before me.

"Really?"

"Did you guys go out for a long time?"

"Yeah, awhile. I'd say I made some big changes in her life."

None of this new information made sense to me. She was with Ryan up until she died. All of a sudden, I felt as if I was hallucinating, because I could hear somebody laugh and I recognized the voice. "Big changes"? My heart froze for a split second and a coldness engulfed me. Ignoring the feeling, instead, I raised my glass and sent my drink swishing past my tonsils. I continued to laugh to maintain my intentional blindness.

8.

"Tay, you weirdo!" Alyssa laughs.

I stick out my tongue and the March wind freezes my taste buds. We had jogged out into an empty field in the Catskills.

"I'm getting tired, Tay, can you stop?"

"What's the magic word?"

"If you don't stop I'll punch your face in?"

"Funny."

I stop and fall to the ground, and then we lie parallel.

"We should do this more often."

She agrees in hums.

"Anything to get away from everything."

Alyssa remains quiet. I've started to notice her eyes never look at me anymore, the irises don't face mine. I used to be able to look into my sister's eyes and know how she was doing, what she was wrestling with. I could rupture a feeling just by seeing her, by taking her in. Now she avoids my gaze, looking around my face—nose, freckle on my cheek, the line on my forehead—splitting her stare into two different eyeballs. Thing is, maybe I don't really want to know what's going on.

"I wish this is where I could live. Just here." I say it to fill in the gap. It's not the truth. I want to ask her how she is, but I'm lying. I'm trying to buy time.

I am faced with her silence again. After a few moments, she asks me a question.

"What do you define as freedom?" Cryptic. I take in that she's been philosophical recently, pondering life's mysteries.

I pause: "Something with no boundaries, I guess."

Alyssa nods her head. "Like a bird."

Ryan was often at our home, knees to his chest, sitting on an armchair with a shearling shawl swung over the top. The first time it happened I remembered it so clearly, because he looked as if he sat on a cloud, radiating a sadness that loomed over us all. He would come just to sit in the house, like a statue, always the first thing I saw when I came home for the weekends. I could not face the buzzing social world of university. We all felt so purposeless. The unhappiness was so alive. It had taken over the big bright void that Alyssa left behind.

I began to cook for the family and sometimes Ryan, who had become our family. I was helping by doing something tangible.

I learned how to cook soups and stews like minestrone or turkey chili. Sometimes I'd make a paella in a cast-iron pan or *my* version of a chicken curry, the way that Dadi-ma had once taught me. The trick was all in the sautéed tomatoes mixed in with the curry powder and garam masala. You had to mix it right at the beginning of the dish to give the curry the extra kick, the depth of spice.

The first time I made it, ad-libbing the ingredients from memory, I was nervous to have Baba taste it. Not a cook himself, I wondered if he would be disappointed by the dish. I cooked basmati rice as well, and in a medium-sized mason jar we had some of Dadi-ma's mango pickles, sticky and fermented, from years ago that I clawed out with a fork, placing them on a shallow dish next to the chicken. We ate in silence.

The steam from the heat of the dish felt like a cleanse, absolving us of our internal torture. I watched everyone quietly take more. Then, as Baba inhaled some achar with the cooked rice, a tear emerged.

"Taylia, this is very, very good. How did you learn to cook this?"

I briefly paused. "Dadi-ma taught me, Baba."

He was shocked. "She taught you? When?"

Everyone was looking at me.

"Remember, they were very close, Adi," Mama said. "But your father is right, Tay. This is so tasty."

Ryan agreed, and it was a moment of serenity in a time when there was none.

Later, as Ryan and Baba cleaned the dishes, I fit the rest of the food into glass containers. There was a pathetic grace in how they moved: swiftly at times, then—mimicking the other—racked by sadness again.

Perhaps this, this pain, was a shared intimacy that the other took solace in. In many ways, Ryan, like Simon, had become the son that Baba never had. And though I knew some part of him did wish we were boys, we had achieved so many of those genderless milestones.

In those ways and others, Dad was a feminist. He liked that Mama was assured, robust in her beliefs and patience. Ironically, the one thing he didn't like was that she'd sometimes wear things that were just *slightly* revealing—the only times they ever fought. I remember, clear as day: they'd be heading out to a dinner party, or we'd all be nearly out the door, and if Baba saw something he didn't like on Mama, he would sit on a little ottoman by the door, looking toward the floor, silent. Like a bratty child. It was a sign of disapproval, but maybe worse: embarrassment. At first, when we were young but able to comprehend, Mama would resist. She'd yell, "My body, my choice, Adi!" Slamming doors until she calmed. For years, it was a fight. A declaration of independence. Baba would condescendingly claim that he had no desire to thwart her, that he was *merely suggesting she look more proper.* It's where I could see what a schmuck he truly was. But, slowly, she amended herself. I witnessed it. How, through the ages, Baba began to slowly change the way Mama dressed. It was a series of small requests or concerns, mostly cleavage based (truthfully, Mama had great tits), but the classic Indian pashmina move became a habit Ma embraced, generally making it look all kinds of Georgia O'Keeffe chic.

Through time, Baba slowly turned his gaze to Alyssa and me. His was different from Mama's survey; this was purely a sexuality critique. Offhandedly, he'd make odd comments about how our pants were too tight in places, how he could see a bra strap peek from behind the edges of our clothes or the shadow of underwear revealing itself from underneath, like an imprint. I began to feel disgusted by myself, now again burdened by my own body. Alyssa, on the other hand, never cared. She'd mock Baba's sensibilities in a jovial way, creating zero tension with her charming comebacks, always knowing the boundaries of every situation. She knew how to temper them both and get her way.

"Eh, two daughters, it's a hard life, nah?" Rakesh spoke, and Baba cocked his head. A pink smear revealed itself in the sky, as the sun set far into the distance.

"Don't tell me you're a misogynist, Rakesh." Baba's teeth gleamed.

"Arré! Come on, man, you know what I'm saying."

I was home from Columbia for winter break reading *Sleepless Nights*, by Elizabeth Hardwick, in a nook near my father, far enough for the two friends to be quaintly coarse with each other without being worried that their disdain would reveal itself.

"I'm just saying, eh, I wouldn't want daughters. Simon is hard enough."

"Do you mean Sly Si?"

Rakesh guffawed. "Eesh, is that what your daughters are calling him?"

"He looks shady, nah?"

"Adi, don't be rude."

Baba changed tone. "Having daughters is not hard..."

"You think having daughters isn't hard? Have you met any boys recently? Arré, didn't you hear about what happened in Delhi? She was with her fiancé on a bus..."

"Absolutely reprehensible."

"They don't teach them manners, no common decency. Completely uncivilized, filthy, so filthy. Actual dogs, *kutha*." Rakesh spat the word out.

"What was she doing? You know, when it happened?"

"Who knows what kids do these days. What nonsense they get into. Girls wear short skirts..."

"And boys are what?"

Rakesh was silent, and Baba didn't probe.

Nonsense. The word struck me, it felt so clinical, given the context. From what I gathered, they were talking about Jyoti Singh Pandey. I'd read about her rape in the news. I remember it vividly, it was the last time Lyse and I would both be together for winter break.

"Things like that never happened to girls we knew. This world has changed."

"There was this girl, Dolly... medical student, more of a lothario than all the men in the *entireeeee* department."

I could hear Baba shirk at the very idea. "Sex, pex... nobody has any self-decency anymore. Kids these days don't respect themselves."

"Adi, you sound like a Muslim... so repugnant."

"I'm serious! Women like that deserve to be raped, eh-nah?"

Rakesh growled, laughing. "Mate, the New World hasn't made you more liberal."

"No, I'm serious, it's not about liberalism. Women should be admonished if they aren't more careful with their bodies."

"What would Kathryn say if she heard it? Isn't she a *feminist*?"

"She would agree. I'm sure of it. We used to laugh at girls in our college days, wearing short skirts in the dead of winter, freezing their skinny white legs off. What are they trying to prove? Besides, she was always the meanest, tearing them apart. It would enrage her. I've always liked her because she never wanted to be like that, you know? *That kind of woman.*"

Jyoti's death made me want to learn more about what it meant to be Indian. I saw her as an emblem for the feminine that was under attack. I wanted to understand the culture Baba came from even more, because I needed to know how men became like this. I didn't know that there would never be an answer.

Yet, here we all were again, cleaning the dishes, chanting mantras to calm our hearts. Ryan, disassociated; Baba, darkened into an uncomfortable quietude; Mama, catatonic and bipolar; me, assailable, broken in misery. Here we all were, unabsolved by Alyssa's sacrifice.

9.

We'd go to our house in the Catskills as often as we could. I loved that we had a home in nature; the trees, the cabins of iridescent design around us, were all beckoning with a life that I wanted to lead. Whenever we were up north, I felt for a time that I was sincerely alive, and it was there that I understood what infinity really was. I would look at the stars and dream of the impossibility of the universe, of the cosmos. On one of those trips I became obsessed with Carl Sagan and asked Baba to find me books about string theory and quantum physics. He complied with my request. I felt there was so much beyond me, without much to lose. In those moments, I felt purposeful.

I can recall sitting at the edges of our patio, hanging from the timber like a stretching cat; I would find corners, lost sections, places I could carve as my very own, and read for hours, turning pages with fingers or the nub of my nose. We owned a great big wooden house and everything was insanely symmetrical, lined and traced with the blades of the tree bark on the sides of the wall—a reminder that this world was theirs before it was ours.

I heard Baba come up behind me, but we rarely talked, so I ignored him.

"I have something for you," he said.

I was stunned, but I didn't turn around.

"It's a book."

I quickly looked at him, and it was true—in his hand he had a small paperback, black with bright light blue swirls on the cover. It read *The Elegant Universe*. I sometimes felt Baba to be a man in the military. So composed, showing little to no emotion. Sometimes he'd pat me on the head, but today he smiled.

"I had a look inside. You know, it's very interesting." Over the years he had developed a more American-esque transatlantic accent, and I liked hearing it.

He gestured for me to come along, and we began walking down the steps toward the lake that was just a few yards south of our place. We were silent as we walked, but I cherished this time with him. We stopped at a bench, and he sat down and looked at me, his eyes telling me to do the same. Baba communicated so much without words. I sat down as he spoke.

"I'm very scared of deep things, Taylia, of deep, unknown spaces."

I didn't ask why—I always knew that if he wanted to tell me something, he would.

"The ocean. Space. These things terrify me."

I was amazed. My father never shared emotional anecdotes with us.

"Maybe it's because I don't know what's out there."

I let that sit with me. I didn't know what was out there, either, but I wanted to believe that whatever it was, it was something worthwhile.

"Life is cruel, Taylia. You have to get used to knowing that. If you're prepared for that, then you're prepared for the worst." He looked at the ground. The lake was so still, a dark navy smudge like ink, a mystery. "I sacrificed a great deal to get here, Taylia. We were not a rich family. Your Dadi-ma and Dadi-ji didn't have a lot of money, but they made do. They sent me to America to have a better life, because that's what people in our culture do. They give their sons and daughters opportunities for a better life. But they sacrificed a lot to get me here. And I owe them everything."

I wondered if he was talking to me anymore.

"Nothing is as important as honor, Taylia. I owe my parents everything, and I will never forget that." This time he almost whispered it: "Nothing is as important as honor."

He didn't embrace me, but instead left it there—that statement—to hang in the air, fragile and explosive in its honesty.

As he said it, I'd remembered that the year previously he'd uttered the same words. We were in a taxi van in Malaysia, on our way to India, Alyssa holding on to Mama as we swerved to the airport. Earlier that day I saw a man with no eyes, hollowed out like ice-cream scoops. I was still ruminating over the way his waxy hands gripped on to my shirt as I walked by, begging for money. Baba looked at us but also past us, declaring one thing only: "Don't plan your lives, girls. Don't ever plan your lives."

He and I would eventually return to the house, after our talk by the lake, where Mama was smoking a brisket, greasy in a cerulean-blue Le Creuset dutch oven. Alyssa was barbecuing corn, next to a pyramid of sweet potato latkes and a wooden salad bowl of creamy cabbage slaw. A smorgasbord of options, all feast-worthy. I watched as Mama and Alyssa sang ballads together, perhaps lovers in a past life. Baba drank Scotch, and I laughed, too distracted to grieve being an outsider. There were moments like this, when there was a semblance of normalcy. When we felt like a family.

It didn't last long when it happened, maybe for a night, sometimes cascading into the next morning, and often it came to an end with a remark from one parent about my body, my gait, the way I opened and closed cabinet doors ("They're *teak*, Taylia."). To that, Alyssa would defend me with a spitting verve and eloquence I had been denied, speaking for me like a justice-loving saint. I knew I could defend myself, but I deferred to her because maybe it felt like love. It felt more like love than anything I'd ever experienced. My parents, much like Alyssa, loved a good debate—and they were on their own team, fortified by their adult intelligence.

"Lyse, it's great you love your sister, but, honey, I'm just giving some advice."

"Ma, can't you see you always attack her?"

"Lyse, honey, every critique comes from my heart. And, look, Tay isn't saying anything!"

Neither would even look at me, to glean my truth.

"That's because she's probably upset!"

At a certain point I'd walk away, my mood already ruptured. I wanted to belong to something. To a unit. I wanted to have something to rely on. My birth family never felt like that. I was somehow always labeled "overly sensitive" because I was quiet. If only they would see the strange and adorable parts that were emerging in me. If only they looked up and saw what was in front of them.

Instead, they haunted me like a mystery. Even still, there was a voice, deep down, that felt I must've been born into this family for a reason. I remember having this conversation with Liza, Vijay's sister, years ago. I heard she had left her family house at eighteen to live with her then girlfriend. A taboo act, unlike any other, especially within a conservative, wealthy group of Indians like Baba's friends. Liza's parents were both architects and owned a firm in the Financial District. But, behind the guise of modernity and approachability, they still had their Pandora's box of dos and don'ts. The remnants of caste based standards. It's what no parent, especially those who consider themselves fair or liberal, wanted to admit. It's another one of those tiny hypocrisies they dare not unlearn, otherwise the entire Jenga monument would fall. So, instead, they pretended in public and admonished in secret. She was a few years older than us all, but I saw her at a gathering of families, her hair chopped into an *Amélie* bob, wearing all white—a band T-shirt with no logo and white Dickies.

I made eye contact with her for a split second, enraptured by the oddity of seeing a girl who didn't care what she looked like, yet who remained still so beautiful. She came toward me, maybe witnessing solidarity. As she sat next to me, she smelled like jasmine and rose. She was irreverent; the tattoos across her arms were scattered like constellations.

"Hey, Taylia. Right?" she asked, her voice a little deep.

"Yeah, hey... Liza. Right?" The awkward dance.

"That's right." She smiled.

"I like your tattoos..." I drifted off, getting lost in them. She had a star on her hand and a moon on her wrist. I wanted to touch them, I wanted to lick her skin.

"You think you'll ever get any?"

I laughed. "No, no way."

"Alyssa's your sister, yeah? I think my baby bro is in love with her." She laughed, but I didn't want Alyssa to derail me in this conversation, so I just nodded. After a few beats, I spoke.

"Sometimes I feel like I wasn't supposed to be in this family." I don't know what emboldened me—maybe knowing she could relate. Or maybe because I wanted her to take me seriously, to know I understood in words of recognition.

"Oof, well, don't I know the feeling."

"How'd you work through that?... The feeling, I mean."

She paused. "Huh. Well, I guess just time, really. Sounds like a cliché, but I find life kind of is. Like, time just sort of heals things, you know? Besides, my friend Frankie says that we're always born into the family we are supposed to. Like, it's karmic. Which is mad Hindu, right?"

I laughed.

A year later I'd hear that Liza was disowned by her family for wanting to marry her girlfriend. That her parents would rather die from shame than allow it. Feeling sentimental, I asked Alyssa what she knew of her. "I heard she went to Tisch to become a director or something." There seemed to be a sense of awe in Alyssa, too, that she was astounded that people could choose themselves. Those days, I guess, we were both learning how to be outside of ourselves. I know I was longing for it more, for a handbook, for an example. I craved understanding myself more clearly. Maybe I was also beginning to *want to* understand why I was in this family. Thing is, I was beginning to feel like there was no reason. Just a sad twist of pathetic fate.

10.

I felt a tingle alight my senses. As I came to, I noticed the weight of a medium-sized hand on my back. It was a rough hand that felt strong and caustic against me, callused with slight indents across the tops of the fingers. The pressure of the hand sent an eerie sensation through me. Something felt off. It felt peculiar. Unnatural.

I knew I'd been sleeping for a while: the dryness of my face pinched as my eyes flickered against what little light existed in the room. I was silent, trying to identify my surroundings. Underneath a curtain of my own hair I gathered that it was a small room. Like an attic. There was a strange draft coming in, and the shadows of the clouds on the hardwood floor made it clear that we were high up, above somewhere.

I was still lying down, rawness enveloping me, my ass to the sky. I lightly brushed my tongue against what was beneath me; it was *salty*. The floor tasted *salty*. The hand on my back now moved toward my shoulders, as if massaging me, then pushed down toward the small of my back with one quick motion. This hand did not plan to treat me right. I remained still for as long as I could, until he suddenly spoke.

"I know you're awake."

My heart pounded rapidly and I knew I was in danger. I didn't speak.

"Do you know how I know you're awake?"

Simon paused, as if wanting to allow me to answer. I didn't.

"I know, because *I* like bodies when they're lifeless. Wait, no—that's too morbid, let me start again—there's a beauty to a woman's body when she doesn't fight back, when there's no hesitation. That only happens when you're asleep or dead."

I felt his face look up, the acoustics of his voice changing slightly. I couldn't help thinking he sounded sociopathic.

"Get up, Taylia, I want to tell you a story."

My mind jumped from one plan to the next. *Should I run?* But I didn't and instead sat on my feet. I'm not sure if it was my inert body or fear that kept me there. I slowly lifted my torso up, my hair still a cloud around my face, refusing to look Simon in the eye.

"God, can you hurry? You are so fucking annoying."

I was distracted by the ambient sounds outside; I wanted to know where I could possibly be.

"You are even more annoying than *Alyssa*."

I was back inside of myself again—she always brought me right back.

"Alyssa and her fucking tight pussy. Jesus. What a girl." He sighed. "I loved Alyssa. I think I really did love her. She was needy, like you, but you're not hot like her. What's wrong with you? God!" He laughed. "What a fucking disappointment you must be."

I gritted my teeth, fearing this was true.

"I see it. I see what a loser you are. I saw how Alyssa would look at you, the way she'd talk about you, as if you were a burden. You *are* a burden. But you know that already." He paused. "And I'm a nice guy, Taylia. I'm generous. I have influence, and I wanted to use that in kindness. I wanted to give them some hope about you. It's been two years, it's time to move on. The way your mom walks around constantly on the clock, hoping you'll get a life, it's pathetic. So I asked you out on a date, Taylia. As a favor. No harm, no foul, right?"

A man of idioms, what a relief. I looked to the ground. My eyes were glassy as I took in what I could within my perimeter: everything was wooden, it looked and felt like an attic. The draft was persistent. I needed to fucking get out of here.

"You know she was a nympho? God. *A fucking nympho*. She wanted it everywhere. Once we fucked outside of your house! Did she ever tell you?"

I heaved a sudden shake. Thinking of her alive pained me. How could I have let myself get into this much danger? I felt ashamed. It came from the very depths inside of me, and before I knew it, my whole body pulled against myself as I shook. He noticed nothing.

"A cock-loving skank who wanted to be caught red-handed, with my dick right up her ass. Don't you get it, Taylia? Can't you see how desperate your sister really was?"

I started to cry. I didn't know what was happening, but I knew none of this was good.

"Do you like it up the ass, Taylia?"

His voice was not condescending—he was sincerely asking. He continued: "No, you're not a whore like your sister, are you, Taylia?" This time he was silent for a longer time. Waiting for me to answer.

"Alyssa wasn't a whore." It was all I managed to say.

He moved even closer and sat down with his legs crossed. He pushed my chin up with one finger and brushed my hair to the side. I looked at his lips. They were still red but no longer desirable. Now, those lips were ready to eat me, and all I wanted was to run.

But I didn't.

I looked at his shirt; he was still wearing the crisp blue oxford from dinner. I wondered if it was the next morning or if I'd been here for days. I quickly glanced around me. The room was empty, and I had been right—it was small. There was an old wooden chair, its cream shellac flaking, in the corner of the room underneath a row of white hooks.

He moved my head back to his face with his right hand, squeezing me with just enough pressure to frighten me. "I want to know if you're a whore, Taylia."

I looked him in the eye, but my face remained expressionless. I didn't want to fight—not for this, not for anything. I couldn't handle this life anymore, and maybe this moment was my way out. He came toward me and kissed me violently, sucking on my bottom lip before he pulled away.

"Are you a good little whore?" he asked as his hands began to separate my shaking legs.

I complied; I wanted to suffer. He pushed his fingers inside of me with a quickness, crawling.

"I'm asking you a question, Taylia, and you're being very rude."

"I'm not a whore." My head nodded as I said it, I was so ashamed.

"Of course you're not. Who'd want to fuck you?"

Nobody, I thought. Absolutely nobody.

"But I'm feeling generous today. I'm going to fuck you, Taylia. I'm gonna do you a favor."

Without warning, he pulled my body against him and then to the floor, slamming me against the ground. I lay crumpled and disgusted by myself. Just as quickly, he lunged inside my thighs and began to take it all away. The dryness built up a natural wall, but he pushed his way through, tearing me open. My eyes glazed over as I lay there, again, no longer in control of my own senses. The searing bluntness moved through me in waves, and with it the knowledge that I might die on this shard of hell. So I let myself drift, to remove myself. His heaving echoed through me, reverberating within the hollow of my chest, the floor groaning underneath the full weight of his body, and me, me—was I a me anymore?

Detached but still cognizant, I noticed a darkened shape, or two, coming toward us. I couldn't see their faces, only the blackened, threatening shape of them. One looked like Vijay; the other, I realized, the white guy at the bar, was Alton, a rich Italian. Both were Simon's boys. But I couldn't look, I couldn't take it in. If this was going to happen, I didn't want to know anything. I felt Simon pull out of me, and my eyes burned as I shut them tight, and then another, maybe Vijay (he smelled like fresh coffee and cinnamon), entered me. Simon sat beside us, watching, his eyes venom and burning through me. The girth of this man was different, and he kept repeating *"good pussy, good pussy, fuck, fuck, fuck."*

Somewhere I passed out.

"Baba told Mama to give me *the talk*."

Alyssa was eating grapes from a bowl, slicing each piece in half with her teeth before swallowing one part and examining the other.

"Grapes are so juicy," she muttered to herself. A charm of hers.

"What do you mean 'the talk'?" I asked, my eyebrows slightly arched.

"The talk talk, like sex talk."

"Huh?" Sometimes I acted dumb, I don't know why.

"Mama told *me* that Baba told *her* that she oughta give me the sex talk. He doesn't want me to have sex. He told Mama to tell me that I can't have sex."

"With Ryan?"

"Yes. God, Taylia, why can you never get things faster?"

I shrugged, feeling suddenly hurt that my charade backfired.

"I'm sorry. That sounded mean. Anyway, isn't that hilarious?"

"Why would he tell her to tell you that, though? Baba never talks about boys."

"Right? That's what I told Mama. But she said it's because sex is a big thing to him and he's really weird about it because it's 'cultural' or something. As if Indians don't have sex! I mean, they invented the Kama Sutra, come the fuck on, man!"

I had read that South Asian culture was super sex conservative in *Newsweek* once. There was an entire article about boycotts and riots when a Canadian-Indian director released a film that was deemed "sexually deviant." To me, it made sense that Baba was protective about this, of all things. It seemed in line with his beliefs about the sanctity of a woman's virginity. I was sure that's why he fell in love with Mama—there was something so angelic about her.

"Are you going to listen to them?" I asked.

"You mean am I not going to have sex?"

I nodded.

"Well, it'd be too late to do that now, wouldn't it?"

She seemed amused, or pleased, or both, and I was reminded again of how Alyssa contained multitudes. I hid my surprise—I didn't want to give her the satisfaction. "So what are you going to tell them, then?"

"Taylia. There's only one option, and it's the best option: deny, deny, deny."

Baba was, for all intents and purposes, a cliché. As a young socialist, I learned, his nickname was "Lenin" in school. His politics were radical, because he believed in Bengali liberation, the future outside of Pakistan. Dadi-ma had indicated as much to me when we were in India, taking me to a dank corner of the study where all of Baba's notebooks and Penguin handbooks on socialism still lay, dusty in a sad pile. I read through the diaries mainly, but a lot of them were in Bangla, a language I had never mastered but was one that was integral to Baba's identity as an intellectual. He was obsessed with the poetry of Rabindranath Tagore and the films of Satyajit Ray and Ritwik Ghatak. And like many other young Bengalis, he had very intense political views. There was still a faded, yet oddly indelible, poster of Mao Zedong hanging, the colors bright, a smiling kaleidoscope.

Sometimes I wanted to ask Baba what happened, what changed. It's not that he was completely lacking in politick, but the father I knew was lazy. He seemed to have had passion, a drive to make this world better, as a young boy. It's something I felt Mama once had, too. But they both enabled the other in their bad habits, both neutered the other of self-possession, as if it was easier to fit a mold of a person rather than to be one. I wondered why he'd never worked in Brown liberation in America, supporting the Black Panthers, creating programs that facilitated conversations about actual revolution. I wondered why they both stopped caring.

As much as I know he loved Mama, I wondered if he had jumped to go back to India when Dadi-ma was sick as a way to engineer a possible return for us all. He never voiced it, but he secretly hated America. On top of knowing he was a hypocrite, living in a country like America, I knew he must have experienced racism so unfettered that the only way to not combust was to marry a white woman and assimilate into society rather than confront all the parts of a life that made no space for him. No nuance. In the United States he was an Apu, a caricature of a person, broken and slimy, who became a token no matter where he went. Always an immigrant, the other. From servers mimicking a head nod behind his back to cashiers commenting on the thickness of his accent (which was, for what it's worth, untrue), Baba was in a perpetual state of embarrassment. That's what it meant to be Indian in America.

Maybe that's what gave them permission—the fact that they were both unwanted, so why not steal from the system and have a good life? The United States is a racist country and also an anti-Semitic one. They both instilled in Alyssa and me an understanding of that. That our identities would always be different. Yet, all their unconscious actions, all their biases, reeked of wanting to be white. As in more white, as in normal. They were tired of fighting, and finally, in each other, they found redemption. They also found a mirroring of needs, a holy thing indeed.

Once I heard Rakesh, my father, and my mother in the living room. There we had a big old bookcase that lined the entire living space, floor to ceiling. When I was a child I'd pretend that we had a ladder, and in my private moments, when nobody was watching, I'd pretend I was Belle in *Beauty and the Beast*. I'd swing from book to book over our Persian carpets, thick with bloodred wool and intricate, geometric Muslim details, padding my steps deftly as I pranced.

I don't know why Rakesh and Baba spent so much time together when they so clearly despised each other, like mortal enemies. Their entire relationship was antagonistic, and yet, within that insufferable, toxic bond, they seemed to find reprieve. That day, Mama was in the mix, a strange but appropriate addition. She was just the right bit of incisive, but still intellectually flirty, which Baba loved, because it was something that both Rakesh and he could admire. It was also a quiet way to be petty, to show who had the smarter, cooler American wife. After all these years, I didn't know much about Marissa or her marriage to Rakesh, though I could tell she wasn't happy. She always seemed abandoned, as if her spirit had been dimmed.

"You cannot possibly compare Partition to the Holocaust!" Mama shrieked. That's what caught my attention. I could just imagine Baba's face, shocked at his wife's lack of holistic understanding. I'm sure this pained him.

Rakesh cut in. "Americans always think—"

"Are you not American?" Mama mocked.

"Let me finish," Rakesh spat, annoyed. "Americans"—by which I knew he meant to say "white Americans," but because he was partially talking to a white American, and was married to a white American, he coded it in generalizations (this was when many, especially those of Baba and Rakesh's generation of Indian Americans, felt that they had to be delicate with white folks)— "use the Holocaust as the be all end all of barbarism and genocide, which is a limited belief. It is simply not true."

"Ask any country that confronted colonialism—"

"We're also talking about complete displaced chaos where you were taught to mistrust your neighbor if they were a different religion." I still saw this in Baba and Rakesh, especially the latter, the way he contrasted himself against Muslims after 9/11. There was something to be said about the Brahmanical order of Hinduism.

"The English destroyed us for centuries, taking our lands, our gems, looting us and putting our property in the Victoria and Albert Museum, exploiting us, raping our women, killing our children. Partition was just the boiling point. But what they really wanted was to make sure that Indians would never be united, so that we could never collapse the British Empire and take what was taken from us." I sighed shivers as Baba finished that sentence.

"Partition was an orchestration of sectarian violence."

"Yes, but also savage sexual violence, too," Baba uttered, which surprised us all, even me. I was sitting in my favorite place to read and listen to family gossip, the stairs.

"I actually heard that women were mutilated..."

"Arré, women's breasts were hacked off with machetes, pregnant women were stabbed in the stomach, babies were roasted alive.

Then what happened in Bangladesh in 1971 is the worst account of genocidal rape in the history of the world." There was almost a sense of thrill in his voice, a sense of palpable excitement at retelling this shocking gore. There was a short pause until my father's mild voice erupted. "Kathryn, it's not useful to use the Holocaust as a litmus test, because there has been so much genocide that has not been reported, and many of those are not white people's deaths."

My mother scoffed. "Adi, that's insensitive."

"But it's also the truth."

"One is not worse, all death is death, it's all bad," Rakesh chimed in.

Everyone was silent again.

Alyssa had not yet died, so the gravity of this conversation remained hypothetical, rooted in the past, but one day they would realize that all death was death. Even rape, as an act of death. And it was all bad. Nothing was truer.

For Mama, the Holocaust had been sort of an abstraction most of her life. It was so terrifying, so noxious, so cruel, that it was easier to accept that it had been bad, but to not let herself be beholden to the memory or the trauma. I could tell she admired being Jewish in a way ancestral lineage gives you a purpose and direction. She imparted that wisdom to us. I didn't feel Jewish because I wasn't white, and that isolated me, but the older I got, I saw how it defined me. How it, maybe, also gave me a sense of purpose.

In more ways than one, Mama enjoyed the Jewish identity of Bernie Sanders, of revolutionaries like Emma Goldman, of thinkers like Freud, Noam Chomsky, Hannah Arendt, Max Brod, Judith Butler, and Kafka. She looked at the inclusive, future-thinking Jewish parts. That's what she passed down to me and Alyssa in her small ways.

I felt her spark, I felt her need for change, but I also saw her complacency. How she had gotten used to a certain kind of life—

of fancy cocktails, of spring galas and board meetings with art investors. She got used to the thrill of her Maria Cornejo splurges and expensive candles with bold labels and collapsing letters. She masked the slight shame she felt, but I saw how she changed after Alyssa. Some part of her let go, sinking into a depression that at times consumed her. I felt she was weighed down by the loss because it fed into an ancestral fear. Like a curse, a deep voice in her soul, that, despite all her might, she never truly silenced. One that was dark, like a small demon: *How could you ever be happy? You don't get nice things.* I could sense this feeling, as I could locate it in my own body. It tasted like sulfur, the voice emerging from a tiny cave, questioning your validity to be alive. I think Mama was always expecting tragedy. It was historic, this feeling. And when it escaped it was like a dark crescendo. After Alyssa's death I saw Mama fight with the fear that she'd never have a good life.

Mama's parents, my grandparents, whom I had never met, I knew had had the same fear, but I also understood that their lives had been harder. Mama would always remind us of that. In her own way, she still showed respect.

Her parents, Marty and Den (short for Denise), had grown up during more rampant anti-Semitism, which they both battled within their respective fields, which galvanized their singular investment in a good life. Marty was a psychiatrist, and Den was a CEO of a womens wear brand similar to Spanx, but with clothes made in the old-fashioned style of ugly cream nylon. Den was a Gloria Steinem feminist, but she was also extremely, sycophantically obsessed with being the best wife to Marty that she could be.

Both were born in New York, and both were the first generation that started to pull their families out of poverty. Raised in the Lower East Side tenements, they dreamed of a better life, of having money, power, a nice house, and a family of their own. They both had that desire in common, so in many ways were ideal for each other. They worked hard to pull themselves out of a tough situation, and they both believed it was their trust in God. So they felt entitled to success, to a good life. Because they were people chosen by God.

Marty hardened in his old age, and his desire for a better life poisoned his ability to enjoy the moment, which only made him even crankier. He loved Den, she was a wonderful wife. He even loved his strange daughter, Kathryn. He admired her quiet tenacity. But the moment she brought home an Indian? It was too much. He had worked too hard to be betrayed like this by his own daughter.

That shift in her father, I believe, was the catalyst that turned Mama against him. She saw it as a betrayal and as being politicized in ways she felt motivated by. She'd been the best daughter she could be, but she chose Adi. She would always choose Adi.

11.

I hate Simon. I hate him in a maddening way. In my dreams he has a mercurial disposition, like death. His natural evasiveness, the smug way he holds himself, chokes me. The tortured viscera of my body makes me want to scream, *AH, AH, AH!* I want to scream endlessly across canyons and valleys, to feel the torment of my internal self play out in front of me with a destructive force.

I want to kill him.

In one dream, I'm in the desert and he's following me. *Am I weak?* I ask myself this question again and again. I turn, and he's brazen, the sun shadowing across us and the great expanse of mustard-colored soil. I stumble in fear, and as I do so, I fall onto a cactus, the needles cutting into me with decisive stings. One just misses my heart and I pull out the rest, plucking out the spines, watching as my blood spools like gold. Then something else pours out of me: "I believe in myself like a religion." I whisper it out of nowhere, like a prayer I once forgot. "I believe in myself like a religion." I repeat it.

As I stare at the same rounded eyes I've known all my life—all mine—I feel a kind of love that I've never experienced before. *The early stages of change may mimic deterioration.* I read that once, somewhere, and now I hear it everywhere around me like a Buddhist mandala that rings around, and around, and around, pushing us into our uncomfortable center.

I look back at Simon; he's no longer there. I'm alone in the desert, but the holes from the splinters shine like rubies on my body, glinting red in the heat. I am alone. *Loneliness is an abstraction.*

I opened my eyes the next morning, remembering who I was, what I was, where I was—in my room—and that I wasn't dead. Not yet. I felt momentarily safe, but then felt the sudden thud of my vagina's soreness, and that's when the deluge of memories flooded in. My mind was desperate to fill in the gaps left by the preventative efforts of traumatic shock. It was as if subconsciously, I didn't want to disappear into that moment in time, like a portal. But his body's imprint was still on top of me like a skin-crawling sensation of numbness. He was still there, his hand around my throat.

I looked around my shrine, this room. Books littered the ground near my bed, the most recently read novel on top of the pile: *The God of Small Things*, by Arundhati Roy. I scanned the rest of the corners: my perfume station, with its various types of incense and dried roses in mason jars. The curtains were slightly ajar, and the light filled the top triangle of my bed. I played around with my fingers but they were heavy; I felt groggy and out of sync. I couldn't stop having short, sudden flashes of the night before, and as each moment flew into my mind, I knew that life would never be the same again. This was my event horizon. I placed my fingers on my cracked lips and slid my tongue across the remnants of the blood that had dried over. Every muscle in my body ached unbearably. I began to cry, the tears stinging the small cuts on my face, followed by a wave of dread. Every thought was swirling, like a gnawing fog, crashing into my impaired self.

The house felt still, more quiet than I remembered it to be, which brought me some respite. I was hungry, I needed to eat. I needed to forget.

After a few tries, I successfully gathered myself into a big ball, my comforter a styled heap, a soft bulwark between me and the world. With that buffer, I opened my door slightly to hear the sounds of Mama and Baba, but I couldn't hear them. No sounds of a Beethoven concerto, no loud voices on MSNBC or NPR to fill the gap of silence. I went to my window to see if Mama was in the garden; she wasn't.

All of a sudden, I felt safe. Ever since I was a child, I craved an empty home. I loved the feeling of walking around unobserved, finally free. Where were they? It didn't matter. For a few moments I could be still and I could be alone. I could be in this room, a quiet sanctuary, and comfort my entire being, something I had become quite good at since the loss of Alyssa. I would just go into another world—I guess you could call it dreaming.

I began to think about life, about safety. Without directly thinking about what had happened to me the night before, I wondered where women were truly safe, when some of us weren't even safe in our own homes. Where could we rest? Outside of these prisms of expectation. Of violence. Of fear. Where could I lay my head and not feel coldness usurp me? In that moment, I was grateful to have a bed, to have a home I could return to— even if it wasn't ideal, even if I didn't have love, at least I had that.

But a beat skipped, and all of a sudden I was concerned about my parents. How would they react? What would they say? Something felt dangerous. My insides sat like a knotted pretzel. I gently coerced myself out of it; I knew I couldn't linger on these thoughts. Not now.

Eventually, I made my way downstairs and still found no trace of my parents. Maybe they went out, which was strange, they usually let me know. Something felt wrong, deeply wrong, but I breathed through it. As I walked into the kitchen, I suddenly became voraciously hungry. Scavenging for food, I found some cold roasted chicken that I picked apart, piling it on a plate with a piece of toast sloppily dressed with mayonnaise. I ate watching the leaves outside fall and rest on our patio. Mama would complain about them dusting about later, fixating on the smallest interruptions as a sign of impending doom. I understood why she did it. She was filling in the gaps of Alyssa's absence, which hung on to her life, a ghost.

After washing the dish, I went upstairs and slowly began to unfurl from my cocoon. The food had helped me return to my humanity, or what was left of it. My body didn't feel like my body anymore, it felt like an outlier to my system. I wanted a spaceship, a body that was mine and mine only to control. I closed my eyes. I wanted to disappear. I couldn't keep still, and my mind was suddenly erratic. It wanted to go to the pain, the lingering one just south of my belly, but I wasn't ready to face it.

I must have fallen asleep because I awoke to a knock on the door. It slowly opened soon after, and my mother stood, staring down at me. She had been crying, there were streaks underneath her eyes that lined her skin. She looked broken, like she did soon after we lost Alyssa. Over the last couple years, she'd been making a slow recovery, as Baba's health was now dissolving. Maybe that's what kicked her into action, the idea of mothering someone she wanted to save. She looked past me now, as my father came in behind her, his hands on her shoulders. They were like a sad human centipede. As they stood for a few moments, the feeling of knots returned to my stomach. After years of practice, I had memorized every facial expression of my father's. I counted to three in my head. *One.* He is looking down. *Two.* He is looking down. *Three.* He is still looking down. I was in for bad news.

"Taylia," my father croaked. His focus was entirely on his shoes, as if suddenly finding interest in their manicured leather. The air in the room was stale and bent, and a singing began in my ears to deafen the blow that I knew was to come. *Because*—of course I knew. I knew how it would look to them. Me, Taylia Chatterjee, a deep blundering mess. I knew because I had listened to Baba, I had heard him loud and clear: *Don't ever plan your life, Taylia. Don't you dare get used to this.* This. *All of this. You can't have it, it's not yours, Taylia.*

They must have gone out to discuss their plan to throw me out.

I could imagine the smarmy look on Simon's dumb face. *She just got too out of hand. She was at my place, but I'm sorry—she was so out of control.*

Mama would believe him because she wanted to believe men and their lies, and Baba would believe him because he was trained to not plan his life.

After losing Alyssa, nothing mattered.

"Taylia."

He paused for an eternity. I heard it in a daze.

"Taylia   your mother
                    and I have

                              decided

that it is b e s t

you no l o n g e r stay with

u s

or are c o n n e c t e d

with this family."

I looked at my mother; she was witnessing something she didn't have the stomach for. We stared at the deafening quiet together. I wanted to scream at her, scream at him. A black question mark hovered before me: *Did neither of you plan your lives, so this is easy?* My mother, now brittle, ugly in her betrayal, certainly not as defiant as she once was when her roots were thick and she stood with a power that announced itself. I remember the menace in her eyes when Baba and she would sometimes fight, her eyes spitting venom. *Don't you dare tell me what to wear, Aaditya.* Now, she was ravaged by weakness, ravaged by loss. She couldn't lose Baba, too. I knew that, but I hated her for it. I knew that she was protecting him. I was just always the last one to save.

"Please, take what you need and... get out."

"What did he say? What did he tell you?" I stumbled, lost.

"It's not important now..."

"No, it is." I was filled with rage.

My hands went to the back of my head, like a tic. I felt the spidery matted hair behind my ears that I had a sudden desire to play with as I prayed in front of my parents for mercy. There were so many inconsistencies in my appearance, how could they refuse to see the damage done to *me*? As I swallowed I felt the chemical aftertaste of blood in my mouth—the cum and saliva—it was the taste of iron(y). I looked over at my mother again, imagining her hands between her knees, jittery and swollen after she'd been fucked by an army of men. Was I being strong, sitting there, still alive? I wasn't sure anymore.

My father's voice croaked. "Simon explained that your decorum was..."

"Was *what*?"

"Disgusting."

"How?" I was defiant, still. I would be till the very end. They couldn't throw me out this quickly.

"Because, Taylia"—his voice leveled up, strained—"you threw yourself at him. You made a mess. He told us everything. Do you have no shame? Didn't I, or your mother, teach you to be better? And you repay us like this? Rakesh is my friend of more than twenty years, how will I show my face to him again? Huh? Taylia, this is incomprehensible."

"So you're throwing me out? For something *he* told you?"

"Why would Simon lie?"

"So what did he tell you, *exactly*?" I asked instead, wanting my own clarifications.

There was no response.

"Baba?" I asked. I craved closeness. Now more than ever, I wanted my father's care. "Baba, please." This was a nightmare, and I felt myself release a beg. "It's not what it looks like, I promise."

"He said you couldn't stop drinking, that you became so sloppy that you began to come on to everyone at the bar, like a dog. That you started to take your clothes off in front of them all, being a *slut*... This is so far from what we ever expected from you. How could you do this to me? To us? To your *mother*." He hissed the last part.

I tried to remember the real events of the night before, at least knowing that Simon was lying, and was momentarily confused. Had I, at all, acted inappropriately? Had I allowed this to happen to me? My truth was too far and too clouded to reach. So I stayed quiet and kept listening, hoping for a breakthrough, for a clear memory that was my own. Simon was pathetic. I was right, he was sociopathic. This was a different level of deranged pettiness. I suddenly remembered Vijay's face, bored, as he loomed over me. *Good pussy, good pussy, fuck, fuck, fuck.* Now, all of a sudden, I wanted to look him in the eye.

"He said you made his friends feel deeply uncomfortable. He said he'd never seen a young woman act so poorly. He was embarrassed *for* you. Can you imagine what you put him through last night? After he had reached out, acted like a gentleman, and you disrespect him, me, your mother, your family name and legacy..." He stumbled. "We can't have this kind of behavior, Taylia. This is unacceptable. I have no patience for this kind of thing. You always knew that, and I will not be the one to remind you of that again. You want to be a... a... slut? You can do that on your own dime. This won't take place under *my* roof." The *my* had a poetic vengeance. He was competing for an American life even against his own daughter.

Nothing is as important as honor was ringing in my ears. *Nothing.* It was as if all the years of advice had led me to this point. Had he always wanted to throw me out? And did she always want to let him? I didn't care about his mind anymore, the way it broke my spirit to see him stumble on the easiest pronunciations or the small, tempered shake his hands were now rhythmed with. I didn't care. My grief knew no limits, too, yet now it was being yanked like a weed out of the topsoil.

As I began to move about my room—*their* room now—my mother wheezed into the wall opposite from me. She was kneeling over the floor, sobbing, contesting, her body writhing with sorrow. I felt sick watching her cry. There was no room inside of me for sympathy. I fumbled and found my wallet, walked to my wardrobe, grabbed a jacket, and put it on. From the depths of my closet I pulled out my raggedy JanSport bag, having the intelligence to pack some underwear, a hairbrush, jeans, a sweatshirt, and a few Uniqlo tees. I was grateful for my beautiful noise-canceling headphones, which I put around my neck. I would drown myself in music. I would survive this. I thought of Vijay's sister, Liza, and how she had been disowned, too. I would be okay, I repeated to myself. I could walk away and survive. The coldness of the moment enveloped me. The warm jacket didn't take away the chill, goose bumps visible as I moved. As I walked away from my room, I took a quick glance at myself in the mirror— I didn't look *that* bad; I knew what had happened to me, and that was much worse. I paused for a moment, my back to my parents. I would be okay, I would be okay. I believed in myself like a religion.

How do you pack all the memories you have and contain them? I thought that over and over again. How much I wanted to start again. How I wanted a different life. Not this, *not this*. Not this fucking pain. I felt simultaneously lost and virulent—my rage a shield against the agony of starting again, alone. Alone. *Here you are again, fucking alone, Taylia. Can you do anything right? What is wrong with you? You've done it again, you've fucked everything up, you dumb, dumb bitch*. I wanted to scream, I wanted to vomit. I wanted a hug. I pushed through that feeling and returned to rage, a sudden numbness enveloping me. I pushed my needs down with the puke. I didn't want to die. I knew that. Not now. I wanted to survive in the face of this injustice. I had to. I had nothing else to lose.

I turned to look at them. My mother's face, with her soft skin, milky, soaked with tears. Her red hair ruffling to the rhythm of her shivering body. My father stood there with his eyes unfocused, staring out the window as the leaves fell to the floor of Mama's perfect garden. Their names felt foreign in my mind: *baba* and *mama*. Had I ever known such things?

Moving quickly, I walked out of my room, looking at the floor as I passed my father. I leaped down the stairs, embarrassed by my body, the weight of it and what it represented: shame. I spun around in circles taking it all in. *My house. My life.* All this that is, all this that was, all of it that was now being taken away from me. I pasted the picture of it all in my mind's eye. The life that could have worked. If only. *If only.* I let my eyes scan everything thoroughly, making sure I'd be able to close them and see Alyssa.

Alyssa sitting at the window.

Alyssa coming home from school.

Alyssa brushing her hair in front of the hallway mirror.

Alyssa smiling.

The smile that made you feel a surge of elation, no matter what mood you were in.

These are the last memories. I suddenly remembered a word I had learned only a few days earlier.

atomization

(noun)

The process of separating something into fine particles; to reduce to atoms

I opened the front door, allowing a gust of wind to wash over me. I looked over at my parents on the top level and nodded my head in a last goodbye and walked out—just like that. I heard my mother howl. But I didn't look back. I couldn't. The sun shone in my eyes. My mother screamed. I walked on.

12.

"What's rape?"

Alyssa stopped outlining and put down her pencil. "Where did you hear that word?"

I shrugged.

"Tay?"

"There was an interview with a woman on television."

"About?"

"She'd been raped."

"What did she say?"

"She's Pakistani. She's trying to bring justice to herself."

Pause.

"Is Baba Pakistani?"

"No, he's Indian, Tay."

"She dressed like Dadi-ma."

"Who?"

"The raped woman."

"Don't call her that."

"Sorry."

Alyssa picked up her pencil again, twirling it in between her middle and forefinger.

"So, what does it mean?"

"I'm trying to think of an appropriate way to explain it to you."

"Just explain it to me however."

"It's not that easy."

I felt uncomfortable, like I was prying into business that didn't involve me.

"Do you know what sex is yet?"

I shrugged. When you're young you think you know it all, even if you're insecure about everything to do with yourself.

"Well, rape is when someone wants to have sex with another person and forces it on to them."

I immediately understood. One of the things I had always hated was when others forced me to do something. It generally involved eating the food at my parents' friends' houses, brandishing me with dishes like it was a competitive sport. I sat down on Alyssa's bed, hoping for more information.

"I've read awful stories. Sometimes men are so vicious that they cut you open with knives and sticks for no reason. Then those women get stoned to death because society is siiiiiiiickk and they think the women were 'asking for it.'"

"'Asking for it'?"

"Men are gross. They want to punish women because they think it's their fault that they want to fuck them."

I didn't know what *fuck* meant yet, but it sounded ominous. I wondered if it was an onomatopoeia, *fuckfuckfuckfuckfuckfuck.* Alyssa's face lit up when she said it, rolling it off her tongue like a prayer, her cheeks flushed over and her eyes widened. I watched her, entranced, chewing my nails in fear.

I never used to understand the importance of believing in oneself. I knew I lacked self-esteem, but I never saw how that affected anybody but myself. I didn't know a life without that lack. It felt like how people have allergies their whole lives and become accustomed to the chronic uncomfort of it all: the phlegm caught in the throat, the constant pull of a sneeze lodged against the chest. That was me, the ache of dissatisfaction had become a common thread in my existence.

A few times when I was younger, my parents—out of fear, maybe—sent me to a child psychologist. She was a haughty woman in her mid-fifties who looked eerily similar to Gertrude Stein. She had no patience for my sadness and would often become frustrated with me. I would feel the urge to tell her that she was in the wrong profession if she had no tolerance for despair. But I lacked the chutzpah. So, instead, there I was— nine years old, silently suffering from depression.

We get so lost in our own universes, unaware of the troubles that surround us with every heartbeat. Not a soul in the world has a life devoid of pain. I tried to focus on that as I felt the misery overwhelm me in the days following leaving my parents. I knew the only way to push out of the grief inside my heart was to look to the sky. I wanted to look up and see twilight, the beams of a blue sky and the green, green trees. I wanted to see growth and cycles and *change*. I wanted to focus on my future.

I remember walking around the streets after 9/11. The city felt vacant, as if entire swathes of people had uprooted and left. That palpability of anxiety, of loss, of traumatic fear—they were left in those streets, mellowing out the anger, burying the loneliness under their ash. I felt them, even as a kid. There was a very poignant smell to that loss, to that sadness: a dank, unfettered human smell, musty and unkempt. When people mourn such massive tragedies they tend to forget to look after themselves—they revert to a more primal state, forgetting what a toothbrush feels like. They forget who they are, bound by pain and pain alone.

Alyssa and I went out with Mama maybe two, three weeks after it all happened. At first, Mama pretended as if it were just any normal trip downtown. We took the subway to Battery Park, maybe as a ruse, an excuse to see what the city smelled like now, what the fabric of the air felt like against our skin, so close to where it happened. We didn't do anything once we got out. Mama didn't do or say anything—she just *walked*. We sulked past the Staten Island Ferry and she paused. "Are you okay?" asked Alyssa. Mama stayed quiet. There was something different in the air—you could feel the absence, you could feel the hurt festering around us. Everything about the city felt dark, cloudy. We stood next to the railing by the water and held Mama's hands, one on each side, as she cried muted, soft tears that floated down to her chin. She looked out past the skyline—way, way past.

As I watched the water move around this city, I thought of how many people had died in the history of the making of this country: Black people who built this nation under enslavement, the Native Americans robbed of the land that was theirs, and now innocent people caught in the cross fire of political ambition and white supremacy.

After 9/11, everyone had become an unknown patriot. Even then, I wondered how the United States could have a finger in every pie and not know that it would backfire. I said that to Mama over dinner a few nights after our trip downtown and she screamed at me. "Do you know how many people died, Taylia? How could you possibly be so heartless?"

Alyssa looked at her food, glum, but Baba glared at Mama, as if to challenge her. There was a flicker, a moment, and though Baba spoke no words, I knew he was thinking the exact same thing. Maybe Mama sensed it, too, because she never said anything like that again.

I understood that I could both love this country but still see people like Baba—Brown people—and Black people and people like me, the in-betweeners: people unloved for what they represented, even with all the benefits of class privilege; who were neglected and then chastised for being mad. Baba didn't say anything because I knew he still wanted to be an American, but it was clear: he knew that he never would be. Especially in the aftermath of such hate. In the days, months, years post-9/11, things changed for him. Alyssa never had any trouble, but I felt the stares in school, and I caught wind of the rumor that Baba had family back home in India who were terrorists. Alyssa didn't care, but I did. I felt the weight of the shame. I wore it for all of us.

Living and going to school on the Upper West Side meant that I was irrevocably cut off from a large part of the New York experience. I had heard that other kids, other kids not like me, roamed the city—farther than I had gone—to the edges of its greatness and its vast expanses, its corners like museums, those blind spots. Reaching out, sprawling, advancing as they got older to other sections. Using the streets in the same way kids growing up in the country used rivers, forests, large rocks, and caves, mapping their world out completely.

I hardly ever spent much time below Sixty-Third Street. I walked, but New York never excited me that much, so I was happy to live in a bubble. Surprising to some, maybe, but I craved consistency. When we were in India, I was confused by my relatives and their obsession with New York. I couldn't imagine the thrill it brought others, how to them, their imagination spoke great wonders. My reference point for super, super downtown the last few years had been the Whole Foods on Broadway and Fourteenth, the Staples—everything else was a bit of a blur. As for the Lower East Side, I was a complete fool. I remotely knew the few places I had been to in the East Village during my high school days, when my friends and I would sneak out and shop at Trash and Vaudeville. St. Marks and the dirtiness of the East Village seemed worlds apart from my New York, that of pristine brownstones and greenery on the Upper West Side.

I tried shoplifting in the Lower East Side once. There was a bodega, around the corner from this Indian place called the Punjab Grocery and Deli, on East Houston that my high school friends and I would go to. Once I tried stealing a Gatorade at the bodega but chickened out at the last moment. I wondered if it was still there or if it had also been caught in the gross gentrification of the LES. My friend Carolyn was with me when I attempted to steal a Gatorade of all things, a hasty decision on my part. I wanted to impress her, as I always wanted to impress girls my age; besides she had hair like Kate Moss's. It framed her face in perfect angles. She laughed when I couldn't do it and said it was fine that I *couldn't* steal. I felt thankful for her laugh, it felt like a commiseration. Afterward, she jokingly lamented the absence of the Gatorade to all our other friends, who were sitting outside on the curb: "Taylia pussied out!" She shouted it, her punishment. I was so shocked, a tingly reservation came over me as my spine rounded over and my shoulders began to slump. This was a memorable moment of friend betrayal for me. You know, when those Shakespearean moments in your life happen.

Luckily now, years later, I still had the Punjab Grocery and Deli, which was mine (a thing I could rarely claim), and it became an LES haven for me, cheap food for my lonely days. It had really good samosas and pakoras, things that I missed about India. Delicious, fragrant street food wasn't such a novelty in India, costing close to nothing. On the streets, Mama would sometimes let us buy things, but very often would redirect us to packaged foods for "our own safety," and Alyssa and I would resent her for it. I used to love these chips, which were shrimp flavored and crunchy like a Cheeto. But I craved the hot foods, the sizzling fried pakoras. Even Baba held back when it came to the devouring of jhalmuri or jalebi—supposed favorites of yore. He would incongruently pat his tummy and tell us that his stomach had grown weary from the time and space away. He never referred to India as home, which always surprised me. I felt bloated with a blue love for India.

In the Deli I experienced a certain kind of solidarity. The servers were kind, talkative. One or two had asked me where I was from in a direct and nosy way, with a familiarity that spans borders. Whenever I mentioned that I was half Indian they would beam—"Indian! *Yoo-aare-Indiaan???*" It would become one phrase linked together like a stringed banner, the words mashed up and fast. I would imagine many question marks as they stood suspended in motion, some with tea-colored eyes, others with skin dark and waxy and with teeth black from paan—a chewing tobacco made from betel leaf—lining the gaps around their gums like caves. Their grins comical in their extended friendliness. Halfness didn't matter to them; I was one of them and they accepted me. They could see me.

In my expansion of learning about New York, which was really just a way to fill my days, I started off with the Highline. I knew it was a sign of a gentrifying New York, and as a New Yorker, I felt I was betraying my city—but still, I didn't care what people said about it, it was beautiful: a refurbished train track with a view of the Hudson River, a cascading cement dream. The first time I came here was soon after it officially opened—when it was still closed off past Thirtieth Street. I came with Mama and Alyssa on a brisk early spring day. Everything felt magical, alive. Alyssa wore a black puffy vest and a bright red hat, her hair trapped like silk in her clothes. Smothered with warmth, we caught the subway to Fourteenth Street and walked to Chelsea Market, bought some snacks, and made our way to the Highline. Mama was overjoyed, cooing at every corner, pointing out every buried weed and fragile flower. Alyssa and I laughed, throwing salted peanuts into each other's mouths, taking pictures on the bridge, and dreaming about the West Village and Chelsea apartments with their rooftop gardens and cascading vines. She was so much fun. *That's it.* She was so much fun.

The days kept arriving, even if I didn't want them to. No matter how far I ran, I couldn't escape the perpetual tide of time. Luckily New York City provided a form of catharsis. The momentum of the streets kept me awake, kept me from completely succumbing to my pain. I don't think I ever walked as much as I did on the day I was disowned. It was like a meditation. I didn't have an objective or a destination. I just walked.

For the first couple of days after, I would go to the Highline, returning each day between roving from diner to diner. The memory of Alyssa attached me to this place, and it put things into perspective. As I sat on those postmodern benches overlooking the Hudson, or on that lawn facing the West Side skyline, I'd be reminded of her. Napping in the sun, I'd lose myself. In the rogue flowers and the sultriness of the earth and grass I'd see Mama. Of course positive thoughts were fleeting and transitory, lasting but a few moments throughout the day, though they were enough to keep my stamina up and running. To keep going.

I scurried around from place to place like a rat. For a city like New York that's so overexposed, there are a lot of hidden corners. But I couldn't sleep; my body felt like it was in overdrive. I felt tense, like I was locked in anxiety, so I closed my eyes intermittently and went to another realm instead. I couldn't fathom it ever being different, but I knew I had no choice but to keep going. I didn't want to die, I kept telling myself. I remembered Dadi-ma, I remembered Alyssa, and knew that they would guide me; I knew I would know where to stop to rest.

Walking through the West Village and the Meatpacking District reminded me of the beautiful juxtaposition of the city. The grit near the glamour, the seediness cut open by the Jeffrey boutique. I decided to pay Magnolia Bakery a visit, remembering that Alyssa used to love buying desserts there because of *Sex and the City*. She was a Carrie; I was a Miranda. I liked being a Miranda, because she was the bluntest. I wanted to be that blunt, that real, in my own life. Upon reentering the bakery, without Alyssa, I felt tattered and dissociative. I focused on the interiors. It reminded me of 1950s glitz, the employees buzzing with alacrity, and the subdued softness highlighted my inadequacy. I felt as if I were insulting its innocence, so I ordered quickly and sat outside, enjoying my treat while watching the people go by. I can't explain what I wanted. I needed normalcy, comfort. I wanted a home. I watched a couple in love and felt my mind slip and wander to the pain in my womb, instantly transported back to that night. I clenched my jaw and stopped myself from going any further. Breathing heavily, I looked down at my cupcake and was saddened by what I saw. I no longer felt hungry. I sighed and threw it away.

The day had made me feel annoyed. Whenever I remembered the pain of my body, with a quick assaulting flash, I really just felt betrayed by it. I didn't want to feel the sting of the tiny tears on my vagina rub against the unruly cotton blend of my ugly underwear. Everything felt insulting, as if it were mocking me.

So I took brief moments of gratitude for my music, for the wondrous sounds that shielded me from the world like a buffer, and began to walk toward NYU. Although I had heard quite a few complaints from my parents' friends about its desire to colonize Lower Manhattan, I quite liked it. I felt it gave New York a new character, and that's essentially what made New York what it was: diverging characters. As I walked up West Fourth Street, on one side of me there was Washington Square Park, a true New York icon, but I had entirely forgotten its existence. How many movies had I watched that panned over its stone exterior? I walked across the park and peered at the many different faces that had congregated there. I watched as a few kids played near the fountain, which served its part as a modern-day watering hole. After a few moments of admiring the Arc de Triomphe–like figure in the middle, I walked farther north, toward a tree that stood on the corner. It was a beautiful, majestic tree, and as I got closer, I saw Dadi-ma resting, meditating, with her eyes closed. I knew she would tell me when it was safe. Getting her signal, I felt steady. I plunked down in front of her, deciding that this would be *my tree*. I christened it with the name Cillian, an homage to Alyssa's favorite actor, Cillian Murphy. We both fell in love with him when we rented *Disco Pigs*. Alyssa always thought he was hot, but in a "murdery kind of way." I even had a crush on a boy once *because* he looked like him, following my faux Cillian from school to the gates of his place. I thought he was so handsome, so quintessentially cheekboned and Irish.

As I sat down underneath Cillian, pulled out of my trance, I slowly allowed myself to recall what I had been through in the past few days. I was still wearing the same clothes, and they stuck uncomfortably to the sweat and grime that had built up around me, like a protective wall. Suddenly embarrassed, I sat wondering what a vision I must have been on the streets, walking aimlessly, like a forlorn wilding. I was alone. I was completely alone.

I looked around, searching for answers, but all I saw was the city's arrogance. Now that I wasn't in motion, finally still, the blurriness began to form distinct pictures in my mind. Suddenly I was angered by the cars, by the people with their venti lattes, expensive textbooks, and by the stupid and domineering Bobst Library with its shapeless blood exterior. I felt like shouting, so I did, a loud bellow. A few looked around, but mostly everyone went about their business. We were New Yorkers, we understood the natural law of the universe. *Sometimes everyone has shit—doesn't mean you have to stop and stare.* I looked around, humored by the lack of judgment. I sat back against Cillian, resting my head in my exhaustion. Does it matter whether the weight of living is overwhelming?

It felt strange to be so close to a school, when my own hopes of schooling had been so altered by the shocking loss of Alyssa. I felt like my once intense ambition had been abducted and replaced by a pathetic, mercurial dullness. I felt robbed of all hope, like a toddler who had heard too many no's for one lifetime. It had once felt special to commemorate Mama and Baba through the intensity of fierce education, to walk the halls of Columbia like them, like a poem or a sweet hymn, but I had no desire to do that anymore. I was no longer tied to that coiling archipelago of what it means to have generational legacy. That terrible myth of blood family, as if that meant anything.

When I dropped out, it felt shameful. I had missed too many French literature classes, and my haughty professor had no desire to give me any leeway. "This is Columbia," she would say, her face a mask of white paint, like a Venetian doll's. Her eyeliner was always a pencil-dotted streak under her eyes, kohl the color of blue china, and her hair, a coiled wig. She looked about ninety, the bones in her fingers like tiny birds that jutted out of the skin. "At Columbia, we don't make excuses."

Had none of these people heard of depression, or did they just not care? After Alyssa passed, I perpetually felt as if there were no air left inside of me. All human interaction felt heavy and charged. In all honesty, I didn't feel safe anywhere I went. She had left me feeling like an empty vault, but one in constant search for some warmth. It felt disarming to lose the only ally I felt I had. What little life I had was sapped out of me, and I dropped out a few months after she died.

Though, sometimes, before I left home, when the sky was tangerine pink, I felt the longing surround me like a faint air— like the smell of the oily couches creased with age that sat in the halls of Columbia's vast libraries. Temporarily, I clung to that feeling—of wanting so badly to be held, to be cocooned, by an institution, a legacy. What was I without it? I had, in many, tragic ways, bought into my parents' thinking. Like them, I craved validation. I tried, after Alyssa, to return to ambition, but it was too hard. I couldn't focus, I didn't have it in me to live for something anymore. When I left school, Baba wouldn't look me in the eyes for weeks, only saying, "My daughters are failures," while walking, in a huff, to his study. He couldn't stand it, he felt like I was betraying him. Like Alyssa had.

I sighed, looking far into the distance, and noticed a small café. It looked so warm, I could practically smell the fresh croissants, the chemistry of the yeast and flour, the golden edges browning over the curves of its hump. I wondered what it would be like to eat, to live, to survive as Taylia now. I had never *really* felt like a Chatterjee—and now the feeling of distance and confusion was thoroughly intensified. I felt removed from the identity that had been carved out for me. It was the feeling of endlessly swimming, a buoy amid so many promises, so many aspirations. The whiplash of loneliness struck me, beating against my bones, my spine hinged against all the dissatisfaction—but I sat there, the smell of baked goods evoking some kind of earthly nostalgia inside of me. It was not something that I remembered Mama cooking, but it felt like home. A home that I had built in my mind—maybe one we all built, about the lives that we felt we deserved.

I inhaled the wind, the smell of fresh bread. Maybe I could do this, I thought. I knew what I needed: security, money, a place to live *permanently*. I remembered some Dutch foreign exchange students who had told me about a youth hostel they'd be staying at in the interim as they waited for Columbia lodging. I realized I could do this, there were options for nomads like me. But I would need a job. That's what brought me to Kat Armand.

13.

Kat was short for Khadijah. Khadijah with a *K*. That's how Kat introduced herself, preemptively knowing the beats in conversation, the rhythms of the *hey*s and *how*s. She knew how predictable people were when they'd ask how to spell her name, their faces simultaneously showing they didn't really care, their expressions droopy, the corners of their lips dancing with a twitch. I really liked that about Kat; she didn't seem surprised by people's bullshit. It wasn't good or bad, it was just data to her.

Kat had grown up in Brooklyn and been in New York her whole life—like me. She had bony hands and skinny legs but a wide, luscious chest and generous upper body that she adorned with cotton-blend T-shirts she bought from Uniqlo over cool black slacks that were "all Lemaire, baby." She told me that last bit with such panache.

When I met Kat she was wearing all black and her hair was natural and short. It was more red than brown, like a burnt auburn, suntanned and warm. She had on several silver rings that she wore even despite having to take them off when she worked. The one on her ring finger wrapped like a clasp over an entwined lemony-yellow citrine crystal. Kat said she wore the citrine because it strengthened the "crown chakra and heightened intuitive perception." She said this matter-of-factly, without loftiness. She was stylish, boyishly tailored, and together. *Together in a real way.* She wore Nike sneakers with high insoles that elongated her thin-like-straps ankles and curved calves. I was enraptured by the way Kat moved, she seemed stately, assured; she was like Alyssa. She told me her love for Eartha Kitt and how they shared the same birthday. This was all in the first ten minutes of meeting.

Feeling connected to her, via her food and energy, I had been visiting Kat's café and bakery for a daily treat all week, usually ordering a chocolate croissant (or sometimes even an apple Danish, or a slice of pumpkin bread, or a salted caramel Rice Krispies treat—always with a small almond milk latte). But that day, as I sat under Cillian and felt protected by the tree—a caryatid, like the mother figure I never had to protect me—I had an idea. Maybe like Siddhartha under the tree, Dadi-ma, my oracle for safety, had brought me here and I was listening to my visions, or intuition, more ardently. And something was drawing me to Kat. I had been reading a book about astrophysics that I had picked up from the discount trolley outside of the Strand, and I thought of how her café, Milk Thistle, was my desperate daily reminder of self-care. In the days right after leaving, it was agonizingly lonely. I longed for direction and asked the stars to give me something, anything. Kat was always personable, always welcoming me into her sacred space, and being around her were moments of the day I took solace in. This felt like a connection worth investigating, even if it didn't lead to anything more substantial.

I took showers every day at the Blink around the corner; I had decided to join after I heard it had decent facilities, and for twenty-six dollars a month, I figured it was a necessary purchase. One thing I had always feared, ever since I was a child, was being laughed at because of my smell. I think that was part of the Indian shame—smelling badly—and something I had picked up from Baba. He loved eating fish but was always scared of the way his hands would stink after. The reaction was exaggerated, almost traumatic. I'd watch as he'd obsessively wash his hands and smell his fingers, grossly inhaling as if he were in that movie *Superstar*. Now that I no longer had my perfume corner, I was devolving a little, and I wanted to feel clean and smell good. I also needed a job to keep up my pastry habit, acquire some scents, and all the other expenses that spilled over.

"Hello." I greeted Kat with an openmouthed grin as I walked in. The smile stretched from ear to ear, an eccentric Taylia smear on my face. I felt like I looked like the Cheshire cat.

She squinted up at me, a smile slowly appearing on her face. "Hi."

I knew she could sense my hesitance.

"How's your day been?" I said, almost breathless, bopping on my toes like I needed to pee. The café was almost empty, which I knew it would be. Kat would close up shop in an hour, and I knew it would be the safest time for me to stumble, to be earnest.

She leaned onto the counter. "Not bad." She paused. "You've been coming in pretty often lately."

I nodded, fake enthusiastically, already way too nervous for my impending rejection, slight and jittery. "Yeah." I coughed a croak away. "Every day."

"Are you okay? It's Taylia, right?"

I breathed and toppled right in, oddly fearless: "I'm looking for a job. Do you know anyone nearby that's hiring?"

Kat took a minute and then suddenly burst out laughing, like I had told a joke. I followed suit, my chuckle racking my nerves, overly fast.

"Just to be clear, you're asking me for a job, right, Taylia?"

My laugh stopped short. "Yes. That's what I'm attempting to do."

She smiled and then softly pouted. "Tell me, why do you want a job?" Her tone had now morphed into something serious. In the little while since I'd been coming into Milk Thistle, with its prime real estate by bustling NYU (and its equally entitled students), I had witnessed Kat's way with people. It was something that I envied, like I had envied Alyssa or Zeina. Women who knew how to be, without question or pause. Women who had no puff of anxiety breaching every interaction. Kat was gregarious in a way that was inspiring.

I stumbled, as I always did. "I... like you, and I like this place... and well, frankly, I need the money."

She was short, direct: "Have you ever worked in the service industry before?"

"Yeah... I mean, I worked at the Body Shop near my house in the summers." It took me years to get on cash duty. Those registers were complicated and seductive, with their wads of cash just floating in a plastic tray.

"But you've never worked in food service before?"

I paused, marking my words in my head.

"I only ask because it's not easy. You have to put up with a lot of personalities."

I nodded, profusely embarrassed that I had taken so much of her time already.

"Buuuuuut, it's funny you came in... Kind of magical, actually. I've been looking for somebody for a while to help me with shifts. I was even planning on putting a sign out there. But I haven't because I knew it'd eff with the vibe. Believe it or not, I wanted to hire someone organically."

I pursed my lips, wondering if this was organic *enough.*

"This"—she giggled—"is pretty organic, though."

"Yeah?" I asked, slightly desperate.

"You have an endearing frankness to you, Taylia."

I smiled weakly, already afraid of the job I hadn't yet started.

My first shift was early in the morning the next day. As I polished silverware, Kat prepped scones for the oven. It was close quarters, so we quickly became acquainted, and I admired her openness. She was a divorced thirty-seven-year-old mother of two. She had a joviality to her, like people with higher frequencies who just buzz different.

"Man, the Body Shop, you remember when it was *all* the rage?"

"Yeah, I mean, I bought those body butters in bulk."

"Hmm... Mango..." we both muttered, shaking our heads simultaneously, looking at each other in glee. "Throwback!"

Smiling, she made us some coffees, showing me how to do it a few times, allowing me a couple of tries as well, before we officially opened. We were leaning toward each other drinking perfect milky coconut lattes, zero foam, all cream.

"What's your situation like?" She hesitated, I could tell not wanting to pry. "As in, where do you live?"

I hadn't been confronted with this question yet. My tongue rolled like a sardine trapped in a can. Finally, I blurted out, "I left school, so I'm between places. It's temporary."

"Well, I'll need an address for work purposes..." She paused, slowing her words down to enunciate her thoughts. "You know, for taxes and your paycheck. But we can see how we get on for now and go from there..."

She was cut off by a bulky white woman who stormed in with a bad mood, despite the sign on the door still saying CLOSED.

"I fucking just saw some dude that looked like fucking Bill O'Reilly! Bill ugly fucking O'Reilly. I really think it was him!"

"Oh, wow, um." Kat was a bit dumbfounded but took it in stride.

"As if we needed to see another fucking Republican around here, am I right? Are your cupcakes vegan?"

Neither Kat nor I thought it necessary to say anything else. I was used to compartmentalizing white entitlement. After the woman left, Kat and I burst into laughter.

"Get used to that right there. Also, watch out for the NYU brats. Jesus. Some of them are entitled little..." She made a face. "But... a lot of them love pastries, so... ?" She said this next part seriously, though: "Also, never, *ever* call the cops. No matter what. If there's a problem with any of the customers and I'm not here, call me. I'll always guide you through it. But just never call the cops."

I nodded my head, taking it in fully.

There was an intimacy we had with each other that was unnerving to me. Maybe because of how fluid it was, how easy. I felt safe around Kat in a way I didn't with most people. She didn't make me feel anxious; she made me feel heard. We talked about real things. Or, rather, she talked about real things, and I listened.

I was still too shell-shocked, maybe, to let it all out, but I enjoyed her trust in me. It made me feel worthy of being talked to. I found out that Kat had started seeing someone relatively recently, but she didn't know where it was going. She didn't know if *she* wanted it to go anywhere. She wanted to be in the throes of it, the throes of love and whatever it came with. I couldn't help agreeing and, somewhere in the distance, wanting the same for myself. Not that I knew what that looked like for me.

"Taylia, I'm a romantic."

The café was closed and we were cleaning up. The soles of my feet felt brittle, like I might collapse, but my spirits were high.

"I used to think it was so easy. Just find the right person and fall in love. But there's no right person. These days I think love is nothin' *but* holding on. If you have two people that can hold on, then you got yourself that *sustainable* kind of love. But then you gotta remember not to hold on too tight. We all gotta die one day, so don't hold on too tight, but hold on just *enough*."

The lady Kat was seeing was a professor of literature at NYU named Claudia Pierre. She'd come in regularly at the café, and then one day, she asked Kat out. They had gone on two dates, and Claudia had paid for both of them, Kat told me as she showed me how to pull espresso again, even though we had already cleaned up the machines, because she wanted the "coffee perfection of Australians." There was a determination in her that I admired—it was motivating. On their first date Claudia took Kat to a nice little West Village restaurant where they shared smoked hen-of-the-woods mushrooms and preserved lemon on a duck breast, accompanied by a silky piece of white fish ("It was a delicious, buttery hake!") with pickled fennel.

"She's quite something, though. She knew I was a foodie and she took me to this place that I had heard of but didn't realize it'd be so damn special. She pursued me, Taylia. I can't tell you what it means to be pursued, for someone to be romantic. To show up and want to impress you. To want to make you come alive. I've never felt that way with a man before. *Khallas*." She crossed her heart with the tip of her right pointer finger, like a crossbones, *cross my heart, hope to die.*

They hadn't slept together yet, and Kat seemed happy to take her time. "I can't do what I used to do in my twenties. Sometimes it's good to wait! Before Voldemort—that's what I call my ex"— she smirked at her statement—"before him, I didn't know what it meant to wait. Then we met and we waited. He left my ass anyway. But with women, it's different. With women, waiting is fun. Means all the juices get a little time to settle and develop."

She tapped her tongue on the right side of her lip seductively. We laughed—and I felt a blush come over me.

Although ultimately I knew I had had "sex," it didn't feel like sex. It hadn't felt like sex at the time, either. It just felt like something that I had to do in order to survive. Like a level on a video game I needed to pass to move on, except if I didn't do it I'd die. And also it was a terrible thing to survive. I still didn't have words for it, it's as if everything about my body was blurred. The baby cuts on my vagina from the dryness were the worst part, because I had to walk around like I wasn't carrying several open wounds daily. I hadn't even touched myself near there since it happened. Even when I went to the bathroom I avoided touching, brushing past the padding of hair, grateful for its existence. Mirrors became things I avoided, and car windows, too—or windows in general: reflective buildings, big huge revolving doors. I didn't want to see myself. I couldn't bear to look at what I had become.

Kat and I spent hours together those first few days. I liked the routine: I finally had a bed in a hostel where I could leave everything but my phone, and I would get up, go to Blink for a shower (the ones in the hostel were unisex and therefore felt unsafe), and then walk to her café for my shift. One day we ate stale olive oil cake and almond croissants on the floor of beautifully symmetrical white tiles at the end of the shift. She had great ambitions about her "tiny home," which was just a little bigger than a hole in the wall. She wanted it to become a part of people's lives, an important New York outpost. She felt as though she had created something special—and she wanted to share that with others. She had the right personality for it, too. She was ambitious and unabashedly so. "I make good shit, Taylia. I know that's not what gets you far all the time, but I actually make *good* shit. So help me God, nobody's gonna stop me from making what I wanna be making."

She told me she came from a lineage of folks who were entre-preneurs. In the '80s, her aunt Sydney had become a realtor in New York, encouraging all her sisters (she had three, including Kat's mother, Oriah) to buy property. They listened. Oriah and her husband, Franklin (an Afro-Panamanian art collector), bought three properties across Brooklyn, all brownstones: one on Carlton and Dekalb, one on Bedford and Putnam, and the last one a block down from the first one, right across from Fort Greene Park on Willoughby Avenue and Washington Park. Over the years, their accrued familial wealth had generated more in-terest in properties. So, when the hot little pocket of NYC real estate became available, right near NYU and Washington Square Park, Oriah found out through Sydney and then told Kat, who would ask her mother for a loan to build her tiny café dream. It was this determination to not just pay back her mother but also succeed like her that encouraged Kat to be ambitious, *and* to make the best product. No surprises there, she was a Capricorn.

We were both smart, but Alyssa had been tenacious. She was good at getting what she wanted, but she liked to fight for it, too. It's strange how we individually processed how to fight. Alyssa and I had learned the same things, and yet our styles were so completely different.

Each night at the hostel, I was afraid of the noises that'd wake me, afraid of men banging on the door, of touching me in my sleep. I made myself invisible, which had always been a survival tactic. I had to be aware of factors that I didn't necessarily have the energy for, but I had accepted that this was my new life. Just as I was thinking this, Kat started talking. It had been about ten days straight that I had shadow-worked with her. The day was coming to an end, and I was beginning to stare into the distance, completely fatigued by the physicality of the labor involved in manning a café.

"Taylia. In all honesty," she started, "and please don't take this the wrong way, but I know you stay at that hostel on Bond Street." She bit her lip. "I saw you walk out once, even before you came in and asked about the job. You have a memorable face. Those strong eyebrows! So I recognized you from coming into the café. When you asked for a job, I was intrigued, and you've been really great so far..." She paused dramatically, and a lifetime of fear built up until she spoke again. "I hired you because I like your energy, which these days is everything to me. A lot of people talk the talk, but not a lotta people walk the walk. There's something about you that's very honest. Sure, you're a lot more private than I was expecting, but I respect that."

She was so insanely transparent. I stayed silent, not daring to interrupt what I felt like I knew was coming.

"So, listen, this isn't something I'd normally offer someone I don't know very well, but until you have enough money saved, you *could* stay with me. I told you I have space, and the boys would love a houseguest."

I was shocked, though not entirely surprised. I had clocked Kat as much as she had clocked me: we were people of the same ilk. "What do you mean by that?"

"I mean, we'd figure out a system. And this wouldn't be a handout as much as it would be a push up—"

I cut her off. "You can't possibly be serious."

She smiled slyly. "This isn't a favor. I'm gonna make you work for it. You know that I will. I just want you to know that I see you."

With a long exhale, I started crying, covering my face with the palms of both my hands. For the first time in a long time I felt dumb lucky. I felt hopeful. She didn't come over and embrace me, but just let me cry until I composed myself, and I was grateful. I was full of emotion, maybe because I had been subconsciously praying for something, somebody, to reach out and show me I wasn't alone. This statement from Kat felt like a lifeline, one I hadn't been afforded since Alyssa's death.

Later, I explained to Kat that I did have *some* money, so that I *would* pay rent, but that I could do with *more* money. She acquiesced, confused as to why I'd live in a hostel if I had *some* money, telling me that was some "white people shit." I couldn't yet explain, to anyone, the rough shapes of my past and how they haunted me. How I had grown tired of expectation, so I meekly expected nothing, offering myself nothing.

I realized I had never known what it was like to choose oneself, having always bitterly deferred to someone else. Watching Kat, I wondered if anyone had ever told her that she had to fight for herself or if that was an inherent understanding. I felt tired of not knowing *how to fight*, but knew I soon must. Maybe when I walked out of my parents' house that day, I was trying to redirect my narrative. I was tired of being a victim.

That night, at Kat's, I took a hot shower and tried to look at myself in the foggy mirror. I wanted to become my own witness. I had visions of Dadi-ma as I washed and grasped at my old talisman, my chain with two rings on it that I always wore around my neck. I thought back to when she had gotten very ill. She lived in Kolkata, and Baba, full with filial piety, insisted that we move to give her moral support in her last days. So we relocated to India for a few months during the summer holidays in my early teens, leaving our Upper West Side brownstone for a home in bustling West Bengal.

It's strange how death was such a sly interloper of feelings. At the announcement of impending mortality, Baba's sense of duty was suddenly forced into motion with a fortitude of longing and soured regrets: regrets of not being physically closer, regrets of leaving his mother and father. Perhaps, also, the misgivings of marrying a white woman and not being able to bear sons—nothing to continue our name or his and his parents' culture.

I was soon enchanted by India. Growing up in New York often provides you with the conceit that no other city is worth venturing to. The busy streets of India were, unlike New York, filled with an unnameable exuberance and a strong, dreamy energy. The rickshaws, the cars, even the raucous fumes, felt like home. I grew fond of seeing lakes, cement, and sloping green trees (the secret Mughal gardens) with a readied excitement. Outpacing the chase, what resided in the streets of Kolkata was also a kindred resilience. The people were friendly and cared for you, and that was the strangest part of it all. Dadi-ma, someone I had never met before in my life, cared about me. Her love was so thick I could feel it, slick and stretched out, floating past me even when I was away from her.

The first night I was there, she sat me down and combed my hair, lovingly caressing my temples to my roots, slathering my hair with coconut oil. The light through the venetian blinds traced our bodies as I sat at her feet, my torso enveloped in her shadha saree. She smelled of burnt cinnamon and her hands were soft and rubbery, like a toy—comforting, as she drew me to her. Gold bands lined her delicate wrists, hanging off her body's ancient tapestry, clicking and clinking every time she moved. Every night after that, she'd kiss me good night and call me her puuthul. She never fretted over the fact that I wasn't like Alyssa; she loved me unconditionally for *who I was*. I meant something to her. And that meant everything to me.

Within the cracks of my childhood, my relationship with my dadi-ma was the tangible kintsugi to my healing. Like gold glue, the veins of a leaf, she filled me with an intense, overwhelming serenity, but more—she initiated a healing of sorts. There was something powerful in being seen by her—the theme of my life. The need for my body to be seen in all of its varying dimensions was like a drug I was hooked on; it gave me permission to like myself, too. A diminutive me, Dadi-ma and I even had the same thick, fuzzy brows, the same button nose, the same petal-shaped lips. She spoke mainly in Bangla (not because she couldn't speak English, but because she didn't want to) and would argue with Baba for not teaching me and Alyssa the language. "You must read Rokeya Sakhawat Hossain, Taylia." That was one of the few things she ever said to me in English, both a suggestion and a command.

I also liked the way she clearly loved me more than Alyssa. Possibly the only person where that was the case. I had never needed to prove my worthiness of love to my dadi-ma as a faulty Alyssa, a less exceptional, diluted version of her. To Dadi-ma, I was me, in all my clumsy glory, and in days where we napped, lined by milky mosquito nets, I remembered that I was loved.

She passed away five weeks into our visit. Although I knew it would happen, I never believed it really could. Here was a strong woman, never submitting to the demands society put on her sex. She went to school when women weren't allowed to; she raised a son and sent him to America despite growing up relatively middle class. She was strong-willed in every sense of the word and had a great understanding of herself and what she wanted to contribute to the world.

I remember, because I understood there was something violent in her. I could see it in the way she went walking with me through the woods, the ways in which she could still cut the throat of a chicken and pluck it for dinner. She was fearless, but she was also wise. She wasn't petty. Baba's cousins were brats, and their children, Alyssa's and my second cousins, were living nightmares who had no interest in us, the foreigners. Alyssa's charms wouldn't win them over, and she resented them for that. Despite the hardness of the family around her, Dadi-ma was just. She rarely raised her voice, her sternness was all in the looks. She seemed so incapable of deteriorating. I was determined to believe that she would prove everyone wrong and live an eternal life of forthrightness and certitude, equipped only with her chewable vitamin C tablets and four golden churis, two on each wrist.

A few weeks before she died, she gave me a necklace grooved with indents, her fingers lacing the chain around my neck—from hers to mine—spooling the golden strand underneath my hair. There were two rings: one yellow and the other silver. When she showed me the former, she pointed to me and said, "You." Then she indicated the silver one—a twine of longing—and said, "Husband." I understood her and nodded, my breath catching up to the excitement of knowing that somebody cared. There were pockets of her that would always be mysterious to me— invisible, yet still somehow tangible in a ghostlike way. I could sense her even when I couldn't see her. She taught me her Jedi tricks, she picked up on my psychic-ness.

She took me under her wing and taught me to meditate, to do yoga—training me, simultaneously, to feel her pulse move through the airtight corners, to feel the friction of space and time, to see the void but know that she was watching me, my skin goose-bumped and blue, my calf muscles flexed, knowing that death was not the end. In those long afternoons with her, it's hard to explain—but it was the first time I witnessed magic. We communicated with nonwords so much, my attunement began to exponentially radiate.

The night before she died, she spoke to me again about love. Her hair was out of its braids, the mosaic of silver strands spar-kling, splayed across her red cashmere sweater. She wiped away my tears and told me things would change. I rested my head against her fleshy waist, her belly exposed only slightly. I knew that she understood my pain—she could see it in my eyes as we lay there underneath the layers of tulle like bandages, protecting our wounds against the outside world.

The day she died, a storm of mosquitos rose from beneath her bed as I felt her take her last breath. The last soft whoosh passed through her with a melodic hum; I was lying next to her, watching with my eyes wide as it happened. I peeped through the sheets and saw Baba crying silently, his head in his hands, and my mother on the floor at his feet, snot dribbling as she clutched at her salwar. There was no stranger malady, I assumed, than watching a parent die, metamorphosizing, shifting from this world to another. The maids stood crying, too, their lilac- and rose-colored sarees strangling their emotions as they whispered prayers. I remember the smell of her charred body, the bright flames burning, licking through her body on the pyre, devouring like a cruel animal. Turned into ash, emerging as a jewel, she had left me—and this world—allowing me to feel hopeful.

14.

I craved stability but continued to fear the dependence that came with finding it in someone else. I admired Kat and could feel the good emanate through her skin, undulating with kindness and morality; but our friendship made me nervous. The conversational intimacy, the brutal candor—things that come so effortlessly to some—felt like a bone stuck in my throat. I knew that if I could speak like the Alyssas and Kats of the world, it would obviate the chance of confusion, miscommunication, hurt feelings (on both sides), and my general embarrassment—but I had never been able to compel those gears into motion. I had never found myself interesting enough. But with Kat, it *was* different. I was still the same, but she somehow accepted me. It felt exploitative, to feel this organic human connection, a synchronicity so uncommon that it felt forced, fraudulent. Next to her candidness, I stood filled with reservations, my tightly locked box of secrets clutched so desperately to my heart, and yet she made space for that, never once using it against me. I accepted this new dynamic, this new friend. In fact, I welcomed it, because I was hungry for real love.

When I woke up, it was my second week at Kat's—early—before Kat and her children, Luc and Isaac (whom I was beginning to care for deeply), rose. I felt an itch. Thankfully, it was a weekend, which meant the café was closed. As I began to scratch, I felt it rise right into my ass, into that raw, cavernous hole. Shifting like a diffraction, the itch moved through me, showing no signs of slowing down. I fell back against the unhelpful comfort of my pillows. I wanted to cut myself out. *Scratch, scratch, scratch.*

Kat had emerged. "Babe, are you okay?" She had heard a commotion, knocked, and opened the door to find me defeated, my eyes pale with pent-up tears. I began explaining to her my bodily dysfunctions. She half laughed and said it in one way: "Sounds like a yeast infection, baby."

"I thought I had had them before... but this feels really, *really* bad."

She had a habit of researching things on Google and explaining to the boys, so she began reading off her iPhone. "Yeast infections are caused by the fungus *Candida*. This fungus is associated with intense itching, irritation... blah blah blah..."

I stopped listening, in pain, and instantly began to think of that night again. Fingers, slimy groping fingers. Those diseased hands. I was going to die. I mopped my wet brow as she read, squeezing the place between my legs as if I were a human-sized tweezer pushing down on the multiple ticks that were pulsing through me. It started burning, but I kept pushing with sweaty urgency. I was drifting. *Don't think of that night, Taylia.* Everything tasted sour.

"Your eyes look like white disks. Are you okay?"

Her voice sounded distant, her tonsils jiggling as she coughed. "Taylia?"

Tell her, Taylia. Tell her what? *Tell her about that night.* No.

My eyes were zeroing out and I could feel the life pumping, the blood flowing like a beat, in my down there. It felt like a boom box, bouncing pulses of sound and goop. I needed to get out. I felt like I was about to suffocate.

"What do I do?" I asked her.

Kat suggested medication, carefully giving me instructions to the nearest pharmacy. I could sense she wanted to volunteer getting it, but I was profusely wanting to prove that I was fine, so she patted me on the back with a kindness that she wanted me to feel, and I walked out. Outside, the city felt like glass and light, the windows high. The air made a sizzling noise as I walked on the pavement, and everything felt fuel-shimmered and smoky, hot to the touch. I walked into a Duane Reade on Dekalb Avenue and bought Monistat, skipping out like Wile E. Coyote. I wanted to pull my pants down right there, but instead I waited until I got home. Kat cooed outside the bathroom as I plied open myself and layered on swathes of the cooling cream. It reminded me of when I had had a burn as a child; Mama had run swiftly to the garden, cutting open the flesh of her robust aloe vera plant. She came back with such grace, holding it in her left hand, floppy with juice, and gently placing the transparent lobster-like flesh on my gibbous burn. The crustaceany aloe felt so cool, so right, on my bony little arm. I remembered her vividly for a brief moment, then cried by the chlorine-stained toilet seat.

Later that day, momentarily cured, I found books on the tarot in Kat's bookshelf, which I wanted to look into. I was impressed by her ability to juggle life so effortlessly. At the current moment, she was in the backyard with her friend Crystal, who also had a young boy about Isaac's age. I could hear them both roaring through the ecosystem, the boys playing with plastic lightsabers, doing the *zhoom-zhoom* sound as they waved them around like batons. Kat made me feel welcome. It's the ethos she had with the café, too, of allowing people to come and create a haven against the harsh city. She'd seen the way the city could make you feel unwanted, she understood the perils. I think she longed for a community she could rely on, which is why she made her home an offering as well.

Our friendship was quite fortuitous simply because she trusted me and trusted that I could handle things for her in the absence of her ex, if need be. I was always good at filling in the gaps for other people. We came to an agreement that I would pay cheapish rent (since Kat's family owned the place) for my room and that I would get paid an hourly wage for my three-month apprenticeship. If things worked out, I would get on the payroll, maybe even become a manager. We were both open to possibilities.

I felt grateful that, although I had left in haste, I had a small, sober inheritance that Dadi-ma had left me when she passed. Thank God I was naturally frugal—except for my apparently new pastry addiction. The inheritance from Dadi-ma of $15,000 had seemed negligible when I first received it. I had turned snooty after time with wealthy peers. But now, it was a godsend, and some part of me was relieved it didn't come from my parents. There was a part of me that wanted to start anew. Dadi-ma must have known that I would need it one day. All of this made me feel that I had struck a good deal with the universe.

When I hurt, I let it hurt, but I tried—with Kat's suggestion—to take my ego out of it as much as I could. And it was paying off: I didn't know why, but the city was making me feel things were possible; it was reviving me. To make something of myself, on my own, and by my own definition, when I previously (just a few weeks ago) had felt like I was nothing. I knew investing in myself was a worthy pursuit.

Kat and I started a nightly ritual. We would smoke hash when the boys went to bed and Kat would read our tarot, teaching me the energetic science of it all. One night, as we sat at her back porch with a beautiful Oriental-style blue-and-white pipe, she asked me what my question was for the night. Up until then, my conversations with the higher forces had been naive, unformed, but tonight I was tender. I asked, "When will I find love?"

Kat cocked her eyebrow, teasing. "You mean like a *boyfriend*?"

I snorted the Bloody Mary I was drinking right out of my nose, the gin firing through me with fusillade precision. *"Noooooo!!!!!"* I had not thought of men in an eternity. I shivered.

"Why'd you just shiver?"

"I didn't."

"Uh-huh, yeah, you did."

She stared at me, and I felt my cheeks begin to burn with memories.

"Taylia."

"It's nothing."

"Hmm..."

I sighed. "I don't know if you've ever realized that I'm not good... with men?"

"Is anyone good with men, honey?"

"My sister—" I stopped. I hadn't even realized what I was saying when it came out.

"Oh... You have a sister?"

I didn't know how to answer that. "Hmm... But men are awful. They're scary!" I said, changing the subject.

She laughed, by now fluent in my conversational swerves. "Ugh, women are scary, too."

I felt the question rise through me like a wave; I wanted to know. "Kat, have you ever been in love? If so, can you tell me about it?"

I rarely caught her off guard, but here she was, suddenly silent. There were many pauses before she finally started to talk, hesitant.

"Yeah. I think... If I'm going to be frank... as much as Elijah is a major S.O.B...." She looked toward the boys' room to see if the door was closed; it was. "We were massively in love. Hell, maybe that's why it hurts so much. Even if you love somebody it doesn't always work out." She paused. "He was good when he was good, you know? *Like good.* And it doesn't make any sense why he left me with two kids, scurrying off like an effing rat... and you know now that Claudia and I are getting more serious, or I don't know... more intense or whatever... I find myself thinking about love again, but with fear. So much fear." She had started crying. "And I hate that he took my faith away in love, Taylia. What if it doesn't work out again? I hate being scared."

She cried silently, composed. Her huffs like rhythms as she gently rocked herself back and forth. I went to her knees and pressed them gently, laying my head at her thighs. That was the beginning of our enduring connection.

I didn't really know if I had the capacity to fully love, if I really had that ability to let go. My heart felt gutted out, concaved, yet at the same time I was tired of my grief. At this point, I was almost bored of it. I wanted so much to say something to her—to say that I understood, that I knew what it was like to have someone leave you with no remorse. To wake up one day and find that what loved you yesterday was no longer there. That the perversely banal life that you led was outshadowed by the one person who cared for you so supremely, but who had also abandoned you. I could never have fathomed the pain Alyssa would leave me in; I could never have imagined how her absence would make me feel.

Kat cried, and we sat together, cradled, watching the moon.

As I entered work the next day, trash bags swelled with decay near the back door. Kat must've forgotten, which was unlike her. The smell was so pungent that I felt temporarily hit by its tenacity. The dry heave of puke almost made it to my mouth, but I stopped it just in time. I had a whole day's work ahead of me, I couldn't afford momentary nausea.

Kat was off getting emerald-green polish on her toes and watching a movie at the Film Forum with her friend Frank, which she kept trying to back out of, and I—well, I was paying my necessary dues. She assured me I would do fine without her, and sincerely, I was managing. I was never good with people, but I had always been curious of others. I was trying to lean into this quality, into the thrill of new experiences. There were people coming in and out on the regular, and for the most part it was stimulating. Tracking the gentle back and forth of old customers who loved Kat and newcomers who were impressed by the place was enjoyable. My answers were always short, tamed, rehearsed, and yet still so stickily uncomposed. I didn't have the conversational lucidity of Khadijah with a *K*. I took a breath and told myself, in my head, to have some compassion for myself. It's the first time that ever happened.

Around eleven I was in the store's back area, taking a quick break after the morning rush, when I heard a voice.

"Hello?"

Caught off guard, I ran to greet the person.

I got to the cash register and faced her. Her hair was dark and ponytailed, eyes round and cat shaped with eyelashes that were elegant and delicate. Her lips were pasted with freshly applied lip gloss, probably fruit flavored. I wondered if it was one of those sweet ones you could lick off.

"Hi." I smiled. "Sorry, I was just—"

She cut me off. "I'm here to pick up a special order."

Kat hadn't told me about this. "Ah, sure, what's your name?"

"Jade Leung."

I was buying time. "What was your order?"

"A baked Italian cheesecake with a raspberry coulis." She paused. "Wait, isn't Kat here?"

I frowned, buying time. "You ordered it with Kat?"

"Yes," she replied, "I ordered it with Kat."

I turned around and made a face, mimicking her now imperfect-lipped drawl. I walked to the fridge and took a peek inside: nothing. As I started freaking out I heard a commotion in the front of the shop. It sounded like another person had entered and I could hear that Jade was squealing. I rolled my eyes and felt frustrated. As I reentered I saw that there was a man talking to her, and as I came closer he looked up and smiled. I didn't smile back. The man was tall and was wearing a brown jacket and pale denim. His hair was the color of dark, unmilked coffee. Long and matted at the sides. As he looked at me again, I noticed his eyes were a strange hue, and even from a distance I could see their peculiarly green-brown-colored gaze. He smiled at me, now for the second time, and I looked down quickly, pretending to not have been eyeing him.

"Did you find our cake?" Jade asked, milder now.

"No, I—I'm sorry..."

"Can't you just call Kat?"

"Yeah..."

"Because she said today, and I'm not coming back again."

"Okay. Yeah. I'm sure everything is fine." I said it with a little too much reservation.

"Yeah, I'm sure it is, too," she said curtly.

I called Kat desperately on her cell. *Dinnnnnggggggggggg.* It kept ringing, but she wasn't picking up. They were both eagerly waiting.

"So?"

"She isn't picking up..."

"Ugh, I take a chance on a local place—"

Just as she said that Kat walked through the door, a paper box in her left arm. "Hello, darlings!"

My heart pounded.

"Taylia, I hope you have been entertaining."

I smiled a weak, thin line. I wanted to punch Jade in the face.

"She's been great," the man chimed in, looking back at me, smiling.

"So, here you go. All as requested. Raspberry coulis made, like, a minute ago."

Sometimes Kat was like a magician—wasn't she supposed to be at the movies? I watched her astounded but inspired.

Jade squealed again. "Roman is going to love this!"

"This is for Roman?" Kat asked. "You didn't tell me that. He was my favorite regular, but I haven't seen him in weeks."

"*We know!* He's been on this huge case, so he's been in another zone, working nonstop. But this is why we asked for this cake from you. He just loves this place so much, and he's been missing his daily dose. We're actually going to go surprise him now! It's his birthday and we're so happy we could get this cake from you! Thank you."

"Oh, what a sweetheart. Well, tell him happy birthday!"

As Jade and Kat talked, the man came up to me. "Hey, I'm Ky."

I stared at his hand for seconds; the cuticles were well trimmed, and the moon-shaped part of his nail was pronounced, almost like Zeina. His hands were slightly tanned and laced with veins. There was even a tattoo in between his thumb and forefinger that looked like two bows and arrows crossed over each other. I looked back up at him, momentarily shocked by the giddy feeling that moved through me. He seemed unfazed, but his stare was intense. Like he was taking me in in a noncreepy way.

"Taylia."

"Taylia? Cool name."

I shrugged inelegantly.

In the background, Kat worked her charm—that's why people flocked to her. She was genuine.

"How's your day been, Taylia?"

I had not done this in so long. "My day has been fine."

"How do you mean?"

I shrugged again.

"Your eyes tell secrets, Taylia."

I assumed someone as empirically handsome as Ky would say this to women and they would feel understood and flattered by his observation, and even though I knew that, I felt that he really meant what he had said to me. Still, my guard was up. "Hmm, maybe."

A loop went through my stomach, multiplying into a figure eight. I suddenly felt so immeasurably happy.

"Ky." Jade broke the spell.

I felt embarrassed by my hypnotized state, like a deer caught in headlights. I felt seen again, an anomaly in this city. But that was it: I felt seen.

He turned to them both.

"Ky, you should start coming by more!" Kat cooed.

"Oh, I definitely shall."

I heard them giggle and chatter, but my mind had gone, drifting in ethereal blackness, in a black hole; I felt like a star spinning through it all with such languid ease.

A few weeks later we were sitting inside the café, picking at an olive oil cake and sipping on a shared iced cappuccino. I was about to head out for a break when I felt compelled to ask.

"Kat, be honest, do you think I've put on weight?"

"What?" Truly astonished, she just stared.

"I feel so—so..."

"*Fat?*"

"Lethargic," I corrected her.

"Why?"

"I don't know. I always feel out of breath, I think I'm getting sick..."

"You should maybe go see a doctor, my li'l principessa. Is there anyone you can go see?"

"Yeah, I'll think about it." I hadn't even begun to comprehend what health insurance and accessing doctors would be like now that I no longer talked to my parents. But I also didn't want to think about it, so I put it to the side.

"Well, honey, here's the thing—if you think you're fat, maybe you are and that's okay. You gotta rejig that thinking and look around you. You are beautiful! I promise. Don't let the man tell you otherwise." She winked her left eye and blew a kiss. I laughed, rolled my eyes, tempering her mildly, and walked out.

Moving toward the park, I eventually sat down next to Cillian. The warmth under him, like in those first few days after I left, filled me with an immeasurable spirit. Now, he felt like the steadiness of family, like grounding; I felt connected to the earth through the roots of him. The first real spiritual experiences I had were through the narratives of Indian culture with Dadi-ma. Tales by Kālidāsa and *Shesher Kabita* by Tagore, the rhymes and wordplay like stringed songs she'd sing, fluid poetry that was a gilded part of Bengali culture. Being under Cillian reminded me of India, the trees and nature such a part of its loamy terrain. Dadi-ma and I would often sit by big jackfruit and mango trees near the house, guarded by a small pukur filled with fresh, gulpy fish. The trees such a bright lime green, the tall palms bending across the waters in prostrated salutations.

Dadi-ma had a rounded knife with a cherry-red handle that she'd pull out of the belt of her petticoat to swiftly cut apples into halves and halves again, eight times in total. I'd count *one, two, three* every time. She put a slice in her mouth and then spit out the seeds through the whistle of her lips. Then she'd pass a slice to me, clucking with joy. In her presence, I learned that small, beautiful things could be treasured, too. There, I began my love for sitting on uneven grassy plains, the ants and soil-colored bugs crawling past my chubby limbs. We'd never talk, but she'd recite to me dramatic verses, her words resonant and voweled. Intermittently she'd smile and pinch the middle of my cheek with two clipped fingers, cackling at the annoyed faces I'd make in return. I started to learn broken Bangla: আমি ভাল. তুমি কেমন আছ? She'd give me a thumbs-up for good, thumbs-down for poor, her bangles *clank clank clank*ing as she laughed her haughty, rapturous guffaw. The trees near the deep lakes, the water dusty and a lukewarm brown, made me think of death. Even in moments of bliss, it haunted me. Maybe it was the realization that this woman—in so many ways a soul mate—would soon be gone. I liked everything about her, even how much she despised us being American, rolling her eyes whenever we spoke English or said "wow." She found English to be so unuseful, so unromantic, unfeeling, and callous. She felt like a role model, someone in opposition to Alyssa, and felt maybe more aligned with the person I wanted to be. That made me both joyous and sad. There'd be moments I'd stare into the infiniteness of the pukur and wonder what it would feel like to suffocate in its muddy, opaque waters. Living without her felt impossible.

Yesterday the light was heavy from the moon. Today, as I looked at the sky, again under Cillian, almost dusk, I thought of the solar system. The spinning plates of Saturn, the braille exterior of Pluto—so, *so* far—the lip of the galactic system, mystical orbs in a continuous loop in the blackness. I used to hate touching *National Geographic* pictures of space (Baba had stacks of them in his study). The onyx glossiness of the page, like freshly potted dark soil, terrorized me. I felt that if I touched the deep space, I'd suck myself in like an apparition, every picture my personal portkey. I was absolutely terrified of space, but I loved the mystery of it. There was a full-sized poster of Uranus on the walls of my school that I'd walk by silently, sometimes only darting quick looks at its mountains drafting shadows onto my fear-based theories of life and death, my eyes dizzying. But now, under Cillian, I felt so calm.

"Who's Cillian?" Kat asked me a day later.

I gave her a widemouthed smile. "How on earth would you know of him?"

She passed me a poem that I had offhandedly scribbled on a shift as I waited, evidently bored. Small love hearts framed his bolded name.

"So, who is he?"

"He's not what you think."

"What is he then?"

"He's a tree."

She looked at me strangely. It was one of those slow Tuesdays, an hour before close, when the lull of foot traffic felt frustratingly slow. Days like these, Kat and I clinged to each other, sharing stories of our youth, of our dreams. I mainly listened to Kat's glorious retelling of growing up in Brooklyn in the '80s, of the perils of Fort Greene Park, with health-conscious parents who forced wheatgrass down her throat and made her take French class because of her Martinique ancestry. She told me her father wanted her to read Frantz Fanon, Aimé Césaire, and Édouard Glissant to understand her roots, to understand radicality in the context of the Afro-Carribean diaspora. It was something that was coming up with Claudia, too, who was Haitian. At the reminder of Claudia, Kat zeroed in on me. I knew she was about to ask me about romance. I sensed the poem about Cillian had made her feel sorry for me, so all day she had been figuring out a way to broach the conversation on how to date in the city. There was a cupid trapped inside of her, and I needed to leave.

"So, any cuties been catching your eye recently?"

It was so funny because it was so sincere. If I wasn't so embarrassed by the question, I'd find it endearing. "And that's my cue to leave."

"No! Where are you going? Don't leave me!"

"Don't know, window-shopping or something." Today I felt like I had to move, like there was energy trapped inside of me. I swung my bag over my shoulders.

"I'll see you back at home! I'll probably go to all the shops the cool kids go to, you know, like ABC Carpet and Home for a sec."

Her eyes narrowed on me, like she knew I was being avoidant, but she merely said, "Hmm."

We both knew it really wasn't where the cool kids went, but I craved a home of my own, and I wanted to be lost in the place that housed the most beautiful home decor I had ever seen. I also wanted to see if I could afford a nice perfume treat.

"Okay, whatever makes you happy!" she said, a bit glum.

I liked feeling needed by her, I liked knowing I added value to her life. I also knew Claudia was scheduled to pick Kat up later, and I was avoiding our inevitable meeting. Maybe because I was embarrassed. I wasn't sure she'd like me. What did I have to offer anyone besides my sometimes thoughtful (but mainly cursory) tidbits? I felt ill equipped to talk to a professor, fearing she'd remind me of my parents.

"Do you want anything while I'm out?"

Smiling, she said, "Nope. But have fun gloating at what rich white people buy!"

As I walked closer to ABC Carpet and Home, there was a rabid dog barking, cowering, its leash almost in shreds. I tried walking around it but tripped on the leash, almost plunging headfirst onto the sidewalk. Bleary-eyed, I shuffled away, my heart beating fast like a vibrating plate. I felt distracted as I pulled at the door, walked inside, and let the rush of this place silence my thoughts.

ABC Carpet and Home. Sigh. I don't know why I liked it so much; maybe it felt nostalgic to come here, like I was closer to Mama. She'd bring us here to buy goods for home (not ironically; she loved the corner filled with "Indian" goods that was always manned by brutish white women), and the cascading chandeliers, the panels of silk and crystal, and the chic homeware cocooned me in safety. Big doors shielding the opulence inside. Rows and rows of unique one-off pieces the price of average New York City rent or facials from Goop.

Expensive things felt nice to be around. Sometimes.

From a young age I was engaged by smell. My aesthetic praxis, through the controlled tenderness I'd show myself (albeit rarely), was in pursuit of smell. I'd walk around after school to those small Tibetan hubs, or to natural health food stores with their wall dedicated to my dizzying fetish, and pick out perfumes: jasmine, sandalwood, lavender. My favorite spot was in the West Village, just near Bleecker Street. It was unassuming, yet bright. The outside was always decorated with Himalayan threads, triangular patterns of calm design. The colors evoked vibrations of the streets of Kolkata—alight, colorful, and alive. The store, like Punjab Grocery and Deli, reminded me of the nebulous, hollow scabs that patched me, reminders tethering me so tightly to India.

My mantelpiece, back at my parents', housed my many trinkets, filled with sweet and oily perfumes I'd scavenged over the years. I loved the fragile glass bottles with thick gold etchings, ones that looked like miniature Russian castles, the colors diluted.

My morning ritual consisted of creating my own scent, my fingers sticky from the bottles. Like drawing blood from a vial, I placed the teardrop of oil across my body, a sign of the cross in my own private ceremony. I gravitated toward a certain smell intuitively each morning, and it became my earthly companion, heightening my state of euphoria throughout the day.

I began to read about Muslim perfumery, how it was extracted through steam distillation. I read about Jābir ibn Hayyān and Al-Kindi, who established the perfume industry in the golden age of Islam. I even tirelessly looked into how to collect the mysterious odor of plants and flowers, wanting to make my own salves and perfumes. It was fascinating to read about resins and wood; about the sacredness of perfume in the Arab world, which brought the art of perfumes to Europe; about the way that Muslims used smells and incense at mosques, how elevating fragrance was a way of dedication to one's exterior body but also to God. I noticed how women in abayas, stunning and statuesque, bodies erect in majesty, always smelled so mellifluously sweet, a fragile muskiness pervading their path—*swish, swish*—as they moved.

There, within the wonderland of ABC, I again remembered the sudden rush of jubilation my morning creations would give me. I wondered, with a stab, what had happened to my perfume corner after I had left. I blinked at the objects near me repetitively to stop my eyes from welling up and caught them on a dainty, crooked piece, standing right in my sight line. I picked up the glass-like wonder and immediately lusted over its curves and crushed edges. I was transfixed by its splendor, until I could sense a hand reaching toward me. Like clockwork, my heart jumped, and I felt dread wash over me. I spun around quickly to see who it was and the bottle fell and smashed on the floor.

"Oh, shit," I whimpered.

"Ugh, sorry."

He leaned down to help me pick up the shards of glass. I didn't look at the man. I was crying. I was crying over something so menial. He got out a *New York Times* from his bag and brushed all the pieces onto it with a natural swerve. All I could see were his hands. They were brown, with fingers that were elegant and well-cut circular cuticles. A tattoo. Momentarily fixed on them, I felt a strange, ethereal surge push through me, past the tears, and suddenly the hands were up my leg. I stopped myself from dreaming and pulled back. The man with the hands was turned away from me and talking to someone behind him. I slumped, feeling humiliated. Getting up slowly, cautiously, drowning myself with a heavy head, I looked up at him. He was broad shouldered with a toned back, and as I watched him the sensation moved through me again. My desire, although transitory—and uncommon—pulled me into a blissful tension between my legs, a slow and easy tightness lingering like a mild sedative. Even though it subsided within moments, I felt so uneasy by this sudden lack of control. I mean, I was attracted to *his back*.

I was so lost inside my mind's conversation that I hardly heard my name being called.

"Taylia," the man said, coming toward me.

I pulled my head up with a jolt, suddenly overwrought. I slowly and reluctantly focused on his face. It was familiar, I knew him. He was the guy from Kat's bakery last week or so.

"Hey, how are you?" Ky paused. "Are you okay?"

I wiped the tears that I hadn't noticed were still on my face. "Er, I'm okay," I answered, concentrating on his jawline. He had stubble growing around and on his chin. I looked up at his eyes and noticed they weren't as green today.

"Upset about the prices, huh?"

I looked at him, confused but smiling. "No."

"That was a joke."

"Okay."

"I followed you here, kind of."

I felt my body go cold.

"That's creepy. I mean I went by Kat's and was hoping you'd be there, but she said that you might be here. So..."

"Kat told you I was here?"

"Yeah, I even got a coffee and we talked about you."

I felt my face physically frown.

"We didn't talk *about* you... Okay, wow, I don't usually make so many failed jokes in one conversation, but, wait, let's go outside... ?"

I didn't want to go outside, and my body felt like it was slowly crumbling in the heat of this man's unwarranted attention. "No..."

"Only just it's getting crowded."

I looked around; he was right. "Okay, wait. I think I have to pay for that stupid bottle."

"S'all good, I got it."

I looked at him in the light that was coming in acute bright angles through the store window and nodded. We walked outside and stood near the left-hand corner of the entrance, me on the ramp, arms tightly wrapped around my body; him on the street, leaning toward me.

"I didn't get to talk to you much the other day."

"Okay."

He laughed. "I..." He stopped. "Hmm, this is going to sound so unrehearsed and like such a weird request, considering we don't know each other, but I just want to get to know you..."

I was sure my face was the shocked emoji.

As if he heard me: "I—I can't explain it, Taylia. I... all I want is to be your friend, obviously, that's it. I, um, don't even really know why, but I was pulled to go back to the café to go see you and that kind of thing doesn't really happen. Like, I don't do those things, normally."

"Like, you're not a stalker. Normally," I said coldly.

He chuckled nervously. "Yeah, exactly. I'm not a stalker. Thanks for clarifying..."

He looked at me, his face sharp. A wave of goose bumps moved past my body. He was silent for eons until he said it.

"I feel like we could be friends."

No.

I was going to puke. The acid of my stomach, like a tongue whipping at my insides, curled with dissatisfaction. I broke my stance and leaned against the railing, suddenly incapable of standing.

"Whoa," Ky said, coming toward me, his hands reaching out.

"Don't touch me! Don't touch me!" I whispered.

"Okay, I'm not touching you. Taylia, are you okay?"

I could feel the winds changing and the energy shifting. My body swayed.

"Taylia. Are you okay?"

No.

"Taylia, should I take you somewhere else?"

No.

I leaned against the cool stone wall, shaking my head no, wishing away this feeling of unkempt, vibrating nausea.

"Ma'am, are you okay?" The security guard was behind me, and the thudding in my head began. A ticking beat. I felt the slimy hands, the visions bringing me back. The white chair, the line of hooks. The rancid taste in my mouth, and that bleating hangover. I felt Simon's fingers inside of me again and again and again. At the roots of my hair I felt him pulling me across fire and earth, along pointed grainy stalactite; his body was pinning me against all the pains of the world.

"Fuck no. Fuck no. Fuck, fuck, fuck." I leaned my body toward Ky and whispered, "Take me somewhere *safe*." I hissed the *safe*.

As if taking orders, he immediately wrapped his left arm around my waist and pulled my weight onto him. We lean-walked down a few blocks and then he put me in an Uber, which I hadn't even known he'd ordered, coming around the other side.

The beats of my heart were spaced far apart, spread out and bumpy. I felt my physical limpness ease as I now sat. The cars moving, Ky not saying a word. The ghosts were still there, strident, but my body no longer felt like trembling goop. I was getting back my definitions. The limbo of existing was intoxicating. I realized how much more work I still had to do.

15.

We moved over the Williamsburg Bridge and I watched the waters of the East River shiver beneath us. I wondered what it would be like to drown in that water and thought of the muddy pukur, of Dadi-ma afloat. I hadn't felt her presence in a few days. I imagined the river was quite filthy and, at the same time, filled with mysteries. Bones patterned with verdigris, blood staining the moss-lined cobbled walls. The toxicity of greed and untimely deaths. All those lost, lost souls. As we came over the bridge and entered Brooklyn, the driver took a few turns before he came to a complete halt.

Ky got out and came to my door, fidgeting his fingers before he opened it and took me out with patient delicacy. "Come on," he said, his hands gently pulsing at the corners of my back, a loose grip. He held my right hand as we walked to the front door, stopping only to take out his keys. With one hand he opened it and with the other he brought me in. I could feel his left palm gently pressing against my lower back, and in that moment I felt an irrevocable sense of solace. There was something undeniably comforting about a body against your own. A firm touch; a lighthouse.

We walked in, piles of books lying on the floor greeting us. The organized chaos gave the house an unassuming, open vibe. There was a lot of wood, a lot of steel, and a lot of greenery. The last was surprising. As I stood, mouth gaping, I looked across the wall closest to me. There was exposed brick and a large, dilapidated wooden mirror hung across it, the glass shattered with age. I took in the image that was staring at me from within. Her eyes were bloodshot; her skin splotchy, exposed with open pores, swelling with an inflamed pinkness that looked like an impending rash. I felt embarrassed. Had I looked like this the whole time? Ky came behind me and asked me to sit anywhere, and I did, collapsing onto a nearby bourbon-colored leather sofa, with a slump.

Ky went into the kitchen. I watched him gliding around through a crack. He came back out and handed me a glass of water and a big block of Lindt (sea salt, my favorite). "My mother says chocolate usually helps with most things."

I sat up properly, looking around. I sensed him staring at me, searching. Suddenly bold, my eye contact was direct. I was challenging him to speak, to probe the beast.

"The sadness is real."

I suddenly retracted, knowing full well I wasn't ready to be challenged. *I think you should shut the fuck up* is what I thought.

"I don't think you're normally this quiet."

You think a lot of things, don't you?

"I think you're probably a little wild. First to get drunk, last one to leave?"

 I lied: "I don't drink."

"Drugs?"

I shook my head, annoyed.

"Rock and roll?"

I shrugged jokingly.

His eyes leveled with mine. "I don't want to sound arrogant..."

"But you're going to power through it anyway, right?"

He smiled a small smile. "I think you want someone to talk to."

I didn't answer.

"So, what's your story, then? Are you an orphaned wizard? A fox on a mission to undermine some humans?"

"Why am I even here?"

Now he shrugged. "Maybe you just needed someone to ask how you're doing."

"You assume a lot."

We both snickered a little, but then the room was met with silence again.

"Or we can just sit he—"

"I don't have anything to say." I realized, then, that I wanted to tell him.

"One thing I keep learning, Taylia, is that every person on earth has a story."

"So then, what's the point?" I was suddenly defiant. "What's the point? If all of us hurt, what's the fucking point? Why do we go on?"

I had been thinking this for months. In moments of stillness, despite how far I'd come, I felt myself drifting, plunging into that dark, unforgiving hole: the wretched wrath of self-pity. I hadn't forgotten or absolved anyone of their sins, but I was focused on moving forward, and yet it wasn't that easy of a fix. At this moment, I didn't need Ky to answer anything for me, but I felt calm knowing that my misery could be felt by anyone. My story wasn't exceptional, and there was something undeniably liberating about accepting that—but also terrifying. Everybody wanted their pain to be hagiographic, perched up, anthologized. So, how to carry on when human pain was so universal? How to feel, when the only option was to push through and not fester? Still, the pent-up energy lay coiled around my throat, like a weed springing to life, wrapping around my esophagus; I wanted to speak.

I looked up at him. His eyes were a hazy nebula, stringing me together as we watched each other, silent, the moment pulsating with thick nerves. I wanted to speak to him and be heard. Fiercely, and ardently, I wanted him to know me. I wanted him to feel close to me, to embrace me. To be let in like no other human before. Suddenly, as if a light went on inside of me, like the strums of an orchestra, I wanted to share myself like a lover. To be open, close—for an eternity, or even a moment. I wanted to be loved by this man. But I remained quiet, unmoving.

He persisted. "Taylia?"

I didn't answer.

"Taylia? What's going on?"

I inhaled deeply. "I..." I started again. "I..."

My breath felt like a bloody tightrope. How much *is too much* to share with a stranger? Each mouthful that I would begin to stutter was a recognition that there was no way back. Each sweaty syllable was a deep acceptance of my death. Living really was a manual on learning how to die, and I was about to forgo my facade to an outsider. Once what was said *was said*—I would not be able to crawl out of its black and blue depths. All the bluish hues of pain, the bruises of life that sink us into a deeper melancholy, I would not be able to escape. Like a blow that builds the bruise, the words I was about to utter would enter us both into a steep plunge of intimacy. Yet, I was still afraid. Afraid of that commitment, afraid of the responsibility that came with closeness, or more: the expectation that resided, on both parts, in its aftermath. What if it was rejection? Dismissal? I didn't want to be pitied, I wanted to be *seen*. Seen for all that I was, trepidatious out of necessity.

"I'm sorry..."

"Whatever you need to say, want to say, don't worry. Just say it. It doesn't need to be coherent."

He looked so earnest. It made me want to kiss and slap him at the same time.

"Okay, fine... I was..." I paused. "Fuccckkkkk."

I paused again, unable to quite form the words. I dug my nails into my right hand to stop it from happening, but the tides could not be stopped, I began to cry. My bottom lip trembled and I bit it, embarrassed. My tears slurred the words. Why the fuck did I want to tell him?

"I got kicked out of my parents' house."

He was silent, but his eyes asked why.

The ultimate question that defined me in other people's eyes.

"I..." I stopped and started a few times. "I was r-raped."

I didn't say anything for a few seconds. It came out like a statement, not a question—which is how it had sat in my mind, coiled around my amygdala. Right now, I felt everything: I wanted to barf, I wanted to cry, I wanted to kiss him, I wanted him to touch me, to ravage me. I wanted to run. I wanted to disappear, like lost time. I wanted to be invisible, so I stayed silent.

He broke it.

"And your parents kicked you out?"

He waited for an answer. He didn't get one.

He mumbled, "What the fuck is wrong with them?"

Theoretically, I thought it'd make me feel better. To tell somebody. But it didn't. I remained silent for the next few minutes, but in truth we were both quiet for a huge chunk of time. After the combination of our mixed awkwardness, I understood that to stay any longer would be too emotionally imposing. I felt that the words spoken had a gravity that I had not anticipated, a reality that, perhaps, I had been avoiding. Its tumultuous weight felt unavoidable, and yet... I'd come so far these many months without even stringing the words together. I'd avoided all feelings of this because what lay beneath the surface seemed incorrigible. Buried, the memories of the night my life fucking changed were suddenly resurfacing—like an earthquake, a ten on the Richter scale. They began to move through me like waves, and so I let them, I let them flow, with no judgment.

He gently placed his hand on my shoulder.

> 1. *He's touching me.*
> 2. *He's touching me.*
> 3. *I'm okay.*

I was altogether ready to go. Maybe Ky's purpose was purely to allow a safe space to unfold, so that I could put words to the brash pain that still lingered, gloating.

"No one really wants to listen to other people's pain." I stood up, but, like a chain reaction, his fallen hand grabbed hold of my right trembling paw, securing it with his.

"Stay, please."

"Taylia." He had been calling my name for a while.

I returned to the moment. He was standing over me as I lay on the couch.

"You're here," he said quietly, smiling.

My mind was filled with a song and its humming. I wanted to suddenly laugh, raucously. "I'm here," I said.

He'd made linguini from scratch, drinking a beer as he cooked, and I obliged. As I ate the food I felt the emptiness inside me buzz with warmth. We were sitting and watching the light become dark outside in his garden. David Bowie's cover of "Sorrow" played, mildly, on the fuzzy speakers inside. It was a beautiful scene: potted plants all around, a large array of vivid green cacti and herbs. I recognized thyme, rosemary, and a wild card: thai basil, pulpy and pungently purple. Mulberry leaves leaned over the back fence, while aloe vera spilled out of mason jars and pale-colored succulents bloomed in tiny little tin cans, corrugated on the sides. Flowers in colors of aubergine, fuschia, and rose hung in fitted hanging pots, and lightbulbs laced the enclave in a full circle, beckoning me to stay. My full attention, however, was on the continuous stars, a string of them, the black sky and its godly pearls. In a hungry way, I watched them. How to drift into that endless tar pond? My exploration was always through the pulsating vacuum of space.

Ky told me his mother was an architect and that his parents had bought this town house for $250,000 in the early aughts; now it was worth a few million. Ky's agreement was that he paid off their mortgage. I thought of what it would be like to have parents who cared for you, who looked after you. Ky, a bit tipsy, interrupted the silence with a maelstrom.

"Taylia, w-w-what if you stayed here with me?"

My eyes favored the stars. I was unable to move. "What?" I asked distantly.

"I've been looking for another roommate..."

"What do you do again?" I was being coy, but also wanted to embarrass him with my bluntness.

"Um, oh. I'm a writer."

"Oh."

"So? Is that a yes? Or do you have something against writers?"

"I can't afford this place." The sounds of fear rang across my mind.

"That's a nonissue."

There was something so annoying about him, and yet I was enamored by his arrogance. I needed an excuse. I started running through a gamut of excuses but decided to tell the truth. "Look, Ky, think about it, you don't *know* me, and living with Kat has been truly healing and maybe what I most need right now."

"Taylia, I know you must feel uncomfortable. You've had a difficult past, and I am a man and a stranger asking you to stay with me. You don't want to get yourself into another bad situation, I get that..." His voice trailed off. He wasn't looking over at me anymore, but as I watched him from the corners of my eyes, I wondered if he had a savior complex: his generosity was on the brink of absurd. I looked fondly over at the white bulb in the sky, the now blurry stars, and asked for holy guidance.

He mumbled with sedated solemnity: "I don't know why, but I want to help you."

I didn't look at him. I didn't know how to answer him. Not believing him, I sat with my heart full, lighting up as he continued to speak. But still, I knew he saw me, the weak Taylia, and he, for whatever reason, accepted me for this. I looked up steeply, toward where the moon lit the power lines, and felt a calm wash over. Each muscle of mine felt fluorescent, tendered in kindness, suddenly, with a sadistic urge, trusting this man.

"You can just pay whatever you were paying Kat. As long as she's okay with that, by the way. I want Kat to be my friend forever."

It was the earnestness that got me. And besides, I had been feeling like I was taking up too much of Kat's space and kindness. Maybe this would be a welcome break for her?

"Well, do you even have a room for me?"

He looked at me again, surprised and elated, nodding a wrinkled yes.

There was not a lot to do or say at that moment. Happiness had won. We sat there as the penumbra lingered over us, descending into the invisible, washing the bitterness away.

16.

That night I slept without waking up in the middle of the night for the first time, tragically, since my rape. Alyssa was back, and I felt her there, in the dream plane. She'd found me, as Dadi-ma had found me by Cillian. As I fell asleep, fidgeting, my pulsing, red-veined eyes finally staying closed, I still held on to some doubt that this feeling of satisfaction would last. Ky's energy, his outlook on life, certainly gave me hope, but I still wasn't totally sure about him. In all honesty, I wasn't sure if I'd ever feel safe around men ever again, at least not fully. It was too soon to tell. Though I still stayed the night, maybe because I wanted to feel free.

"Tay? Tay, wake up. There was an interview with a woman on television."

"About?"

"She'd been raped."

"What did she say?"

"She's Pakistani. She's trying to bring justice to herself."

It was a conversation we once had.

"So, what does it mean?"

The next morning, I woke up thinking about how Alyssa was back, in my dreams, but I wanted to know if she'd appear before me in real life as well. I looked around the room. It was eight A.M. Only half awake, I was already searching for her. The room was bland with striped linen sheets, like how spare bedrooms are often set up. As an east-facing room, there was ample sunlight. A giant monstera sat like a king near the window, but otherwise it had no character.

"Psst, Lyse. Are you there?"

There was nothing. But I felt a humming, a resolve. She would appear soon. Maybe she was trying to tell me something.

Though blanketed by warmth, there was an anxiety that festered within me, not yet ready to greet the day. With a jolt I remembered: *Fuck, Kat.* I needed to tell Kat where I was. I looked at my phone, and a little calendar reminder for work popped up, as if I had known I'd need to be reminded. As well as seven missed calls from her. I knew I owed Kat so much, and I didn't want to disappoint her. She had high standards because she was offering me more than anyone would. So I was indebted, and I carried that responsibility. I got up, hastily rewore my clothes from the night before, and waddled to Ky's room.

A few knocks later he stood at his door, shadowed in blue, a soft red light against all that felt sad and weird about this world. He leaned into the doorframe.

"Hi," I muttered, nausea usurping me.

"Hey. Did you sleep well?"

"Hmm."

"Okay?"

I felt lost. I needed to get to Kat. *What is even the address here?* I needed to learn to navigate my life now from this compass, and Ky's place felt too abrupt. How was I supposed to accept this? I didn't know this man. Feeling disgusted with myself, I was ashamed of wanting his attention.

"I need to get to work. What's the best way out of here?"

"Oh, wait, I'll head out with you then."

I did the math: Did that mean we'd have to talk to each other? The entire time? The thought of it gave me more anxiety.

"Of course," I said instead, and he followed me downstairs. As I slowly maneuvered myself into the kitchen, I was met with a man in gray pajamas.

"Hello! I'm your roommate."

"Oh." I looked at Ky, aghast, and mouthed, *Roommate?* I had sensed he lived alone. Ky nodded and mentioned Emi was a semipermanent resident as well, as if he'd been recruiting roommates into this giant space. Maybe he was just lonely. I felt embarrassed to think I was special to this man. All of a sudden, I felt a strangeness engulf me. Could I share space with two men? I didn't even know if I could trust Ky, let alone whoever this was. I felt all of this, but also found myself wanting to drown the voice of hesitancy. I just wanted to rest somewhere.

We made small talk with this roommate called Emi after a quick introduction. He seemed nice enough, jovial, almost annoyingly so. Like a puppy. Even though there was a sadness present, too. He was in between places after his girlfriend cheated on him. He looked like a schmuck, all doe-eyed and pathetic. It was beautiful. Maybe that added to my acceptance of the situation, too. I knew I must not have had the best intuition, since, in one way or another, it was hard not to blame myself for trusting Simon. I had had every reason to listen to my gut about the sliminess I knew lingered inside of him, but instead I listened to what others thought. I let Alyssa override me. But since that night, I had been trying to change. To listen. So that's what I did. With Emi and Ky I listened, and I would keep listening.

Ky finally looked at me, ushering us to get a move on. I nodded sedately, but yelled *on y va* in my mind. He was meeting his agent in Manhattan, so we shared an Uber into the city. He told me he was working on a novel but that he also worked at a huge tech company, brainstorming creative projects. From the sounds of it, he was paid very well, which I weirdly resented. It didn't sound like he deserved it. He dropped me off first, and as I got out of the car to face Kat, there was a song playing in the distance. Was it Patsy Cline playing on repeat? "She's Got You," that's it. Faint through the wind past the loud snoring sounds of the city heat, the percussion of the traffic, the bus pounding rhythms mundane. As the city roared on, Patsy played like a David Lynch dream, languid and cool, smooth across the rooftop of Ms. Cline's mouth. Moving closer toward the café, my face met Kat's, and I braced myself as we made eye contact through the glass before I even entered. Like a small animal cowering in a ruckus, the tic in my anxiety was as evident as her annoyance. I walked inside and she waited until Arnold, a local actor, left. Then, through gritted teeth, the question came out in one string: "Where-have-you-been?"

I smiled at her, but her response was dull. "I can't even imagine how to tell you."

"Well. Imagine!" The curtness came out shrill.

"Look, Kat, I'm so *sorrrrry*."

"Okay, but, where were you?"

"Ky's." I said it with an embarrassing assuredness; maybe I knew she'd like the gossip.

"Ky?" She was shocked. "Okay, *woof*."

She grinned a big toothy snarl. I had known she'd want to know every detail—that's something I loved about Kat, she was present. She watched me as she clipped the sides of her short nails (which she had to keep short for the baking, she hated it) with her teeth, and then she shrieked as it hit her: "Wait, did you... ?" She just stared at me, without asking further. What could I tell her? I didn't even know what it was that I felt. He had a girlfriend, so clearly there was no reason to assume there was a hint of romance between Ky and me, and truthfully, I didn't know if I *even* wanted that. I mean, what about Jade?

I sat down in front of her, looking for approval. I felt frustrated by how much I didn't know how to be a person. As in, how to talk about lust in an intangible way. Crushes had never been a possibility for me before, I felt so unworthy of attention. Now, I was aware of my body, of my tender parts. It's as if a scratch had turned bold: I was yearning for something. I had never really had the experience of feeling my heart quiver, so I was suspicious of even the idea of love, even though I wanted it. But, much like my new perspective on Ky (despite how I *was* beginning to feel about him romantically) and Emi, I was beginning to pay attention to myself, even in the smallest ways, to the signals in my body. Surely that's how you started to build intuition.

"Macchiato?" Kat asked to fill the void. I must have dozed off into my dream reality.

"Please."

"Next time—text me, let me know you're all right."

"I will."

She started buzzing around. "Okay, so, tell me—if you weren't *ahem*-ing Mr. Ky, then"—she said it languidly, like she was reciting Shakespeare—"what the eff were you doing there?"

I admired the way Kat would occasionally PG rate her swear words, a habit she had picked up for the boys.

"He, um, wants me to move in with him?"

She was dumbstruck. "Huh?"

"You heard right the first time."

"Wait, Ky..."

"Yes."

"...wants you, Taylia..."

"Yes."

"...someone he doesn't know..."

"Correct."

"...to move in with him?"

"That's it."

She cocked her eyebrows again. "And y'all wanna tell me you ain't fucking? Tay, please..." She looked upset.

"Kat," I assured her with the labored emphasis of my hands. "*T-r-u-s-t meeeee.* I'm not hiding anything."

Her eyes went small, the pupils hardly visible, and she gruffed. "Okay then, what does he want from you?" I liked how she enjoyed a sense of drama as much as I did. Besides, I had been asking myself that very same question.

126

Kat had written out a poem on a piece of ripped yellow legal pad paper:

> *To keep up a*
> *passionate courtship*
> *with a tree*
> *one must be mad.*

I found it on the way back to hers and laughed. That night I decided I would sleep at Kat's. I wasn't ready to face what an offer like staying at Ky's would mean, and I was trying to give my intuition time to work. I texted him about giving myself some time to think it through, and he replied that he understood.

After work a few days later, I sat underneath Cillian, daring myself not to touch any of my baked goods, and I let my mind wander. I had decided that I would start dipping my toe and feel out living with Ky. Kat and I had discussed it, and I explained to her that it felt important for me to see how it would feel to explore something unknown. At first, she voiced judgment, but, over time, I was able to convince her that something was calling me there. To Ky. I think because she was romantic, she got it.

Dadi-ma used to practice meditation under the teachings of a guru Saraswati. So I had always been interested in the mysticism of meditation and its effects on the human body. Especially after witnessing the effects it had on her. In just five weeks she was able to convince me so thoroughly of her living standards, providing inspiration, that almost a decade later I still remembered her in day-to-day life, like Scripture. Nobody occupied my life like that. She was so agile, so sprightly; her senses were so keen—right up until she died. I admired her ability, her strength. Through her, I was able to understand God existed. I went back to these memories as I began to track my instincts; it was as if I were relearning old magic. So there I sat, under Cillian, meditating, trying to remember how to conjure the data she had passed down on to me.

I longed for family, I always had. But I don't know if I ever really believed that I'd get it from my parents. So, at a certain point, I let go of trying. Also their trusting of Simon over me, their own daughter, felt like the worst blow yet. So I let go even more. In the last moments, as I had accepted my rape, I also accepted my fate-to-come without real resistance. Otherwise I wouldn't have survived. What my parents decided felt like an actual betrayal. And maybe that's what made me stand up for myself, made me leave and follow Dadi-ma, and Alyssa, in the stars. I needed them to really hurt me, and they delivered.

All in all, I know I had it lucky. Others had given their lives to this. I thought of Jyoti Singh Pandey. *Jyoti, Jyoti, Jyoti*, I heard myself ringing. I couldn't sleep the first time I had heard what happened, like I felt it in my body. Like it had happened to me, and the many versions of me before. It's hard to explain what I felt. It's as if the agony of all women had seeped into me and that I screamed their pain in vengeance. Gutted out with a steel pipe, *Jyoti, Jyoti, Jyoti, my sister*. I still remember overhearing, like it was yesterday, the conversation between Baba and Rakesh, two Indian men with such little compassion. Women were not believed, were hunted and killed, and I had survived. I would do something of this life, I would make it mine. I had to learn how to do that, at the very least.

And with that, all of a sudden, under Cillian, I started crying, unstoppable. It was the first time since the rape that I had felt it again. The burden of what had happened to my body. I wanted to forgive myself, but I couldn't yet. I felt I had betrayed myself as well. Maybe that was the hardest truth to face. I felt I had let what happened to me happen to me. Even though I could theorize that it was more complex, right now I still only had myself to blame.

My body was burning. Thinking of Jyoti, then myself, I felt a dull ache of resistance as my bones started vibrating. I felt as if I owed Jyoti something for surviving. I resented myself for living and breathed in, shrouding myself in my misery. It was okay, I told myself. I had to carry on, I had no other choice.

I didn't understand why I felt that now that I was *trying* to pay attention, to listen for instructions. But I knew I was being directed to Ky's. So, with Kat's blessing, I moved into his place with all my belongings that still fit into my old JanSport bag—a few books, a sweater, two dresses, one pair of jeans, and under-wear—and placed them on the striped linen bed. I was excited to make something of this space, to carve out a home. With the boys, I secretly felt I was always in Kat's way. She never made me feel it, but I knew I was. I felt irresponsible that I had let her help me, but I had taken it, selfishly. At Ky's I felt like there was an equal exchange, or at least I could make sure there would be.

I placed my belongings in their relative places, and after a half hour of lying on the bed, I decided to make myself something to eat and claim the home further. Being in another space was exciting: there was such a nice layout to this home, different from Kat's, whose was more chic, almost French; Ky's was like a millennial's take on midcentury modern. I guess Ky's mom had converted the inside of the triplex after buying the entire building. The interiors were clean and linear, the ideal vision of adulthood in your twenties. I felt, again, a bit spiteful. Some people's privileges astounded me, and this was coming from me. As I walked down to the kitchen, I brainstormed ideas for the room. I'd get a hanging plant from the farmers' market, maybe go down to Brooklyn Flea to find some nice keepsakes. Building a room was a metaphor for all the ways you had to rebuild your-self, and it was daunting. I felt out of breath. Still excited, but my nerves were getting the best of me. And then when I got into the kitchen I realized I wasn't alone.

"Hello," a voice whispered out of the corner. I looked over cautiously: it was Emilio.

"Oh, hi," I said with relief.

He smiled, his fingers sticky from Triscuits smeared with purple grape jelly. His mouth was full. "You're seeing me at my worst."

"Oh, no judgment, seriously."

"You hungry?"

I nodded a half nod.

"Let me cook us something real," he said, gesturing.

I nodded my head because I wanted to be a woman who could accept care from a man. I sat down on a nearby stool, lightly combing my hair with my fingers. He stood, mildly ashamed, licking his fingers one by one, hastily finishing off his ritual by sucking on the webbed side of his palm. Swiftly, he reached down to his pants, rubbing his fingers against the denim three times before he started. There was something on the stove, and as I inhaled, the sweet smell of coconut milk wafted through me and memories of India floated through the room. The busy streets and the air filled with humidity and spices; the acid reek of petrol and random rot that smelled like garbage, mixed in with the aromatic bliss of cooking cardamom. It filled me with an intense nostalgia. In that instant Dadi-ma's face drifted in and around my soul, and in mere moments she was there with me, sitting clear eyed, the lines on her face tracing upward to her smile. The hem of her saree brushed against my right forearm, and as we watched each other, her eyes gelatinous, everything felt resplendent for a moment. With her presence, again, I was beginning to trust myself to the situation I had found myself in. Her pale wrinkled left hand, spotted with a solar system of smudgy dots, lingered near my right, and the calmness emanated, *at last—at last*.

The three of us sat in our silence for a while.

"I'm making a coconut chai rice pudding."

"Okay, wow."

"I may be a mess, but I can cook."

"That's usually an impressive quality."

He laughed. "Usually."

There was a pause.

"Are you okay?"

"Yeah..." He seemed unsure. "I've just been filling my days with my work. I'm a graphic designer, so I can basically be lazy and have flashes of inspiration, then be lazy again. It's a nice cycle of productivity."

I laughed, I related. It had always been hard to inspire me, but there'd be moments when I would feel it, and it would pay off. I knew I had talents; I just needed to learn how to harness them.

"Ky went out with Jade, they'll be back later."

Ugh. I looked at Dadi-ma. She looked regrettably unfazed.

"It's her birthday," he added.

"When did they go?"

"A while ago."

I sat silently, wondering why Dadi-ma was here, placid.

"So tell me about yourself, Taylia! This is exciting, new friends."

I came back to myself, biting the left corner of my lip. "Oh."

"Let's start with when is *your* birthday? LOL. What's your sign?"

Birthday? I forgot I even had one.

"June twenty-seventh... I'm a Cancer." I coughed, drawing the awkwardness out. "Are Jade and Ky serious... you think?" I cringed at my abruptness.

"Oh... I think you'll have to ask him that," Emi answered blankly.

I wondered why he said it like that.

Jealousy came over me. I let myself steep in the pettiness that was coming up. I bet Jade was one of those girls who would say Ky's full name to establish intimacy, to establish a past, to establish a history that nobody else knew of. I imagined her begging, *Eat my pussy, Kynan, baby, please.*

"Girlfriends are... tricky?"

I came back to myself again, feeling uncontained. "Oh?"

"After this last breakup, I'm just not sure if I could do it again."

"Date, you mean?"

"Yeah. I mean, I loved her and she just fucking..." His voice began to break.

I was stunned, so I observed him in his softness, in this moment of delicacy. From the corners of my eyes I saw Dadi-ma's force field fading around me. "I'm sorry."

"It's okay."

He reached his wet palm to mine, swollen with sadness. He reached for comfort, but it was too fast a movement and my body reacted in a convulsed outrage, jolting back into my seat. His look was generous despite my outbreak.

"I'm sorry, Taylia, I didn't mean to startle you..."

The absence of saliva was making my throat dry. I sighed through the words: "I just don't like people touching me... all of a sudden. You know?" I wasn't really asking, but it came out that way.

"Of course." A stream of sweat passed through the side of his face. "I mean, that makes sense."

It was how he said it: it was suggestive.

"What do you mean?" An unbearable acidity began to rise in my cotton-dry mouth, suddenly raspy.

"Because..." He looked at me fully this time, "...of what happened."

We made eye contact, and in the connection I felt extreme rage. I felt like the wind had been knocked out of me. There was no refuge here. Feeling the blood move through my face, I wanted to scream. I wanted to run.

He was judging me, I knew it. I could feel it. I knew in the back of his mind he was looking at me with disgust, wondering what Simon had seen in me. I could see him talking but nothing was registering. I slowly pulled myself out of it and looked at him again, tremulous and sick. My mind rolled with one thought:

That son of a bitch, Ky. My senses were dilated and I wanted to run from this internal heaviness. *It's your own fault nobody likes you, Taylia. You dumb bitch, you thought you could trust these men? Huh. Nobody loves you, especially not Ky.*

Dadi-ma flickered with an eerie velocity, becoming transparent, until she disappeared.

"I gotta go, I can't be here."

Endowed with a composure I forgot I had, I walked out.

17.

A car pulled up, "Raspberry Beret" blaring, and Alyssa sashayed over from across the street. She swayed, moving to the beat like a clock ticking to time. Her face was a myriad of baroque expressions that transported us to a stage.

"Tay..."

I looked up at her, my face full of questions. "Yes?"

"Do you think we were raised with class awareness as a construct, but we were just never told we benefited from class privilege?... I've been thinking about it a lot. About this farce we've been born into."

I stayed silent.

"You know what Mama is like with money, and, well, Baba..." She trailed off. "It's about so much more." She paused. "Don't you think? So much more than what we've been allowed to see."

She was looking over at me. Her eyes were bloodshot and her face was strained. She looked tired and lethargic, her eyes a bit sunken in. I very rarely saw my sister looking so weak and lifeless. I was afraid. Something had recently changed in her.

"I've been feeling so, so disillusioned."

My breathing was slowing down.

"I'm beginning to realize how much I don't know."

I was starting to feel faint.

"How much I didn't get to learn."

We were both silent after that. We both wallowed in our own pain, our hearts searing with disappointment. I knew what I was too afraid to say out loud: Alyssa had become tired of life, and now it was too late.

I was beginning to see myself as someone who had no one, cared for only by women who were dead, besides Kat. I decided to go back to Ky's, but to maintain a quietly hostile demeanor when I returned. I knew I was being a brat, a little passive aggressive, but I also didn't care. I wanted to be a person who owned her feelings. I had to stay alert; I no longer felt comforted by his kindness or his and Emi's feigned concerns. For a second right after Emi told me, I thought I'd go back to Kat, but welcomed the free months of rent Ky offered, as a means of repair, and I felt some kind of justice taking it. I knew that my silence was confusing for him, but I also didn't really care. I wanted to stand by what was coming up for me. I was tired of accepting disrespect.

A week later, I caught the A train down to the beach at Jacob Riis. I felt empty as I sat on the subway, people-watching and daydreaming. When I finally arrived at the beach there was a cold sting in the wind, a black surf in the distance. The fear of drowning enchanted me. There was so much destruction attached to the waves. The water was smooth and cunning; its seduction could pull you, hold you down, and kill you. In two hours Ky would come home and maybe knock on the door, perhaps say sorry yet again. I sat and watched the water.

You'll like it.

The blood drained from my face like sand in an hourglass.

You'll like it.

The images were vivid. Recollections of that night flashed in front of me. I felt the hands searching me again, their insipid cocks living vicariously through their fingers. I closed my eyes and thought of something good. I needed to transport myself to happiness. But there was nothing. The feeling was too strong. These bad memories were indelible. I lay down, submerging myself into the sinking sand, splaying out across its majestic vastness. As I parted my arms like an angel, I hit something along the way. A piece of glass scratched my hand lightly. I picked it up and eyed the crystal-like object closely as it reflected the sunlight. I turned the glass at an angle and then sliced it down onto my arm without skipping a beat. The divine pain was my gateway drug; blood poured out next to me as I saw stars.

This was it: the sweet spot. I had entered the red room, I had entered actual melancholia. To wallow in it sedated me in those nanoseconds. I looked up again toward the stars, through the sun, the clear skies, trying to concentrate on a bird. I longed to be free; I longed to forgive myself and let it all go. I moved to my side so now I faced the water. Out in front of me was a small boat, the cruel waves slowly crashing against its hull. I focused on the sea. The persistent tide gradually mesmerized me, the subsisting force awoke a hunger inside of me. I fell into the hypnotism of the never-ending waters that stirred the small boat. It floated in the middle of nowhere, abandoned by mankind, neglected of its purpose. There, in the middle of the water, that's where I was in my life.

I recalled Valéry, *"The Sea, the sea, perpetually renewed."*

I took off my clothes and the necklace with the rings that Dadi-ma had given me and placed them on the sand. I walked to the edge of the water, completely bare, offering myself to this power. Hoping to be renewed. I cleaned myself, rubbed away the grime from my skin. Blinking in fury, I resigned myself to this moment. I didn't care who was around me, I was one with the moment. The water had a judgmental sharpness to it, as if it sensed my weakness. It remembered me, it consoled me. *You are strong*, it told me. *No, I'm not*, I screamed back. The cut along my arm burned senselessly, the salt in the water piercing deeper, but I meditated on that pain. *Please don't get infected.* I screamed, wanting to self-destruct.

The moon was low as I cleaned the blood off the shard of glass and brought it to my hair and chopped, chopped, crunched it off. My hair was thick, but I got to the end of it. I needed it gone, it lingered from that night. The memory of their hands still groped me in the silence, it still mauled me on this empty beach. The cut was uneven. There was hair peeking out at all different hesitant lengths. But mostly, it hung below my ears in a do akin to a bob, but not quite. For now it would suffice. What was done was done. *Khallas,* as Kat would sometimes say. I was entering a new beginning. I realized that my parents would never know my story. I hated them for not caring enough to find out what really happened. Here, on this beach, I felt bitter and hard, and even as my eyes scanned the horizon, the savage twilight failed to soothe me.

Hatred was much better. It gave me resolve to move forward.

"Last Goodbye," by Jeff Buckley, played in my ear—*Taylia, you have to go home, you have to go back to Ky*—

I awoke abruptly. The sharp wind was on my face. Immediately, I stared out onto the water, monumental, opaque, like a sweeping ghost, and the depth and breadth of it stared back at me. The blackness of the crepuscular ocean, like thick tar, no longer enchanted me. A hypnotic fear rose up inside as I heard myself say I didn't want to die. As I ran from the beach I only faintly remembered why I awoke so quickly. I'd had a dream, and Alyssa was in it. She had spoken to me, she was there, along the constellations. I ran from the night, this time in search of warmth, wanting a home so badly.

I couldn't find my keys, so I knocked on the door. Ky opened it. The muscles in his jaw bunched up when he saw that it was me. I felt a fleeting sense of elation wash over me, gleefully malicious, as if I enjoyed that I had an effect on him. He ushered me in, closing the door behind.

"Where have you been?" he asked gravely. There was a tinge of anger in his voice.

I glared at him.

"Taylia, where were you?" He paused. "And what happened to your hair?"

I turned around and started to make my way up the stairs, enjoying the drama of it all, but he grabbed me by the hand with a measured tightness, holding me back.

"Taylia?"

"Let go," I whispered, and tore my hand from underneath his. He again pulled at me, this time along the now crusty cut on my arm. I cried out, enraged.

He looked down, the tension of the unknown building up in his body. "What is that?"

It looked gruesome, not infected, but pulsing. His voice was stern, like an army general demanding answers. I didn't like his tone, but some part of me also did.

"Tay?"

"What? Just let go of me."

"What is that on your arm?"

"What does it fucking look like?"

He continued, alert and impatient: "What the fuck... You did that to yourself?"

I stayed silent. I didn't know what I wanted at that moment, maybe a shared grief. Maybe sympathy. Maybe I just wanted to be taken care of, but I didn't know how to articulate that.

"You did this to yourself?"

"Yes."

"Why?" He sounded broken.

"Because I felt like it."

"You can't do this to yourself. This isn't right."

"Ky." I paused, tired. "You can't begin to imagine what I'm going through."

"If you shut me out, then I never will."

"Shut you out? I opened up to you and you fucking betrayed me!" It came out like a deluge; all of a sudden, I wanted to punish him. He inhaled deeply as I just gawked, waiting for an apology.

"Life isn't a fucking John Green novel or whatever the fuck, Taylia. I didn't betray you. I told Emi—yes. Should I have asked you? Yes. And I'm sorry. But I wanted him to understand the situation. I wanted him to understand *your* situation. I care about you, that's why I did it."

He watched me solemnly and I felt mute. My emotions lay jumbled. Despite how much he annoyed me, I felt connected to him, I felt close to him. I felt the sadness of not getting what I wanted usurp me, and the inevitability of what was to come sank into me like an etching. I would get hurt, there was no doubt about it. But I felt open to him, more open than I had felt in years.

He took my silence as anger, which it both was and wasn't.

"Taylia?"

Besides, what could I say? Could I even dare to feel this way about him?

"Taylia?"

I had read about the path of the lovers' discourse. Love was tinged with sadness, it bled with uncertainty, and I had always been too weak for love. Fuck, I sounded like Alyssa. But I liked it, I wanted to be more like her.

"Taylia?"

He put his hands on my shoulders, knocking me out of it. I looked up at him. I wanted him to think I was powerful. That I didn't need him.

"Go to hell." I didn't shout it, I whispered it with spying eyes.

The next few days felt excessively aimless for me, and I hardly knew how to interact with him anymore. I didn't know where this intensity of feeling had emerged from. I felt stuck. In love. In this horrendous feeling. Each day, he did his part to be nice, as if he were paying his dues. Every morning I'd hear him breathing through the door, post-run, pre-shower. I had memorized his schedule defiantly, believing that if I mirrored his actions in my mind I would somehow be there—not just in spirit, but with him at any given or precise moment. I would feel his thumping heartbeat and it would be as if we shared an experience together; his shadows began to define my reality. I'd imagine how it would feel to have his flickering breath linger on my face, how his eyes would hold mine in conversation. How maybe he'd laugh and put his hand on my shoulder and then brush my blood-warmed cheeks with his fingers and stroke the happiness that radiated through me. The ache I felt was tangible. I could feel it wail and grow stronger in its disobedience.

I had heard quite a bit about Ky's darling brother, Roman. Even after hearing both Emi and Ky (and sometimes even Jade) bring him up like he was a hero, I was suspicious. I wondered how sincerely admirable this man, or *any man* (Ky included), could possibly be. At the café, the few times I'd had a glimpse of him, he seemed completely normal. Was it merely an exaggeration they had all accepted?

"Taylia, you grew up in New York, too, I hear."

It was a Sunday, and the leaves were bright like tree frogs, glossy like them, too. Ky and Emi had invited Roman over for dinner. I was also invited. Jade was supposed to attend but was caught up with work, so it was just the four of us.

I was in charge of making the potatoes, Emi was doing the chicken, and Ky was doing the salads—we had two: beets with goat cheese, dill, and mint, as well as a kale and walnut Caesar. I began prepping before Roman came, and by the time he was at the house, the chicken was already in the oven, roasting; the potatoes were in a cast iron, toasting; and all the salads needed were their respective dressings. We were good to go. Now, we were sitting, waiting for things to cook and bloat with tenderness. Roman and I were sipping on a biodynamic Riesling (that's what he called it) he brought; the other two were sipping rum, El Dorado 12, also a gift from Roman.

"I mean... I sure as hell didn't have the excitement you all had." I laughed my awkwardness off, but he seemed calm in my response.

"We really did have an exceptional childhood. This city in the early nineties was daaaank!" Roman looked toward Ky, then Emi. "Our parents kind of let us run amok, right?"

"I mean, y'all's parents let y'all run amok... My Catholic immigrant mom didn't want none of that shit," chimed in Emi.

"Oh, fuck off!" Ky shouted.

The three of them laughed.

"You were a brat dude..." Ky added.

Roman interjected. "I mean, Emi's kinda right. Mom and Dad let us do a lot of things. Remember Mr. G?"

"Holy shit! Mr. G. We were so mean to him."

"See, perfect example. I never joined in on your bullying escapades."

"Emi, I don't know what dutiful choir boy charade you're trying to pull, man, it's not working."

"Listen, my moms wouldn't let me do shit!"

"She was pretty judgmental of us..." Ky added.

"Nah, that's not true... she was just... she was busy, she was sad. She was lonely, man." Emi paused. "It's crazy how you begin to understand them years later."

He looked at me and briefly smiled. I looked away, training my eyes unnaturally on the food not yet on the table, a hallucination. My voice was suddenly gorged inside my throat like a scratch.

"You know, for years I thought she was angry, but nah, man. She was just mad sad, dude. She was just scared, too. Can you imagine coming to this country and being so damn poor with kids, and then no matter where you go you're a dirty fucking immigrant and nobody wants to give you shit and resents you for *everythiiiiiing*. It makes me angry. All the things I never had to even think about because I'm American straight off the bat, or whatever."

I wanted to say it was because he was a man, too, but I didn't. Because some part of what he was saying was true. We were all children of immigrants.

"The ridiculous thing is, we don't understand all the unconscious bias there is against us. We think because we're born here it's different..." Roman trailed off. "But it's really not. This country is fucked at its foundation. Only rich white people have true, unadulterated access. All the rest of us beg. Tahsin..." He paused, then looked at me to explain whom he was talking about. "My wife, Tahsin, and I were recently talking about the sort of sacrifices both our parents made. She's Lebanese, and her family came here after the civil war... Though a lot of her family is back there, in Beirut, which, you know, has been under siege for so long. So, it's this wild juxtaposition where you're split, always longing for a home that you can never return to, but being here and never being fully accepted. She's Muslim as well, so that just adds an entirely new dimension of racism on to her experience."

We were silent, grappling with our individual experiences.

"Yeah, I mean, the kind of racism she's had to overcome, man. That shit is real, that shit is deep," Emi added.

"Tahsin is always randomly selected for extra screening... you know, shit like that, and now with Sufjan, our kid," he said, turning to me again, "we're like, 'What's good, America?'"

"You're just like, 'What's good, Ameriiccaaaa?'" Ky asked.

"At the airport, 'What's good, bitch?!'" Emi added.

Ky started laughing. "You're so stupid."

They all laughed, brothers. In this moment, I deeply missed Alyssa.

"Where's Tahsin?" I asked, hoping for a comrade of my own.

"She's with her sister, who is her best homie, no kidding."

"Oh, how's the sis?" asked Ky, and I felt a pang of jealousy at his sudden interest.

"I think she's good, we should all hang out, she's super dope. Maybe I'll bring her by next time."

I smiled fakely alongside the other two.

"How about you, Taylia... what's your story?" Roman met my eyes, asking me directly.

I didn't move. Clearing out my throat with a tick, I bided my time. "Um, well, what exactly about me?"

"About your parents." People were always curious to know where I was from. I looked South Asian but ethnically unplaceable. Maybe it also had to do a lot with people not knowing much about the history of South Asia, me included. The bare minimum was what exotified us, but in many ways we were still seen as subhuman because we were so easily erased.

"Oh..." I cleared my throat again. "Well... my dad is Indian, from India. Kolkata to be exact. So he's actually technically Bengali... though not from Bangladesh. It's this weird thing where the Hindu Bengalis stayed in India and the Muslims stayed in Bangladesh." I gauged the room, and they all seemed interested, so I went on. "See, India was split up by religious lines during Partition, so Bangladesh was known as 'East Pakistan.' It was literally considered Pakistan's property even though it's, like, a completely different country, literally on the other side of India from Pakistan, like thousands and thousands of miles away, so it was completely unfair and unjustified to separate the country like that." I paused again. "So yeah, my dad's from there. And my mom is white, well, she's Jewish. She grew up in New York, on the Upper West Side actually. Which is where I was raised. Her parents kinda hated my dad, my sister, and me. They weren't ever outrightly racist, but we were raised knowing that they didn't want our mother to marry my father. So I guess she was protecting us because we never met them. Which kinda sucks..." I trailed off.

Concerned, Roman asked, "Where are your parents now?"

I couldn't face Ky, not entirely, but I felt his glare as he cut in. "Before Taylia answers that, we should set the table, food is going to be ready soon."

I cherished his interjection, knowing he had done so intentionally. I couldn't acknowledge it, so I kept my head down. Ky got up immediately, and I followed, aching a few feet behind him. He passed me the plates in silence, and by the time I got to the table, Emi and Roman were already on to something else. My heart skipped a beat knowing that Ky had saved me from this moment.

Later Jade joined us. The evening had moved into the backyard again, and as the stars sprawled I lingered on how strange the last few months had been. Emi and Roman were smoking a thin joint, and Jade was eating a plate of dinner while Ky massaged her shoulders. I watched them, frustrated but also, I noticed, more open than I had been in a while.

For so many years, I presumed I was unlikable, maybe even unsociable. Living with Alyssa, I guess, had made me feel dispirited, like I'd never be good enough, so why try? But nothing had changed, I was still me, and yet people found me interesting, maybe even charming. Emi passed me the roach, and I inhaled, taking comfort, but was soon sideswept a few seconds after the puff, perhaps regaining my tiny levels of unconscious anxiety. Suddenly, I could tell Jade was suspicious of my presence, and I was annoyed by that and by her. She was so beautiful, her skin so plump and glowing. Like a moonbeam. She had freckles like Lucy Liu, and she was beautiful in a way I could never be. There was a small part of me that wanted to hurt her, but of course, I resisted. I knew my feelings toward her were unfair, because I was really just comparing myself and feeling unworthy. I didn't want to be this simple-minded. Which frustrated me, the feeling like a loop. I let out a shallow sigh and made eye contact with Roman. He smiled at me, and suddenly I felt relieved, temporarily acquitted of the sprawling judgmental thoughts of my brain.

Maybe because of my latent envy of Jade, I realized I needed to avoid Ky at all costs. What I was feeling for him was a seizing of fierce, concentrated passion, an ever-present throbbing of constant distress. Especially in my vagina, an area I still refused to touch or even really acknowledge. When I wasn't around Ky I felt a yearning—a nostalgia for the infinite, for him. But a part of me also wondered: Did he deserve this? Did he deserve my pining?

When I was in my early teens, just coming into my anxiety, Alyssa would often point out how intense I was. Her inflection would reek of disapproval. I knew it was her way of telling me to change, as if my attributes were malleable to her whim. I think, as a result, my intensity was deeply foreign to me.

"I feel grotesque, my limbs are all tangled."

Alyssa was sitting on my bed in Ky's place. We were always so dramatic with each other, cosplaying Yeats and Lord Byron.

"Taylia, why?"

"I don't know how to let this feeling settle."

"God, I wish someone had said this to me: *enjoy it!*"

I pleaded, "Untie me. Will you untie this knot?"

"Between me and you, or Ky and you?"

"Both."

She howled; I sneered.

"Listen closely, my little Taylia: there is nothing else quite like the horrors that love blooms."

Wide-eyed, I gulped and then watched her evaporate. She had said that to me once before when we were living in India. Both Alyssa and I would read incessantly, sometimes competing with each other, sometimes sharing the books or the family Kindle. We were building a tiny library in Dadi-ma's home, and though Mama thought it was a waste, when we could be exploring the city with her, Baba thought it was encouraging. "Let them live a little," he'd tell her. Of course he thought reading literature was akin to really "enjoying life." It was during this period that I saw Alyssa become a little more melancholy than I'd ever seen her before. Ma, especially, overcompensated. When we weren't reading, she'd take Alyssa out on day trips to the Marble Palace, the Victoria Memorial, or the Kalighat Kali Temple, while I preferred to stay home with Dadi-ma. Alyssa did not take to life in India, it made her feel claustrophobic and watched, two things she hated. With all that reading, perhaps she lived in a second universe; the pages became her new home, closer to the life she'd grown so fond of having in New York.

One day, when I was sad at the prospect of Dadi-ma dying, an ever-looming reality, I shared this with Alyssa, hoping for a detailed summary of how I'd be fine or, at the very least, for some compassion. Dadi-ma, outside of my sister, had been the only person in the world I had felt genuinely close to. She'd been reading *Tender Is the Night*, and her tone was mildly incredulous in response to my sadness. She simply said, "There is nothing else quite like the horrors that love blooms," plumping her lips into a heart shape.

About two weeks after the first dinner gathering where I met Roman, I walked home to Ky's from Milk Thistle. I had, since my beachside incident, with Kat's guidance, received a haircut akin to a short bob, less triangular than Amélie's but a similar style. I briefly thought of Liza in admiration, wondering where she was these days. Personally, I liked the way the wind wept on the nape of my neck, a cathartic whisper. For a few months now, I'd also been wearing some of Kat's old clothes she was going to donate to Beacon's Closet. Some of it was perfect—formless, genderless, but also chic. The way my body swayed in Kat's extra Pleats Please (ones she let me borrow; she really knew how to live), along with my white Stan Smiths, made me feel like I was finally carving out who I was. With every new day, I was coming closer to the person I envisioned myself being. This Taylia preferred walking, maybe because it allowed my body to feel like it had agency and direction. I also didn't like the closed spaces of the subway. The forced intimacy of the carriages made me feel disorientated, the meandering eyes of the passengers and the self-imposed awkward body dances at every jerk of the track struck a strong discord deep within me. So, instead, I enjoyed the walk through the history of New York's streets, particularly the vivid and welcoming buzz of the Lower East Side: the cascaded blocks, the young basketballers—even the grime of Delancey Street was charming. Walking over the East River each day reminded me of my mortality; I knew that with the slightest of pulls, I could be dead, drowning from asphyxiation. But as I walked over it I felt alive. I felt like I was beginning my life.

I approached the front door and noticed that it was open. I breathed in relief, knowing that it meant a quick and jolted escape to my still almost empty room. Yet in these last few weeks it had become my sanctuary. I crept up the stairs and crossed the hallway. As I placed my hand on my door I heard faint, eerie crying from Ky's room. It felt familiar, like a moment trapped in time: the dark room in the corner where a deep pain resided. I put my ear to the door, pulled by the cry—the utmost bloodcurdling sound of human exhaustion, the ferocity of loss. Frustrated, I edged closer to the door, wanting so desperately to know what had happened. My senses were in overdrive; the replay of life quietly taunted me.

"So you heard," a voice standing next to me whispered.

As I turned sharply to face Emi, I realized he had been crying too. "What's wrong?" I said, afraid, wanting answers quick.

His eyes were peaked with tears as he detailed the events of the night before. As I listened I stood horrified, my feet glued to the floor and completely unable to process any form of movement.

"He's so fucked up right now."

I watched him pause. The short intake of breath, the excess of saliva, the subterfuge of the tongue, and the impulses of the body, releasing under the stress of misery. I wanted to hold him, Emi, but I hardly knew what to do after. Instead I communicated with my eyes, staring with my full intensity, hoping—in some small way—to communicate my condolences.

Emi left to get some air, so I walked downstairs.

The quiet was deafening, the silence usurping this sleepy cavern. I watched the stillness drift past for minutes, hours. It was so strange how we fear and yet still anticipate death, in some ways

146

believing that for us, and that for our loved ones, it will be different. Despite these preparations it's never what we thought it would be. The air in this apartment had shifted, the energy of this place responded to the loss of Roman. The house grieved, as we all did. Though Ky's crying had stopped, the residue of the wretchedness lingered. I knew, because I could feel it like tree sap dripping all around me.

Just yesterday, Roman had come over for a minute bearing gifts. As the eldest brother, I could tell he was a caretaker of sorts. Or, at least, the responsible one. He and his wife, Tahsin, had gone to Sahadi's, a giant Arab grocery store, picking up delicacies like juicy, taffy-like dates, salty labneh, and über-green za'atar. After dropping off Tahsin (who had their son) at home in Park Slope, he came to Ky's to say hi and offered everything from squeezable harissa to fresh, smoky baba ghanoush to a fat packet of lemony Marcona almonds.

Emi had known Roman and Ky since they were kids, as they all grew up together near a housing estate on Avenue C speaking Spanish. Despite the common language, Emi's religious Venezuelan mother was skeptical of Roman and Ky's liberal parents: a Peruvian and Japanese couple who had left cosmopolitan Lima to test their fates in the New York art scene.

I hadn't had many moments with Roman, but I could see a generosity emanate from him that I had rarely seen in men. It had not been an exaggeration: he was the brilliant, gregarious big brother invested in his baby sibling's life—and I had grown to feel guilty of my earlier cynicism. For Emi, I could see how he looked up to Roman all his life, with no filial obligation or sibling defiance, so the love was pure and unfiltered. It was a love of someone you idolize, who has the life you want, but you're free from jealousy because you genuinely admire him. Perhaps it's easier, too, if he isn't *really* your sibling. Ky was less forthcoming with his adoration, but you could tell that he relied on Roman for all manner of things, as a stabilizing force, as a brother, and now he was gone.

The next day I walked upstairs toward Ky, my hands laden with a freshly baked (that day!) olive oil cake that I brought home from work. I sensed how he must be feeling toward this immeasurable loss. I paused at his door, inhaling strength. I knew that my past experience would allow me to have some perspective. I could help him with my wisdom. I almost laughed at myself. *My wisdom?* Jesus.

I knocked lightly on the door and entered, I didn't expect him to open it. It was dark inside, the curtains firmly drawn together. My eyes adjusted to the darkness as I searched for him. There was a dim light on at one corner, but no sign of Ky. I peeked around his room. Taking in the art that hung beautifully from the walls, I noticed a large unframed canvas that rested on the wall to my right, the colors raw and fleshy, like fresh salmon. I wondered if he had painted it, but remembered Jade was an artist, so it was most likely hers, and suddenly wanted to groan in annoyance. I again resisted. The rest of his room was neatly put together. It was spacious, and even under the circumstances, it looked beautiful. There was a door on the other side; as I looked toward it, it opened and Ky came out. Light stubble tinted his jaw, making him appear disheveled, and his eyes were tired—the usual warmth had subsided, the bright green now a warm hazel. Surprise struck him as he noticed me; at first he faltered, but eventually—reluctantly—he came out.

"Hi," I said awkwardly.

He stayed silent, walked to his bed and sat on the covers.

"How are you feeling?"

I staggered up to him and halted, keeping a respectable distance. My hands were shaking, but I extended the plate toward him. We hadn't talked directly to each other since the night I told him to go to hell.

"I brought this from the café today." I paused for him to answer. He didn't, so I continued. "Olive oil cake is kind of Kat's thing." She often served it with fresh whipped heavy cream and wild strawberry compote; it was delicious.

He glared up at me dangerously, but didn't answer.

"You should eat."

"That's an odd request."

I made a face of confusion.

"You've avoided me for weeks, but now you want me to eat?"

"Ky, come on..."

He shrugged sluggishly, pouty.

"Ky, I'm sorry. I just haven't been in a good mood." I paused. "Look, I know I'm tough to be around—"

"You're actually not."

I was almost certain he'd agree with me. "I'm not?"

"No."

I was excited. "I..."

He sat waiting for me to finish my sentence, but I stopped myself, quickly changing tone.

"I'm sorry about Roman."

I felt like a fraud. I hardly cared about Roman right now. He was insignificant to me. In this moment all that mattered was that after all I had done to Ky, he still didn't think I was crazy. Life felt promising. I wanted to smile, I wanted to embrace him and tell him how much I appreciated his facial hair and how handsome he looked even when he was completely unkempt and melancholy.

He sighed, exhaling with a "How's your arm?"

His voice pulled me out of my daydream.

"My arm?"

Slumping onto his bed, he pointed to his arm. "Your little... indiscretion."

That was a very tempered way of saying *your self-harm*. I smiled, fully knowing how inappropriate my timing was. But I didn't really care. The fact that he remembered filled me with happiness. I shook myself out of it. "Do you want to talk, Ky?"

He looked down at his hands, completely hopeless. "Is it worth it?"

I played with the dry skin on the sides of my nails. "Depends."

"On?"

"Whether or not you want to allow yourself to be okay with whatever comes out."

I could sense him watching me. I knew I had moved him; I could feel his warmth respond to me.

He sighed again. "I don't know what I want."

I knew how he felt. "I think talking will help sift through those feelings."

"I guess I am afraid of what might come out."

I peered at his shirt, thinking it was a happy medium between his face and the floor. "Maybe those things need to be said."

"Maybe, Taylia." He paused and then sang: *"Maybe it's because I don't know you at all."*

I was struck with familiarity. "Jeff Buckley."

"'Last Goodbye.'"

The regret of the unsaid.

"What a face." Ashamed, I realized I had said that out loud.

Ky seemed amused. "Unfortunately I concentrated more on his songwriting skills. And that falsetto..."

I salvaged the moment, smiling crookedly: "Your loss."

Ky gave out one loud bellow. There was a long pause. "Roman used to love Buckley."

Ironically, Baba had introduced me (and Alyssa) to his music, through Nusrat Fateh Ali Khan. As I thought of that, with a pang, momentarily, Ky grabbed hold of my hand. I noticed how tight his grip was and realized he was also crying.

"Fuck, it's past tense. Taylia, it's fucking past tense... He's in the past. His life is history. Fuck, fuck, fuck. Taylia, fuck..."

I held on tightly.

"Roman..."

He jerked his hands out of mine, pulling at his hair. I fumbled with my hands to give myself something to do.

"What the fuck. Oh God, what do I do now? The last time he was on the phone he said, 'I love you, Ky,' and I scoffed. I'm such a piece of shit."

He had collapsed onto his palms.

We were quiet. After a while I decided it was time.

"The pain might not subside, but the absence is easier to bear after a while."

He seemed unconvinced.

"I know because when I was nineteen, Alyssa, my sister, committed suicide." I breathed in. "She was the only person that I think ever came close to loving me, you know, like how I wanted to be loved. Or maybe... something like that. These days I'm not sure of that, either."

He looked up at me, tears rolling down his face. I watched them stop just at the curve of his jawline and trickle down just below his neck.

"You lost your sister?"

I wanted to say that I had lost a lot of things. I had lost, in the past few years: my sister, my virginity, my dignity, both of my parents... and, potentially, also my mind.

I got up. "You'd better eat that cake. It's super fresh."

"Don't go," he said unexpectedly.

I was surprised but thrilled. "Don't worry. I'm just getting you some water."

I remember waking up to the sound of my mother crying. Something was definitely wrong—my mother never cried, not like this. I tried to think of what day it was. *The twenty-sixth of October,* the day after Alyssa's birthday. I sat silently for a while, replaying the dream I'd had the night before. Alyssa had been in it, wearing a white dress. As I replayed the dream I could hear her voice, but nothing she was saying was audible. Screeching wheels, shattering glass—the dream was filled with sounds that struck you painfully, on repeat.

I pulled myself out of the warm refuge of my bed and went to where I could hear the crying. The door was locked, so I slithered onto the floor. But all I could hear was anguish floating from under the crack of my parents' bedroom door. My mother's senseless huffing and puffing, her expressions of devastation, resonated. I was stuck in her pulse, and her heartbeat moved through, shaking me into an involuntary convulsion. I was drifting in her screams as they gnawed like parasites. What was wrong? Mama wouldn't have been crying like this for her parents, and Dadi-ma and Dadi-ji (my father's father) were both dead. Then the horrible thought entered my head: something had happened to Alyssa.

Suddenly and without warning, she seemed incredibly far away to me; I couldn't feel her smiling face, I couldn't feel *her*. As I moved slowly back to my room, I was flooded with questions, so I opened the door to hers and crept in. Hope swelled inside of me, *she's there, she's there*. I moved over her covers, but they were empty and the room was lifeless, I could feel nothing. And suddenly I knew—how sisters knew—that Alyssa was dead. I looked around her room; the previous day it had been filled with people, and today it was empty. On the floor I saw the box I had packaged her present in. It had been a white dress, like I saw in my dream. I bent down toward the box and looked inside. It was empty. I went around her room, searching like an outsider. The space was a complete void, the gaping kind of immediacy that absence brings.

I cried until I had nothing left in me.

Every object in her room was a sign. Had she left a message in the way she opened her curtains? Was half open a half mast? She couldn't have left without saying something significant. Seized by the hope that there was something more, I moved my shaking hands through everything. I trolled through her carefully selected jewelry box, her table, the notebook on the side of her bed, her bookshelf. I picked up the book she had been reading by her window just a few days earlier.

"What are you reading?"

"*Kafka on the Shore*."

She was distant.

I was bored. So, I walked out.

I walked out. I walked out. I walked out.

Before I left, which would turn out to be the last time I'd lay foot in her room, I went to her wardrobe and touched her clothes like they were a living organ. Her life was pulsing through their veins. They still lingered with the smell of her. She had been alive in these clothes. She had bled in these clothes, laughed in these clothes, cried in these clothes. They were the only tangible part of her that was left. I looked outside her gloomy window and watched the leaves fall to the ground for moments, hours, gone by. It was finally beginning to feel like fall; the garden ground was covered with leaves as if they, too, had been mourning her.

Mama's pain was insurmountable. In those days, weeks, months after Alyssa's death, it felt like a burden, a dark cloud whenever I was near her, spilling over onto me, the emotionally susceptible one. She slept for days at a time. Baba rarely disrupted her, instead choosing to sit in a fog of cigar and ash in the private confines of his office. The loneliness was stifling, compounding the feeling of loss even more intensely. In my grief, perhaps in the only way I knew how to grieve, I learned to take care of my parents. I cooked, I cleaned, and I cared for them in remembrance of Alyssa. But nobody looked after me.

One day, a few weeks after her death, I went to my parents' bedroom. No one answered when I knocked, so I opened the door to a hollowed silence, almost a void. Like the hum of *om* during meditation, the silence was unnerving. The curtains weren't drawn, and inside the cavern sat Mama, like a pallid *Flaming June*—eyes closed, in a sleepy repose. I walked in, close enough to smell her, although she didn't wear her perfume—a mix of saffron and musk—instead she lay still, heavy lidded, almost dead.

"Mama?" I whispered.

Nothing.

"Mama?" I whispered again.

I don't know what I wanted, maybe to be seen. To be looked at and remembered as the other daughter. The one who was still there. I touched her gently and she shrank from my touch so rapidly that I felt like I had committed a sin.

"I'm sorry—"

"Taylia. Not now, just go away. Please, I beg of you."

I shuffled away, and by the time I was back in my room, the door sealed, tears had begun to stream. I plummeted to my own bed. Looking for ways to ease the pain, I screamed into my pillowcase.

Zeina was over, and Mama was lying on her lap, cracking her toe knuckles against the side of the sofa. She seemed both depressed and mad, her body on fire, emanating heat; I could feel her as I sat and listened on the stairs. They both couldn't see me, and I preferred it that way.

"All my weaknesses were distilled into her. She was my Trojan horse. I don't have anything to live for anymore. I have nothing."

Zeina just told her to hush gently. In lulling Mama out of her sadness, she threw in my name, like a lifeboat. But I couldn't help but feel the venom in Mama's silence, which made me believe some part of her wished it was I who had died.

"Do you think Dadi-ma was burned alive?" Alyssa asked me on the staircase.

"How could you even think of that?"

"Could you feel her breathing stop?"

"Lyse..."

"Don't you sometimes wonder what happens in the moments after? When life leaves you, when you've finally surrendered? Don't you think it's such a beautiful thing to leave a body, a space, that can no longer hold you?"

"Um, no. That's fucking weird."

"It's just, don't you ever wonder how odd it is that she died in our presence, like on cue?" I felt an anger rise up inside of me.

"I'm not sure I know what you're trying to say."

"You always pretend as if you don't get it, T... but you always do."

I filled a glass with water and took it back upstairs. Ky had gotten out of bed. Still sitting down, now he was leaning over his knees, sobbing softly into his hands as if to muffle the sound. Someone else's pain is always so much harder to bear than your own, and I felt the pang settle in my lungs, smothering me as I breathed. I crept down in front of him.

"Ky, have some water."

He took the glass, putting it to his lips and tilting his head backward as he swallowed in big, spaced gulps. He put the glass down and collapsed into his hands again.

"How do you get over it?"

My attention was on him again. "You don't, unless you throw yourself into things. People say time mends it, but I'm not sure if it does. I mean, while time goes by, when you think about it again the same feelings always come rushing back. It never really fades."

He sighed heavily. I watched him, surprised and delighted by his emotion. My father was the only other man I had known closely—maybe not intimately, but enough—and he was completely devoid of feeling at all times. After Alyssa's death I often stared at him, hoping to see a sign, a revelation, but nothing. He just wallowed in his empty cavity, playing the heroic lead. As I currently examined Ky, it was heartwarming to see how moved he was.

Something came over me. "It's okay."

I cupped my hands around his jaw. I always assumed that my touch repulsed others, but here I was, touching someone. I felt surprise exude through my very fingertips. Ky responded to my kindness eagerly, craving assurance. A small part of my caged self let go.

"It's okay, I'm here," I whispered.

He drew back and looked at me, his eyes moved and slowly focused on mine. With precision, his fingers brushed my face and he reached out toward me, clasping his hands over my neck, slowly touching his lips with mine. And I responded. I responded with no fear of rejection. He tasted different, in a foreign but comforting way. I remember wondering if this was a moment that I would remember for the rest of my life. People always say that about these kinds of things, but I wondered if it was true. He moved one hand to my cheek, and I wanted to fall into him. I wanted to disappear in his lips, into the folds of his tongue and the crevices of his mouth.

His perfect face was all of a sudden frozen in my mind: his high cheekbones and that skin that looked like bright toffee, his dark hair bleached mildly from the sun. He had a surfer aesthetic to him that added to his coolness, his hair always long and shaggy. He was so beautiful, I wanted to cry.

He has a girlfriend, Taylia.

Remembering, I pushed him off me. He stumbled as if in a trance. I sensed him pulling back toward me and I felt wanted, I felt safe.

I had nothing to say: no words could explain my elation and simultaneous fear. I finally moved, avoiding all possible contact when I got up. I didn't see his face, but I could feel his eyes on me, burning my skin. I ran reluctantly down the stairs and adrenaline shot through me like traveling light. I rushed to the back door and released myself. Making sure I was clear of hearing distance, I let out a primal scream, hoping to free the aggression that had been cooped up inside of me. I felt ready to combust, a speeding force that needed to hit the ground and shatter into a million fragments. I sat on the concrete hoping that what I felt had been a reality. I couldn't bear it if this was a dream. I pinched myself, savoring the pain for a few moments. I felt the wind on my face and the dew of the grass wet my knees. I knew that the best of dreams, even among some of the most vivid ones, were never colored with this much mundane yet beautiful detail.

18.

I woke up that morning feeling unresolved. Happy, in a state of wild bliss, but like a thread of loose yarn I was being yanked. I couldn't believe what had actually happened the day before. *Had I truly kissed Ky? Could it be real?* I bobbed my head up to look at my empty, cavernous room. A new beginning. I wanted to feel settled, I wanted to feel embraced. I yearned to make this room a home, this home a home. But now I had gone and kissed Ky, and everything felt both meaningful and *too* loaded. The light was coming in from my window, the trees like guides, a star constellation that ushered me in to my higher self. I lay with the shattering feeling of remorse, or maybe more shame, which overcame me. I knew I had to tell Jade. So I called her. She had given me her number offhandedly, in a spooked way, as if to keep tabs on me. I felt angry at both myself and her for knowing.

"Hello?"

"Hey, um, Jade?"

"Yes?"

"This is Taylia."

"Who?"

"Uh, Taylia."

"Oh right. Ky's roommate."

I took an unacceptable pause.

"Taylia, I'm sorry, but I'm on another call with a client, I thought you were somebody else so I picked up. Is everything okay?"

She annoyed me so much.

"Uh, Ky's not doing too well."

"What do you mean?"

She still didn't know.

"Roman died."

"What? Are you serious? The fuck... Oh my God... How... the fuck?"

"I—"

"When did it happen?! How did this happen?"

"To be honest, I'm not so sure."

"Tell Ky I'll be right over."

He kissed me. He kissed me!

"Okay."

I heard her fidget on the other side.

"Poor baby." She was sniffling.

I winced. Her romantic vernacular seemed so forced.

"Thanks for calling me, Tahlia."

"Taylia."

I heard the irritation in her voice. "Sorry, Taylia. I'll be there soon. Let him know that, won't you?"

But I wouldn't.

What if I was sidelined by her? What if what had happened in his bedroom was just a reaction? What if it was just his way of numbing the pain? What if he had mistaken me for Jade, hoping to lose himself in me, not caring who or what I may be, only craving the satisfaction of blanking out for a few seconds so that the trauma could be overwritten by nonparalyzing mistakes? I didn't want that to be me. For once I so desperately wanted to be a positive choice.

Jade stayed over that night. I wondered if she fucked him. I thought about that until I finally allowed myself to fall asleep. I waited for sounds of moaning, my ears turned to the door, red with impatience. I watched the stairs, but I was confronted by silence. I imagined Jade in bed. I wondered if she moved sinuously like actors in the movies. Did she ask for more, did she get on her hands and knees and get him to fuck her hard? I couldn't picture her talking dirty and I couldn't imagine her coming, her face contorted into forms of passion; everything about her seemed so wooden, almost mechanical. An image kept playing in my mind. I thought of her on the bed, hands trembling as she clenched on to the old Pendleton blanket in front of her, Ky's cock bruising her beautifully. I replayed the image of him sweaty and broken, fucking her to ease the pain. I felt the wandering lust savage me. The image was no longer Jade. I was now in front of him, knees to the floor, waiting for him to devour me.

I woke up.

I felt wetness between my legs. I hadn't had a feeling down there that was pleasant since it happened. The wetness felt viscous and sticky, the heaviness weighing down my panties. I got up and fast-tracked myself to the bathroom, closing the door behind me. There was a warmth between my legs and I felt a gravitational pull toward it. Mouth ajar, I placed my hand to see if that comforted it at all; it didn't. I needed something harder. I placed myself against the bathroom sink and rubbed myself up and down against it, and after a little while there was a release, a sigh passing through me. Afterward, I sat myself down next to the toilet. With my lips twisted, I pulled off my underwear and put my fingers to the wetness. I hadn't touched myself in so long, but right now, it felt so good. I moved against my own flesh, circling the ridge, so tiny and yet so overwhelming, feeling the undulations move through to my chest and head. I kept playing with it, this time picturing Ky. I felt him entering me, I watched him move in and out of me. Focused, he was hovering like a hologram above me. His hazel-green, now almost orange, eyes sunk into me like teeth. Tears scattering past my flushed cheeks, I felt the tides move through my skin, lifting me off the ground into serenity. I sighed a big, greedy sigh and sat for a few seconds in awe that I could be transported like this. I looked down at my fingers, spliced with come. I could smell it on me. It was a very human stench and lasted even after I washed my hands of it. I got up, feeling lighter than usual.

After getting ready, I went downstairs to prepare breakfast, smelling my hands, again and again, as I rushed, happily transported to the bathroom tiles. Hoping to avoid the early-morning traffic of an overnight guest, I planned to beeline for the fridge, but when I got to the kitchen my view was suddenly blockaded by an indecent amount of exposure. I felt my body shrink and my heart sink. Jealousy riddled its way into me. Her hands were awkwardly placed on his body. He was holding her gently, his lips even more beautiful when they moved against skin. I couldn't look away. I stared unconsciously for a while when someone said something.

"Oh. Hi, Taylia."

I was back in that moment. "Oh, hey." I rushed the words quickly out of my mouth,

They both stared at me. I made eye contact with only one of them.

"I'm sorry, I have to go."

"Won't you have breakfast?" he asked.

"Not that hungry."

I charged to the front door and walked to the bakery. I was back in my head, the most solitary place to be.

After work, I took an extra-long route through SoHo, exploring the cobbled streets and the expensive boutiques. New York, on my own terms, had an incredible effect on me. The streets were always so healing. I thought of the other lost souls who had walked through these passages, hoping to be saved by this city's enduring charm. I was soothed by its sibilant sounds, knowing things would be okay. This was a new feeling, one of home. Even if I lost everything, I would still have the city. I would pick myself up and reemerge again.

As I walked into the house, instantly glum, remembering the details of the morning, a voice interrupted my depressing meditation.

"Hey."

I gazed up. It was him.

"Hi."

I knew my voice was a few octaves higher than usual.

"Did you just get back from work?"

"Uh, yeah."

"That was a long shift."

"No, I actually went walking around the city."

"Find anything interesting?"

"Yeah." I smiled a thin line. "The city's secrets."

He smiled. "You seem like you're getting comfortable here."

I rested one hand on the skinny banister. "Uh, yeah, I am."

"Good. I'm glad that you're here."

Please don't do this to me.

I stayed silent.

"About yesterday..."

I nodded my head profusely. "It's whatever. Don't worry about it."

He was piercing through me.

"It was nice of you to call Jade."

I nodded my head again.

"I can tell you don't like her."

"She's whatever. It's whatever. I thought you just needed some, you know, love."

"Yeah."

"I'm sorry, I was there on the bed. You probably thought I was Jade, I mean you were so emotional and—"

"I didn't think you were Jade."

"Oh." I let it out without realizing.

"I knew it was you, Taylia. And you don't have to apologize. You didn't do anything wrong. I was in the wrong. It was inappropriate of me to do—"

"Where's Jade?"

"She's out somewhere. She said she was going to get me a surprise."

"That's exciting."

He smiled. "Do you want to hang out? I don't know when she'll get here, but we have some time to just hang out. If you want."

I paused. "I actually have a lot of reading to do."

He smiled again. "Oh, reading."

"No, I do. I have a lot of reading."

"I'm sure."

I laughed. He followed.

"How are you feeling today?"

"I'm..." He paused. "...numb...You know how it is."

I nodded, I did.

"What is it that you're reading, Taylia, that you can't make time?"

I stuttered. "I—I am reading Jhumpa Lahiri's *The Namesake*."

"Oh."

"So..."

"Too busy, huh?"

His brother just died, you bitch!

"Seems like it."

I could feel him staring into me. But I knew it would be problematic for me to stay, to linger, to want more. Jade wasn't so bad, and it was unfair that I hated her.

"I can't tempt you with a movie?"

He walked toward me and brought his hands to my cheeks. I watched his hands move to my face in slow motion. He rubbed them softly, brushing the redness away. I was transported to the smell on my hands earlier that morning as I thought of him.

"You're warm."

"I know."

He laughed. There was a long pause.

"*The Namesake* is calling me..." I was still looking down.

"Okay."

His hands were still on my face.

"Okay."

I moved away swiftly and his hands fell to his sides. I felt him watch me walk up the stairs. I wanted him so badly that I was afraid I would keel over from the desire moving through me like fire. I closed the door behind me, and my body shook against the beat of my fast-moving heart.

19.

I was lying on her floor, among her clothes, leaning on a plush hoodie as an armrest. She was applying a red Chanel lacquer to her toenails. Mama hated the color because she thought "red nail polish is tacky," but Alyssa didn't seem to care. She had recently bought pumps, knockoff Louboutins, where her toes peeked out, and it was for an occasion. The occasion of looking good. I watched her, then broke the silence.

"How does it feel to be in love?" I asked.

She lingered on her baby toe. "It's just that, a feeling..."

"A feeling?" This didn't seem right.

"It's a state of mind, I guess."

"Does that mean that people have a choice to not be in love?"

"Oh no, of course not. The whole idea of love is that even if it hurts, you can't help it."

"That doesn't make any sense."

I watched her moisturize her hands. She seemed frustrated by my questions.

"Tay, you're young, okay? You don't get these things. When you're my age you'll know."

"Know what?"

"What love is. Gosh, Taylia. Why the twenty-one questions?"

I paused, giving her space to breathe. "Do you love Ryan?" They had been dating for a few months. I watched her closely: she was resisting the urge to chew her bottom lip.

She shrugged. "Sometimes."

It sounded like a choice to me. "Well, how do you know when you're in love?"

"You just know. It's like when you're with the one person, you're whole... you're complete. That's just when you just know. Capisce?"

It sounded awful. I was scared at the idea that I would never be complete. How did it feel to be fragments of a person? Only half whole? I wanted to ask her what the feeling was between two siblings. Was that the same love? I wasn't sure. After Alyssa killed herself, I tried to convince myself that it would have to be enough, but I felt weary and insatiable.

I had always had crushes. Those schoolgirl obsessions with teachers, like Ms. O'Neil, my history teacher. Alyssa hated her, but I loved the way she smelled—like crisp cinnamon. She had short hair that parted to the side like bleached grass, so she looked like Nick Carter. I always had crushes on older women when I was younger, and perhaps that stunted and confused me. I knew I liked men, but they seemed so unattainable, so my misery felt like a more reliable companion. In many ways, I hadn't changed.

I walked to the bathroom, sensing that someone was inside. I looked in and saw Emi washing his hands, using water frugally, fingers slight and swollen.

"Hello, lovely Taylia!" He was all smiles.

We still hadn't properly talked since the incident, and it was a few days later, I managed to smile back.

"We never really talked after..."

"Oh, I know."

"I'm sorry about it all, Taylia. Maybe I've been too self-involved."

"No way! How?"

"I don't know... I've been so nonexistent, I'm sorry. I've just been binge-watching *The Wire*, working on my work projects, and crying..." He chuckled. "I haven't even properly spent time with Ky. I'm being an asshole, I know I should be more attentive to him since Roman, but I've been going through it, too, you know? I'm sorry."

For the first time I saw Emi as a person outside of Ky. I'd been so focused on what I could get out of him, as a proxy for Ky, but now I took him in completely. Contracting my eyes, I pulled back. He was handsome and round-faced with large brown eyes that tilted down at the sides, almost drooping, like Goofy's, but it gave him a charm, a warm absurdity to his looks. I stared at him, head to one side, noticing his calm tenderness that seeped through every lopsided grin. An expression of purity shone through him.

"Earth to Taylia."

"Oh! Shit. Sorry, I disappear sometimes."

"I just said that Ky told me to say hello. He couldn't catch you before he left."

Left? My heart sunk a little. "Oh?"

"He was going to say goodbye but you weren't awake yet."

"Where did he go?"

Emi paused. "To make all the funeral arrangements for Roman. He decided to go take some time with his family. His parents live upstate now, so he's there for a few days."

I nodded my head.

"We should have dinner. I wanna know how you're doing."

It sank even further. "He's gone for that long?"

"He didn't tell you he was leaving?"

"No."

"That's strange."

I nodded my head in cautious agreement.

"He must've forgotten."

My innocence was suddenly exposed. "Hmm..." My smile was faulty, I could feel the edges quiver against their will. I knew Jade must've gone with him, and that maddened me. I caught my breath mid-sigh, and Emi moved past me, speaking. Feigning tiredness, I warded him off, and he seemed keen to get back to work, or *The Wire*, anyway. He walked away and I heard the dialogue of the TV show start again. I stood still, my pulse at my tonsils, beating like a splaying frog. The salty residue of my saliva, runny, sat at the back of my throat. My body was reacting. It was ready to shudder, to break down, to cry, to torment. I bit my pettiness away and went for a walk, tracking the weeds along the sidewalk right to McCarren Park, a few blocks away. The hair on the nape of my neck stood against the breeze as I watched joggers on the ochre-red track. My gaze was searching for Ky. I inhaled, smelling the leaves of sassafras shake through me, fragrant with desire. I felt his kiss on my lips, repetitively, preferring my dreams on this cool, cool night.

At work the next day Kat cried in my arms about Roman. It was strange to see how this man's death affected the two closest people in my life in unrelated ways, punctured by the same pain. We stood by the grand baking ovens and took a reprieve from the business of the lunch rush. I pulsed her hand (in the space between her thumb and pointer finger, as she had taught me, for its unique acupressure) as tears scattered across her face like lost stars.

Death was a strange beast that I didn't know how to tackle. When Alyssa died, the mourning overtook my soul, but consoled me. Grief was a consolation back then, but now it felt insincere. I felt detached from the pain and therefore much better at being a stand-in, like a death doula. Maybe that was my fate? I thought of the intricacies and formality of funerals, what Ky must be going through balancing it all. I held Kat as she cried.

After work, I walked across the East River, moving past the gentrified Williamsburg pads. They stood upright like vapid tin intrusions, littering the corners of the place I called home. As I walked idly, I caught the eye of a biker careening down from Greenpoint and felt myself blush. I cursed myself, feeling pathetic. Any kind of human interaction always made me feel strange and giddy, like I was sharing a secret that nobody knew. There was something oddly sensual in that fantasy, nerves jittering in the aftermath.

I turned toward a narrow park on my left, making my way across the cobbled stone path down to the bank. The greenery was overwhelmingly placid. I faced the city's profile, rapacious buildings protruding out like jigsaw pieces that didn't fit, I stood, insignificant, against the tide of life, the tide that kept coming. "Bulletproof... I Wish I Was" blasted in my ears, the song accompanying the breeze, mirroring my disposition. Vaguely annoyed,

I took the headphones out of my ears and stuck them into my pocket. Right now, I wanted to hear the actual sounds of the city. Sitting down on a big blackened log to my right, I caught the eye of a guy sitting in front of me on a makeshift bench made from dried branches and scattered driftwood. I looked away quickly, thoroughly embarrassed. He was wearing fitted corduroys with a hooded khaki jacket and a maroon beanie. He looked back again, this time smiling. Fingering his pocket, he took out some tobacco, and gesturing toward it, he asked, "Do you want one?"

I was mute.

"They're not as nasty as the prepackaged ones."

"I don't smoke."

"Oh, but you should."

He came and sat next to me. We made eye contact again. The feeling enveloped me.

I concentrated on him and his actions. He was delicate with his craft, his fingers surprisingly nimble for a man so tall.

"You live around here?"

"Yup, North Ninth."

"Near Cafe Colette, right?"

An unease came over me.

"Don't worry. I've seen you before, you look familiar."

"You live around here, too?"

"Yup, at the north end of the park, just where it forks out."

"Oh, near Five Leaves?"

"That's it."

"Cool."

He exhaled and gray particles dissipated into the air. "You walk around a lot. You're always in your own world."

My hands went to my face as I muffled my laugh.

"What?" He asked as if he really wanted to know.

"No, nothing. It feels weird that I've been watched."

He exhaled again, a wolfish grin played on his face. "Well, it's not like I stalk you. I'm not your personal *stalker*."

I giggled, loud. "Aren't all stalkers personal?"

"Yeah... Okay. I don't know your life like that."

I laughed.

"Whatever, my point is, I am neither of those things. I've just seen you from time to time, that's all."

I gave him the thumbs-up, and a smile crept onto his face.

"Yup. It's pretty sweet."

He lifted the cigarette back to his lips and held it there as he wiped his right hand on his trousers and extended it toward me.

"Ralph."

I laughed unnaturally. I think I was trying to flirt.

"What?"

"*The Simpsons*..."

"Fuck, really? That's what you tell me? You can't be like, 'Oh, is that pronounced *Rafe*, like Ralph Fiennes'? Instead you compare me to a... cartoon?"

Baba hated *The Simpsons* because of Apu. He never explicitly told Alyssa and me that, but the theme song would come on the TV, sliding us into a dream, and a silent commotion would start as Baba would rush to bark, "Turn that off, *please*, both of you. I don't want to tell you twice." Alyssa would always smirk quietly, but I would feel sad. Sad for the traumas we can't face.

"Well, I wouldn't ask you that, because you just pronounced your name like Ralph anyway..."

"I could be tricking you, you know?"

I sighed. "Taylia." I delayed extending my hand.

"Tay-what?"

"*L-i-a.*"

"That's actually nice."

I lifted my eyebrow. "Sure."

"No, really."

"Okay, *Ralph*."

I felt comfortable. Better yet, I felt confident.

After a few inhalations he put out his smoke on a rock and wiped his face with both hands. "It's a filthy habit, but God, do I love it."

Getting up abruptly, he fixed his jacket as he straightened out.

"Come to the bar at the Wythe one night, I bartend there on weeknights. They have a great rooftop bar, drinks on me. "

I smiled.

"I'll see you around, Taylia."

"Yeah."

He walked past me and I didn't turn around to see if he looked at me again. Prurient, and suddenly warm, I watched the waves wash past and looked out at the New York skyline. I'd done it! He was no Ky, but he was cute. Maybe I was getting better, maybe I was conquering my weaknesses. As I sat on the shore, I wondered if I would see Ralph again and how often in life we hope for things to be better, to be different.

Alyssa had taken up smoking. Buying overpriced Marlboros and leaning out of her bedroom window, coughing, spitting, but mainly reveling in her newfound habit. It gave her an edge, and I liked it. It reminded me of the girls in the movies, like Ally Sheedy in *The Breakfast Club*. Alyssa was cooler, though, but there was a severity she displayed that felt opulent. Like, it was a newfound zero-fucks attitude that was less mean and more defiant. In those moments, I still believed she couldn't hurt me.

She got a record player for her sixteenth birthday. It was one of those gifts that she felt truly described her: *I'm eclectic, I'm alternative, I listen to vinyl, I watch Ingmar Bergman films, I read Allen Ginsberg. I'm different. I'm different. I'm different.*

One of her earliest albums was *The Velvet Underground and Nico*. She bought it on First Avenue, in a dingy record store. The look on her face when she came home that night was irreverent. She sprawled onto my bed, eyes shining. She smelled like Tommy Girl.

"I know you're not old enough... but love is so great."

I wasn't listening, I was worried she was ruining my bed, which I had made earlier. I had creased every edge to smooth perfection.

She started singing "I'm Waiting for the Man," then walked out of the room singing even louder. The shift was palpable, her strutting around, indignant, entitled—something dark inside of her had begun to shimmer out. Was it the determination of love? The way it must embolden you *to be beloved*. To not have a question of doubt in your mind. I heard her chanting louder, fully aware that it was late, and Mama and Baba would do little to reprimand her, a mere hiss of disapproval. I could hear the lyrics echo against the panes of glass and mirror in the bathroom. *I'm waiting for my man.* I sensed her staring narrow and pointed toward her reflection, basking in her mirrored delight, her hair in smooth waves.

I was destined to be forever waiting. Why do we wait, and who is there to wait for? Doesn't the very idea of waiting imply that there is something or someone on the other end? Like gravity, was she who was waiting being pulled closer at lightning speed to whoever she was waiting for? Waiting felt useless. It felt cumbersome. I could feel the ache of the love that I was not having resonate, cold, in my bones.

But then I smelled him when I opened the front door. Ky was back so soon? I was surprised that Emi had not gone to the service—maybe it had been small? I wondered these things as I entered, suddenly wet, desirous.

I walked in cautiously. My nerves, like hot oil in a skillet, put me in a dance. Up the stairs—*no, what if he's there?* Down, okay. *Wait. Who's that in the kitchen? Fuck, fuck, fuck. That's him.* He coughed as if he could sense me waltzing. I balanced myself up the stairs, biting my nerves until I was in my room. All things would be easier handled once I was out of the apprehension zone.

I sat on the bed and waited. I picked up *The Namesake*, opened it, and placed it near me to ensure that if he were to come into the room I would have an alibi. *What are you doing?* I would look at him with no sign of affection, no sign of tenderness. *I'm reading, can't you tell?*

I waited on the bed for hours, my mind unable to process anything other than memories of him, past, present, and future. I listened to music, I flipped through several books, but nothing calmed me. My breathing had slowed to the point that even the slightest bit of exertion burned a hole through the rest of me. Perversely I lay there, drawing him in. Ky, my custodian, my companion. I waited. But he never came. Inquisitive, but tired, I fell asleep in dreams, mouth wide open, my saliva staining the pillow, arrested by him fully.

Later, I awoke with a start and said aloud, "It doesn't make any sense."

"What doesn't?"

"Did you see him kiss me?"

"I did."

"And?"

Alyssa shrugged.

"I need some input here."

She played with her hair. "I don't know what you want me to say."

I was annoyed.

"Come on, Taylia, this is what men are like."

"Ky's not like that."

She raised her eyebrows. "That's what we all think."

"No, it's not a fucking cliché, Lyse. It's the fucking truth."

Dejected, she lowered her voice like she was speaking with authority. "Okay, T."

I closed my eyes and focused on our whereabouts. We were in the Catskills at our summer house near the lake. We spent those days dusted in grime and dirt, our clothes stiff like cardboard from the buildup of the earth around us. We sat in the woods, lodged in between the trees, and hid as young brats do. Green pines, pungent, and the smell of fresh mildew, musty rot, damp leaves stuck together days after a rainstorm. I savored this memory. I was glad I remembered it.

She broke my meditation. "I never anticipated you'd feel like this."

"Like what?"

"Heartbroken."

"Is this what it feels like?"

She nodded. "I've been watching you."

"I just don't get it. He kissed me. He was so keen, and then nothing. Nothing! Did I do something? I wish I could go back and take it away, do whatever I did differently."

She sighed. "I know how you feel."

"Have you ever had your heart broken?"

She nodded.

"By Ryan?"

She was silent.

I didn't care, I was in my own head again. "It would have been easier if he hadn't said anything. If he hadn't shown he cared. Then he'd be like everyone else and right now I wouldn't feel so rejected."

She sucked on her bottom lip. "Life was never meant to be easy, my love."

And then she disappeared

I woke up to moans. It was as if she were being purposely loud. The rhythm of the bed headboard knocked me awake. The sounds of wood hitting the wall made it hard to concentrate on anything else.

"Ky."

"Harder."

"Yes, fuck me."

Jade sounded like a child who had just learned the word. I felt myself blushing and silently crawled out of bed and opened my door with a steady hand to ensure no creaks were made. The panting was instantly louder. It was as if I were in there with them, watching guilelessly as Ky moved in and out of Jade. Moments later I heard the panting lower; this time it was coming from him. He moved with urgency, his breath a pattern across my ear's soul. There was something so distinctly animal about his call: he sounded wounded. I could picture his face, a score of painful expressions and an inextricable joy pulsing through his radiating body.

I headed out with the sun that morning. I didn't have work, but I also didn't have any thoughts that didn't concern him. I walked up Wythe, along the bike trail, and watched the skyline move past me. I took every step with an anxiousness that crept through me. I was cautious to look a certain way, because I wanted Ky to happen to see me and feel desire run through his vast and tenuous body.

Every tree, every sign, every car reminded me of him. I walked past a coffee shop and remembered how he had mentioned the coffee served there. Foolishly, I walked in, believing that I could forget about him for a few seconds as I tested the macchiato skills of the pink-haired barista. She said her name was Amber and we talked for a few minutes about the beans. I asked her what was good to eat around here and she mentioned a place on the right, just a few blocks down. "You won't miss it! It has one of those great New York awnings." I saw La Superior a few minutes later and walked in and ordered fish tacos from the waify white girl who served me. She winked at my choices, adding in that they were the best tacos she'd ever had. I smiled absent-mindedly. I wanted a distraction. *Anything.* I was desperate. But he was everywhere, on the grimy walls, on the ugly graffiti art, in every smudge that marked my reality.

I came down the same route back to Ky's. My steps were still cautious, still calculated. I'd force my mind somewhere but it would always move right back to *him.* When I walked into the house he was playing "Please, Please, Please, Let Me Get What I Want." I hated Morrissey and I wanted to groan at the universe's joke. He made no sign that he knew I was in the house, or that he even cared, and I walked up the stairs, sullen. I was frustrated by my loyalty. This man had shown me affection and now I was locked in, unable to muster any thought that didn't concern him. I went to my room and paced around, hoping something would lift this weight off my chest. Almost maniacal, I opted for a bath. Crumbling what was left of my bubble bar, I prematurely climbed into the bathtub and sat in the lukewarm water with a frown. Waiting for the water to rise around me, I slapped my headphones onto my ears and lay back. The water finally got to the right height and I turned off the tap. Closing my eyes, I tried to transport myself into his thoughts. Was he thinking of me? If he was, why hadn't he come to see me? He could just say hi. That would be enough. Or a smile. He could knock, come in, and just smile. I would fantasize about that hello and smile for days to come and put meaning to the syntax and sound, to the rhythm of his voice. Would there be a hidden message in the pull of his smile? If the left side edged upward, was he trying to tell me that he loved me? *He kissed me. He kissed me. He kissed me.* He put his delicate, swollen pink lips to mine. I felt his eager tongue slide into my mouth, never once overbearing. That meant something. I was transported there again.

"Taylia!" A voice behind the music in my ears screamed my name. I didn't know this part of the song. *How odd—how had I never picked that up before?* A hand came out of nowhere, like a wave, and pulled my face up. I woke up and saw Ky kneeling before me. His hands were tightly clasped around my jaw and I was looking back at him. I pulled my headphones off and slowly realized what had happened.

"I—God. Fuck."

He had gotten up and had one hand on his hip and the other resting on the wall. He leaned into his hand and I watched him, groggy. The door was off the hinges.

"Taylia."

I was in the bath.

"What were you doing?"

Naked.

"I was so worried."

I was in the bath, naked.

"I thought you..." His voice trailed off.

Ky had seen my naked body.

He looked at my face again. I wanted him to see me, all of me.

"I thought you..."

I wanted him to touch my puckered skin and love me for all my inadequacies.

"I was just taking a bath," I whispered.

"I was outside and I was calling your name. And you didn't reply... and that got me nervous."

I smiled up at him, but he was looking away.

I wanted to come out of the water and stand there. I wanted him to look over at me and I wanted him to want me. I wanted him to watch me with desire me as I stood in the cold water, my whole body visibly crinkled, and tell me how much he wanted to fuck me.

He was still looking away.

"Ky, I'm fine."

He put his hand through his hair. Looking back past me, respectfully, he said, "Well that's good to know."

All serious, but there was a small hint of a smile at the edges of his mouth. I beamed up at him.

"How have you been?" he asked.

I haven't stopped thinking about you a moment since you've been gone.

"I've been good," I lied.

"Good."

"How was... the funeral?" I felt already stupid, but I knew it had to be on his mind.

"It was as expected."

"So, terrible?"

He made a sound like *hmm.* He had his back to me, and we were in silence for a few moments. I hesitantly moved my legs closer to my seated body, turning myself into a lopsided W to ensure that I wasn't being completely indecent. He turned around and came closer, crouching with widened eyes.

"Listen, I wanted to ask you something."

"Okay." My heart slowed down just a little bit.

"It's about Jade."

"Oh."

He laughed. "She wants to stay here for a little bit, some nights, you know? Anyway, I said I'd ask you."

"That was nice of you."

"Taylia, I would like an honest reply."

I pulled my knees closer still, feeling chewed up. "It's your place."

"It's *our* place. Oh yes, and our other roommate, Emi, is fine with it."

"Why does she want to move in anyway?"

He sighed. "To look out for me in this 'dire time of need.'"

He sensed my lifted eyebrows.

"Her words, not mine."

"We, as in Emi and I, can look after you."

He rested against the bathroom wall. "I know." He gave me a smile.

"Maybe she just wants to use your body." I looked down; I knew my delivery was off and cringed. I couldn't bear to look at him.

"I wouldn't mind that." He didn't say it with a laugh as I expected him to. I looked up to see him staring at me. Now that we were looking at each other, I watched his mouth move: "I wouldn't mind it at all."

I looked down quickly, a rotation of the stars in my stomach. I felt him get up and walk toward the door. Gesturing to the debris, he croaked, "I guess I'll have to fix this somehow, maybe Emi can finally come in handy." Suddenly awkward, he walked away. The space howled between us.

I stayed in the bluish water, swelling from the moment. Awakened, pulsating like a life-sized artery, the idea of his tongue moving through my crevices revived me. I felt sanctified like a Byzantine saint, and I was going to listen to my calling. Feeling this buzz, I got up and wrapped the towel around me with a dull fear. I half-heartedly slabbed on some Tahitian monoi body oil. I didn't know where he was, but I was going to find him. I walked toward his bedroom and entered without an invitation, without a knock. He was standing near the window, present. He was my sexual nexus. I moved toward him unabashedly.

"Ky."

He turned around and his eyes focused on mine. I pulled my towel off and stood there in front of him, a child of the sun, the limpid rays infusing me with power. I could feel my bones trembling. He held his breath.

"Ky."

"Yes, Taylia." I could hear it in his voice.

"I want you to..."

He came toward me fast and put his hand on my face. I knew he wanted to know, to make sure, that this—what we were about to do—was what I wanted before we did anything.

"You sure?"

I responded with absoluteness.

We looked at each other for eons before he sunk down and kissed me forcefully. He traced his tongue up my neck and jaw until he was back to my mouth. I felt his warmth envelop me as his tongue danced around mine for a millenia. He pushed me down onto the bed and brought his legs to mine, entwining them together. My hands went up his back that was suddenly bare, up his spine until it led me to his full head of hair, where I felt it move under my skin. He kissed me strongly on the mouth again, exploring every detail, then moved toward my pussy. There was a pause, and I was almost panting, suddenly hungry. I never wanted something as much as I wanted that. He felt perfect, just as I imagined, his tongue a dance, a slow, perfectly slimy beat. He sucked me like mango and got me so wet I could feel it drip down my thighs, sliding down to my crack. He stopped and raised himself onto his knees, suddenly regal, hovering above me. He opened me up, and my body followed him, and as our torsos met I felt him rising against me. He fumbled and found his way inside. Suddenly we were together, breathless. *No hurt, no bruises.* The provocation of my skin ruptured through my very fibers, but it was dazzling. I was seduced by his rhythms, by his mercurial disposition, as his eyes caught mine, filling me with longing. The animal in me was moving and dancing on my chest, a puppet on a string. The rush I felt squealed against my nerves with pleasure. Just slightly under full consciousness, I lay, being fucked and feeling no edge, no hurt. And I embraced him fully as I felt him again. It was more than I could bear. He surged into me, again and again, watching every bit of tension move through my eyes. Our legs, tangled, and his body gently moving in and out, swaying to the tide of time.

Truth is what you've experienced. It's what you know. In the years of feeling unworthy of love I grew to believe that I was unlovable. My theories were proven and sustained by every bit of mistreatment I'd ever felt. Even Alyssa couldn't do much to dissuade me. *You're overreacting,* she would tell me. Code for: *You're exaggerating.* That's how people gaslight you. They do it in the subtlest of ways, making you doubt your intuition, your knowing. Alyssa had no desire to drive me insane, but sometimes, even I knew she wanted me to shut up and take it. I felt like sometimes even she was bored of me.

After everyone had gone to sleep, sometimes I'd stand in front of the bathroom mirror so long that my whole body would feel numb. Like when you're out in the cold for too long and the feeling overtakes you so much that you can't remember what it felt like to be warm. I'd trace my hands up my thighs and to my stomach. *Je me dégoûte.* I'd say it over and over again. I was afraid to say it in English, some part of me didn't want it to be true. I didn't want the ghosts to hear me say it, and know it, and see it.

I'd stand on the side and pull my stomach in as far as it would go. I reveled when I could see the lines of my rib cage, skin like cheesecloth being pulled over the edges of a rough surface. I was definitely bigger than the girls in the magazines. Dark hair shaded my lower back to my crack, and visible stretch marks bruised my hips like spiderwebs. I had big arms that stuck out and medium-sized, semiround tits that were set far apart from each other, giving them a disproportionate distance. How could anyone ever make love to this body? I felt that deeply, at that time, as my eyes lingered painfully on my tortured unappeal. I knew I would never be desired and loved simultaneously.

Ky was asleep when I woke, so I got up and walked to my room. Unsure of whether anyone could see me stark naked, I moved fast, trying to make no sound. I put on what was closest and plonked down onto the floor. It had happened, it had really happened. Life felt strangely intense, but positive. I looked down at my thighs and found them half unshaven and prickly. Out of laziness I often skipped shaving the backs of my legs or even large anonymous sections of the vast space of my thighs. I put my head to my hands. But shame couldn't fester in my current state. My heartbeat felt large in all the places where the energy was suddenly pumping. I felt embraced by the universe, the furtive voices of my self-disdain weak in the moment. The blood in my face moved with a throbbing madness; the tiny blue vein in my left temple pulsed as I thought of *that* night in waves. That night, with its terror, was like an eruption.

I replayed my sulky, brutalized self, a close-up observation of my agony, as I lay opposite Simon, hoping to be saved even in that moment. In my replay, he was a body with an all-consuming pride. A deathly pallor with an aquiline nose and that deranged gray glare. The overture of the night rung on repeat. But, now, where was I? In this moment, I stood suddenly at the edges of my dreams, soaring. I couldn't believe how the pendulum had swung. That I, a girl who could have felt *that* low, felt good, felt surreal, right now, *right now.* I got up and walked downstairs. I felt famished. Agitated, I was met in the kitchen with a pile of dirty dishes. So I started washing them, existing for a time in my thoughts.

"Taylia."

I had not heard him come downstairs. He now stood behind me in the kitchen doorway. I had a soapy plate in my hands as he approached me.

He reached down and wiped a bit of foam off my dress, caressing me softly as he did so. I felt scared, anxious, momentarily unaware of myself again and of what to do next. I faced the other way so he couldn't see the questions on my face. I felt him come up from behind. With one hand he took my wrist and turned me to him. Tracing my skin softly, he pressed himself against me. I don't remember how we got upstairs.

Toward the end with Simon, I was bleeding under the loss of myself. And, for a split second there, I thought I saw *the* white light. Frankly, the notion of death, in that moment, seemed comforting. I had toyed with suicide for so much of my life, because anything had to be better than the life I had been dealt, even silence. Like that scene in Amélie where she thinks of all the people crying at her funeral, I felt sorry for myself, of course I did. So, dying felt like a solution, an absolution. As I looked toward the white light, my body bruised like a bashed-up fruit, my vagina blaring hot, hot heat, I felt myself transcend to a time so similar. *Alyssa, I'm coming for you,* I thought, as her breath was suddenly fixed in my pulse. I could feel her; in her moment of dying, she was all adrenaline. She was with me, even my blurred vision could tell. But then, all of a sudden, she was running toward her freedom. Without me.

White light, white light, white light.

I came back to myself. To Simon. But I was alive.

What surprised me about him the most was that he didn't talk about his mother with contempt; he didn't casually slip in how he dreamed of slaying her while she was on her knees after he'd stabbed her thirty-seven times across the top half of her body. Surely the violence that he had administered to me would be detectable in his voice or the linger of his sneer. There had to be signs. Like a smoker's odor that always reeked through every perfume, the undernotes of tobacco lingering, there must be a way to sense terror in a man.

What was so shocking was that it was obvious, and I *had* always known he was a piece of shit. I had just pretended not to. Simon had an alchemical taste to his aura. The air tasted of steel when he was nearby, stale, like all the air around him trapped. I could see the violence in his eyes, like a glimmer. I just hadn't properly intuited the depth of his ferocity. How was he able to hide the pitless and unappeasable psychopath that lay dormant within him? And was there something wrong with me that it took me so long to recognize it, but really—to fear it?

20.

Kat and I sat in a restaurant near her house in Fort Greene. Beats of music passed through us, sinking us back into our wooden chairs. We had closed the café early that day, deciding on curried rice with saffron and raisins, chakalaka, and mojitos. Kat brought me here, the walls covered with variegated maps of Africa and pop-style portraits of the madiba himself, Nelson Mandela. The guitars hummed while we devoured our food like starved animals, drinking the fresh sweet-and-sour slush that tasted like the booze of a crushed flower. Then we ordered some more, and more.

"I brought some tarot for you *today*, my sweet Taylia."

I was drunkenly thrilled.

"Tarot—to be honest—should be the regular practice of *ev-ory-bo-day*." She sang it, and I joined in. We were drunk.

"I feel you."

"Are you ready for some spiritual praxis, hun?"

"Yes! I am!"

We were both definitely very drunk. She pulled the cards as we sang rhythmed oohs and aahs in response. "Page of Cups!" "Ace of Cups!" When the final card came, she placed it near my left arm and breathed in. "Two of Cups, all cups." My fortune teller gasped, "A suit of all cups, all upright." She paused. "This is quite something."

"Is it?"

"Oh, yah, Tay."

"Okay, okay, tell me!"

"Well, the cups represent emotionality, love... water signs..."

"I'm a Cancer!"

"Yeah, I know—wait, what's Ky?"

"Fuck... I don't know?"

"Okay, find that out, Taylia. Find that out!"

"Okay, okay." My mouth twitched as I repeated, *Ask Ky his birthday. Ask Ky his birthday,* in my mind, blasting it through the coils of my memory center. "Please, what else?"

"Okay, this is all positive. Seriously."

"For?"

"For *lurvve*, my baby."

I was in a trance.

The sky was suddenly luminous, and the screech of cicadas rushed in the late summer heat. A man on a bike went past our window and I watched him zigzag, his safety light blinking like lightning. The moon shone through the park ahead of us and framed the silhouettes of the cars on the street. We were both distracted in unison.

I smiled. "Kat."

"Yes, my love?"

"I feel happy."

She fluttered her eyes, as if she were Samuel Morse himself, mimicking the *tip tap tip tap tip tap* of the first Morse code message. She was now quiet, aureoled—my darling friend. "You're finally seeing what you have to offer this world, my love, and it's pulling you out of your manic, er, cataclysm, or what have you."

"I didn't know... Honestly, I didn't know that I could ever feel like this."

"When you're young everything feels impossible because they're things you haven't experienced before. Then, as you get older, you see that life is worth relishing, and sometimes there are patterns you can almost intuit. The noise dies down after a while, then maybe it picks up again... but sadness, these days, feels far, far away... Another drink?"

I nodded, slowly drifting.

"Just one more, right?"

We both grinned mischievously at each other.

It'd been more than a few months since Kat and Claudia had started dating, and there was an ease in Kat that I mirrored, well not entirely, but it was inspiring to see someone be so relaxed in love.

"Is the whole dating a woman thing hard?"

"Not entirely, like... there's more emotional honesty than before. The sex... is different, maybe more intense than with men. She only dates women, so sometimes I'm worried that I'm disappointing her."

"What? Impossible."

"Girl, it's been a transition. I don't know why being with a woman feels so different, but it does. It feels more weighted, you know? Because this shorthand exists: she understands me better than all the rest, maybe because we're similar. I don't know, but I love her deeper, I feel more aligned with myself than I ever have before. I just feel this intensity consumes me all the time. I don't know..." She slurred her last words. "Am I talking too much?" As confident as Kat could be, she had moments of self-consciousness, especially when she talked about

Claudia. She was giddy, in love. It was sweet, we were both reflections of each other.

"Are you serious? This is all I want to talk about," I assured her.

Kat smiled. "Being in love feels like such a feat."

"You *are* in love..." It was confirmed.

Her eyes lit up brighter as she touched her right incisor with her tongue, a little cheeky. "Maybe."

I watched the golden hour light move along her hands to mine, past my fingers. My body had always felt as if I were trying it on for size, never quite fitting, but now, beneath this honeyed glow that shone across us both, I felt full, thinking of love and its majesty. I grinned, seeing the light of the city change before us.

"How are you finding the job, by the way?" she asked. I liked how she controlled moods. It was her Capricorn nature, she steered things.

"It's good... I don't know if I'll ever have the rapport that you have with the customers. I feel like some of them are bummed out when they see it's me and not you at the counter."

"Well, they can suck it!"

I howled. "No, but seriously, I mean it's about them, but it's also about you, about us, this community you are cultivating. It's made me confront a lot of things about myself."

"Like what?"

"Like my fear of being unlikable."

"I think that's a burden put on all women, Tay."

"Really?"

She smirked.

"What?"

"Sometimes you feel so outta this world. Like, these things that are so simple..."

"You mean basic..."

"Yes." She giggled mercilessly, and I shook my head.

"I mean, I feel naive... most of the time."

"It's a Taylia charm. Because then you're not. Then all of a sudden it's clear you've seen some shit. But, truthfully, I've never met a kid from New York like you, so you're an anomaly."

"I'm not soft..."

"No, you are not. But you're you."

"As are you!"

"We're both unique... Also, is it just me, or does the air taste like champagne?"

We paused and took a moment. There was something about the sky. Just as I looked up toward it, a fleet of birds cuckawed above. There was a serenity to the moment that I didn't want to lose. Something about it reminded me of Dadi-ma.

"You know, you're really the first friend I've made since the death of my grandmother."

There was a beat. Kat, with her unique brand of patience, didn't say anything, almost stubbornly. I knew it annoyed her that she always had to cajole things out of me, and I was trying to be more accountable to my secrecy, to my fears, my anxious awkwardness. So I told her about Dadi-ma. About how this, our relationship, was one of sincere ease and something that I hadn't experienced in my adult life, ever.

Kat told me about the girls she had grown up with in Brooklyn, told me stories of grief as well as stories of generosity and community. That spirit was palpable in everything she did. So she told me about her youth and how much she loved Brooklyn, how there's a certain respect she had for Black people in Brooklyn.

"Honestly, if I could get something for Milk Thistle in BK, dude, are you effing kidding me? I'd get it in a heartbeat. Well, with the help of Ma, but you know, it'd be a worthy investment. The woman was born with a gift." She scratched her chin, in super planning mode. "But, okay, imagine more seating. Imagine a bigger menu—as in not just drinks and pastries. I'm thinking sort of like a nine-to-four eatery, you know, like how the Australians do. Those Australian lunch menus... kimchi fried rice with an egg and shiitakes roasted in bacon fat... I just made that up, but just these elaborate, beautiful, luscious meals, pouring out with delicacy. I want this to just be good, like runny yolks on a chicken congee. I really want to play, I really want to maybe try and do the real cook thing."

I was incredibly moved, seeing her in her element, when she was linking ideas, inspiration, movements together to create something different. This was an exceptional quality of Kat's. There was a reason Milk Thistle had gotten prime real estate, for quite decent rent, in Manhattan—Kat was doing something invigorating. Yes, she served pastries as well as the highest-grade coffee—inspired by international baristas, using perfectly sourced, truly fair trade beans—but the space was also alive and Zen in a way. I could also see the vision clearly for her future Brooklyn outpost. She was dreaming, and I knew I had to ask her logistical questions to help harness the manifestation.

"Okay, what color walls?"

"A pale pink."

"A garden?"

"Absolutely."

"Ideal location?"

"Near the house. Are you kidding me?"

"Waffles?"

"Yeah, but, like, with buckwheat and a raspberry coulis... and crème fraîche."

"Grits?"

"Yes, but more authentically Cajun with a vinegary avocado side salad to cut the creaminess of the grits."

We continued the back and forth. Eventually tired by our visions, we sat silently, both looking out into the neighborhood. We both felt comfortable in our silences, a habit we had developed in the café, and I thought about how grateful I was for our connection, something that I believed was a true kinship. After a while she told me what was on her mind.

"What we have is so special." She paused. "I benefit from you being just as good a friend as a work companion. You're someone who can help me through my rough patches, but also my creation period. You've been someone I can lean on privately... and I really appreciate it—"

"You're the same for me." We were psychic. We both smiled at each other, in love.

"I know."

A few days later it was hot, and Ky and I were in a deep, meditative semicoma when we decided to watch a movie, both craving satisfaction through entertainment. Jade had left after dinner last night, which meant she wouldn't be back for a few days. I don't know what had happened to her plans of staying with Ky, and I didn't ask. Besides, she was acting weird. My anxiety was coasting on a low setting, so I didn't care, even though I could tell something was off. I was numbing myself to the situation. I had told myself that it was okay, that I was okay in doing what I was doing, because Ky and I had a special kind of love.

She had looked at me funny the entire time we ate dinner together. Emi had cooked a paella and we were drinking Prosecco. There was so much parsley in the paella, tenderized with the mussels and shrimp, it was perfect. But, as we all ate, basically the entire time Jade's eyes scratched at me. Did she know something? It didn't matter; after dinner, she decided to leave, and I was relieved and excited to watch her go. I was going to fuck her boyfriend. It felt terrible to admit it to myself, so I danced around it. Ky and I had a connection, it was true. We still hadn't fully addressed what was happening, but we both knew *it was happening.* Our chemistry was rude. It was so greedy and lustful, but we hid it well. Both playing the part. Whether Jade knew it or not (which I momentarily felt bad for), she decided to leave us easily caught in each other's grasp. Now, after fucking three times in a row, Ky nominated watching *In the Mood for Love* by one of his favorite directors. I acquiesced, feeling paralyzed by the heat, and my plump pussy needed rest. By the end, I was marooned in this tale of love, loss, and regret. The music held me for the whole damn movie, and those beautiful swaying hips of Maggie Cheung were intoxicating. But the end left me gutted, my skin tracked with tears. As the credits rolled, Ky spoke. "Thoughts?"

I felt hollow. "What does it mean to you?"

He was silent for a few seconds. "I guess, to me, it showcases life."

"How?"

"Well, the characters are complex, and in the end none of them get what they want."

I sat, numb from the words. "And that's life to you?"

"Well, yeah."

"That just sounds so sad."

He smirked. "Life is sad, Tay."

I knew this was true. Of course I knew it was true, my entire life had been a questionable mix of painful events. Even then, I hoped for something more, for something to be better.

"What did you think of it?"

"I fucking loved it."

He smirked.

"No, I did. I thought it was a beautiful love story, but..."

"But they're never together."

"Yeah, well, that part sucked. But they had love!"

"That's it? They had love? That's enough for you now?"

I looked over at him, disheartened. If he didn't believe in happiness, did that mean that he would never be happy with me? I mistook Ky for someone who believed that things could be better. Now, I felt consumed by a black surf. I felt fooled, suddenly sunken.

"What's going on in there?"

He was trying to be sweet, trying to lighten the mood. But I just shrugged. I felt scared to talk, afraid that my vulnerability would scream in the break of my voice.

"Life is sad, but still, sometimes there are extreme moments of serenity that make these shit lapses in time bearable. You know?" he said, trying to salvage the moment, but suddenly, again, I felt brandished with the truth. I wasn't ready.

"One day I want to be happy." I said it with desperation again: "One day I want to be happy."

He looked hurt, like he was a parent telling his child the inevitable truths of the world. "Okay?"

It wasn't the answer I wanted to hear. Was it even an answer? I wanted to hear him say that I would one day be happy. That he would be the one to make me happy. That no matter what, he would try to do whatever he could in his power to make me happy.

"I can't."

It was as if he read my mind. "What?"

"I can't, Taylia."

"You can't what?"

"Do what you want me to do for you."

I felt halved in two.

"It doesn't mean that I don't care. But I can't do that for you."

I was hardly listening anymore. There was a ring in my ears.

We hadn't yet talked about it, but because he hadn't broken up with Jade, it became increasingly difficult to force the conversation about our relationship in any direction toward permanency or stability. At this point, his cavalier-ness had become a trigger point for me. I craved stability, like one craved fur coats. For me, stability was a declaration of something, a hymn of one's purpose. I didn't like the feeling of uncertainty anymore. I had spent too much of life living in that space. Now my heart felt creased, signaling weak arteries. I wanted permanence, goddamn it. I wanted to feel stable. At least, in one place in my life, I wanted to feel settled.

I assumed he felt nervous, and a little guilty, too. About the turn of events, and how this implicated the both of us. But I felt guilty, too. I knew Jade sensed something, and I knew that's why she had been so judgmental of me in the first place. Maybe she had been trusting her gut. It wasn't fair, but if she only knew how much I dreaded facing myself each day. How, as time passed, that feeling had lessened, but that it was still a stubborn oak, with branches and roots right into the very depths of my heart, lodged in between my veins and flesh. If she only knew how much I had hated myself my whole life. How this was a response to that, too. She had just been in the cross fire, and I just wanted something to work out for me. For once. And, as much as doing this behind her back wasn't making me feel like a good person, it was making me feel desired. But I despised being a secret and blamed her for it. The cabin fever was setting in, costuming every emotion with a terrible feeling of simultaneous dread and sadness.

Dadi-ji had a thin, stark face and once told me, in between stagnant puffs of a cinnamon-colored cigar (like father, like son), that every man is on earth not just to exist, but to live. I remember him sitting in a "chair of ugly comfort" (as Mama would call them) against the washed-out wall. Kolkata walls looked tea stained, tapestries of brown-and-gray watercolors. In my memory, Dadi-ji sat and just continued to smoke. He died a few years after Dadi-ma, but we didn't go back to Kolkata as a family, just Baba. When he returned he had shaved all of his hair. He looked so weak, so lifeless—deflated, I assumed, from the sadness of losing both your parents.

There was a time in my life when I thought that living and existing were the same thing. Two plus two equals life. But as you grow older, or wiser, or maybe both, you start noticing the nuances between living and existing. I thought that once I met someone like Ky—a man to save me from myself—my life would have meaning. Pure, striking, pulsating meaning. I'd have purpose. Better yet, I'd be exempt from suffering, from my all-encompassing, boring pain. I was naive to think that being happy meant the absence of misery, because, well, it doesn't. Our next-door neighbors' youngest daughter, Maddie, died when she was twenty-seven years old from a tumor the size of a Milk Dud lodged lumpy in her left lung. Diagnosed at twenty-five, she was dead two years later. The cancer ate her away, drifting her in and out of a semicoma in the last stages, distilling her body down to dusty sediment, like a sponge drying out in the sun. Her mother came by crying in variegated fits during the chemo, then through remission. By the time of her death, her mother's tears were more stunted; the misery had been subdued through its continuity, the heart striated by the agonizing dullness of repetition.

When I was younger, I envied Maddie. Even Alyssa was in awe of her. A summa cum laude graduate from Yale, she was an older girl with a tepid coolness that white girls with money from New York often had. She looked like Bijou Phillips and wore Missoni prints with a sense of fashionable ease. Maddie's parents were fiercely proud. But the coolest part of her life (or the thing I most envied) was that she had a college sweetheart, Matthew, whom she lived with.

He had bought them a two-bedroom apartment in the West Village with his inheritance three years into their relationship, filling it with midcentury furniture to Maddie's liking. It had a second bedroom that she used for writing, overlooking a diamond-shaped courtyard in the middle. It felt like a hacienda, misplaced for New York, but misplaced in a good way. I saw it all on Facebook.

I imagined she enjoyed the way the skinny, leafless trees shook in this courtyard during the fall's wind, how they muttered secrets to her as the seasons changed. On weekends Matthew and Maddie would sleep in together, *New Yorker*s stacked on their respective bedside tables. Matthew would make coffee in their stovetop Bialetti, pouring almond milk in his cup from a refrigerated mason jar, distilled out of a batch he made earlier that week with their trusty Vitamix. Sometimes they would promenade like real locals up to Chelsea Market and pick up bottles of cold milk from Ronnybrook (which Maddie preferred in her coffee, using the glass bottles to hold tulips around the house afterward) and fresh loaves from Amy's Bread for the week ahead. They would walk past the traffic toward their home that they had built together, past the billboard of lifeless Calvin Klein models, and talk about their future children, about new restaurants they had to try; they were happy.

But none of the projected dreams came true. Maddie died against the backdrop of a pale dawn in the hands of Matthew, who no longer had anything to live for. I wondered if people would recall Alyssa's life like that.

21.

Alyssa's face was once alive, expressive.

It was almost spring, and she was smiling at the effervescent sun. Her eyes crinkled at the sides; I knew it was hurting her to look at the brightness with that much intensity, but she want-ed to. She wanted to convince herself of her mind's perfected drama.

"Look at that cloud."

I followed her fingers to a large, slightly ominous off-white mass. "It's so big!"

She wasn't listening; she ran off, chasing. "You can almost fool yourself into thinking that you're spinning the speed of a thousand miles and circumventing the sun."

She had run so far ahead that I could only just make her out in the distance. The wind moved through her like a snake.

"What?" I yelled.

We were upstate again. This was one of the happy times, just before she changed. I remember the before and after so clearly. How there once used to be a charming ease to her. But when she realized she was beautiful she did what a lot of pretty girls end up doing. She punished herself for the sin of beauty.

It was the summer solstice and the tilt of the planet's semiaxis caused the back of my shirt to dampen. The air was dulcet and warm, and I was peeling an orange, the light citrus blending and wafting through the space between Emi and me like a live spritzer.

I broke our cave of silence. "Does Ky ever talk about me to you?"

There was a spark in Emi's eyes that contained a deep, unnameable something I couldn't quite place, but it was very palpable. "Oh, this game?"

"I'm not playing games..."

"Hmm."

"No, seriously, I'm just asking."

"Oh, *okaaaaay*." He sipped on his grappa, a pure distillation of grape pips. My mind wandered to when I was a child and I asked Baba, "If I swallowed a seed and some soil, could I grow grapes in my tummy?"

"I sometimes wonder..."

"Wonder?"

"What he thinks about me."

"Well, I think it's pretty obvious."

"Obvious, how?"

He paused and bit his lip. I could sense him slowing down, the energy palpably shifted. I started to feel nervous, like I sometimes did as a child when I could intuit Mama's or Baba's anger like an electric shock in my body, pulsating on a low sedateness. For a few seconds, I was aghast, not knowing how I should broach him, but he finally answered.

"Have y'all told Jade anything yet?"

I felt slapped across the face, but I also knew I had no right to. "I... don't think he has..." I stumbled in half words. Though, it was also *the truth*. I rarely wanted to bring it up with Ky, and I could sense and understand Emi's frustration, now that I could finally place it.

"I obviously don't want to overstep, Taylia. Kynan is his own person. He's a grown-ass man, so I'm not gonna give advice. But I think it's shitty to Jade, if I'm gonna be honest..."

He paused. "I don't think I ever told you what happened with my ex, but, basically"—he took a deep sigh—"she cheated on me. And Ky knows that, so it's weird to sort of witness it on this end. And, okay, Jade is a hard one to like immediately. But she's really fucking nice when you get to know her... Ky wouldn't be dating her otherwise. Or dated, or whatever the fuck you're doing... Like, is this a throuple, are y'all in an open relationship?" He paused again. "Okay, and I really, really mean it—no judgment— but I can't help but relate to Jade, and nobody deserves this. Okay, maybe All Lives Matter people deserve this shit, but, like, ordinary nonracist nonshitty people don't! It's dishonest and disrespectful to everyone involved."

I inhaled, knowing what he was saying was true, and it was hard to deny it. "I know. I agree, and I'm sorry."

He groaned. "Don't apologize to me! Figure it out with Ky, though. Before it hurts Jade more than it already will." Immediately after saying this, he threw down about two fingers of grappa, refilling the glass again. I could tell he was in pain. I could tell he resented having to tell me this.

"I'm sorta doing things I'd never imagined I'd ever do," I muttered, embarrassed. I wanted to tell him I felt ashamed, but also resisted being too vulnerable with him. There was a part of me, if I'm being honest, that felt adult to be in this situation. It felt gratifying to be in a position of some kind of power. I felt crazy, because inside of me existed a duality. I knew how unfair I was being—but maybe there was a part of me that felt justified. I deserved this. I deserved love after the life I had led. I knew that wasn't something to voice to Emi, he wouldn't understand. There was something so boyish to him, and it annoyed me. Ky had it, too, at times. But Emi felt like a big, goofy idiot, guileless and gullible. I didn't respect him. I didn't know why. Maybe I was just witnessing him at a time in his life when he was removed from his best self, bloated in pain, and I found that quite weak and boring and was unsympathetic toward his turbulent emotions, and clearly his latent drug and alcohol abuse. In this moment, however, I paid attention, maybe because some part of me wished to be scolded. I wasn't sure.

"I mean, listen... I know Ky isn't a bad guy. He's my best friend..." He trailed off. "And I don't think you are, either, Taylia."

A voice came out of nowhere. "Yo, Emi. What's going on?"

We both swiveled toward the sound. It was Ky. The music froze dramatically, the Leonard Cohen record skipping on the last beat again and again and again. Emi threw back his head, this time sharply, gulping down the rest of the grappa. By the time I watched him take his second swallow I felt water standing in my eyes. I looked toward Ky but couldn't discern his full face, so I stared past him, toward the world I had dreamed up between us. He came toward me and paused.

"I'm sorry, man, I'm just being real." Emi took the bottle of grappa, with its bold blue Romanesque label, preparing for something.

"Dude, don't you think it's kinda whack that you're dragging Taylia into this?"

I felt like I was being wrapped in a heavy, itchy shroud. My breathing was quiet with a dull fear laced with excitement.

"Nah, man, it's the both of you... right? Two people in a relationship..."

"Yeah, okay, but I don't think Taylia deserves this, especially not from you. As much as I do, maybe..."

"Maybe? Okay, look, I'm not trying to be a dick. And I'm sorry, Taylia."

I shrugged.

"It just is alarming to me. That's all! And I think Jade oughta know."

Alanis Morissette played in my ear, I was distracted. I looked at Ky: he was in pain.

"I mean, I'm not disputing that. I'm just saying that you're coming for the wrong person."

"Okay, fair. My bad..."

I remained silent, detached.

Ky exhaled. "For what it's worth, this is not my proudest moment and I think of it all the time. It's just... it's hard." He paused for an eternity, then turned to me: "If I'm being honest, I don't know what to do." He paused again. "I don't know what to say, but I feel like I have to say the truth."

I was back in my body, but this time I felt so sad. He came to face me, searching for a light in my face, an entry point.

"I guess I'm having a hard time figuring out what I want..."

I guess I had also known this. Kat had said something to me about customers being predictable. It was a metaphor.

I heard him speak. "I'm not trying to say I don't want this. I do, but it's complicated. I was in a long-term relationship with someone. I absolutely thought Jade and I would be together for a long time... then you came into the picture, Taylia... and something shifted. I started wanting you in a way I no longer wanted Jade. Which is so unfair to her. But that's what happened. You and I fell in love, and who's to say that won't happen again and again?"

Emi pulled the air through his teeth. "Come on, bro, now you're just being selfish."

"I'm... I'm just trying to be honest. All I'm saying is this isn't easy for me!"

"Ky... truthfully"—Emi's words were comedically slurred—"you're being a dick, man."

It felt like that was my cue to exit. I had wanted to leave for a while but couldn't move, and now a sob kicked into my chest. I muttered an excuse and scuttled upstairs. Neither of them tried to stop me, which was a relief. This whole interaction was involuntarily thrust on to me, and I needed to process it. For myself.

That night we didn't make love. When Jade wasn't here, we'd sleep in my room, which should have been a sign. I respected Jade for knowing something felt off and avoiding it. She had class, she was giving it time. Maybe she was giving us time for reflection, to compose ourselves. We were all cowards, but I blamed Ky for his hallucinating inaction.

The moon shone through the curtains. I couldn't sleep. At a certain point in the night he curled up behind me but soon pulled away, my body frigid to his touch. Something felt off, suspended and frozen. I couldn't do this kind of instability again. Had I come so far only to be treated like dirt, *again*? To not be chosen, *again*? I felt like a turd on the side of the road, but unlike the other times I had felt this suffocating feeling, now I was alive. No longer a dead intention. I changed when I walked out of my parents' house. I had started betting on myself.

When I woke up, breakfast was beside me with a note that read, *I love you*. I kept running it through my head, hoping to settle my nerves, but instead I was distracted by the repetition of the word *jinn* in my mind, which in Arabic meant "hidden from sight." A word I had found researching the real meaning of *jihad*. What was opaque to me, hidden in sight? What had me arrested in motion? *I love you?* I called bullshit. Why now? I was traveling on my Möbius strip of thoughts. *I love you...* Ky had once said to me those were just words. It was everything else that counts.

With psycho-spiritual clockwork, Kat brought up Jade as well the next night. I was over for dinner. Claudia, whom I was meeting for the first time, was making ragout de truffles accompanied with pommes dauphinoise, delicacies she learned living in France. She poured a Crémant du Jura into a sleek, chandelier-like glass as an aperitif for both Kat and me. I watched the way Claudia looked at Kat, even while cooking, like Kat was her compass. Wearing a face of readied hunger and also constant awe, she looked like she knew she was so lucky to have the woman of her dreams. And she was.

"I made something very simple, I hope you don't mind," she said. Her hands were delicate, lined with veins like my mother's. I could understand why Kat was attracted to her. Like a vortex, she was so embodied that she had a gravitational pull. It's a strange quality, but it was in the way she calmly arranged the plates onto the table, using silverware like a frame. She had a presence. I think I was forming a tiny crush.

As we all inhaled the food, sipping on a wonderful, cloudy, appley pét-nat from Portland, Kat asked me, gently, "Babe. I've been thinking about this for a while... What's going on with Jade?"

Maybe I had expected it, so I felt ready. "I don't know, I—"

Claudia interjected. "Wait, who's Jade?"

"Honey, let her speak..."

Claudia nodded, and they both looked at me, an audience.

"No pressure, LOL." I was trying to deflect hard, looking at Claudia, embarrassed by her inevitable judgment, any by handsome she was. "Ky's been cheating on his girlfriend, Jade, with me."

I felt like shit. I had intuited right, I could see Kat was trying to lessen the blow to Claudia, who seemed unnerved.

"Baby, it's complicated," she said, protecting me.

"How?" Claudia wasn't having it.

Kat looked at me, probing me to explain.

"I... I don't know, it's not like I ever thought I'd do this to someone. It's not like I get turned on by breaking up relationships. Ky and I... it's different." I guess I had never tried explaining it to anybody. "We're just really compatible. Our intensity matches the other's, which is a big one for me. I've never really met anyone that could face me with that feeling." I guess that was it, Ky could hold me. He had the capacity, the want to. Ever since the beginning of our relationship he had made such space, and I realized that's what bonded us. This awe-inspiring feeling we both felt around each other, or at least what I felt around him.

"But... Taylia, men who cheat are unreliable. It's simple."

I felt slapped.

"Okay, Claud, wait a second. Frankly, T—I like Ky. I really do. I don't think I would be so supportive of you if I didn't. I liked his brother, Roman, too. Clearly they were raised right. And to be completely honest, Ky is hot, and I think you guys are good together. And, so, I'm excited for what's to come. Because, and I really believe this, no matter what happens between you two, this is an important milestone for you to go through. It's an important transition to usher you into the next part of your life. That much is clear to me."

I looked at her, astounded, because I had been feeling that so much recently myself. It was as if she had the articulation in language that I understood abstractly. I agreed profusely, and she paused, gathering her thoughts,

"I know it's complicated, because nobody deserves this, so I'm sympathetic to Jade. But, over these last few months, you've really helped me understand Elijah, if I'm being honest."

Claudia held Kat's hand gently as she talked and tears began to stream. I moved closer to her in my chair, wanting all of a sudden to cocoon her, and so Claudia and I both held her at each side.

"I think it's easy to fall into narratives of people. And if someone's hurt you, then it's easy to replicate that." She paused, turning to Claudia. "My love, it took me such a long time to trust you. I trust easily in my life for most things—I mean, I'm not an idiot, I'm obviously psychic af —but I haven't always been lucky in love and the wound is deep."

She started to cry now, stuttering. Claudia and I shielded her more, wanting to make a haven for her to let it all out.

"But, my God, did I feel so fucking low when he left. I was in disbelief. Just pure effing disbelief. I couldn't believe this man I built this home with didn't want me anymore. And the hardest, hardest, *hardest* part was that I don't really blame him. It got too hard, we just were compatible to a certain point, but that's it, and we had surpassed that marker. We just didn't want to admit it to each other, because it's not as if we hadn't both tried to salvage what we had, but it just wasn't working, and it's been easier to believe he was Voldemort than to see his perspective. He was a good man, but he was just a weak, indulgent man. He didn't know how to stand up for me, or us, and he grew lazy. But a lot of people grow lazy in love. And that's the problem. But for a long time he was good, and he loved me. It's taken me a long time to see it, and, Tay, truthfully I wouldn't have been able to have this kind of compassion if you weren't in this situation. Because seeing it from your side, and seeing your naïveté and maybe tenderness, made me see how complicated any given situation is. Honestly, so thank you. You've given me clarity. You've made me remember that people are complicated."

I was in shock. "Kat..." I started pulsing her hand, my full face on her chest, resting against her collarbone.

"Thank you for sharing that, my love," Claudia said, kissing her on the cheek, then on the mouth. Their love was so wholesome, so pure. "I guess I don't get it, but I get it... if that makes sense. Clearly, Taylia, I don't know the specifics and I'm sure it's much more complicated... as most interpersonal relationships are. I didn't mean to be judgmental."

I felt floaty and so held. "Thank you. But you were just being honest, and I get it." I smiled. "It's not been an easy road, because I know I'm in the wrong. I don't feel good about it most of the time, and I don't know if I ever will, until he tells her. And then I'll still feel like shit because I will have hurt her." That was the truth. But then some part of me lingered; that's when the anxiety started, and I felt restless. *Would he tell her? What if he never told her?* I felt suddenly panicked, but unwilling to share it with Kat and Claudia. I didn't want to ruin their night, this beautiful night.

"Anyway, it's a lot. Let's talk about something else..."

So I changed the subject and steered things in another direction.

The next morning, back at Ky's, I walked outside and watched the puffs of milky white move leisurely across the sky. I was thinking about the conversation from the night before and the anxiety I had felt, wondering if Ky would ever tell Jade. I hadn't been the same around him since Emi's outburst, and it was as if he was being cautious. Alert. I thought he had been writing, but I felt him come up behind me, curious but also mildly suffocating.

"What are you doing?"

"I'm watching the clouds."

"Just in case?" He mirrored my gaze. "I think there's one that looks like Bowie!"

I laughed despite my nervous mood, playing along momentarily. "Where?"

"There." He pointed at one that resembled no part of David Bowie.

"He's singing 'Velvet Goldmine.' Look, he's got the microphone to his face!"

Ky anticipated a laugh. I myself was expecting a laugh to come out. I waited for it to rise in my chest, but my mouth hurt at the crease and I didn't want to stretch the sides of my pitiful emotions and deflating self-worth.

"You okay there, kiddo?"

"Sure am."

"You're not overworking that pretty head, are you?"

"You mean with thoughts?"

It was supposed to be funny. We had fallen into a comedy routine in our daily banter. But today one member was slightly off; the show would not go on. My voice broke, and I ended up sounding sad rather than sassy. He picked up on it but stayed silent.

We stood together for a while, both in our worlds of imagination. I wanted to say what I wanted to say, but I couldn't. There were too many outcomes and answers that I was not ready to face. Not yet, anyway.

"What are you thinking about?"

I'm ten days late for my period. I'm ten days late for my period. I'm ten days late for my period. Fuck, fuck, fuck, fuck, fuck.

He suddenly seemed very far from me. My poker face was secure, but I felt like a mockery of myself. There was no suspicion in his face, but he knew I was blatantly lying. He could hear the echoes of my weariness play in the silence. Sorrow had become me, but the tension was unspeakable. Besides, I would deny everything. *Deny, deny, deny.*

Eventually, he smiled and kissed me on my forehead. "You mean the world to me."

As he walked away, I heard him hum "Sorrow."

In Arabic, etymologically, the word for fetus comes from *jinn.*

The next day there was a peculiar sense of metamorphosis. I had awoken that day tender, in tears. My mind was a labyrinthine explanation of terror. I had once heard that a lot of women don't generally know, but for me it was an intrinsic knowing. Like when you can taste the rain in the air and the clouds bloom and rise and the darkness embellishes the sky. The water pours only seconds after you realize it's going to gush and then it does, washing the bad away. Just like that, there was a shift. I felt a pull in my lower abdomen, like the hands of a ghost pulling at my womb. There was a distinguishable heaviness as a tangible weight began to crawl inside of me. The baby's soul was inhabiting my insides. I didn't react. I just numbed myself to the point that I was no longer exerting anything. No energy, no thoughts. I was just *overcome* with stillness.

We were so young. And Ky was still so dumb. I didn't know so much that I wanted to learn. Like ikebana and playing the guitar. I wanted to be able to say that I ran every day, to be fit and not have to hide my thighs, to be proud of my body. I wanted to be really good at chess and do crosswords and listen to Bach and not forget to take (or buy) my iron supplements. These were all things that I still wanted to do, to learn how to do. I wasn't ready for this.

The reality struck me and caused me to halt.

I wasn't ready for *this*.

The moment I knew for sure I was pregnant, just a few days later, the air was dense like liquid. I felt the tears I was crying evaporate into the air and hollow me out like a cave. My tears, my sweat, were rising to the surface and I was drying out like clay. I felt so low. I felt as if an energy had overtaken me and now controlled me. I was no longer Taylia. I was at the whim of the universe now. I was weak, I was nothing. *Me, have a baby? I couldn't even face myself.*

I walked past the cars with my headphones on. I was listening to *Figure 8* accidentally, and as I walked underneath the Williamsburg Bridge, "Everything Means Nothing to Me" came on. I smiled at the irony, at that little Spotify sign. I was in a lake of my own misery, but the song was pulling me through, sinuously, for two minutes and twenty-four seconds. When it stopped, I was in reality once more. My legs felt like stilts, pieces of bark, coarse in their fear of the unknown.

I walked onto Broadway, past the Marcy Avenue stop, and kept walking.

Finally, I reached my impending doom. I saw the stairs to the doctor's office and could already taste the metal against my tongue. I hadn't trusted the two take-home tests I had done a few days earlier. Those little plus signs meant nothing to me. Those stupid pink plastic pieces of shit meant nothing to me. I needed someone to shake me and scream at me and tell me, *YOU ARE PREGNANT.* Even though I knew I was, I still needed to hear it. I needed someone to know what I needed to do. I needed someone to ask all the right questions like, *What the fuck are you going to do?*

The office was busy with women with children, women with no children, and women who were very obviously about to have children. I swiped at my tears with the back of my hand.

"Taylia Chatterjee?"

I looked up as a pretty woman gestured me into a room. I felt slightly embarrassed that she was clearly South Asian, but some part of me wanted to be ruthless. I couldn't care right now.

"Hi, Taylia, I'm Dr. Kumar, nice to meet you. Please sit down."

"Okay." I looked at the floor and there were vacuum marks on the carpet.

"So, what can I do for you today?"

"I'm pregnant." I blurted it out in the hope that if I did the baby would miraculously leave me. *Then I would be free.*

"Okay."

"Am I pregnant?"

"I thought you just said..."

"I did the tests—you know, the take-home ones. I bought the packet with two of them in it, just in case, you know, and it was like, I don't know... like twenty bucks or something. It was from Duane Reade. I don't think that's really a reputable source for someone to tell you that you're pregnant, don't you think?"

"You mean *Duane Reade*?"

I nodded.

"Well, Taylia, they're formulated tests and they're pretty accurate. What did the test say?"

"Tests, I did both of them."

"Okay, well, what did these tests say?"

"They said that I was pregnant." I started to fully cry.

She passed me some tissues. I didn't want her to judge me, I was scared of that.

"Listen, it's okay, Taylia..."

I stopped listening. I looked toward the window. It was slightly ajar, and I could see the Williamsburg Bridge and that gigantic white savings bank. There seemed to be a thin screen blockading me from out there. I knew, by just looking at it, that there would be no issue to break it. I could catapult out the window like in the movies. I could play a song in my head to make it easier. *She's like the wind*... I'd fly out, pretending like I was in the arms of Patrick Swayze, limbs flailing unnecessarily, my heart in my chest, and a fetus I would never know in my body.

"Taylia. I know what you're going through is difficult, trust me, I know. Unplanned pregnancies are always hard, and I'm guessing by your reaction that this was unplanned... You really need to figure out what exactly it is that you want to do from this point onward. You need to make a decision as to whether you'd like to keep this baby, or... not. Have you thought any of this through already?"

I was silent.

"Do you have a partner, or..."

He's going to leave you, Taylia.

He's going to leave you.

He's going to leave you and your sorry ass, and then you're going to have to look after your good-for-nothing baby by yourself.

"I..."

"...or family?"

They already left you.

"No."

Why do we ever do anything? Something always pushes us to the answers. But what are those answers, really? They're nothing of substance, right? In the larger detail of our lives, the decisions that we make are nothing more than that. Decisions that we made.

Made, past tense.

They're not the puzzle pieces forming together, or the corners that we cut in the maze to come to some realization. When we were younger, Alyssa loved watching *Labyrinth*. She was probably thirteen or so when she said that the labyrinth Sarah moved through symbolized human life. She sounded so smart to me then. But I realize now that she wasn't. And it doesn't. Life is random, with no meaning, no purpose, and definitely no point.

He was going to leave me. He was going to leave me and not Jade. He was going to leave me like my parents had. He was going to leave me. I was almost certain that he would.

So. I left him first.

22.

I walked from the doctor's office (equipped with my JanSport backpack, I had come prepared) to the café and sat there as Arnold and Elliott, and all our other regulars, came and went, sipping espresso, discussing books and articles by Ta-Nehisi Coates. A day earlier Kat and I had talked about the politics of being the neighborhood friendly Black woman and the psychological impact of being nice to white people all the time. It made me defensive of her as I watched Elliott and Arnold talk about *Between the World and Me* like these white men truly understood and actually wanted to unlearn the smearing unjustness of white privilege. That madness was a good way for me to temper the insanity I felt.

I struggled with the whiteness that lay dormant in me, and it was something that I didn't want to talk to Kat about. I guess I was embarrassed. Embarrassed by a lot of things, like how little I really knew, but also the overwhelming fear of facing racism in America in a way that was beyond theoretical. I wanted to be a person who could stand by my politics; I didn't want to be like my parents who had grown frail and ugly. I also didn't want to lean on her, even though I knew I would, and I pre-emptively felt shitty about having needs and not knowing who else to turn to. I focused on that thought—a loop, a complete distraction—and maybe it was a way for me to feel sad without acknowledging the real root of my sadness. I couldn't let the fear of leaving him overtake me. I had to be strong. For this baby, for me.

I could tell Kat sensed something was off; she kept looking at me with thin, concerned lips, but I avoided her stare. Taking orders, boxing pastries, I remained steadfastly particular, focusing on the details. But inside I felt like a madwoman. I felt fucking uncontained.

When the lull of the day came she asked me what was wrong.

"I'm pregnant," I said, looking away, focusing on the invi-olability of motherhood, this deep moon inside of me that was growing like a bean. I tried to meditate on Kat's impressive poise.

She embraced me. "Oh, baby" was all she said, letting my face fall to her chest as I disappeared from the world momentarily like a quiet ghost.

Some part of Kat understood that there was a dark under-belly of my life that I was not ready to share. A puddle of black ink hovered over me, and even just a brush of a fingertip could be transformed into my hurt. So I avoided it. She understood the volatility and knew I couldn't afford that kind of interference, not now, not in this state. So she propped my spirits up with her love. She didn't ask questions. When I asked her if I could come and stay with her again, she nodded silently, maybe slightly afraid of me or for me. Or both.

From the very beginning there were endless hours when she would stay up late, massaging my back with her deftly soothing fingers. I'd wake up sometimes, my sheets and my body succored with Tiger Balm, tingling slightly. A trace of a faint smile would sometimes peek through the cracks, giving me an awareness that I was alive and that that, at the very least, was something.

I woke up, uncomfortable in the position I had been sleeping in. The clock showed the time: 6:56 A.M. As I looked around my darkened room, the same one I had stayed in before, my eyes adjusted to the shapes. Kat had taste, so the spare bedroom was nice, with heirlooms and linen, and even the ceiling, with its expansive crown molding, felt comforting. I was reminded of Kolkata, of sleeping next to Dadi-ma during her daytime nap. We wouldn't use the mosquito net then, so I'd stare at the ceiling, an archipelago of stains and leaks, of muddy water lines, as she snored. As I remembered her, a glimmer of light seeped through the shutters, outlining some objects on my nightstand. The hit of the early-morning rays in the room at Kat's made everything look ominous, creating shadowed illusions on the walls. I made out the round curve of a big leather chair, an Alvar Aalto stool. I felt greedy, I felt lacking, in Kat's home. There was an incredible void that I needed to fill, and nothing fit, nothing was the right size. I wasn't quite showing yet, which only continued to breed a fickle uneasiness right through the very bones of my body. I was beginning to face myself.

I sat in bed for a while, my thoughts pushing me into an alternate reality. I had one daydream that I would replay in my head until I was satisfied. It involved Ky. It was a reality that I knew would never exist, and yet I continued to dream it, hoping that one day, soon, it—the dream—would be enough for me. I moved myself over to the armchair and lulled myself into my fantasy. The horizon peeked through the clouds, and I witnessed another beginning without his presence, without his comfort.

"Hey, you're up." Kat stood at the doorway.

"Yeah." I forced a smile.

I wanted to say, *Do you hate me? Do you hate how much space I'm taking up in your already busy life?* But I didn't say anything.

"How are you feeling?" she asked. "No headaches?"

"No headaches," I said.

"Hungry?"

"Sure am."

I got up and followed her to the kitchen and immediately looked at the microwave clock:

7:37.

Luc entered the kitchen. "Oh, you're up today," he said with surprise.

Next it was Isaac. He looked at me happily but kept his distance.

"What's wrong, Isaac? Come here." I gestured him toward me. He ran, halting at my feet, and looked cautiously over to see if his mother had seen him run. She hadn't. He relaxed his tiny bony shoulders, like a small bird, and grinned up at me. I brought my fingers to my lips and mimed *ssh*. He smiled and nodded.

"So what are you going to be doing today, dear Taylia?" Kat asked, passing me some eggs and day-old lavender polenta cake with homemade clotted cream.

"I'm gonna watch daytime television."

She smirked. "Sounds exciting."

"Television has a life of its own, Kat."

"Evidently... I mean, arguably, everything has a life of its own." She smiled, knowing something, taking a pause. "I've got a new crew member coming in today!"

In my absence, Kat had hired a new employee. I was glad that the pressure of performing was gone. It also meant that she was beginning to slowly, ever so slowly, start to rely on others. To ask for help, instead of putting too much on herself. I knew that, after me, Kat had realized she could afford to slow it down, to meet Claudia for lunch at Balthazar or catch a matinee at the Angelika. Before my very eyes I was seeing her resistance to life a little bit less and her floating in the feeling of abundance. It was extraordinary to watch her and Claudia bond, too. For their heads to sometimes lean on each other as they read their different newspapers together in the morning, after nights when Claudia had slept over. Or massage each other's feet as they watched TV with the boys and me, us all one big random-ass family. Claudia would bring by natural wines (her new favorite find) and lavish Kat with gifts: Palestinian za'atar, the book *In Praise of Shadows*, and a multicolored hexagonal pepper grinder. It was like they had memorized and rehearsed each other's love languages to a T. She reminded me of Roman, which made me think of Ky.

Kat never made me feel like I was in her way, but there were moments I felt it. I felt uncomfortable that I was there, just lingering. Like a disease, or a bacteria sitting, innocuous. My fat blooming body blazing from heat, deliriously eating food and demanding attention. I felt ashamed. To accept and embrace the love somebody gives you was half the battle. I knew both Kat and I were learning how to do that with each other, so that we could learn to do it with others, too.

In the mornings, depending on our interactions, Kat would sometimes pull one tarot card for herself, for us. Today she pulled the Magician, winking as she slid it in front of me. I googled the card and the explanations were littered with positive messages like "new beginnings" and "great expectations." I hummed a soft tune. The air had the intoxication of tuberose, an incense that Kat would light in the mornings. All of a sudden, I felt pink, I felt luminous, and in that moment I sat, calm. I turned on the TV and watched back-to-back episodes of *Love and Hip Hop: Atlanta*. The day felt inspiring.

23.

It happened on a gloomy day where the rain stuck on the windows like pristine, clear goop, crystal bindis in a row, teardrops, symmetrical. Kat was off at work, and the boys were at their grandmama's. I remember, because I was attempting to read Kat's copy of Bertrand Russell's *The Conquest of Happiness* when the voice on the radio, just as I hit the curve of a sentence, changed from the soft humming of Mozart's Fifth into the sweet, mellifluous sounds of Alyssa's soft vibrato. "Taylia?" she called as I sat still; she'd never come to me through the radio before. The line cracked and she repeated, in a higher, more rushed tone, "TAYLIA!" It was cacophonous. The voice repeated, in waves, an old adage that Alyssa would say when everything felt bleak. She'd impart this wisdom with her quintessential lightness. A naïveté that was always undercut by so much pain, so much torturous emotion. "Life will turn out!" She said it again and again, circling through the radio sounds like a calming saint. Then she was gone. *Life will turn out*, the faint whisper of life's inevitability.

I got up and walked out of the room. I went to the kitchen and opened the cupboard where the snacks were stored. Making a big mess, I helped myself to Triscuits and jelly, in memory of Emi, filling my mouth with the fancy fat raspberries from the jam Kat bought at the farmers' market. She liked making her own (and, frankly, hers *was* the best), but every now and again she'd treat herself, and by extension me. I ate the jam blissfully, laughing. Alyssa had just spoken to me through the radio, she'd never done that particular trick before. I gawked at everything like they were alive. Spout mouthed, I laughed and laughed, plummeting berries down my throat.

"Taylia!"

Out on the street, I turned around, bursting with hope. Instead I was faced with a familiar face that I had no memory of.

"Hey..."

The man sensed that I didn't know who he was.

"I don't know if I should be wounded that you very clearly don't know who I am."

"I'm sorry?"

"I'm being a jerk. Ralph. I'm Ralph. We shared a moment on the... er... shores of the East River that one time."

I suddenly remembered. "Oh, Rafe!"

There was a beat as he smiled. "What are you doing in this part of Brooklyn? Have you moved?" He was joking.

"Uh, yeah, I guess I have."

"Oh." He looked away and then back at me. "Well, what are you up to?"

I thought for a second. "I'm on my way to meet a friend for breakfast."

Kat and I had arranged a brunch date: the boys were at her sister's, and Claudia was out of town.

"I was just about to get some breakfast..."

"Yeah?"

"Yeah. Where are you going?"

"Buttermilk Channel..."

He smiled. "Oddly enough, me, too. I swear it always seems like I'm stalking you a little bit."

"How do you know you're not?"

"I don't."

I laughed appropriately. "Are you meeting anyone?"

"Mm-hmm." He pointed at his ragged old notebook.

"Well..." I paused. "Look, I'm sure my friend wouldn't mind if you joined us."

"Really?"

"Really."

"That'd be chill, Taylia."

I laughed loudly in public for the first time in a long time. Something about the way he said it, said *chill* so nonchalantly, tipping off his tongue, evoked a tender youthfulness. A youth that I realized, right then and there, that I'd never had. It struck me like whiplash. How fast I had grown up, how much I had been burdened with, because I never had "chill." Never been it, either. We were standing at the edge of the street, and it was awe-inspiring, like seeing the sky in front of you turn pink, like seeing a kaleidoscope for the first time. I couldn't believe it, couldn't believe how much time I had wasted on pain, on being in the purgatory of my family's decided disinterest in me. But I didn't want to be that version of me anymore. The one always in slight pain. I didn't want that for myself—or this baby. I wanted to learn how to be chill.

That day I managed to decrease the amount of times I thought about Ky. There was something endearing about Ralph that made me focus on him; he had an energy of being young and living in Brooklyn that was contagious. It was all in his demeanor, in his street wear, in his embrace of his twenties. We were wearing the same Stan Smith sneakers, and after years of feeling as if I were from another era, I felt my age in his presence. I was easing the burden of the last few months. I was someone I had never been.

While Ralph was in the bathroom, Kat announced she was going to leave and let me do my thing. I resented her for leaving me alone. She said she needed to go get her hair done at her salon, her ritual, but I also knew she was pushing me toward Ralph, and I was annoyed.

He was back at our table, about to sit down, looking a little too hopeful that Kat had left. "Oh, she's gone?"

I feigned an excuse.

He smiled, pausing. The tone shifted, more intimate. "I was hoping you'd come and see me, one day. At the Wythe."

I squinted, looked away, and chose to be earnest. "I don't do well in most social circumstances."

"You seem fine to me." He was serious.

I laughed to fill my turn to speak.

"You're cool, Taylia. Really," he reiterated.

I made a face.

"That's not a pickup line, but..." He was leaning in toward me. I wasn't sure what he was going to say, but I wasn't ready to hear it. "...I want to see you again. Not accidentally. Would that be all right?"

I wasn't sure what was all right anymore. "I don't know," I whispered, wanting to be heard and not at the same time.

"Taylia?" He hadn't heard me.

I breathed in everything around me and swallowed past the lump in my throat. "Yeah?"

He sensed my reservation. "It doesn't have to mean anything more than a getting-to-know-each-other kinda thing."

"I think that'd be better."

"Okay." He was hurt but still hoping.

I watched him from the corner of my eye to see if any part of him resembled Ky. There were some similarities, but there were also vast, vast differences. We were up, and Ralph slid on his heels, impatient, nodding to a tune as he shrugged at me cheekily. I'd never really been attracted to white men before, and maybe that had something to do with it. He wasn't my type, but his eagerness excited me.

"I want to kiss you."

I came out of it. "Not today."

I wasn't sure what that meant, though it seemed to be enough for Ralph.

"I can live with that." He dared to come closer, lingering near my face. I was ready to elbow him away, but he kissed me softly on the forehead and pushed my hanging hair behind my ears. His fingers were eager and slick like a pianist's. "You have very pretty eyes."

I kept my gaze down, modest, saying nothing. He rolled up, his sadness an answer to my silence.

"I guess I'll see you soon."

I nodded and smiled up toward his general direction. He stayed there momentarily, gazing back and puncturing me with his direct stare. I refused to lock eyes with him. Eventually, he turned and walked away.

"So?" Kat asked when I got home.

"So, what?"

"How'd it go?"

"Fine." I was still annoyed.

"And? Taylia?"

I shrugged. "He wants to see me again."

"And?"

"And I said that sounds nice."

"That sounds *nice*?"

The frustration was crawling up on me, like a rash. "I don't know if you realize this, but I'm pregnant. I can't start a relationship now, especially when all I do is think of him—" I stopped myself and put my hands to my face. "When I think about..."

"Tay?"

I pushed her voice away.

"When I think about..." I was hyperventilating. It felt all-consuming.

"Taylia, I know you're upset. But please remember that I'm your friend. You came to me, remember? But, just be conscious of that this is hard for me, too, so please don't push me away, it's not fair to me otherwise."

I suddenly realized I was treating Kat like the mentor I never had, and I knew it was unfair. I wanted that relationship so badly, I replicated it without her consent.

I breathed in, hurt, but knowing. "Kat. I need to sleep, okay? I'm sorry, but I need to sleep."

I was already out before I heard her speak. I went to my room and stayed awake for ages, replaying old memories. For hours I stubbornly shook the sleep away and thought about him. I knew it was my own fault that I missed him, but I did, and that was that.

I had created a near-perfect image of Ky, and as I lay, the blue volts of my love's rage racing through me, I traced him on the ceiling, on the window where the fog had shaded the glass a mossy terra-cotta color, on my stomach so I could tell my baby who its father was, who its father *is*. I missed the half-intense gaze he'd give me every morning, when Jade wasn't home. I cringed over the detail but still missed him. He wanted to be present, batting his eyelashes so many times I could almost make believe he was singing me a love song in saturated blinks. The way he'd throw that smile at me, his lips a shade of peachy pink, and the way his jaw would feel under my hands, stubbled and comforting like a cat's tongue.

"Hi."

It was early and I had already been waiting a couple of hours to make sure it was an acceptable time to call. That morning I awoke from the baby's presence, my face patterned with creases from the sheets, my stomach burning from hunger. Later, I threw up, my internal skin puckered by the acid. Lying down on my arm, exhausted, I fenced myself off from the world. I wanted to be asleep, I wanted to make my bed there on the stale toilet and cold bathroom floor, but after a half an hour of stillness, I got up and faced my day.

"Taylia?"

"Yup, is this a bad time?"

"Not at all. I'm just half awake. What time is it?"

I looked at the clock on the microwave. It blazed a bright red 7:51 A.M. I probably overshot the acceptable time range to call someone in the morning.

"It's almost eight."

"Oh, whoa, I don't think I've been up this early in a while." Strike one. "Okay..."

"I mean, it's good to hear from you."

"Listen, Ralph, I was wondering if you wanted to hang out later today." I expected a no, I had already given up on my invitation.

"Today?" He paused. "Yeah, that could work. Where are you staying now?"

"Around the general Fort Greene area."

He laughed, no doubt thinking of our stalking joke, as I had intended him to.

"There's this really great place by Dekalb..."

"Okay, how does twelve-ish work?"

"Can you do it earlier?"

"You're a morning person, aren't you?"

"Does eleven work?"

"Whoa! Okay. Well, I'm sure I can shoot for eleven for you."

"See you then... then."

I planned it out. Fifteen minutes to walk down, which meant that I had about two hours and a bit to figure out what I was doing in the other spaces of my day.

I texted him the address, and I got there before him and sat down outside. The chairs were warm from the sun, and I could see Fort Greene Park, the spirulina-green grass still milky with morning dew. The variation of the sky's patterns gave the city a different kind of warmth. When Ralph finally came he kissed me on the cheek and scanned my face for answers, resigning himself to his nearby seat when he got nothing.

"You are something else, Taylia."

I paused, taking my time. "I don't have many friends, Ralph. Actually Kat is my only friend. And I had another friend..." I regrouped. "I don't really have any family. They're all... gone. So I'm not good with this people stuff. I don't know what to say or when to say it. I know you don't believe me because you've only seen one side of me, but I am just learning... all of this... you know?" I paused. "Like, to let people in again, I mean."

When I had the courage, I looked at his furrowed brow, then focused on something behind him. I looked away shortly after.

"Are you trying to make me run away?"

"Are you going to?"

"No." He said it matter-of-factly.

"I guess I just want to get to know you and I want you to get to know me. I want to be friends and for me to learn more about myself. I feel like I don't know anything about myself, really."

"You think I'll teach you things about yourself?"

"Human interaction usually helps, right?"

He shrugged. "I don't think I know much better than you."

I felt apprehensive.

"Well, what do you want to talk about?"

I blinked. "What do you people talk about in these situations?"

He stopped and thought. "Tell me about yourself."

"Me?"

He gave me a confused nod.

Fuck.

And for the first time in my life I thought rationally: *What do I have to lose?*

I brought flowers home for Kat. Tulips the color of daffodils, because she loved tulips, and it was the season. I felt alive in a way I hadn't felt in a while, the way your body fills with adrenaline. I also felt grateful, in a strange way, as if the sun had nourished me with its radiance and courage had coalesced inside of me.

The pregnancy had been a tiny eternity; these last few months away from Ky were a way for my body to settle and shift the emotional construction toward something that felt grander than just me or him. I was becoming my own compass, and I could feel it. Weirdly, Ralph was helping me with this, as he was seeing me during this transformation. "You're smiling." It was Alyssa, who had returned to the hallway as I checked to see if Kat was home. I guess I was.

"No, I'm not," I said, swatting her away.

I had walked through to the back room, which was brightly lit, and there was Kat reading an anthology called *This Bridge Called My Back*, which was creased all over like it had been through the wash then hung out to dry. The red cover was bright like blood. Lemon oil laced through the front room and the kitchen.

"You're making lemon squares!"

She was beaming. "Hi, what did you do today?"

I looked around; Alyssa was gone. I was back in the moment, and with a snap I realized Kat had this remarkable way of getting me to apologize and confront my inner brat with her use of kindness as a tool for self-reckoning. I passed her the tulips, understanding this incredible journey she had started before the boys were born, to always be present with kindness, to emanate it—while not taking shit. I knew I had recently been moody. I wanted to tell her that the lack of unconditional love in my life had left me heavy, weary with the need to be seen. I wanted to tell her that because I had spent so much of my life walking on eggshells with my parents' moods, the presence of her compassion was jarring. Sometimes I shirked her kindness, like a fly, out of arrogance and fear of vulnerability. Maybe because I expected her to still hurt me. Like I was suspicious of what she gave me.

In the past, we had discussed this "power dynamic" between us and how miraculously we each played a role in the other's needs. Love—feeling it and having it—was a source of power. People just didn't realize it was the most honest source of it. So, with her love of transparency, we had concocted ways to help aid each other. From me, but also in general, she needed reliability, care, and thoughtfulness. No mess in the house (or the café) and constant consideration (i.e., making sure I was on top of the shopping list and our everyday needs like paper towels or laundry detergent, or, most important, a ping to remind her we needed coffee beans to crunch at home).

Definitely an act of care first, gifts and quality time coming in second—she welcomed flowers and skin care products (she loved Goop or Josie Maran) and books. But dates? She *loved* dates. Dates from Egypt, from Yemen, from the Emirates. Dates paired with good biodynamic wine at local Brooklyn restaurants.

And me? I just needed to feel like I was worth loving. That was all. Or at least, that's what I was starting with. I was learning that needs could, and should, evolve. Sharing space with Kat made me realize that we both had to develop a shorthand. At the café, but also at home, with the boys. In many ways, I had become an aunt to Luc and Isaac, and they treated me as such, sometimes requesting my reading of the bedtime stories (we were going through the Harry Potter books in order; Kat had started on them young, to get their heads full of magic, and you can see how the Elijah-as-Voldemort metaphor was even more apt) and to accompany them to the park. We had become a family; in many ways, they were the first real family where I felt valued for being my own person.

"I just want to say, first, I love you." I didn't want Kat to feel like I was using her generosity and began to feel quite humbled by our relationship. She didn't owe me anything and yet here I was: I was well, there was no other way to describe it.

She kissed me on the cheek, laying the bouquet gently on the table, making a mental note, I knew, to find the perfect vase. I could tell, because her mind was so good at making checklists. There was a pause. I liked how though she wanted you to, she never really made it easy to apologize, there was a sternness to her, but a gentleness, too. She appreciated effort, she appreciated the earnestness that I had. As I thought this I knew that all she wanted was for me to tell her more about my life. She had told me so many times, and I was trying to be more open with her as well. She got up and stood, facing me, snagging the ends of her navy-blue checkered sleeves. We both yearned for intimacy, and we hadn't had one-on-one time in a while. So, I acquiesced, and talked about the easiest conversation starter: Ralph.

"He's doing his master's at NYU, he's a TA."

Kat smiled. "You like 'em smart."

"Yeah, I do!" It came out effortlessly, with no hesitation from me. "It makes sense because Baba's really smart."

She pulled her eyebrows into a question mark.

"Baba is what I call my father..."

She nodded slowly.

"Both of my parents are smart, actually."

Her voice was quiet when she spoke. "I guess I just always thought they were dead."

Pinching fingers went up my spine. "Oh, no, no... they are both very much alive."

Clearing her throat of more questions, she said, "Well, it makes sense that you're smart then."

I exhaled. "I used to be smart. In school I was really smart. But in the last few years I've felt so displaced, I guess. I feel loose with energy but none of it is directed."

We were both still, together. She was the first to break the silence. "All you have to do is direct it somewhere. Take me, for example. I did it with ambition. I did it 'cause I had to. I want Isaac and Luc to see that life won't be handed to them but that *that* shouldn't stop them from going out there and getting what they want."

Sighing, I released something. "I know, but with myself? I don't know what to do. At school I wrote a lot, mainly poetry... but these last couple of years... everything feels stunted."

"I haven't seen you write in the time I've known you. Except that poem to Cillian."

I snorted. "That's because I don't... write..."

"Why? There's so much going on in that head."

My eyes were wide. Sometimes I still felt so scared of life.

"It's your prerogative, but sometimes you gotta let people in. You're carrying around this guilt and it's weighing you down. I know I'm not an artist, per se, but guilt is not inspiring." She sensed I was overwhelmed and changed direction. "Okay, let's change the subject... back to Ralph."

"What about him?"

"Girl, stop playin', are you, Taylia, going to sleep with Ralph?"

I shuddered at the thought of having sex. Chewing the inside of my cheek, I let it out like another exaggerated sigh: "I'm not ready. I mean, for him to see me"—I gestured at my body—"like this..."

"Oh, this crap again." Sigh. "I know this is your big lesson, Taylia. But! You really need to start letting that go."

"Maybe I'm just not a sexual person." But, thinking back to me and Ky, I knew that wasn't really true. "Besides, I'm pretty sure I just want to be friends with him... You know?" I looked up at her, my gaze direct. "You know?"

She sucked her teeth, her eyes almost blue. Sympathetic, her voice was suddenly tender: "Well, let the poor chump know then, won't you? Don't string him along, Taylia. Be gentle, and be quick. You got him wrapped around your li'l finger, let me tell you."

Suffocating, I coughed loudly.

A week later, Kat, Claudia, and I went shopping. We went to the Park Slope Beacon's Closet, and they both mourned the days of good vintage in New York.

"Though, I have to say Century 21 is lit," Claudia announced to me as Kat tried on clothes in the changing room. Upon hearing this declaration, Kat started to guffaw, which caused all of us to start cracking up loudly; we were a raucous bunch, feeling free. All Claudia could whisper, through laughs, was "It's true, it's true!" I ended up taking them out for dinner, for their passing on of their joy. They had even helped me find a nice floral dress from the '90s. It was long, strappy, and elegant—and the first time I took effort to actively feel better about my physical self.

There was a trendy stationery store near Kat's that I went to the next day. It looked like Kate Spade had barfed on all the items, splotched in glittering colors, stringed confetti splendor. Yet, I resisted my negativity, sincerely needing an outlet to explore the breadth of my interior life, along with all the shapes and sizes of it, via some relatively cool, colorful shit. My lack of direction revolved around my lack of real purpose. So, I wanted to *try to* write. Or to document some of my feelings, somehow, somewhere. Even on a fluorescent green page.

Suffocated in the tight, bright place of the store, I stood forever at the pen station, testing a variety of pens with lavish colors like fuchsia rose and orange blossom. Though, through a composed stillness, I went for a monosyllabic pen color (vert) after a few brief tries. Accompanying my purchase of vert was a medium-sized camel-colored notebook with red letters bolded on the outside that read NOTEBOOK (no shit!). I headed home in a vague fog of acrid ink fume.

When I got home I sat at the kitchen table, and for the first half hour I stared at a sliced avocado that sat on an orange ceramic plate. I knew that if the pit was kept in the avocado it kept it's *green*-green lime green, but this poor guy was pitless, its flesh a barely dull brown, a sad sight; avocados went from God's gift to putrid real fast. Before my pregnancy, I used to love avocados, their silky interior goodness, their cratered baldness. Now they made me sick. Could I use it as a metaphor for something? I opened up the book and scrawled *Taylia Chatterjee* like I had something to say.

"Baby."

I opened one eye and saw that the microwave read 7:27. I put my hands to my sides and pulled myself up. Kat was beside me and I was still in the kitchen. She looked amused, but I felt heavy, my shoulders sore. "Fuck, I can't believe I fell asleep…"

"I tried calling you but you weren't picking up."

"I think I literally fell asleep, like, five hours ago."

With the gentleness of a saint, she put her hands on my shoulders, tenderly circulating her fingers up my strained neck. "You have to think of yourself and the baby now. You can't accidentally fall asleep on a table, boo. Even if it is really amusing to watch you."

I groaned. *Empty hours.* I had spent such good hours of the day asleep and unproductive. Whenever I awoke from a daytime nap my body would react with anxiety, as if I had been cocooned and prematurely disturbed. Always sweaty, the creases of my skin gummed together like melted candy, the baby heavy.

"The position felt nice when I rested my head, popping a squat kinda."

She giggled. "What were you doing?"

I paused, my head filling with water. "Writing."

"You're doing it, bitch!"

"I just wrote my name! That's all!" I placed my face in the comforting gap of my elbow.

Kat cackled. "It's the way of the universe, you gotta keep the momentum going. It's not gonna happen in a day, you know, Rome and blah blah."

The cold gleam of the streetlight shone as Kat walked to the stovetop and hummed a sweet tune, the sound vibrating behind her closed teeth.

"Do you ever feel like what if all this positivity doesn't work? That we're all just doomed."

Kat turned to me and rolled her eyes.

"What?" I said defiantly.

"Enough."

I wanted to whine, but I didn't. There was a long, long pause, then from a clear stutter, she emerged, suddenly serious, as if this had been rehearsed: "I have something I want to tell you, Tay."

My heart stopped. Everything felt incredibly still.

"Some effed up shit happened to me when I was younger, and I've just been moving through it recently, so I thought I should tell you. You're basically my second wife, babe."

Suddenly jolted, I felt her pain. I knew it'd be hypocritical of me to probe, when I, in turn, had shared nothing of my trauma. But... my stomach churned. "Like... what? Of course, we don't need to talk about it—"

"I mean, it's okay..." She paused. "I guess I never really knew—I mean, I had always wondered... wondered why certain sexual things terrify me. Like, *terrify me.* How uncomfortable they make me, or even sad, damn... and it's always been this inexplicable, paralyzing thing... and Elijah always accepted it, and I made sure it never got in the way... but Claudia, she knew. My body just shut the fuck down one night... and she damn right knew, and she called it. This has all been unraveling the last few days."

"What'd she say?"

Kat sighed. "It was simple, she just had this look and said, 'Baby...' Our nonverbal communication, Taylia? Yowwwwie."

I sat, stunned.

"It happened a couple of times, with two different cousins. Tiffany and Stevie." She paused, looking at my face. "Sorry, that's heavy. I'm sorry. I didn't even ask if you're ready to hold this."

"I'm ready," I told her bluntly, looking her in the eye. I was starting to understand that many of us who had experienced this type of sexual trauma—abuse, molestation, rape—talked about it in code. She didn't have to say much more for me to understand completely. I took her hands and breathed in, tears in my eyes. She had started crying, too.

"It's nice to not always be strong, Taylia. I want to share that with you, because I think you need to hear it." She paused. "I like that Claud makes me feel safe enough that I can be vulnerable. Because Black women can't afford to be vulnerable. Look at all this responsibility. The café, the kids. You." We both laughed. "But I want you to see this kind of love and believe it's possible for you, too."

I circled her hands with my fingers. I felt so selfish, like I was entitled to her love, all while she'd been housing this, healing this deep, dark wound. I couldn't believe how she'd handled all of this on her own. With two kids and a business. I felt like trash. "I'm sorry I'm such a piece of shit sometimes. You've given me so much..."

I trailed off, wanting not to embarrass myself and cry more.

"Claudia has been suggesting she wants to move in, maybe? She thinks it might be easier. She wants to be here with the boys more, she says she wants to show up for me more."

I inhaled. "Do you want her to move in?" I wasn't afraid of the answer.

She looked at me. "Kinda... yeah."

A little bruised, I smiled, feeling truly happy for her. I didn't know what that meant for me, but I was also beginning to trust that things would work out. Maybe because I inherently *had* started to trust Kat. I didn't push to know more about what had happened to her as a child, but I felt relieved that I wasn't alone, or something. It was hard to locate the full dimensions of what I was moving through emotionally, but it felt less lonely all of a sudden. Relief and sadness packed into one. Sitting within this rapid, sweaty, sedated feeling, we both sat in it.

It was here that I realized, for the first time fully, that maybe what I had lacked, for the entirety of my life, was the experience and understanding of another's. In all honesty, I had never really thought about it. Everything had always been about *me*. How *I was feeling*. Even when Alyssa died, I never fully contemplated the loss it was for Mama and Papa, let alone her boyfriend, Ryan. I had never reached out to him or looked back. Then after Simon, everything was *even more* about me. I had missed that part. I had missed the part that made me look bad.

Embarrassed, I massaged Kat's feet with shea butter and ran her a bath with Epsom salt and lavender oil. She asked me to bring in the Bose speaker and play some Etta James, and as she soaked her body, I sat next to her, forgetting why I was ever sad in the first place.

The next morning felt like a lurch, and all of a sudden a sinking feeling hit: I wanted to bring up her abuse again, but I knew I couldn't. I knew it wouldn't be fair for me to do that to her, but still I wanted to know. It was an itch. I wanted to hold her and kiss her cheeks. I felt protective of her; the idea that someone had done something to her made me sick, it sparked something inside of me that felt mythical, violent. Like a spirit was shooting through me, emblazoning my soul. I wanted to protect her; I wanted her to be happy.

Instead, she went to work early and left the boys under my care. Playgroup was twice a week, and because I wasn't working at the café, they were with me from three onward. Ideally, Kat would have them for the weekend—but I didn't mind if days, like today, she'd have to sneak into work. Truly, I enjoyed the distraction.

This morning, right after a breakfast of tofu scramble, I took the boys down to the park. As I watched them run around with their mini-lightsabers, baby boys playing—Luc in yellow overalls, Isaac in bright pink shorts and a lime-green T-shirt—I felt their youth, their spirit. Watching children play is magical, because it's so pure, so unfettered. Their energy bouncing like a light source, unadulterated. I was overwhelmed with joy, seeing them come alive fully. I knew in a few months there'd be another companion in the pack. My baby, kicking around, suddenly felt near, more palpable than I remembered.

Eventually the boys and I returned back home. I sat them down to watch an episode of *Adventure Time* as I cooked lunch. I liked the rhythm of doing so, my hand like a lever against my lower back. I fed them at Kat's table where we all laughed like a family. I entertained them, tricking them into eating their healthy meal. The act of caring for them so intimately made me suddenly feel purposeful. It was as if the symmetry of all the mothers before me came to possess me, teaching me things I had not known before this very moment. Like the switch of motherhood came on, a light pulsating. I looked beyond the dining room and saw Dadi-ma smiling brightly and nodding: *See this is how it's done.* I blinked back, nursing a quiet admiration for myself and this achievement: I was beginning to accept that I was a mother. I had always been my own.

Suddenly, I was flushed with a memory of Dadi-ma stealing a ladoo for me from a vendor who was her friend. It was a prank, something ever so innocent, but she picked up this ladoo from its Pyrex container—one perfectly spherical orb, yellow like turmeric—and passed it to me. As I stuffed it into my mouth, the entire thing like a breakable gobstopper, she uttered her favorite American phrase, "*Hot diggity.*" It was always so funny that even she would laugh at the absurdity. She had a comedic quality to her; her access to fun was such a fluid emotion. I thought about how much she had taught me about laughter and play in the months I got to know her. How her innocence and sense of life were compounded by her excitement for it. Even at an older age she hadn't lost her playfulness. As I thought about children— Isaac and Luc and also my own soon-to-be child—I gathered parenting had a similar sense of wonder. Something I had never been given by my parents but now desperately wanted for my own child. As I dreamed of Dadi-ma, she sat before me, smiling, still at the dining table, and whispered, "Hot diggity."

I tried writing again the next day as I stared at Kat's vast plant collection and admired the thin pottery bowls they sat in, the leaves draping down like their own constellations, gravitational, placidly languid, dreaming their green-crushed dreams. I remembered Mama's love for plants. I'd watch her sometimes from my bedroom window that overlooked our garden, puttering along to and fro, a copper trowel in her left hand, red hair frizzy and winking. For her, it was a sanctuary; the dirt and the earthly palette grounded her physically. It was a nourishment for her hands, for her soul, and it connected her to Alyssa in some way. Though, I understand now, it was also an escape from Alyssa, her treachery, her insurmountable, continued sadness. Inside the walls of Mama's garden, her moon-ladened Gibraltar, she created a retreat, a life no longer void of her prodigious daughter. She could have control over the lives of these plants, and, unlike her daughter's life, she could nurse these plants to prosperity and encourage spectacular growth, like jewels glinting, her resplendent riches. She was a bewitching light out there, thriving, grieving in her own way.

"Do you look like your mother?" Ky once asked cautiously. I smiled, and he grabbed at me, pressing his lips delicately onto my mouth. "I wasn't sure how you'd react."

"Right, because I am so moody." I was joking, but I guess I had always known it was true.

"So do you?" he asked, peeling himself off of me.

"I don't know..." I said. "She was—*is*—so beautiful..."

There were no other words to describe my mother. His right hand came to my cheek, brushing his warmth onto me.

"She's delicate and graceful in a way women no longer are. She used to exude so much confidence in a glare, or a smile, or her laugh. I feel like she embodied a kind of majestic aura, like women of a bygone era. Like Georgia O'Keeffe in all those portraits that Alfred Stieglitz took of her, there's this knowingness, a togetherness. Or like Meryl Streep walking out of an office in *Kramer vs. Kramer*, hair parted in the middle and a crisp white shirt unbuttoned a quarter way down. I didn't get that. It was passed directly on to Alyssa. I think—I mean, I know—that's why they both loved her so much... You always love anything that reminds you of yourself. Alyssa resembled the daughter they wanted. One who was astute, composed, smart but coy. They wanted a white-passing, beautiful daughter."

"I asked about you, not Alyssa." He whispered it, his breath lingering in my mouth.

I propped myself up on my elbows, pushing him to the side. "It's hard, Ky. I was always so unappealing. Next to Lyse, I was 'homely.' My hair was always frizzier, my skin always darker. Alyssa was this light-skinned, bright-eyed beauty. She was basically fucking white. It wasn't easy. I didn't feel Indian or white."

Even as I said it, I cringed. I had matured so much, and now I mourned all the time I had wasted hating myself for not being something it turns out I didn't even want to be. I sat silently for a while.

"I remember I had a journal. It was given to me by my aunt for my seventh birthday. Handmade by Bengali village women, I treasured their handiwork, so I would only ever write special things in it, mainly stories..."

"Like?" Ky asked.

"Stories of myself being perfect, or like Alyssa." I began to blush. "I thought if I wrote these stories down maybe they would come true. That maybe this fictional character would take over and turn me into something beautiful or different. But always, *always*, like, better..."

"But why still? You're older now. You know better now."

"I don't know who I am if I'm not trying to be Alyssa, making myself in her image."

"Just be yourself. That's all anyone can ask of you."

I lay in silence. "I don't know who I am."

He got up and stood in the shadows, examining me. "Don't let your wounds make you someone you're not, Tay."

24.

"What's another word for *soaked* that also starts with an *s*?"

Ralph and I were in the park doing crosswords.

"*Sodden*?"

"*Sodden*! Yes, you genius woman!"

His natural inclination was to kiss me, but I turned my lips to the side and he hit my cheek instead. Still, he smiled, unshaken.

"You're in another world today."

"Huh?" I asked.

"Point proven."

"What are you talking about?"

"Nothing, dear Taylia, nothing!"

I put down the crossword and rolled onto my back. My new notebook was nearby and I clutched at it, suddenly feeling the urge to write. Anything.

"Writing now, are we?"

"Mm-hmm."

"What are you writing?"

"Well, I can't write anything when you're hounding down my neck!" I tried to sound nice, but I wasn't sure if I succeeded. Ralph got up soon after, under the guise of thirsting for some ginger beer. I happily accommodated and doodled the nearby trees, shakily, across the lavender-colored hills, when a voice came at my side, assaulting my inner silence.

"Taylia?"

I wasn't looking up, but I knew that it wasn't Ralph. The voice asked me again, but this time it wasn't a question.

"Taylia. Holy shit."

I recognized who it was, though I didn't quite know what to say. I felt sick. I pushed myself up to a seated position slowly, easing my back into my posture. I looked up toward the sun. He stood there, all six feet two inches of him, and stared back at me with a candied smile.

"Hi."

"Hey!"

He came toward me, crouching down on his tiptoes. He was still handsome, still athletic, still Ryan. I took in his springy hair and the long muscles in his shoulders. He hadn't changed a bit.

Well, maybe he was more built. He gave me a steady, unblinking look, and I was transported back to my teenage self.

"How are you?"

The questions were whistling out of him. I extended my palm up to stop him, braced my stomach, and hurled the sticky puke out of me like an unwanted secret. I was a Catholic at confession, I wanted to be absolved. It came in dredges, and as I watched the stink pool up around his shoes, I expected him to walk away, disgusted. I expected him to frown at the string of yellow retch that moved out of me with calculated precision. I was familiar with the process. I welcomed the release. But he, instead, looked at me with a look so tender, so soft.

"Tay..."

Alyssa. Alyssa.

Can you hear me, Alyssa? Help me, Lyse. I can't do this anymore, Lyse.

I felt his hands on my face and then he pulled me toward him. No shyness involved, he opened himself up to me. A flower blooming, waiting. He was unafraid, and so I cried into him, swallowing past the harsh taste of life, breathing in the scent of him. Between the brown cloud of my hair and the landing rock of his shoulders, I felt comforted, I felt grounded. Then I collapsed.

The smell of bleach surrounded me when I woke up. Everything was milky, drenched in the diluted off-white color of limbo. I wasn't in my bed, at Kat's or Ky's, but my blinking eyes were able to make out that I was in a hospital. There were two figures with their heads bowed in the distance: one of them looked familiar, and the other, only just. My limbs felt weighty with an ache. I felt as if I had been smashed into a million little pieces and then stitched back together like a mismatched collage. I coughed loudly and instantly a head popped up.

"Are you doing okay?" It was Ryan. He came toward me.

"What happened?" I was unsure of the events. I remember puking and then drifting out of my body, but that was it.

"You collapsed. In my arms."

"How romantic."

He smiled. It was strange; we were so familiar even through the distance.

I heard a noise behind Ryan and soon saw Ralph's head come up from behind.

"Hey." He walked closer toward me, already marking his territory.

"Hey. Have you met Ryan?"

He didn't look over at him but instead answered with "Yeah. We spoke a little bit while you were, uh, asleep."

I nodded okay.

Ryan interrupted. "I'm sorry, but I'm just going to go and look for a nurse."

Ralph and I both watched him walk out.

"Who is he?" The jealousy was unsettling.

"He didn't tell you who he was?"

"No. He just said he's known you for years."

I shook my head in an upward direction to indicate that I agreed.

"Ex-boyfriend?"

"No. He's my sister's old boyfriend. I have known him for years, though. Family friends and all that stuff."

"Sure." He seemed more comfortable.

A nurse came back into the room. "Heya, you're awake."

"I am."

"You'll be pleased to know that the baby is fine."

I looked over at Ralph and saw Ryan at the doorway, looking away from the nurse, looking away from me. "Okay." I could hardly hear myself.

"You need to look after yourself."

I coughed loudly, not wanting to hear what she had to say anymore.

Ryan spoke up. "We'll be sure to look after her."

The nurse looked at me—"I'll come by a bit later"—and then smiled and walked out. I almost dreaded her exit as much as I also longed for it. I knew answers needed to be given.

"Ralph. Where do you live?" I heard Ryan ask.

"Not too far from here."

"Okay. Great. Well, I can take care of Taylia today."

I could see the tension rise up in Ralph's jaw. He peered over at me to see if I disagreed.

I didn't.

"Yeah, thanks, man." He walked to his chair and picked up his jacket and then came to me and kissed me on the cheek. "Get some rest. I'll call you later."

Ryan looked at the floor, I nodded, and Ralph walked out.

There was an unbearable silence until Ryan broke it. "Pregnant, huh?"

I cringed inside.

"Nobody knows what happened to you... But it looks like you're doing well?"

I didn't answer.

"You just sort of disappeared. Wasn't sure if I'd see you again." Silence.

"What happened, Taylia?"

The inevitable question: *What happened, Taylia? What happened to you, Taylia?*

My throat was locked on mumbles, nothing audible was coming out. It surprised me that Ryan had evidently kept in touch with my parents, which was the only way he must've known any of this, of my leaving. What was even more fascinating was that they had kept the details of my departure very vague, obviously for easier conversational consumption. It was a pathetic way to control the narrative, to keep their victimization intact. I paused for an eternity, marking my words. "I grew up."

Ryan scoffed, though it wasn't mean. "You grew up? Is that why you're pregnant?"

My instinct was to shrug, to run. "I made a mistake."

As soon as I said it, I knew it wasn't true. I was pregnant because I had fallen in love with an idea. With being saved. With the bromides we tell ourselves about a good life. About a family unit. I was curious about what would happen if I had an ounce of control, holding Ky captive, licking his ear, whispering, "Come inside of me," like I was a regular Minnie Riperton. It felt powerful to rewrite the patterns of my skin, of my insides, with his gooey debris, his guttural oohs and aahs, his shaking body. It felt significant to be fucked and in love. But now he wasn't here. He was never really mine. This baby felt like a hollow gift, one that I had not yet unwrapped.

"That's not true," I corrected myself. "I am at a crossroads right now."

"A crossroads?"

"Yeah, a fucking crossroads, Ryan. There are many fucking turns and many fucking roads and I'm not sure which one to fucking take."

A smile crept along his lips. "Do you have any idea which one might be the best one?"

"I don't know. Probably the one that has been least traveled. Or whatever."

He nodded slowly. "Classic Taylia."

We sat in the hospital room for a little while longer. We waited for the nurse to give me instructions, and soon after I was discharged and taken home by my dead sister's ex. He didn't come up but left me at Kat's stoop. I watched him walk away, nostalgia hitting me hard, feeling warm with memories. The moon inside of me was still. I felt content.

"I can't believe they didn't call *me*! I'm your emergency contact!"

The next day, over a pineapple turnover, I was telling Kat the story of my hospital adventure.

"I was there with Ralph and Ryan, so I was just fine... Trust me."

"Who the hell is Ryan?"

How could I explain this to avoid further questioning?

"He's my sister's old boyfriend."

She was confused, I could see it in her eyes, the way they locked tightly on to something in the foreground, the irises pulsing in the particled morning light. She hugged her elbows and her eyes gleamed with emotion. "Didn't know you were meeting up with him..."

"I wasn't. I just saw him randomly in the park."

Her lips were puckered into a question mark, but she didn't string the words through.

"Actually"—I coughed—"he's a really nice guy. Would you, er, mind if I invited him over for dinner, maybe, one day?" I didn't even know if this was something I actually wanted, but I was trying to be chill.

She put her coffee mug down and gripped the sides with obscured fingertips. Her face looked funny with so much confusion. "You want him to come over?"

"Yeah."

"Wait, why?"

I wanted to shrug, but I didn't. I articulated: "I want to get to know him, I guess. As an adult."

She looked at me, wanting more. So, I breathed in.

"I don't think I've ever told you, maybe because talking about death never felt right. I never wanted to spoil the mood or whatever. But my sister killed herself a few years ago. And everything since then has been, I guess, fractured."

She looked at me, incredibly still, subdued. "I'm sorry," she said, mid-sigh. She grabbed my hand and stared into my eyes with a fierce and steady compassion. "I want you to be able to tell me these things. I want us to be able to lean on each other."

My tongue felt lifeless, tongue-tied. I managed to say, "I know." Then, after a few seconds, I said, "I want to be able to talk about this, too... but I never wanted to burden you."

"You can't be scared around me. Sometimes I feel like you're so nervous—where does that come from?"

I sucked my bottom lip. "That's just who I am, I guess. I'm always scared of fucking up, saying the wrong thing. But I'm changing, I'm getting braver."

She smiled, eyes glassy. "My love, the amazing thing about adulthood is that you get to be in control. You get to make your own family."

We were both silent.

"What was her name?"

I looked at Kat, tears suddenly in my eyes. "Alyssa," I said. I felt her, Alyssa, climbing inside of me, my sweet moon. In these past months, years, I realized how I had forgotten her former outlines and had now begun a new perspective of seeing her. A clearer image, where I wasn't pitted against her, even in my mind. I still missed her. Like a long-lost song.

"Alyssa," Kat echoed. "Alyssa Chatterjee."

I smiled, tears like the lines designating lanes in a swimming pool rushed down my cheek. "Yes." I nodded. "The one and only."

We sat, both in tears, through joy and sorrow. I remembered, again, how all life seemed beautiful at a distance, and how easy it was to fall into patterns of solipsism and sadness when you felt robbed of a good life. Kat talked to me about friends she'd lost to drugs or petty crimes, like weed possession, who were now serving lifetime jail sentences all because they were Black. She told me about her friend Nina who was murdered because she was a Black trans woman. Nina had been beautiful, sweet, gentle. Kat had known her through the queer and trans network and explained the cacophony of pain she'd felt when she'd first heard of her murder—the pain of being reminded, time and time again, how uncared for Black life was. Especially the lives of Black femmes. We talked of grief, this grief, that human life—in particular nonwhite human life—incurs and the resilience and weight of living. How, in turn, there was the pressure and guilt

236

of surviving. But also the gratitude for one more day. I told her about my need to give space for Alyssa to move through me. How soon after her death, I felt as if I owed her my life.

"I'm almost forty. My sister never killed herself, but I definitely have felt the brokenness of death. It sounds like Alyssa chose her fate. I know that's harsh, but there's a truth to it. You can't hold yourself back. All I can say, Tay: you just gotta bet on yourself, mourn, give yourself the time. Then be kind to yourself and those around you and keep it moving."

She made a joke about that being the most Capricorn thing she'd ever said, and we both laughed, but I knew she was right. I needed to unlodge Alyssa.

"Oh, BTW, I have something for you." She stood up and rummaged through her custom camel handbag, which sat crumpled next to her, finally handing me a piece of paper.

I looked down at it. There, in large, bold letters, it said SINGLE MOTHERS CLUB.

I didn't read on. "Kat, seriously?"

"Don't judge, Taylia. It'd do you good."

"Good for... How? People are still making flyers? Where did you find this?"

"It doesn't matter. And, obviously, to talk to other women who are going through similar emotions could help you. Besides, I wanna go, too, we can make it a date."

"What do they do?"

She sucked her teeth. "Read the damn pamphlet!"

"I don't want to."

"Namaste." A slim white woman walked into the wide room. There were all types of people in the class, though it was jarringly white. The room was filled with draping saris, and smelled like cheap, suffocating incense. No South Asian body besides my own could be seen, which made me sad. I thought about Dadi-ma, and how white girls say *namaste* with such relish, having

237

claimed the word, feeling entitled to it with such ferocity that we had forgotten the meaning of that which was once ours, all ours.

I looked at Kat with a raised eyebrow.

"Namaste," everyone replied.

"How's everyone doing today?"

"Good," some people replied.

"Her name is Jan," Kat whispered.

How had yoga, a practice of my ancestors for thousands of years, become known as a bougie white thing? My voice felt locked in my throat. *Why was I here?*

"It's quite a hot day, great for our class. We can get an extra workout!" Jan exclaimed.

Oh, how wonderful.

"I see we have a few new members today. Hello."

I looked around. All eyes were on me and Kat. Kat looked at me to lead, so I said hi uncomfortably.

"Welcome to our class."

Her stare was direct, yet strangely comforting. She had one of those soothing voices that you expected annoying (white) yoga teachers to have.

"Is this your first time?" she asked.

I wasn't sure what she was referring to, the baby or the class.

I tactically answered, "Ah, yeah."

"Wonderful." She put her palms together. "And your name is?" she asked.

"Taylia..."

"Taylia, namaste."

"Namaste," I replied, missing Dadi-ma in the softness of that word.

"Now this class is all about doing things that feel right for you, so please, if you feel at any point that you can't do something, just stop. Go at your own pace and don't forget to keep breathing."

I nodded and took a deep breath. Everyone then looked at Kat, who introduced herself with charming reluctance, and soon the class began.

"Judy, would you like to start us with a mantra?"

Jan sat down onto her unrolled mat. A voice nearby, which I figured belonged to Judy, started a Hindu chant. India, its broad temples, darling marigold mandalas, and salty turmeric with burning pungent onions, ignited my pulse. I watched Jan's skinny white body with contempt but then, somehow, extraordinarily, got pulled into the om. The om felt like mine, a rhythm for me. Its roots were embellished in my vinegary sweat, in the darkness of my body's plains, in my yellowed brownness; the om vibrated a frequency of a blessing. I felt the hatred diminish inside of me—*om, om, om*—I felt Dadi-ma's moon-shaped face guide me, her spirit rattling inside of me—*om, om, om, shanti om*. I came out of class, heaving in my own way, and saw that I had two messages on my phone. One was from Ralph, the other from Ryan. I read Ryan's first.

Hope you're doing okay, kid. If you're up for it, we should grab a coffee.

You choose the place and time. I'm flexible.

I felt giddy afterward, a swarm of bees rising in my stomach. I didn't even remember giving him my number, but he wanted to see me. I walked out of the studio with Kat, completely in my own world.

"It wasn't so bad, was it?" I heard her say.

I agreed.

Things weren't that bad.

"I wasn't sure if you'd get back to me."

We were sitting by the window in a restaurant in the West Village. I had let Ryan choose, as I had no idea for cool things outside of Kat's.

"Why not? Why wouldn't I?"

"Well, you've always been a bit aloof, haven't you, Taylia?"

He was wearing a gray fisherman's sweater. His hair was buzzed tighter than it used to be. He must've gotten a haircut since I saw him. He looked like someone who cared about his life. I watched him, waiting.

"How are you doing? Are you feeling better?"

"Yes. Yes, I am." I wanted to tell him it was because of him. I was suddenly excited about things after such a long time of being so absent in my own narrative. But here was someone who knew me, knew me before it all happened. Knew the Taylia who wasn't afraid to dance to Louis Armstrong after Sunday dinners on warm summer nights. Those rare, rare nights I felt truly free. Mama, pink from wine and chatter, dancing to the rhythm; Baba, with a cigar in his mouth, crooning some old Bollywood tune as everyone cheered; Alyssa slow dancing with herself. It was the perfect familial alchemy. Ryan also knew the Taylia who was afraid of the Natural History Museum and the great vastness of Central Park—the Taylia with her unsullied teenage jealousy of Shirley Temple, with her curls all pretty and blond. He knew *my* weaknesses. But better yet, he knew Alyssa's.

"Are you hungry?"

I nodded.

"Good, they have a great falafel here." He ordered.

It was raining and the water pattered the outside of our shell like fingertips in the dark.

"Do you ever think about her?"

My heart braced itself. There she was, she had entered the room. She was truly omnipresent. "Yes. All the time. I think about her all the time..."

He nodded. For the first time in my life, I saw Ryan searching for something.

"Seeing you has brought it all back, Taylia." Pause. "Who she was, what she was. It's all coming back to me now."

I couldn't help singing the lyrics to "Céline." I inhaled slowly, biding my time.

"It's strange when things you think you've worked through resurface."

I nodded. "I know, it's weird." I wavered, looking for the right way to say it. "Actually, it's weirder because I never thought you liked me."

"Oh, Taylia..." He stumbled. "I never knew what to say around you. I could tell that you were protective of her. And she loved you more than anyone. I guess that was hard for me to get over. So, I avoided you."

The rain drummed.

"Do you hate her for it?"

I was about to reask the question, not sure if he had heard the first time, but he slowly answered me, knowing what I was asking. "Yes and no."

I nodded in understanding.

"I'd like to think that I'm way more mature than that..."

"I don't think it's about maturity..."

"No, no, let me finish." I gestured to him to do so. "I don't think it's about being mature in the traditional sense. But you and I both know that in the end... Alyssa wasn't thinking about me or you. Her pain had transcended *her* reality."

I sat there, numb. "Do you really think that?"

"She had a lot going on. Things that you probably never understood because you were so young. Plus, your parents drove her insane. And your mother had this ridiculous tendency to polarize people. According to her, Alyssa was all good..."

"And I was all bad."

"Yeah... I guess. Kind of."

"I do that, you know? I always told myself I'd never end up like them, but every now and then I'll catch myself saying something like my mother, like judging someone's awkward taste in patterns or color coordination with their clothes."

"You even have some of her mannerisms, like the way you scratch your chin with your forefinger."

I laughed. "Really?"

"Oh yeah. I mean, you can't really escape them, can you, Tay? They're your blood."

I looked past him, embracing the truth and inevitability of that statement. Our food came and we sat there, our conversation awkwardly paused.

"I miss her so much. Sometimes it's hard for me to believe she's not here. She just..." I whimpered, tears floating and rising like a tide, half-moons in my eyes. Ryan sat against the backdrop of the rain that beat against the sidewalk. He looked outside, and I desperately wanted to be given answers. "Don't you think she was perfect..."

I knew it was unfair of me to probe him like this. I felt as if I had suddenly turned into an addict. I wanted nothing more than to wallow in conversations of Alyssa with him. He lifted his left hand to his ear, as if blocking a twitch, and looked past me.

"Yes, I guess she was, in her own way." He paused, taking a sip of water. Neither of us had touched our food. We were participating in the awkward dance of consideration. He waited for me, and I, in turn, waited for him.

"Remember how she used to do that thing and lick her lips before she ate?" I said, mimicking her soft charms.

Ryan didn't look up; he knew what I was referring to. Half smiling, he answered me, sighing. "She always knew how to get her way."

From that I knew he was stepping away. His hands, in the air, begging for Alyssa's mercy. *Enough,* he was saying, *I've had enough.* He seemed suddenly powerless, his eyes closed in a hushed prayer. From whatever veil lifted, I understood that Ryan had undeniably been hurt and that I was, again, not the only victim of Alyssa's recklessness.

The next single mothers club meeting was an art class at a local artist's studio in Bushwick. I had often wondered what an artist's studio would resemble. Perhaps a lair of prints and charcoal sketches? A multicolored mosaic of colors, embellished with paint and European postcards? A messy bloom of potted and hanging plants, a green sanctuary within this harsh city?

Alyssa would frequently bring back books of famed artists from school, scattering the pages of her passions, dog-eared and belly open. She preferred artists with a bit more perversion, particularly admiring Egon Schiele, Amedeo Modigliani, and her favorite hedonist, Toulouse-Lautrec. His pictures of prostitutes and nymphlike naked women always exuded a freedom that I could tell she longed for. She would have fit well into the Belle Epoque era. Her face: pretty, yet daring. Her body: supple, eyes ensnaring men with extraordinary ease.

An hour before I was about to head out, Kat texted saying Ruth, her new employee, couldn't cover, so that she could no longer accompany me to the workshop. I felt as I had as a kid when I didn't get my way, huffing the blue expanse of fear and frustration of being alone. I put the phone down, welcoming the feeling like inviting in a ghost. This dread that I had of change was merely a pathetic fixation I had on familiarity, a strange compulsion with reliability. I was afraid of the emptiness of my mind and of the solitude that would inevitably follow. But I knew I needed to honor the fear, surpass it, and move on to my main trajectory, toward a place of halogen-like contentment, a fearless Taylia. I wanted to be strong like the women in the songs, to be redolent of the women proselytized in poetry, mounted in history. Unafraid of my failures or my shortcomings, I wanted to embrace it all: the murkiness, the tepid waters that stood before me. I took in a slow inhalation.

In my flash of anxiety, I imagined what it would be like to be strong. I was strong when Alyssa died and when I walked away from my parents' house, resolved in my resilience and the vindication that I was not to blame. That was the first time I took refuge in myself, realizing that within this broken corpse of a being lay a fire that was ready to emerge. I breathed in the agitation of wanting to be who I was already. In those moments, again, I could feel my sulky presence shifting, and I knew if you blinked you could see me, slowly, slowly. I was evolving.

As soon as I walked into the Bushwick artist's studio, a man came out of a back room, immediately introducing himself to everyone as Mateo. As he talked to another student, I admired the beauty of the main room. With the large windows and high ceilings, it had mostly exceeded my expectations. I slowly began to blink approval of this Mateo character. He had olive skin with tattoos that lined his right forearm, and I could see that almost all his hair was gray. As he spoke, he spun and turned toward me. And then, as he looked directly at me, I saw that his eyes were sober, like a child's, unflinching and honest, resembling a pair of fish oil capsules Mama used to take every night before she went to bed.

"Hello?" he asked with an interesting inflection.

"Hi, I'm here for the art class."

"Well, you're in the right place, take a seat."

In that moment I noticed how needy I was, how much direct attention I craved. I sat down in a seat nearest to me, straight-away immersing myself in this new environment. This studio was a raw, unblemished canvas, with no arrogance attached. As I looked around, with shrill excited focus, I noticed a familiar face from the yoga class a few days earlier, one of the only other blaringly nonwhite faces besides Kat's and mine. Her long hair framed her broad, thick eyebrows and a strong nose. Today she wore a sleeved floral dress that matched her flushed cheeks and her pale pink lips. Just looking at her reminded me of Alyssa; she left me starry-eyed and famished.

Throughout the class I watched her. She kept mainly to herself but would often laugh fearlessly, her whole face transformed into a wide, open gummy release. She painted with verve, an unwillingness to compromise—asking Mateo for colors that weren't in her reach. "I really would love this cerulean blue when you have a chance!" She'd bask in his attention, smiling a cheeky grin. I wanted to be her friend.

In front of us, inside a circle, lay props, and the session was designed so that from every angle lay something seductively stimulating for our imaginations. I sat in front of some grapes and a solo khaki-green combat boot. Unsure of how to frame, I breathed in and just painted what I saw, hoping the rest would come. Cringing at every stroke, I reminded myself that I couldn't be a perfect painter if I never tried. More important, I had already decided I wanted this woman to be my friend, so I walked toward her after class.

"I've seen you at the yoga classes..." I fumbled. "Or, really, just one class."

My words were like friction, which I felt, but she let her guard down slowly.

I stuck my hand out like a lever. "I'm Taylia."

She took it. "I'm Tahsin."

"I've heard that name before!"

She smiled as if she had a secret. "We must have met in a dream."

I wasn't sure if she was serious, she was still half smiling. "Yeah."

I stood there, temporarily feeling strange. I felt like I had known her, a flashing trance. That feeling made me reobserve her, a malachite-green hue resonating as we talked. *Who is she?*

"Are you enjoying the classes?" I asked.

"Yeah, it's a great concept, isn't it? Plus, it's nice to get away for a little bit. I don't really get much time off."

I sympathized. She talked fast, like she was nervous, too.

"But I have a beautiful healthy boy waiting at home for me, and that's enough motivation to remain in high spirits."

"What's his name?"

"Sufjan."

I smiled. "I wonder how many names *he's* inspired."

She picked up on my emphasis. "Oh yeah, the singer... No, not for me, I just liked the way it sounds in Arabic."

I laughed. "Oh! What does it mean?"

"Sufjan means 'comes with the sword.' I think it's a relic from the last bastion of the Muslim empire. I like it for its musicality. Anyway, how about you? Is this your first baby?" She gestured to my stomach.

"Yeah. Can you tell?" I said in my idiosyncratic, self-deprecating manner I had on lock.

She shook her head in an exaggerated no. I exhaled. "I never thought I'd be having children so young, but here I am."

"Right? Some days it's hard. Like really, undeniably hard, but then you come home and your little bub will smile at you with a toothless little grin and then, I kid you not, all of it—the shit on your hands, the three A.M. wake-up calls, the heavy udders that have replaced your boobs"—we both laughed—"will be..." She sighed. "...worth it. But I'm sure you've heard that."

"Well, I haven't heard exactly that." She smiled. "But, yeah, so they say."

"They say it for a reason."

My eyes lingered on her eyes for a few moments. She seemed confident, but always in thought, avoiding my direct gaze. I interrupted our silence. "Are you divorced?"

She raised her eyebrows, but half smiled again. "No." She paused and breathed in. "I'm widowed."

My brain thudded. "Oh, I'm so sorry."

Suddenly it hit me and I wondered if this interaction was even real. She had to be Roman's widow. Now I buzzed with a secret. I nodded with nerves, trying to hide what I knew in my sweaty, exhausted heart. She was Roman's wife! Roman's wife! It felt surreal to be standing near her, to smell her skin—like pure jasmine—and look into her eyes and see something akin to home. Instead of saying anything, I just zipped it up, tight inside my stomach, like vomit was urging to ooze out. This was my soon-to-be child's aunt. I felt mildly high.

"Thank you. How about you? You're not divorced, are you? You look too young to be divorced."

"Never married. It just got too hard."

"What do you mean?"

What did I mean?

"My relationship... it just got hard I guess..."

"It's okay. I'm sure it's complicated."

Was it?

"Yeah. It was. That's an easier answer anyway."

She laughed and I looked away, chewing the rubbery insides of my cheeks. There were words, frustrations, questions, coiled around my throat. I wanted her in my life, and I was desperate for her to approve of me, for her to say that I was her friend. I gave her my number and we told each other we'd meet up soon.

I walked back to Kat's that night with a gentle kind of eagerness. It was a nostalgic stirring, an awakening. I had found a possible friend, another like Kat. She was the type of woman that I always found I was drawn to. Self-assured and proud, and yet with an almost self-effacing sensibility, never detracting from the acquisition of true womanhood. Like a deep laugh in my stomach, a restless sense of wonderment brewed inside of me. She was also the closest link I had to Ky.

I looked forward to the single mothers club more than anything else in my week, and it became a tangible incentive that pushed me into shape. I found myself reading more, something I had not done resolutely for a while. My bad habit had been to offhandedly read the papers Kat left around the house in passing. Whether it was a week-old *New York Times* or a magazine, I would languidly take in a few pieces here and there, and that would habitually suffice my self-imposed reading quota. But now? Now, I was thirsty to read and to feel again. To be hungry and outraged. I wanted to feel life in a thrilling way.

When I got to Mateo's studio again, I worked on an abstract piece, focusing on the same boot that he had centered for us to paint, except from a different angle. I loved the catharsis involved in painting, in the drabness of the wet brushes after I cleaned them in baby mason jars. The swirls of colors oscillating through the water, the paint moving fast like cloaks of whirling dervishes. I wasn't a good painter, but the feeling I had as a little child, the desire of wanting to be good and perfect at everything, was quickly waning. I felt untwisted underneath a golden sun, full with purpose. I was becoming something of my own design. Fucking finally.

Ryan called me the next day.

I was cooking a curry lentils recipe I had found in one of Kat's addictive Ottolenghi cookbooks. The garlic and onions were browning to a soft caramel when the phone buzzed and Ryan's name blinked like a flashing sign.

"Hello."

"Hey, kid, whatchya doing?"

"I am... cooking."

"You can cook?"

"Um, I used to cook all the time for you! Remember?"

"Oh yeah, I guess you're right. Well, what's the occasion?" he asked. I could see the smile on his face, his lips pursed to the side.

"Oh, nothing."

He laughed for real that time. "Wanna hang out?"

"Uh, yeah." And I did, I really, really did.

An hour and a half later he picked me up from Kat's and we walked around the block with a lilac-purple Tupperware container filled with curried lentils and a slightly burned, but still tasty, golden quinoa and sweet potato cake.

He opened the lid cumbersomely. "Don't be mad, but I wasn't expecting for it to actually look, you know, edible."

"Jeez, thanks, man."

"No, I mean, I can't remember if you were a good cook or not!"

I nodded my head, a little annoyed. After all those meals I cooked for him, I felt kinda disrespected. But it was in the wake of Lyse's death, so I forgave him quickly.

"Fork?"

I shook my head, instead passing him some chopsticks.

"Okay, that's strange."

I laughed and watched him contemplate the proportions. He eventually took a bite.

248

"That's actually not bad."

"Right."

"In theory, it could have been bad."

"Maybe."

"So, how you doing?"

"Well, I made a friend."

"That's nice, what are they like?"

"She's a she. She's nice. Friendly. Pretty."

"Pretty girls are always a great incentive."

I laughed. Ryan set down the Tupperware and stared at me.

"Where should we go?"

"Take me anywhere you'd like!"

We walked to a café nearby and we ordered some creamy tiramisu, a dulcet strawberry cheesecake, and a short, sharp espresso for Ryan. The air's circadian sense of rhythm was palpable. I wondered if he was seeing anyone. I wondered if I should ask.

"What are you thinking about?"

"This. This is strange, right?"

"Us? Yeah, this is strange. But a good strange." I smiled up at him.

"It's definitely weird seeing you. You're the same but then you're not."

"I'm not." And I wasn't.

"What were you then? And what are you now?"

I took a few moments before I answered. "I was weak..."

"And now you're not?"

I laughed. "No, I still am."

He joined my laughter.

"But, I mean, I feel older. It's not even a mental thing. It's like I can feel life in my body. My skin has changed, shifted, grown, stretched. Having a baby inside of you makes time a tangible thing." I paused just as the baby moved. She had begun to move. "I mean, I'm still unsure of what I'm going to do with my life, you know, but I'm not as nervous about it as I once was."

"Well, I remember when you didn't talk, not a peep!"

I smiled, remembering also. "I didn't need to talk, Alyssa did all the talking."

"Why did you always step down? Why didn't you ever challenge her?"

I shrugged as if it were obvious. "She was the *chosen one*."

I said it in a joking voice, but he scoffed. I felt defensive.

"She was... My parents loved her!"

"And they didn't love you?"

I paused. "No. They didn't."

"Tay, that's bullshit."

The tight rage, with a sudden jolt, was building. "Listen, you were an outsider looking in. You can't even begin to understand... I mean, why do you think I'm here?"

I didn't want to entirely open the Pandora's box of suffering; for now, I still wanted vagueness to subsume my past.

Without a beat, he asked, "Well, why are you here?"

I sat silently.

"Taylia? I've upset you."

I shrugged again.

"Hey, listen. I'm not saying that your issues of insecurity aren't valid. They definitely painted Alyssa as this—this... golden child and maybe it's unfair of me to question how much that had an effect on you. No doubt it was tough. I'm just saying that though I'm sure it was hard, maybe it would do you some good to look at it from another perspective. Glass half full, maybe?" He paused. "I mean, I don't know... I don't want to 'mansplain' your life to you or anything."

I winced at the usage.

"That's what all the kids are saying."

"You forget... You're a millennial, too. *Sorrrrrrry, dude!*"

He smiled. "Word."

I stopped deflecting, and for a second I indulged him. *Was it all as painful as I remembered?* Truth was, *I didn't know.* I wasn't sure. All I *knew* was this was what I felt, and that *that* was valid.

Ryan strategically moved the conversation away from my family. "How are you doing anyway?"

And I deliberately changed the subject, not wanting to unnecessarily linger. "I think I'm sick of Ralph."

"Ralph? The guy I met at the hospital? Not the baby daddy, right?"

I nodded.

"He seemed like a nice guy. Overprotective, but nice."

"He's a philistine."

"Big word, Taylia."

"Shut up. It's true." I felt myself acting dumb again. I had created my own drama. I was my own Alyssa, luring in a man whom I now no longer needed. I was being strong like her, feminine like her, wicked like her.

"Don't be an asshole to him." I didn't say anything, and he continued, going right back to the wound. "When you have that thousand-yard stare on your face, you look remarkably like your mother."

I jolted out of my daze. "My mother?"

"Yes."

"I didn't know you still had such a good relationship with my parents." I said it with disdain. I said it because, in some universe, maybe I was jealous that they liked their nonbiological son more than me.

I could see the words climbing up his throat: "I loved Alyssa, but I also hung around for your parents." He continued. "Two years into our relationship I began to understand the ins and outs of Lyse's character... She was predictable because, in a lot of ways, she just liked drama. Maybe I was drawn to that, at least as a teenager. Now, as an adult, it's different. But I guess I just really liked being around y'all. You were alive, in your own ways. I don't have siblings, so you became this—this... extended family for me... It felt nice to be welcomed into your home with all of you." As he talked to me his eyebrows pulled in like waves of compassion and immediacy, nudging me to listen, letting the words sink in. "All four of you made up this indistinguishable serenity in my life."

Suddenly, my eyes were rigid against his face. "What the fuck was so great about my parents?"

This unfazed him, like he was almost too eager to go on this propaganda campaign. "Your parents were cool. I'd never met anyone like them before. Your dad was a weird Brown antisocial brainiac and your mom was obsessed with art in a way that was riveting and stimulating to me. They weren't like other parents I knew. You guys were just exciting to me. I don't know what to tell ya!"

I felt like I wanted to bark at him, but I just sat and absorbed this information, putting it into context. Ryan's parents were really rich Black entertainment lawyers who traveled a lot for work. They sent Ryan, their only child, to all the best schools, and I wasn't surprised to hear that even after Alyssa's suicide Ryan graduated (though years later) from Harvard Law. Unscathed.

"Ryan, don't."

"Don't what?" His voice was suddenly tinged with defiance.

My cheeks flushed over. "Respectfully... you don't know what you're talking about."

"Whatever they did, you don't need to keep punishing them for it. You know your father has, like, full-blown dementia now. Early onset. Like it's bad..." It sounded like an accusation, and momentarily my heart curled over. I knew Baba had been show-ing the signs for years, ever since Alyssa died, but I cared little to know much more about it now. My fury toward them had possibly saved my life, and I couldn't let go of it. And now, for the first time, Ryan, my dead sister's ex-boyfriend, was telling me how to think and to feel about *my* life—like he knew what it felt like to *ever* compete for love. Though Ryan's parents were busy throughout his life, and I'm sure the absence hurt, he was always the apple of their eye. They made sure to prioritize him, to love him. I could tell when I saw them engage with Mama and Baba, I could tell that Ryan was loved by the way he talked—

it was similar to Alyssa. Now a powerful executive at a fancy film production company, he had always been outstanding. A little boring, yes, but an overachiever. Like Alyssa. They had that much in common.

I knew it was unfair of me to project, but he couldn't know the traumas of my life. And I couldn't know his. But I also realized he had never even treated me like a person worth engaging with the many years he dated Alyssa. It was easy, in retrospect, to praise our fanciful, exotic life and all the things that *that* had offered him, but I wasn't a prop in a family play. I was a person. I had been mad at myself for never reaching out to him, but now I was figuring out that he had also never reached out to me. He never checked in, all the while still being chummy with my parents. It felt cruel. Why did people so rarely think of my needs? Why had I allowed myself to be glossed over so incessantly?

He was talking about my mother and how she was barely coping. I pictured her, the ghostly image moving through my stomach like a slippery mass. Her hair a dense cloud, and she, on her left knee, lifting the white powdery tights up Alyssa's legs. The memory was milky, delayed, lost in the puddle of a thousand recollections I had of being tossed to the side. Of being second. Of being fucking second. To Alyssa. What had she said to me moments before? *Taylia, come here*? Had she asked me to stand near her? Had she also asked to put the tights on? Had she asked me first? Before Alyssa? I can't remember. What did she say? Momentarily, I was caught in doubt. *Had it all been as hard as I thought it was?* I felt anger rise up again. Of course it was hard! I was a ball of clay that could be carved by the whims and desires of my parents. Too often mothers and fathers want their children to be pliable to their desires, the gatekeepers of their lost dreams. My nonlife—the existence on the other side of Alyssa's existence, the no-space of being where I had resided since I was a little girl—was my harrowing reality. I was the lesser child. Pointed out like an afterthought, a leftover, a messy fragment of the equation... I knew I sounded dramatic, but it was my truth, and I hated Ryan for questioning me. He would never understand. But I was beginning to see my life fully.

Then there was the rape. I toyed with the idea of telling him, but I didn't want the questions. It would hurt too much to see them form. Besides, I felt myself unconsciously judging my own body, my own experience, still. I had to protect myself from being gaslit. I had to protect my mind and my heart from those who couldn't see it.

I knew Ryan hated Simon, but people always protect men. Even the ones they hate. I could see this in the statistics of the people (mainly women) who report rape and the even smaller numbers of people who find any redemption, any remote justice. Violence against women is too common and known, too ubiquitous, and yet the culture of shame creates the cycle of silence. The culture of shame.

I wish I could explain to Ryan what it feels like to have your body taken from you by violence that then lurks—for months, for years—like a ghost in the darkest corners of your mind, galvanizing like invisible smoke. How self-hatred creeps, and you are robbed of yourself. I wish I could explain to him that I still felt Simon as well. That I still had nightmares of their hands and the feeling of being ripped open. Rape is a kind of death. Of the self, mind and body. Survival looks like many things, but sometimes you do believe you deserved what happened to you, as a means of accepting your fate. Which is why there are such high suicide rates for survivors. At a certain point, you wonder what's left living for when your body no longer feels like yours. Where are you safe? To then watch the men, the people, who damaged you live, continue on, is another kind of death. It is to feel gutted out, constantly. It is to feel unsafe and unloved, constantly.

As I thought of Simon now I thought of claws. If it ever happened again, I know I could kill him. But when it came to Ryan and the truth, I saw Mama and Baba stare back at me, wreathed in paranoia, the sham of care circling like a war wound in my stomach. I didn't want to feel judged by them, even if it was via somebody else, so I silenced myself and erased that specific smudge of my own experience. I didn't say any of this, presenting the version of myself who was irrational in her rage instead.

25.

When I was about thirteen, Alyssa found a journal my mother had kept in her early twenties. Inside the very first pages, dated September 29, 1982, my mother, before she was my mother, had inscribed:

> *Today Janice finally talked to me again. She didn't even say a hello when she walked up to me with all her fucking sass... But then she slowly opened her mouth and asked, in her annoying southern drawl, "How can you bear to kiss his lips?" I wanted to tell her how good it actually felt to be kissed by a man who respected you, who hadn't asked for "it" but who had instead told me that he'd wait for me "for as long as you need." But I just laughed her off, laughed off Janice with her stupid gap tooth. Now I sorta wished I hadn't laughed it off. Who does she think she is anyway? Maybe she's just jealous. I always thought she was. The thing is, I love him, Janice. I fucking love him.*

I was too young when I read it and the only thing that really resonated was the fact that my very own mother wrote *fucking*. My second thought was that this Janice was still very much a presence in my mother's life, which meant that Janice was a two-faced bitch. As I noticed the third and final thing, Alyssa simultaneously pointed it out to me. There were tear tracks down the page, blurring the words *lips* and *anyway*, smudging them into blue-inked clouds. For a moment, in that snapshot of time, my mother suddenly seemed very human to me: a tangible being with emotions and maybe even a heart. For the first time, I didn't feel sorry for myself but for her.

I fished around for Tahsin's number and called her, feeling grateful afterward that she happily accepted a meeting that in retrospect almost entirely felt like fate. We set a date, and on the day I waited frantically for her at our meeting place, outside the Whole Foods at Union Square. She worked in the city as an editor for a magazine, and we were meeting on her lunch break.

I tempered my apprehension with my inevitable excitement. I recalled what she looked like, the curves of her haunting face were etched into my brain. I had a day-old *New York Times* in my hand, but I couldn't read a full sentence without having to repeat each word every half a second, so I concentrated on the front page. There was a coffee stain from Kat's favorite ceramic mug creased into the first few pages and unintelligible scribbles written around the headline. I smiled, thinking of Kat reading the paper before work, only distracting myself for about three to four seconds.

Eventually Tahsin walked up to me. At that exact time I was watching the man in front of me sell his intricate crafted jewelry made of vintage spoons, but my glances were only a conduit for what I was actually doing: thinking nervously about Tahsin. She was smiling when she arrived, wearing a burgundy long-sleeved dress with a thin tan leather belt around her waist. Her shoes were strappy, and her hair was down in waves and billowed around the corners of her face. A strand or two were caught in her red lips, like a fly to a Venus flytrap. I had worn a Canadian tuxedo that I thrifted from a Salvation Army. She hugged me first, and I hugged her back. It was a very embracing, full hug.

"I'm so happy to see you," I said, my mouth just above her shoulder.

"And I, you," she chanted back.

I knew it was only a courtesy, but it still felt so warm.

She pulled my arm to hers and asked, "Where should we go?"

I shrugged, so she took the initiative and we started walking.

"So, how have you been?"

"I don't know." I paused, trying to find the right words. "I had an interesting night last night."

"Oh yeah?"

I nodded.

"Like how?"

Where to start.

"Well, see, I don't have a very good relationship with my parents, in particular my mother."

She turned to me, concerned. "I'm sorry to hear that."

"It's okay," I said quickly, not wanting to cause her distress. "It's always been like that, I guess. Well, it's not really okay. But it's life, you know, so it's whatever."

She nodded. I wondered if she could understand.

"Anyway. I left home a while back. Things weren't working out... and my parents didn't want me in the house anymore... So I left, I guess... And, well, a few years before that my sister killed herself... So, anyway, my sister's ex and I recently reconnected, and last night he told me that I shouldn't let my parents suffer anymore, or, well, something to that effect, and I guess for the first time I started remembering my parents as humans who felt and had pain... which is just weird! Because things kind of shifted in my head after that... So now I'm in a weird place and I need to process it all."

I looked over at her. Her face was a blur of confusion. She put up her hands and mouthed, *What?!* "Taylia. Holy shit. That's a lot to deal with."

I shrugged, my safest default reaction, not knowing what else to do, knowing full well that my nonchalance was just a facade. I felt comfortable that she cared, as this was why I had turned to her. Sometimes we just need someone to tell us, *Wow, that's really hard.* It's as if having that someone acknowledge the pain creates a purpose for these things to have happened in the first place. Or that they would, somehow, be things that were lived and not merely conjured. We kept walking.

"So, what's the next step?"

"Nothing. I don't have one. I think, if anything, all I really want from my life is to accept the things that *have* been given to me." I emphasized the *have*, halving the air with my teeth, the two front ones cutting down lightly onto my bottom lip, resounding the whole word.

She stopped walking, the wind blowing her hair forward, and for a second her whole face was masked from me and others to her side. It looked like a curtain being stringed for a closing act, like her hair moved neatly and succinctly to a languid performance. As she turned to me, the music rose in my ears and I watched how beautifully she even turned her head. When our eyes finally met, hers were welled with tears, questions floating at the top.

"Taylia, honey..."

She grabbed my shoulders and pulled me into a full hug, and as we stood there, opposite the Walgreens, and she didn't let go for an eternity. Instead, she lingered in my hair, in my mind, and deep in my heart.

"Is it okay that I'm hugging you like this?"

I said yes. We kept hugging.

Minutes went by, passerbys continued on. Some stared, expecting a scene, an artwork, a remark, a protest. We just stood. Two people connected over pain, over heartache, over loss. She finally let go of me and the timing seemed perfect, each of us fuller with something. We said nothing, but she held my hand and pulled me by her side so that our shoulders touched as we walked on.

"I'm sorry. I just think I really needed to hear that."

"How come?"

She exhaled. "After my husband died, I've been struggling with that idea, Taylia. I've been struggling with my faith, with God. How does a God that loves you take away something that meant the whole world to you? Can I worship a God that betrayed me in that way?"

I stayed silent. I had my own battles with God.

"Are you religious?"

I said I didn't know.

She laughed. "That's probably a good answer. Maybe people with true faith have to challenge God. Or at least that's what I've been telling myself."

We continued walking. Sometimes we were silent, other times she'd point out a store she liked and I'd mention how I'd never been there, or, sometimes, I'd make an observation, like the brightness of a woman's hair dyed a deep and effervescent violet. We were comfortable in our silence together.

We walked into a coffeehouse brimming with color. It was as if I had been transported into the '70s. The interior was wooden with flowers arranged on every table, like some eccentric dining hall at a *Freaks and Geeks*–themed summer camp. We walked through the small café to a quaint enclave in the back and made a place near some plants and a questionably placed fan. I ordered a white peach tea and Tahsin ordered a three-shot ristretto mocha.

She turned to me after ordering with a huge grin on her face. "Coffee is a weakness."

I nodded.

"Not a coffee fan, aye?"

"I just worked in a café, so coffee is very accessible to me all the time. I'd rather try something completely different... like a white peach tea!"

She laughed, quickly turning sober. "I can't imagine what you've been going through with the death of your sister and leaving, or rather being kicked out of your house, it sounds like?"

I agreed, also shifting into "serious" conversation mode.

"Where are you living now, by the way?"

"I live in Fort Greene. A very kind friend of mine has housed me for the last few months. Her name's Kat. She's also a single mother, we should all hang out."

Tahsin smiled a yes. Our drinks arrived and we started sipping. She oohed and aahed over hers. "You don't want to have a teensy-weensy try, do you?"

I ferociously declined.

"So, does your sister's ex... Okay, what's his name? We can't keep calling him that."

"Ryan."

"Okay, is Ryan suggesting that you go and pay your parents a visit, or... ?"

"I guess so."

"How does that make you feel?"

"Horrible. Going back to them would mean that I had forgiven them for everything."

"And you haven't?"

"No, not at all!"

She looked perplexed. "I don't know, love. I come from an Arab family where family is paramount. It's everything that you have. I understand that you never had that, but I'm just trying to look at it from an objective place."

"I appreciate that. Do you get along with your family?"

"Depends what you mean by that."

I laughed, thinking, technically, we *were* family. She and I—our children were cousins. Baby suddenly pushed, and I suddenly got quiet, seeing it as a sign, hoping she wouldn't notice.

"Look, every family has their own drama. It would be naive of me to say otherwise. I have had my ups and downs with my family, but they love me, and I love them. They've accepted a lot of things in my life—I mean, I married a non-Muslim—but we've learned and grown together. We're not an ideal family, but we're happy. Which is something, I guess. Also, and this is the biggest thing recently, they've really been there for me since my husband died."

I deflected fast, not wanting to linger on Roman. "Do you have any siblings?"

"Yeah, a sister. She's pretty great."

I smiled sadly, remembering Roman talking about her around the dinner table.

She put her hand on my hand. "I know I keep saying this, but I'm sorry about your sister. That's just terrible."

"It happened a few years ago, which is weird to say. You'd think I'd be fully healed by now..."

She looked at me with a smile. "You'll heal when you're ready."

The words fluttered past my eardrums, down my spinal cord, and into my stomach. I felt lighter, calmer, and at peace. I felt tears rise up. *I'll heal when I'm ready.* Suddenly time no longer mattered, failure was no longer an option. I felt *with* life. "Ah, and I really needed to hear *that*."

We paused.

"Do you feel lonely without him? Your husband, I mean." I felt bad pretending as if I didn't know who her husband was. But I didn't feel ready to tell her.

She began with a sigh. "Every day, Taylia. It's always really hard when you're reminded of them because of a distinct memory you have of a thing that involves them, or your only memory of that thing is coiled around a memory of them. I'm sure you can understand. Sometimes I just touch things hoping I can feel the echo of his fingertips. When I don't, it's hard to accept that I'll never feel them again. He'll never push my hair back behind my ears or touch my hands... And that's"—she bit her lip—"that's when it's really, *really* hard." She looked down quickly; I knew it was because she was minimizing her chances of crying. I sometimes did that, too. She smiled even amid the tears, and I clasped my fingers around hers.

"I know it's not exactly the same thing, but I do understand. I felt like that after Alyssa died. It's hard to believe a person is dead when you can still feel their heartbeat everywhere. I was crazy. I wanted to relive everything in my memories of her, like go to her favorite cafés, believing that she would walk across the street and scream out, 'Tay, I've been looking around all over for you.' I have that dream still." I didn't tell her that it worked, that that's kinda what Alyssa did do, though not exactly as I had hoped. Apparitions of dead people weren't exactly the same as having them back in real life.

Tahsin closed her eyes so that a stream of tears spilled out of the corners. She was still smiling, but the smile was embedded with so much sadness. She got out a tissue and blew her nose, and then folded the tissue into a square and drew it to her eyes, where she brushed the edges of her soaked skin. She looked like a saint.

"Okay, enough of that." Her eyes were wide and open. "Today's about you."

"We can talk—"

She stopped me. "You." She paused. "So your sister's ex-boyfriend Ryan, huh?"

"I don't know what to do."

She took a sip of her coffee and then asked, "What are your options?"

"Well, to go see my parents, according to him."

"Is that a viable option?" she asked.

"No way. No fucking way."

"May I interject?"

I nodded. *Of course.*

"Sweetie, you're young. I know young people hate hearing this, but you don't really know what you want when you're young."

I breathed in defiance.

"I mean, to be fair, you never really know. But still. There are times when life *feels* right and an aha moment clicks in your head and things fall into place. I'm assuming seeing your parents doesn't give you that feeling, huh?"

I shook my head.

"Why?"

Tell her. Be open, Taylia.

I hesitated. I wanted to tell her about Simon, but I wasn't ready. Not yet. "They loved my sister more than me."

Without a beat, Tahsin asked, "So? I mean, don't get me wrong, love. That's horrible. I know, don't tell me that I don't understand sibling—or more specifically sister—rivalry. It's horrendous when you're growing up, especially when your parents play you against each other, but still. Look at yourself. You're amazing, you're smart, you're compassionate, *and* you're beautiful. What should it matter what your parents did or didn't do when you were growing up? I doubt they really loved you less, it just maybe feels that way."

I was shocked, both by the compliments and by how cavalier she was being of my pain.

"Taylia, sweetie? I haven't offended you, have I?"

I shook my head.

"I know it's easier said than done. I'm just putting my two cents in..."

"No, I want you to be honest."

"Okay, I will be then."

"I guess it's just a lot more complicated than you're making it out to be."

"Of course." As she said it, she put her hand on her heart.

"There was a lot of shaming and guilt-tripping involved. I guess that's why I feel so undeveloped as a person, you know? Like I shouldn't be having these problems in my twenties. So it just makes me feel like I'm slow... at life... or something."

"Honey, it's not a race." She smiled, and I cocked my head goofily. "Tell me about your sister."

26.

Mama is in the living room. She is angry, she is pulsing. She looks tough, the bruises of her anger apparent like swollen lumps on either side of her cheeks. Yet, despite her vexations, there is warmth—and it surges through her. She is a needy love, she is a confused love; the pain of unfulfillment travels fast through her blazing eyes. Every blink, every smile, every thousand-yard stare—is a call, to love.

"Alyssa, please don't wear that."

Alyssa laughs. At her. She is uncompromising to this woman, a stranger.

"Alyssa, don't be rude."

"Oh, Mom." *She's so condescending.* Oh, Mom. You're an idiot. Oh, Mom, what is wrong with you? Oh, Mom, I'm the best thing that ever happened to you. Oh, Mom. You're nothing without me.

So much said in so little words.

"Alyssa..."

"What? You're acting like a fucking cunt."

I am not there and there at the same time. I don't register. My facial expression remains intact, removed. I'm on Alyssa's side no matter what.

It felt like a dream lived, a past life. We were downstairs by the kitchen. The kettle was humming. I couldn't remember how old I was, but I knew I was old enough to do something. Or at least to know that what Alyssa was doing was wrong.

As I lay there not doing much of anything, I replayed it all in my mind. I tried to isolate the images of my mother that had formed in my brain. My mind focused on Alyssa, but I refocused it on Mama. She didn't do anything when Alyssa threw those words at her, assaulting the air, cutting through the energy like the slice of a guillotine. She just stood. The liquid around her eyes rose, creating a film that sat there on the edge of the cliff, floating in the space between the lashes and her eyeballs. I rewatched her every move in my mind, haunted by her composition, disturbed by her preciseness, and for the first time I realized that she was used to this. Her face didn't transform into a mask of pain, but there was heartache etched all over. She bit her lips in a bid to pace the tears, and when Alyssa swiftly exited the room, laughing perniciously to herself, my mother let the tears reign over her.

I was there that day. I just sat as if I weren't. It wasn't my fight, it wasn't my war, but I let my mother weep and mourn, already at a loss for a child who had given up.

I got an abrupt message from Ryan on a Tuesday afternoon. I had ignored his last few attempts to meet again, so was surprised when the message just said, *We need to talk.*

There had never before been a sense of urgency with him, so I wondered what this message could possibly mean.

Why, is something wrong? I texted back.

His next message was as abrupt as the last. *Can you meet up later this evening?*

I felt nervous just awaiting his reply. We decided on 8:00, and at 8:02 he buzzed the door. I ran down, one hand on my belly.

"Hey." Inviting him up, I gestured a *come on*, but he paused. We both paused on the steps of Kat's brownstone.

"I have to tell you something, Tay. I should have told you this a while ago. Or maybe not, I don't actually know. But I'm gonna tell you this now because I think that it's right, or something."

He got out his iPad that had a dated message that read:

> From: Alyssa Chatterjee
> We all bleed for our wrongdoings. If not in this life, maybe in the next. I'm not ready to bring life into this world. It's not yours. I'm sorry. For everything.

I reread it at least five times before he said anything.

"She sent that to me the night before she killed herself."

I was dumbfounded. "Why?"

His head was cocked to the side. He was tired and angry. "Why? Why? Why...?" His words were like a grater slowly tearing at the outer layer of my heart, shredding it to a pulp.

"Ryan?" *Was she pregnant? Was that what she was saying?*

"I hate her for leaving me to do the dirty work."

"Tell me."

His fingers were at his eyes. "A couple of months before she died, Alyssa was sleeping with Simon..."

I shook my head violently, *no, no, no.*

"She was seeing him because she needed him. Simon had something Alyssa needed." I knew he was trying to spell it out for me without saying the specific words, but I needed help.

"What? What did he have?"

His head was hung over the edge.

"Ryan?" I was shouting it at him. I needed to know. The answer was staring at me in the face with a smirk. Simon's smirk.

"She had an addictive personality, Tay..." He stopped talking midsentence, and I let him, my heart grinding to a stupefied halt. "She did it to herself, Taylia."

It was so cold. He had given up. Slowly he explained her pregnancy with Simon's baby. Her addiction. I wanted to projectile vomit. *Alyssa, my darling.* I wanted to weep, *Alyssa, Lyse. I'm sorry I wasn't there.*

"That sounds harsh, but it's true. She lacked self-control. She chose not to take advantage of the good life she was given. She decided to fuck up."

I could hear how hurt he was, but I didn't care. There were small tires of anger lodged underneath both sides of my throat. His response was so mean. Like a plug to my tears, I felt immeasurably sad for her. I knew this wasn't the whole truth, and in that moment, I mourned never getting the chance to know her side. The pain of holding back the deluge, even for a few moments, sent a tight pull up my jaw, like a harness against my emotions. Couldn't he just forgive her and move on? He was still here, he was still living.

"Taylia..."

"Get the fuck out." I wanted to scream it, but before I inhaled another scratching breath, he had already left.

As I began to breathe normally again, I remembered that before she died, Alyssa wrote out, in her notebook left neatly on her bedside table, a quote from Mama's favorite book, *Family Lexicon*, by Italian writer Natalia Ginzburg. It was a line about Cesare Pavese, an Italian poet and writer who tragically killed himself. Though, I guess, suicide was always tragic.

"He looked beyond death and imagined death to the point where it was no longer death he imagined but life." She wrote it at the top of her Moleskine, leaving it open for all to see. It was scrawled with her favorite Kaweco fountain pen. The ink bled a little onto the pages, just the way Alyssa liked it. I remember, I remember reading it. I should have known.

She came as soon as I texted. In one hand she bore a stack of Ritter Sports, the ones with cornflakes in the chocolate, and in the other was Sufjan with an insistent gaze. Luc was behind me, holding on tightly to my stringy dress, hands shoved tightly against my fleshy calves.

"Who are you?" he asked Tahsin.

"I'm Tahsin. Who are you?"

"Luc." His questions didn't skip a beat. "Is that your baby?"

"Yes, it is. This is Sufjan."

"You know my mommy owns this place." Even under the circumstances, it was so cute that Tahsin and I both laughed. I tried to pick him up to kiss him, but he swatted my care. There was another short pause before he sprang off. "Okay, bye!"

Tahsin giggled. "Kat's not home?"

I shook my head. "I've been doing some babysitting to help her out. She's probably prepping the kitchen for tomorrow as we speak. She doesn't really ask for much help, but this is the least my giant amniotic sac of a body can do."

Tahsin cocked her eyebrows at me, judgmental. I watched her plop the chocolates onto the dining table while simultaneously pushing Sufjan upward in a graceful propelling motion.

"How are you really doing?"

"Well, I guess I don't know what to think..."

"Why? Don't you trust Ryan?"

I breathed in. "Yes. I do..." I guess I did, but I also didn't know him anymore and didn't know if I could trust his objectivity.

"Then? What's there to think?"

"I don't want to believe it, Tahsin. I just can't. It would mean too much."

"What? What would it mean? Other than she was complicated, and that she hid things. Even from you. I know that hurts... but you were coming to terms with that. If anything, this is a blessing. I think this is that for you. You just have to look at it like a blessing. Besides, you shouldn't hold her complexities against her."

I didn't. I just felt betrayed that she never told me. That she never confided in me.

"I'm just shocked."

"That is to be expected..."

"I just found out that my sister—" My voice broke.

Was pregnant? Drug addicted and pregnant? With Simon's child?

"Okay, sit down. I'll make us some tea."

I sat down, replaying every memory of her that could have pointed to the truth. How could she have done that to herself?

As if reading my mind, Tahsin remarked, "Taylia, people do stupid things, obviously to varying degrees, but she clearly felt like she was losing agency."

How could I tell her that this was also about Simon? How could I tell her about the disgusting overgrowth of despair that was Simon?

"Oh, and she only just left me all alone in this fucking world."

"Sweetie, please. Would you have wanted to be overshadowed by Alyssa your whole life? It's hard, but you have to find a positive in this..."

I felt a disorienting alignment pull up my spine. "A silver lining..." I said half-mindedly. "I guess. Yes. It's so great my sister killed herself so I can finally learn to be strong! Have you found the silver lining since Roman died, too?" I wanted to be cruel, but the question came out sedately, clear, with a certain piquancy.

"No," she said, "but I see him everywhere..."

My heart started hurting as I suddenly thought of Ky. I noted that she still talked about Roman in the present tense. I stared at Sufjan for a while, my mind suddenly absent. I could hear her speaking, but nothing was going in, she was just a voice outside of my paralyzing shell, her voice mildly operatic. I suddenly wanted to blame her for the fact that Ky never tried to get me back. He never even came looking for me. I guess he never really loved me, and I was also in the midst of accepting that.

"In time, I will heal. It's hard to start your life after death." I was back, listening to her. "Your natural inclination is to die with them, right? Like, you almost don't want it *to get easier*, because how dare it? And the thing is, did I even have a life outside of him? Do I just stop loving him? Do I just turn it off? I know that would make it easier, but how do you stop loving someone you love, and if life would have gone your way, they'd be loving you too... right here, right fucking now."

I could hear her voice stutter at the word *here*, and only then was I fully present again. I stared at her, knowing and not knowing her.

"It's strange, there's this word in Arabic, *Ya'aburnee*, which means 'I love you so much that I hope I die before you because I couldn't bear the pain of living without you.' I used to say it to him all the time, and we'd laugh at its absurd moroseness. *Ya'aburnee.*" She started crying. "You look pale."

I looked up at her, unfazed by her tears. "Do I?"

She nodded.

I deflected by getting up at the zing of the kettle boiling and poured the hot water into two short ceramic mugs, wide with moon-shaped handles. Tahsin had scooped Sufjan into her left arm, drumming his diapered bottom as she cried melodically. I wondered at how much I didn't know about her. How I didn't quite understand the intricacies of her character yet. Was she just wearing a disguise of positivity? And if so, was she actually in chronic emotional pain underneath it all? I felt my eyes numb as I stared at her wiry silhouette, questioning what it was that made us who we are. She was so open, so authentic, but not vulnerable. There was no room for hurting anymore, only room for survival. She wanted to succeed. Even then, on some level I was a witness to her pain. It was deep like a well. I assumed some days the pain must rise more than others, floating to the top, usurping all.

I still hadn't mentioned Ky. I knew I wasn't ready, but I also was paralyzed by the idea of what to do next. Was I actually going to have this baby alone? Kat had done it, Tahsin was doing it, but was I going to actually join the single mothers club for eternity? Money was an obvious question. Kat owed me nothing, but I wondered if she'd let me work at the café again. If I could beg her to let me stay in this brownstone with her. How was I going to pay for everything? For this baby? With the small sum of money Dadi-ma left me? Forever? Life was beginning to come crawling in like an anthem.

27.

As my mother had married a man with toffee-colored skin and a Nehru nose, she knew she needed to prove that her husband was just the same, lacking in no way what a "normal" man had. He may have resembled a cabdriver, but he was a different breed of Indian. An Indian with a Western education, who despised incense and spoke with a well-adjusted transatlantic accent. His skin was sweet and odorless, unlike other dirty Indians (and never sticky on hot days). He despised religion, having never read the Bhagavad Gita or followed the silly customs of his family. He ate beef, drank wine, and never reeked of cheapness. Completely affable, he wore polo shirts that highlighted his handsome physique, resembling a more rugged and darker Imran Khan. He was the Commonwealth's dream who proved the Queen and her endeavors had done well to pillage and invest in Indian and foreign soil. He was cultured like *them*, like *her*. He was no longer barbaric, he was saved.

When we lived at Dadi-ma's, how easily Baba fell into wearing a lungi—a checkered blue sarong with hints of plum purple—in the daytime, reading newspapers with his feet, out of his Bata slippers, leaning like a bridge on Dadi-ma's glass coffee table, drinking garam garam chai. He would visit his mother after breakfast, as she'd lie on her high, hard bed, the mosquito nets twisted like braids to the side. He was lighter with her; speaking in Bengali gave him character that English never gave him. He had humor, he had dimensions. I lamented never knowing this Baba. I knew that he probably felt he had to wear a mask of stoicism to survive in America as a Brown man, and that tormented me.

Every morning I'd feed Dadi-ma red root, to strengthen her blood, and sat with her as the young girl, who usually swept the house, would wash Dadi-ma's floating feet and toes in a shallow bucket. I'd tend to her hair, almost all white, like the beard of Gandalf, while she stroked her soft hands on the hems of her saree. We gobbled food, meals sectioning our days. In other hours, Baba lectured his visiting neighbors (I noticed he had a different vibrato in Bengali), while Mama would often read on the roof, in the rose garden, the peach and fuschia goblets already bloomed, and Alyssa would watch the Fashion network in the back room. In India, Baba's gender took hold again, and he was satisfied with the privilege of his birthright.

Are good memories just moments in time we choose to remember, or are they a sign of something greater? I looked back at the memories of my childhood and was surprised by what I had kept to bear with me through the days. A lot involved some kind of accomplishment. Like the time my fourth grade teacher said that I took *initiative*, and I knew that was a good thing, even if I didn't know what it meant entirely. These embellished moments were simply a result of my stunted self-esteem. I guess what I'm trying to say is if love had been fostered within me at a young age, would my life have been different? And would I look at it differently? I don't really know. But I'd like to think that I would. I'd come to realize that my self-effacing nature had become a roadblock to myself, and I never realized the way I viewed myself was deeply interconnected with Alyssa. So, to let go of that part of my life, the one that I had woven so tightly to my stunted heart, I needed to let go of Alysssa. Of what I deemed her to be. Especially in juxtaposition to me.

Tahsin and I had quickly become like *The Wives of the Dead*, bonded by loss. Both of us understood the disabilities that came with that kind of pain: the unwanted tears along the sidewalk, the accidental somnambulance that occurred in daylight, the confused feeling of one's heart continuing to drop, leaving an empty vessel—a heart-shaped lacuna. Our sudden bursts of emotion were as explainable and natural to each other as breathing and sleeping.

After art class Tahsin turned to me.

"Aye, Taylia?"

"Yes, Tahs."

She looked nervous.

"What?" I laughed.

"This guy, the guy you left. You never really talk about him..."

My positivity had its limits.

That's because it's none of your fucking business.

What I chose to say was the blanket answer to all uncomfortable inquiries: "I don't really feel like talking about it..." I stumbled. "Right now."

She wrinkled her nose.

"What was his name?"

I hadn't said his name in months. What would it sound like to say it again? How would my mouth feel to resonate that heart-twisting syllable, the sound of those letters again? How would my body react to his name being said aloud, and almost more important, how would Tahsin?

"I really... really would rather talk about how much you enjoyed Mateo's ass today!"

I hardly believed I had uttered it, but it had come out of *my* mouth. I didn't know if I should be proudly horrified. But my intuition knew one thing: Tahsin had a weakness for Mateo's spicy white (we still didn't know where he was from, but assumed Italian) butt. Tahsin laughed and nudged me playfully on the shoulder as we walked in the sunlight.

Later, I caught up with Ralph even though I didn't want to. When he called me to set something up, I said, "I don't like you, life," but what I had meant to say was his name. He laughed with familiarity, as if this were a candid joke of mine. I imagined his face as if it were right there. I imagined him smiling, eyelashes sprawled out like a fan as he thought of me.

When we eventually met up, he pulled me into a meaningful hug in a meaningful way. At first I didn't put my hands around him, but then something shifted and I involved myself both emotionally and physically. After a few moments he pushed me forward, still holding on to me, and caressed the part of my cheek that was closest to my lips with his own. I wasn't repulsed; instead I looked up at him and saw him for what he was. And suddenly, it was that obvious. I looked at Ralph, finally clear-minded.

"I'm sorry. I can't do this anymore. It's not working for me."

I was learning new skills now, skills of straightforwardness, of honesty. With the heaviness of my voice, the directness of my glare, I knew Ralph understood me. I could tell he was skipping between words, but in the end he said nothing, so I walked away.

Letting go of Alyssa took a lot more willpower than I had initially anticipated. I had to rewrite the crusty neurological center of my brain, bright against blackness. It was the unknown, the uninhabited wilderness, that scared me. Living without Alyssa reinforced my innate fear of failure. My anxiety always swallowed me whole. My anxieties were their very own majestic organ. I was utterly afraid of ending up at square one again, so I had spent years steeping in my depression, a bitter tea leaf, sunken and rotting.

But, slowly, through the work of showing up for myself, in the smallest of ways, the pink membranes of my heart were starting to understand that I could fail without *being a failure*. That was it. When you accept that you're a real life human—a squishy, mortal, and malleable being of sorts—you begin to accept your mistakes. You accept that your life cannot ever be fixed, not like a fast-tongued solvable riddle. Instead, you must become intrigued by the messiness, the nuances and the in-between bits of yourself and your life, to survive. You have to accept change. At one point, you have to surrender.

I was beginning to understand that my mother wanted for me to excel only in her own image, maybe out of protection. It was a desperate requirement for a woman who, I came to realize, was stuck in her habitual racism, taught to her by her parents. Maybe she was drawn to Baba because of her self-actualizing hatred. So she dedicated herself to a cinnamon-eyed stranger out of a misplaced, fleeting need for *change*. But white was the color she knew. And that permanence would haunt her. She loved Alyssa because she was closer to her, but also of a world she wanted to enter, a world that being Jewish also gave her—but her accidental whiteness, and generational emulation of whiteness, absolved her of. Now, I understood it: Mama was making sure we were all fitting in. She was doing it for all of us. Maybe she was trying to unlearn her racism, but in the end gave up on it. Both she and Baba were complicit. Through remembering that, I was finding compassion for her. I just wish she never stopped trying. I wish she and Baba had stood by their politics. Maybe that's why I felt okay leaving them—what did they have to teach me? I could love and respect them for all I had received, and let everything else go.

I had learned from both Kat and Tahsin the intricacies of being women—Black and Brown women—in a failing health-care system that cared little for your needs or pain threshold. How many women were dismissed, unseen and unheard. I thought of Dadima talking to me and Alyssa about her sister who died while giving birth. Complication from eclampsia. I remember being struck by the word. These days, with my baby, I knew that could easily be me. I had little money and even less support, but I would find a way. I wanted the birth to be a new beginning. To set a new standard into motion. I was optimistic, even when I wasn't.

"I'm going to put you in touch with Naima. She's a doula. She was mine with both the boys. She usually just works with Black women, but I asked for you, and she's down to take you on. You can do this, we will all help you," Kat assured me, with bluntness.

Tahsin was a similar help, conceiving a birth plan with me. I had decided to do a home birth, a forever masochist, and when I told Kat, she told me she'd get the kiddie pool ready. It felt powerful to be held by them both. The trauma of my rape was definitely present as the baby began to get bigger and bigger, and

I realized that there was no way that I could keep hiding. At least not from myself. The more I looked, the more I found myself in dark corners. I was resurrecting. The more I stared at those dark shadows of myself, the more I saw Dadi-ma, with her adoring eyes, mouthing, *Hot diggity*.

On the ground floor of the building right next to Kat's brownstone, there was an old Afro-Panamanian elder who would point at my belly every time he saw me and say, giving me the thumbs-up and harmonizing, "Baaaabycomesoon!"

Now things felt a little more stable, at the very least emotionally, and one lime-filled night, I made Kat a dinner consisting of rosemary lamb cutlets, with mint and peas on the side and buttery homemade gravy.

"Why does Claudia get to have all the fun with you?"

"*I meaaaaaannnnnn...*"

"Okay, okay, I get it. She offers you *things...*"

"And you don't know me like that, boo."

Kat had transformed over the past few months. She looked calmer, more resolved. I had been waiting to have a solo moment with her, so that she could talk to me about everything that had been coming up.

"I guess this stems from trauma, but I kept focusing on how it might end. Instead of embracing the now, the reality. Also, like, why does every 'successful' relationship have to be predicated on longevity? Sometimes it just doesn't work out, and it could still have been flourishing and vital... I just think that fear is our biggest captive, right? Like a dominating fear can stall you from the best kinda life."

I nodded voraciously, and the smell of tuberoses brushed past my nostrils like smelly clouds.

"I want to experience Claudia inside out. Not just date or fuck, but really experience her... and in order to truly do that you've gotta let go, you just *gotta* jump."

Her pupils were dilated, and she was glowing, lucid. Her teeth white against her radiating dark face, shining like pebbles under a haloed moon, she was wearing a fuschia lipstick and eyeliner, and a sixties pink and green smock. She looked beautiful. I smiled at her, knowing that I wanted to feel that sure in love, that resilient. I knew I didn't feel this kind of love for Ky, the one that Kat was describing, but that didn't scare me anymore. Seeing Kat in love made me see the possibilities of future love. Heteronormativity had defined so much of my desire... but was it even my own? Or a projection? I was suddenly open to possibilities. I pulled myself out of the situation and watched the space between Kat and I. What if I was queer? It wasn't something I had ever let myself explore, but the more I thought about it, the more it excited me. There was a tilting gold-and-violet orchid sitting between us, its flower a bloomed curl, stiff leaves buttressed up toward the light. The tiny yellow specks inside the funnel of its petals resembled a birthmark or freckles.

"Also, I want Isaac and Luc to grow up with two Black parents. I want my kids to grow up around Blackness, to be around Black love. To see Black women be strong and beautiful, and embracing. To be vulnerable and, you know, radically honest. To remind them that it's okay to be, and that they are loved. I've always wanted that, but when kids come into the picture it's more complicated, T. You want them to have the best— the best—the best—" Her voice broke. "Because this country won't give that to them, that's for damn sure."

I pulsed her hands with my fingers, wishing I had something to say. We were silent for a few minutes, both wanting to let that settle. She sighed a big, heady sigh, and we both stretched. I loved her, and I knew she loved me, too.

"I honestly don't know what the next few months are going to look like. But I want you to know, we will all figure it out together. Worse comes to worst, we'll help you find another place. You can come work at the café again if you want..."

Her words circled in my head like a prophecy. They hit me right in the bones. She had heard me. She was showing me all change didn't have to be bad, and that all no's weren't traumatic. I wanted to cry; I felt sedated, calm. Even though my belly felt like the ocean, I could feel that the baby was happy. And I was, too. I felt safe.

"I love you, Kat, and I'm here for the ride. Let's do this!"

She giggled, squeezing my hand. We were just about finished eating when she announced, "*Also*, this lamb, Taylia *Chatterjeeeeee*, was Italian-chef-kissing-fingers emoji!"

I grinned a deep grin, tears flaking near my eyes, and as she sipped her light gamay, she whispered quickly, as if to ease the mood, "Tarot?"

I nodded my head.

She shuffled languidly and pulled three cards: Ace of Cups, Ten of Swords, and the Empress. Putting on a British accent, she spoke with a slight lisp, her beautiful lips veiled: "Now what we have here is very simple, my dear Taylia. You have pulled yourself up from the deep rubble of yourself—the pain, the misery, the feeling of being attacked—cloistered in a corner by the deep workings of the universe. And you're untrusting, you've been failed by those forces that were deemed to protect you. You've been picked at, brutalized, hurt and hurt and hurt, but now you are rising, after the fleeing, *après le déluge.* The pain is releasing from the depths of you, and the subterfuge of the universe's design is finally showing you itself and its secrets. You are at the end and you are, my dearest, darling Taylia, ascending. There's just no two ways around it. You are ascending." She broke her trance.

I could see a luminous kind of light surface in front of her. The truth was there, in this suddenly bright room. And with *us.* As I looked directly into her eyes, the truth was resonating like floating dark red dots before her.

"Kat."

"Yes, Taylia."

I didn't break my gaze, but a mist was rising. Yet, for the first time, I felt unashamed.

"I was disowned by my parents. I was disowned by them because I was raped. I was raped by a family friend. Well, no, I was actually gang-raped by him and a few of his friends. And for this whole time, in the almost two years that has passed, I've tried to understand why. As if rape can be explained... But that's just it, we've—we've been socialized to wonder why when acts of violence are committed against us. *Why me? What did I do?* When in reality, I should be asking, *What happened to him for him to be so utterly fucked up?*"

I looked at her. Her eyes were lined with crimson, tears ready to trail down her cheeks.

"I'm not a victim, Kat. But I have felt like one, I have felt like one my whole life. It was a role I felt prescribed to me because I felt unworthy of being a survivor. Even way before the rape I felt like I didn't deserve to even live. That my body, my soul, was only a carrier of pain, and that I would never be good enough." I inhaled, my words broken in two by my heaving. "But I am good enough. I'm so fucking good enough."

Kat suddenly pushed her chest into my face, holding me as I thundered giant, heavy sobs into the groove of her neck and felt the yellow glowing catharsis of letting it all pass.

"Taylia, my love, my love."

I pulled away from her after a few moments, my head still down, curtained by hair. "I didn't tell you because I couldn't even say it to myself."

She pulled a string of hair behind my left ear. "You don't have to explain to me why you didn't tell me, Tay. You don't have to do that. This is bigger than that."

I looked at her and saw no judgment.

"All I can say is that you're not alone. You're not."

I sniffled, and a glistening trail of slime trickled up my nose.

"You knew the son of a bitch?"

I nodded.

"If I knew who he was"—she paused—"I'd fucking castrate him."

I smiled weakly, wanting the same end. I had felt a cold violence reach from the base of my tongue, remembering the copper taste of my split lips spilling blood. My rage felt purple.

"I watched that new documentary, *India's Daughter*."

The movie about Jyoti Singh Pandey, my sister. My sister who had been gang-raped by six male demons in India in 2012, then fucked by an iron rod that turned the inside of her body into red mush.

"I know it's too simplistic, but men are trash," I heard Kat say.

I wondered if the linoleum floor of the bus had marks from Jyoti's fingernails gouging at her freedom. I wondered if she—blinking eyes pooling with blood, as her organs, like bright red yams, failed from the rupturing of cocks and blue steel—prayed to Kali for revenge. Or if she prayed to Shiva for clemency from this unearthly brutality. I hoped those men saw her when they closed their eyes. I hoped her face lingered like a cold gray cough that starts off tight but then takes over, like a hurricane, beating faster and faster as the lungs lose air. I wanted them to suffer slowly. For little paper cuts to split their skin a million times, for them to be run over by the same blistering rickshaw wheel again and again and again.

I had no room for mercy, not for them, and definitely not for Simon. I wanted to slice him into neat little squares and let him rot in the sun so the maggots could slowly chew through his skin. If I saw Simon again, I would spit in his face, cursing him forever through the ages. I would haunt him, his dreams, his waking moments, and I would haunt him with my lips whispering, like sweet nothings, for his demise. I would make him suffer. I wanted him to die, like he killed me. But then, again, Jyoti was not here, and I was. I cried for her and all the lost women. Kat cried with me, too.

That night I dreamed of Baba, smoking a cigar, looking at me with his brown alchemist eyes, handsome and soft-spoken like

I'd never seen him before. "The greatest love is the love that's never shown, Taylia." He was saying it with an expression that was half stern, half earnest—but he felt mildly warm, he felt close. I spun his words around like cotton, fast and messy.

When we lived in India, he would take me to a grand old Imperial Chinese restaurant on a dusty street in Kolkata, carpeted in bloodred top to bottom. Waiting for my spicy wonton soup that was always too floury, I would play sudoku in an American newspaper. Baba would let me sketch the numbers in with his 0.5 mechanical pencil, his favorite width of lead, and I would hum, enumerating my advance.

Momentarily, I thought of Liza. Where was she now, after also being disowned? I thought of her brother, Vijay, and what he had done to me. I always fantasized telling her, the radical lesbian with a rapist for a brother. I wanted her to be angry with me, to feel the betrayal with me. I always hoped I'd see her for a split second in a crowd or serve her a dulcet coffee at the café. I wanted to tell her that her existence restored me. It made me believe I could choose myself, even if my family wouldn't. She made me see that I was—that my life was—worth choosing.

28.

Alyssa and I are watching *Kuch Kuch Hota Hai*. I desperately want to be Anjali, Alyssa is obsessed with Tina, and we both love Rahul. There's a moment during one of the songs when Rahul sees Anjali. There is love present in that gaze, and it's so palpable that my little heart flutters from the excitement that such a love could exist. An empyrean sort of love, reminiscent of an unconditionality that I so dearly craved.

Tum paas aaye, yun muskuraaye
Tumne na jaane kya sapne dikhaaye
...kuch kuch hota hai.

I dance to the TV, mirroring the moves of my Bollywood idols, hoping to adopt a semblance of their ineffable coolness. I glance over my shoulder, idly, and my mother watches, a little smile playing on the edges of her lips. I smile back at her. She whispers, "My little Bollywood queen," and I turn around shortly after. A few moments later I forget about this memory altogether, too absorbed by Shah Rukh Khan's good looks.

Alyssa is also glued to the TV, mimicking the way Rani uses her hand like a wave in that blue lace salwar, and me, the forever Kajol, the schlubbier of the two versions of what a girl could be, decked in a Nike headband and oversized tee. I'm about eleven; Alyssa is almost sixteen, a little more formative, her hips no longer straight but now ripe. I want to be like her, as well.

I remembered Mama watching the both of us, laughing and clapping to a rhythm that seemed cadenced to songs I know felt so foreign to her. In Kolkata, both Alyssa and I wanted kurtas, lehengas, and salwars to match our dreams of Bollywood, the most accessible (and cool) part of Indian culture. It was something that spoke to us, as outsiders who had a narrow definition of what it meant to be South Asian, but nonetheless felt it in our bones. It felt like relief to see some kind of representation, and though I know I liked being in India more than Alyssa, both of us desired the embrace in different ways. I guess what I'm trying to say is I think Mama craved it, too.

Tahsin came over with Sufjan cradled in her arms. She looked at me intensely.

"I don't know how to say this..." was how she started the conversation.

"Ah... say what?"

"I kind of maybe figured this out a while ago. But I wasn't sure..."

"Are you being intentionally evasive?"

"Taylia."

"Yes, Tahsin?"

The snake was right there, at the base of my throat.

"Ky misses you."

I had suspected right. Somebody just uttering his name sent waves of nostalgia/nausea/desire/sadness/happiness down-downdown and upupup my body. I could feel his presence and I missed him.

I looked at her, feeling fragile.

"When did you... *how* did you know?" Finally ready to open Pandora's box.

"He accidentally said your name a couple of times. At first I couldn't be sure. Taylia's an uncommon name, but this connection was too absurd. How could I meet my brother-in-law's... by accident? It seemed *too* strange, too unexpected. Then, after a while, it was obvious. I couldn't avoid the fact that perhaps, in some way, life was handing you to me and I had to figure out what to do with that. I didn't, and still don't, want to compromise our friendship, so Ky doesn't know that I know where you are... but"—she paused—"I think he should... Especially considering he doesn't know you're pregnant with what I'm assuming is his child?"

I nodded my head cumbersomely. Where to even begin.

"I figured it out, too, a while ago..." I muttered.

"You what?!"

I held on to the table in front of me, the big ball of my stomach a moon. Luc was watching *Yo Gabba Gabba!* and Isaac was playing with dominoes, making all sorts of symbols. Tahsin walked over and plonked Sufjan down next to the boys and came back to me. I watched Isaac walk over, sink down, and hand Sufjan a domino, which made me laugh. Children were so innocent, so open.

"Please, Taylia. Explain."

I didn't hesitate, knowing I'd had my time. "Well, when you mentioned Roman, I knew straightaway..."

"But... that was the first time I met you! You've known since *then*?"

I nodded my head. "I needed time, please don't be mad."

"I'm not mad!" Tahsin said with a raised voice, and both Luc and Isaac looked back. They were both *so* intuitive, so sensitive; they understood the good and bad sounds in their environment with very specific precision, enough to turn a head. "I'm not mad, but I'm confused. I'm a little annoyed, I guess, but I'm more confused. Why didn't you tell me?"

"Tahsin, there's so much... you don't know about me. It's not because I don't want to tell you, but it's because I don't know how... I don't even know how to utter everything to you."

"Just tell me..." she said, agitated.

"It's not that easy. I'm not good with questions or interrogation— not that I think you'd interrogate me... but my life has been fucked, kinda, and I don't always want to talk about it."

"But about Ky? Did he do something to you?"

There the snake was again, the ache in my throat.

"No..." I felt like I would cry. "He's great. But he's complicated. *It's complicated.*"

"I think he loves you, Tay. In his own way. I feel like I bullied that out of him."

I hadn't expected to hear that, and I suddenly felt overwhelmed with sadness. Even though it wasn't entirely appropriate to ask her more about Ky, I wanted to. What did she know? What had he said for her to think that he *loves me*?

"He chose Jade over me." I paused, choosing to articulate. I didn't even know if it was the truth, because I was beginning to question if he ever even wanted to choose me. "I don't trust people, Tahsin." I exhaled loudly, my eyes a sudden blur. "I don't trust people, and I'm so fucking tired of it. It's so exhausting to live like this." I had slumped down onto my seat like a rag doll with no spine.

"Where's Kat?" Tahsin asked, changing the subject. Perhaps too annoyed to continue the conversation, which I wouldn't blame her. At the sound of her name Luc and Isaac had congregated near my legs, holding on and leaning in.

"Mommy will be home soon, my loves..." I kissed their ears.

"I have to take a picture, they're so cute! They love you so much, Taylia. Look."

She passed me the phone and I saw the boys and me, a pietà-like figure, all plump, with these angels nursing their tiny heads on my thighs. I loved them both. I looked happy, beautiful. I did look like my mother. That made me feel warm.

I could tell Tahsin was plotting playdate ideas for Sufjan. Now he'd have more friends, older friends who might show him the way one day. She was sentimental like that; she preferred connectivity over stagnancy.

We all played dominoes and the boys showed off their toys. A little later, when they should have already been in bed, keys rustled at the front door, and the beep that indicated that it'd been opened went off. The boys looked at me, cheeky but slightly nervous, miming *shh* to Tahsin, who was now holding a sleeping Sufjan. Kat must've sensed it, because she walked right to the living room where we all sat, huddled near the games.

"Lord Almighty! What's going on here?" She smiled at the room.

"Hi, Mama," Luc, the charmer, started.

"Hi, baby, why aren't you in bed?" She was wearing her white clogs with a polka-dot jumpsuit.

"Auntie Taylia said we could play a little longer."

"I'm sorry, Kat, we were having so much fun. I—"

"I'm Tahsin." She was already up, ready to embrace Kat with a sleeping Sufjan in her arms. "I've heard so much about you, it's so nice to finally put a face to a name."

"Tahsin! Hello, how wonderful. Same here." She sat down by the boys and me, the dim light pouring onto all our faces so that we looked like paintings in the dark.

"How's Claudia?" I smiled.

"Who's Claudia?" Tahsin asked as Kat turned shy.

"She's my girlfriend..."

"Oh, wow! New?"

"I mean, it's been a while now, but it just happened so unexpectedly."

"An unexpected love? Oh, how delicious!" Tahsin hummed as I got up to make some tea for us all, grabbing a boysenberry cheesecake out of the fridge. I zoned out of the conversation, and when I came back in, this is what I heard:

"You know I actually know an Arabic word, and I actually use it a *fair* bit, Taylia will tell you." I slowed down what I was doing to watch Kat pause for effect and Tahsin's eyes alight with a tell omg. *"Khallas."*

She gasped. "Mashallah, your pronunciation is impeccable."

"Girl, I have so many Sudanese friends."

"Makes sense. Plus your name is Khadijah... Taylia once mentioned it to me."

I frowned, not understanding.

Kat explained. "Khadijah was Prophet Mohammad's first wife, technically the first Muslim as well. She was an entrepreneur, a divorcée fifteen years his senior... and she asked him, her employee, to marry her!"

Tahsin squealed. "Mashallah!"

By now, Luc and Isaac had joined Sufjan, fast asleep on Kat's legs. As I sat down, Kat slowly transitioned out of her seating, passing Luc to me and laying Isaac on the sofa behind us. All the speaking was muttered, but we were all enjoying this new modality; there was an excitement of being up when you normally weren't at a certain hour, with friends, cradled by their companionship.

"I hope this isn't too forward, but do you smoke, Tahsin?"

She smiled knowingly. "I think I smoke what you're smoking."

"That's what I like to hear!" Kat loud-whispered, grabbing her beautiful ornate weed box, which she opened only on special occasions. As Kat rolled, Tahsin filled me in.

"Kat and I were collectively agreeing about the fear of raising children in America."

I nodded, remembering what Kat had told me recently.

"The conversations that Black mothers need to have with their children... it's fucking devastating," she added. "I wonder, too, now without my son's father." Tahsin paused and looked at me, the truth all out. "Roman, who wasn't Muslim like me, would have maybe protected Sufjan from Islamophobia, but now I wonder what'll happen."

I cleared an itchy cough in my throat and took the floor, wanting all of a sudden to give Kat some sudden clarity. "Kat, Tahsin was married to Roman. As in Roman... Ky's brother."

"Wait, you knew Roman?" Tahsin gaped.

"I mean... I own a café next to his work and he was always there, almost every day."

"Wait, you made his last birthday cake!"

"Yes! That was me."

All of a sudden Tahsin launched over and embraced Kat, just the one side that was free, but she stuck her head in Kat's nook, cocooning herself.

"Thank you for that cake." She had started crying. "I always get so excited and emotional when I meet someone who also knew him. As if hearing you speak about him will bring him back."

There was a moment of silence as they sat like that, Kat gently pressing Tahsin above her right knee.

"Did Taylia tell you about my ex?"

"No, Taylia doesn't tell me anything!" She was still mad at me, and I welcomed it. Both of them deserved to be mad at me.

"Yo, you and me both." Kat laughed, having a better way of not letting it sting, knowing how sensitive I was, or maybe because we both were. "Well, Elijah left me. I don't know why— well, I do know, he just didn't want to do it anymore. He had enough of me, the kids... Or, really, once he tried to explain that *it*, meaning us, didn't feel right after the kids, and it's like, we got the kids. You wanted them! Don't back out now, ya fool. But he did. So, much like what you're doing, I've raised these two babies on my own, and I keep thinking, all these years, did he think I wanted to do it? All of this? And alone? The effing nerve! But what I'm trying to say is that even folks that knew Elijah—because we were together a long time... it was Kat and Eli, man, we were a team—and even when those people who've known him come talk to me about memories about us... I still listen, because that's the perfect time to miss him. It's the time I allot to mourn him. And maybe that's a good way for you to do it, too. To give yourself the time to remember him."

"Habibti, thank you. That's very sweet, I like that."

I watched them both give each other what they had given me and what I hoped I had given them: solace, companionship, an ear—without a moment's hesitation. I wanted them to feel nurtured in this womb we had created in Kat's living room, a pumping heart.

"I think that's good advice for you, too, Taylia." Tahsin's eyes twinkled. "To give yourself a specific space to mourn."

I closed my eyes with a smile.

My heart beat fast at the memory of her. The tethered leaves on the trees outside my window ruffled and shook, causing my emotions to rupture. Alyssa once told me that love was redundant. She told me that love couldn't withstand *everything*, because in the end, someone always breaks. "And if you break enough times you reach the point of no return." That was said to me sometime around her last days. Then, I didn't know that she believed that hurt was the only consistent factor of her life. I wish I had known. *Fuck, Lyse. I wish you had trusted me.* I had trusted her word, because I thought she knew best. But what I'm realizing now is that she didn't have answers any more than I did. She had been hurt, and she was speaking from within that pain. Maybe by Simon, maybe by life, the unexpected pregnancy.

Had Mama and Baba known? They must've seen it in the autopsy. Their darling daughter. Obliterated by an unspeakable trauma that she couldn't face, so she hurt herself instead.

Eons ago, Alyssa, bangs parted to the side, gave me a wiry smile as her delicate kitten-shaped eyes watered over lightly, innocent, but in pain. "Oh, Tay. What do you think you'll be like when you grow up?"

I didn't know. "I don't know."

Tears stained her light honey-brown complexion, but she seemed unaware, or at least wanted me to be cavalier toward her emotions. She turned to me for a second, searching for me.

"I hope I get to see who you turn into."

When I looked at myself in the mirror, at this present moment, I stood aghast by how much had truly changed. My complexion was a little more freckled, the skin around my eyes a little more unruly. I was a dark golden-brown hue that emanated the endorphins charging through me. My big, fat belly stretched out like a gift I had not yet unwrapped. How did I come here, this place of acceptance? It seemed not so much a foreign entity, but a world unknown and exciting, brimming with hope but still familiar. As if I always knew that happiness resided in the spaces between and within me, even if I hadn't believed it.

Baba had never put much emphasis on happiness, but as kids we stayed on the lake up north on our summer holidays, daydreaming about Cary Grant in *The Philadelphia Story*, three-piece suits, his hair slightly frazzled and greasy. I don't know about Alyssa, but in those moments I would daydream about the feeling of being fully white, not just half white. If I was full white, maybe I could be a movie star? Like Kate Hepburn in a white one-piece. I always admired how sassy she was. She reminded me of Alyssa. We would often sing very loudly, our song of choice being "Ol' Man River," and without a moment's hesitation we would simultaneously both follow up with *"Oh my darling, oh my darling / Oh my darling, Clementine...*" We must have heard the songs back-to-back on a cassette tape that Baba would play during bedtime, the melodies seared into our brains, rolling into one another like a natural symphony. Those days in summer were of happiness. Or as close to it as I had ever gotten.

One night I remember hearing sounds that my little body found exhilarating. At a young age, passion, even sexual passion, is coveted. It's seductive because it appeals to our human senses. It's not erotic, it's life.

I lurked by the ajar door, standing by the cavern of my interest. Inside, my parents were moving in motions unfamiliar to me, but they seemed content, sated. The movements were fast and concentrated, and the sighs rolling off the tops of their clavicles were filled with earnest, palpable desire. My mother ran her fingers across my father's back, tracing the loose hairs that grew sporadically. Navigating with her index, finally she placed her bare palm in the center of his sweaty middle region. They were happy, in love.

Years later, Simon and his parents joined us in the Catskills for a summer. He had started dealing cocaine and MDMA (then, later, heroin), claiming he had a "medical background" as a way to coax all his friends to take it. "I heard that you're trying to write songs. Oh, it's taking a while? Listen, I don't know if you're interested, but I have this thing that's really good for artistic creativity. Oh yeah, I heard Mallarmé used to take it all the time..." I could tell Alyssa and Simon were getting close, but it always seemed so transient, like neither of them had decided on the other.

As a kid I had learned that the samurai who had forsaken their duties were asked to perform a voluntary suicide known as seppuku. It was a ritual that involved slicing a tantō (a small knife) into your lower abdomen and disemboweling yourself from left to right. It was a part of the Bushido honor code, and the samurai volunteered to die like this to ensure that their deaths were noble. I was forever enchanted by this idea, by a people consumed by so much integrity that they were compelled to voluntarily kill themselves. For the samurai, suicide absolved your sins.

Tahsin told me Muslims have a word, *nafs*, to identify the lower self, the unrefined self, the ego. They say that it is a little black spot in the heart that can be removed through the processes of spiritual development, refinement, and mastery of yourself. I didn't know what mastery of self referred to. But whatever I had done, I felt better. I was transforming, and since it began, Alyssa no longer visited me.

Something had shifted as well. In her absence—or maybe more accurately in the face of *my truth*—I realized I didn't need to be like Alyssa to be beautiful. I could be myself and everything I represented. I think this was partially why Dadi-ma protected me. She understood what her culture was like, what the world was like, how it upheld beauty like Alyssa's. The more white adjacent you were, the more you usually were revered. I'm not sure if my parents knew that; I don't know if either of them, frankly, had the sophistication. It took reflection to come to this place of understanding. A reflection I myself had only quite recently acquired. But I knew I was beautiful, with a face like Dadi-ma's, with skin dark and easily browned, with stretch marks, cellulite, and a juicy, fat belly. I was plump like ripe fruit; I was so intensely round like a delicious, cream-filled raspberry doughnut.

Going lingerie shopping with Tahsin, who had (maybe) been plotting a romance with Mateo (I didn't ask), I found myself facing the full-length mirror of a Journelle changing room. There was a cacophony of sounds outside the changing room: the buzzing of insects, that specific *cha-ching* sound from Venmo payments, Tame Impala's "The Less I Know the Better." I raised my dress. I was wearing a long-sleeved psychedelic printed smock that lay tight around my belly, and as I slid it off, slinkily, I looked at myself in the mirror. I had recently purchased underwear from Uniqlo, and the cotton stuck to my body like tiny claws, like the teeth of a Venus flytrap. My skin was tan, so caramel I wanted to lick it. I looked beautiful; better yet, I felt it. My

291

breasts with strong, bold areolas, I looked at my body and it felt like mine.

29.

Tahsin looked at me resolutely. I hadn't yet seen this face of hers, almost like a half-clownish scowl. I looked petulant, goading her. She bit her lip and began. "You know, the only time Roman and I used to fight was when we talked about money." She seemed hesitant, like she was sparing her words. "I think he didn't quite understand what it meant to be an immigrant and not come from a rich family... and how those two things really made my life extremely hard. Class is a deep issue for us. I still pay my parents' bills with my salary job. The sad reality is Roman's life insurance will help me, but I've spent so much of my life poor that I'm also terrified of everything being taken from me again. I mean, I had to lose my husband and best friend to feel monetarily stable. So I'm naturally scared for Sufjan, for his future. I live in that fear, always."

We were sitting on the grass at Fort Greene Park. My belly, at this point, was so big and robust that I had to scoop my waistband down just so I could sit comfortably on a picnic blanket. The boys were squirming out in front of us, the three of them on a mission for bugs, while Tahsin and I sat at home base, eating deli-style beef salami, fresh pesto on a focaccia, and Castelvetrano olives. As she was talking, she took big chunks out of the olives, her two front teeth against the pit, which she stored gracefully in her hand.

"So why did you fight?"

"Because"—she sounded lyrical—"he's rich. Ky and them, they're rich."

I felt my cheeks go red, maybe at the sound of his name, maybe at the rich part.

"And there's this... I don't know, maybe lack? Not sure if that's the right word, but I'll say lack, I guess, of fully understanding the scope of class."

I wondered why she was telling me this, but as soon as I thought this, I let my anxiety and insecurity go to the side.

"And when you're raised with money, it skews your perspective of what's possible and what kind of life you can have access to..."

"But I thought..."

She preempted me: "Yes, Ky and Roman grew up poor for a few years, but by their teens their parents had money, several property investments—you name it. So, for most of their lives, despite being two little Brown boys in New York, they still had nice things. And *that*, Taylia, is everything."

I looked at her, nibbling some of my beef salami. "My parents are rich."

"I can tell," she said, with no hint of sarcasm.

I blushed and looked toward the boys, who were poking at something in the grass, absolutely astounded in disgust and awe.

"How can you tell?" I asked finally.

"Your naïveté"—she paused—"and maybe even your secrecy."

I wanted to be less scared of saying things. I wanted to say what was on my mind and not be scared to fuck up or sound unintelligent. "I mean, for sure, class is real. I think that used to really eat Alyssa up, toward the end especially. Maybe it was some kind of ancestral pain where she felt like she couldn't live her life because of the poverty and pain of our lineage. So she was eaten up by it, by the old trauma that didn't want her to be happy." I hadn't yet articulated that to anyone.

"Uff, that's so deep." She licked some pesto off her finger. "Having a baby should make you think of all these things realistically. That's why I'm bringing any of this up, anyway."

"What'd you mean?"

"Are you going to get back with Ky?"

It hit me like a rock. "I don't know. Honestly."

"Okay, what I will say is: Ky is fine. I love him. He's my brother. Roman and I were together for seven years, so I'm sure you can understand I got to know Ky so well... This is all to say, he's no good as a partner. Y'allah." She smiled, exaggerating it with her eyes. "He's a dummy."

I burst out laughing, because I guess I had come to the same conclusion as well.

"This fake deep writerly shit. You know he's paid almost two hundred thousand a year to write the most basic, benign brand strategy?"

She shook her head and turned to look at the boys, who were now playing in a random pit of sand. I loved watching them roam free.

"Anyway, Taylia, the more I get to know you, the more I love this enchanting, brave person you are. You don't need him. Except maybe for his money."

We sat for a long time in the sun and heat.

"I'm thinking of all the women, Taylia. All the women that have been through what you've been through, habibti. This world is so unjust."

I had recently told her about my rape. I was moved that the story affected her.

We sat in that, as I thought of Dadi-ma and Alyssa, my two dead companions, again.

I broke the silence. "Tahs?"

"Hmm?" she asked, sniffling.

"So you think no more Ky?"

She looked at me hard, all our truths finally present. "He got you pregnant while still with Jade. Honestly? Fuck him."

I grinned. Maybe I had needed to hear this.

"Jade is definitely standoffish, but I think it's just anxiety."

"She's... so austere."

"Aha! *Austere* is the word..."

"She's always felt so rigid." Though, as I said, I knew I was being unfair. I knew I didn't like her because she didn't like me... and

I had fucked her boyfriend (many times) and now was pregnant with his child. So she had a point. Besides, he was still with Jade and had never tried to come and find me, but none of this really bothered me that much. I guess that's how I knew it was really over. He had given me this baby; maybe that's all our karmic responsibility was to each other. Like Kat had recently said, relationships didn't need to last for them to be important.

"Yeah, well, she's not. She's supercool, smart, talented. She's made Ky so much more interesting, and it's all her doing. Ky used to be a fuckboy..."

We looked at each other and laughed.

"Habibti, you don't need him. He doesn't deserve you! He doesn't deserve Jade, either, but that's her journey. But after all you've been through... nurture that heart of yours and fiercely love this baby. Kat, Claudia, and I, we got you." She reached over and squeezed my hand. "Ask him for child support, though." Her eyes glittered. "Take as much money from him as you possibly can."

We stared at each other for an eternity and then simply smiled.

After the park, Tahsin came over for dinner. Claudia was already there, I peeped, reading James Baldwin's *Blues for Mister Charlie*. She was wearing a blue checkered shirt, buttoned all the way up. When we came home she put the book down and started talking to Tahsin, who I could tell was also developing a quick crush. It was something about Claudia's aura. She was more reserved than Kat, with dark lips and a piercing onyx stare. She held gravity. Where Kat's energy was light, Claudia's was dark. Neither was stagnant, both were amorphous, mercurial. I had learned how to handle Kat in her bad moods, vice versa—and maybe our reliance on each other in that sense had led to a different kind of intimacy, a bond that felt like family. But Claudia was more mysterious, opaque to me. It was hot.

I took the boys upstairs to clean them off before Kat got there, and by the time I brought them down, both in their dinosaur one-

295

sies, Claudia told me she'd ordered jerk from the Islands, Kat's favorite take-out place. By the time Kat got home, a bottle of chilled Austrian Grüner Veltliner sat alongside copious amounts of jerk chicken, rice and peas, coconut shrimp, plantains and greens. That night we ate like kings.

On the way to bed, panting started above me, a few octaves higher, like an orchestra of groans. The soft moans wafted as I paused, haunted. My relationship to my body, to sex, was evolving. I got into bed, resolved. There, in that moment, I knew one day I would find what I was looking for romantically.

The thing is, I was grieving while I was preparing to have this baby alone. When I stepped out on Ky, I was clearly over his bullshit, but a small part of me had imagined maybe we would be together. But through time, it felt reminiscent of my parents' mediocre love. I had no time for that anymore, either—to be swayed with "maybes" and "I love you, buts..." I wanted devotion, dedication. I wanted a pulsing, empowered love.

I was rarely in the Lower East Side anymore, but the temperature was cool, and I missed my walks along the East River, over the bridge up to the Domino Sugar factory and past the big white arches of the Williamsburg Savings Bank. I felt weightless. The moon had passed over me, its orbit in Cancer, where it was home, soft and unalloyed. The sidewalks smelled of rain after it passed, and I walked alongside Kat and Claudia, out on an adventure for breakfast. They looked happy in the way companions do, Kat earlier resting her feet on Claudia's thick brown thighs as we drank on a bench outside the Juice Press. The latter's fingertips rhythmically rubbed at the cursed pain from Kat's bunions that were forming from the stress of being on her feet all the time. Weirdly, I was ready to get back to that life. I missed the flow of the café, of working alongside Kat.

We slowly began to walk, directionless, like three women who were free.

"Look at the light," Claudia exclaimed, her voice deep.

With smiles we all cooed, looking at the light shimmer across the city. It looked like magic.

"What if light is just God?" Claudia whispered.

One by one, we nodded our heads, a chorus witnessing majesty. I still wasn't sure what God was, but I was curious to know. Maybe my baby would bring me back to something.

I don't know how I sensed it, this disruption. She slid toward me, and as I smelled her, like a coriander glow, the back of my neck, where my hair met my skin, blazed. I hadn't seen her since Alyssa's funeral, but here she was, dressed in ivory linen, her shoes the color of blue porcelain.

"Taylia," she said in a whisper, and I heard my mother in the cadence.

"Zeina," I said confidently, because I was finally a woman who could meet another woman's gaze.

We stood there, four women, surrounded by secrets, and yet nothing felt cryptic, only open. I looked at her wide eyes and heard her croon an "OMG"; she came to me like I was an altar and embraced me, curling around my spine like a lover. She started crying, and I cried, too. Claudia and Kat held us. We all stood, a flood of grief.

"You're here," she kept saying, like a prayer.

As we circled each other, I felt the baby speak to me, and everything soon felt out of focus. It felt like eons, but I heard Kat say it first, then Zeina, as the water loosened inside of me, trickling to the cement beneath me.

Kat shouted at the two of them, "We need to get her back home now!"

I knew where the kiddie pool was, and Naima was on speed dial. I had been doing the pelvic floor exercises with Tahsin and going to doctor's examinations in tandem with biweekly fertility acupuncture visits in Park Slope. I felt prepared and even had the boys' hand-me-downs—crib, toys, bibs—everything I needed I had access to. I was safe, and so was this baby.

Nothing can shake us; we are strong. That mantra was my catharsis; my pain was being channeled toward the anger I felt in the past and the anger I felt now. I had moved past the cruelty of my rape. I heaved. Here I was in an inextricable amount of pain, but I felt relatively calm. I was present, I was focused. I was not hopeless, I was not lost. I pushed and kept pushing as Naima talked me through it. I looked at Kat and I remembered why I was there. I wanted this baby. More than anything, I wanted this baby.

I heard singing.

Bleeding steadily, the ribbon of red shot through me like puss oozing out of a sore. I clutched at the waves of bodies around me: Zeina, Kat, Claudia, and dear Tahsin, who had come to witness the birth. She must've gotten the signal. Finally, I could let go and there were loved ones who would catch me. I embraced the pain within this strange holiness of birth, with the mothers who stood beside me. The baby screamed to life, echoing across the ecosystem and my galaxy. I felt the towel wrap around me and I faltered, feeling fear at my lips, at my throat—what was I doing? Then, I felt the breath: a stillness perforated the space and I was frozen in suspension, full with love. Slowly, like a pull from a string, the connection was made. Forever tethered by our hands, our faces, our hearts that beat to the same drum, and our same veins of red, I saw my baby.

I didn't cry. I just got it. I could sense Dadi-ma there, her spirit looking at me. *Tumi bhalo aso, tumi bhalo aso. You are good, you are good.* She would often repeat it, as she sainted me with incense smoke from her morning pooja. I always thought she meant, with my broken translations from Baba, that I was a good kid, which I needed to hear then. But now I understood she was saying, *Your life is good.*

For a moment, I couldn't hear my baby.

"Where's my baby?" I screamed. I screamed for the ages, I screamed for my rights, I screamed for the women before me and after me who would bear this beauty of life. For the women and the torture faced by all of us, for our bodies that had been beaten but our hearts that were still strong. Naima slid her into my arms, and as I looked down I knew she was a fighter, with every breath she was a fighter. I bent my head and breathed in the fresh new musty scent of her; she smelled like me.

When I look up the name Taylia, I find no answers. The origin is unknown, potentially Hebrew, as Mama claims—but the name itself is a mystery. I embrace this, this random reality of my name, the rotation of stars sinking into me; I am undefinable. The name, like a loose broken T-shirt feels like it finally fits, it's a punchline that's landed. It is me, I am Taylia. I have felt unworthy of my name, of my being, for too long—but it's mine now, see. My pupils are dilated, everything is clear with a punchy aplomb, I see diamonds.

It's my name, and by God, I'm never giving it up.

You know, when I look at the moon, it's licked and jagged edges like a stone fruit orbiting the seas, I recognize Alyssa's faint curves, I see Dadi-ma in her shadha saree. They are the moon, its kinetic energy fuels me, reminding me of its quaint mercury. I am not alone, I have never been, I was always guided by the moon. Its dull circumference calms my anxiety. I am healing. For myself, for my child. I'm ending the cycle, I am becoming the moon, too.

In my mind, I walk up the stairs that I had hovered over for so many years, without realizing its life blood, its significance. In that moment, on the top-most stair, looking beyond the elegant trees, towards the full haloed moon, I sink into my thoughts, distracting my fear; will it rain today? My eyes scan the foliage, again, drawn in by the silence I breathe in twilight. I feel satiated, I feel poised, self possessed. Right now, there's no refuge in my fear, I breathe in. I knock on the door, a stranger amidst so much familiarity. She opens it briskly, with such ease. Her coloring is different, more sedated in age, but her crimson hair is flying with the wind, her skin is soft and milky, the same, *Mama*. My heart rises. I want to scream, but there is an absence of saliva in my mouth so I smile a dry throated line and she smiles back at me, her eyes watering with a slivered sacredness.

She looks down onto the bundle in my arms, her small body cocooned, Dadi-ma's chain glinting on her tiny neck. Mama fingers the necklace quietly, enraptured by her fluttering red veined eyes. "What's her name?" her voice croaks. I don't say anything, I can't say anything. She's like the sun, she's like the moon, my faulty moon. I named my child something with teeth, and my mother understands this. She ushers me in, one hand on the small of my warm back, the other clutching my weary forearm where my young beauty sleeps, rests, my Alyssa, I've resurrected her. Beethoven's "Emperor" Concerto plays from Baba's study, unbelieving of this bliss my lips begin to tremble. Wrapped by my mother's embrace, frozen in the music, I hear her say: "Your father has been waiting for you…" I nod with a full lake of tears in my eyes, gushing, sublime. *I forgive myself, because I've forgiven you, too.*

"I've been waiting for you," she says. "I've been waiting for you to come home."

I opened my eyes, now in my room at Kat's, resting with my Alyssa. A few moments later, as I was still half lucid, Zeina walked in, sitting on the side of the bed. She brushed Alyssa's cheeks, cooing at her pinkness, and held my hand, pulsing the inner web, exactly where I would often pulse Kat's hand. She said the words quickly, spilling them out like gold stars.

"I'm proud of you mama."

I smiled back at first. Then I began to cry, to sputter, spit came out like a trail. It felt surreal, but important for this moment. I wanted to say thank you, but I just held her hand.

You see me, I thought. At last, you see me.

Acknowledgments

I owe this book to three people.

Firstly, Alexandra Ragheb.

I am absolutely in awe of you. You saw me, and carved me out. Thank you for investing in me, for telling me your truths, and trusting me. I love your Aquarian mind, dude. Here's to expansion, to the truth, to justice, to the takeover. Thank you for walking alongside me. Thank you for being a fire starter.

Oliva Taylor Smith

Thank you for respecting my mind, story and process from the very beginning. I cannot tell you what it meant to me for you to believe in this book that, I know, needed so much work. You've made me understand what I should expect from an editor. Your patience and resilience to help me with this story has moved me, I have so much gratitude for you, Olivia.

Tanaïs

Firstly, you should know I'm crying writing this. To my queer Bangla soul-sister... I'm so lucky to witness your brilliance, your consistency, and your power. You are a genius. Thank you for making this book better. Thank you for asking me to try harder, gently. You are infused in this story, and I am honored that we get to reflect each other. Thank you for helping me create a reference, and for being one, too. You are everything.

*

I wrote this book over eighteen years. I was twelve when I started it, and I've turned thirty the year it comes out. I can't tell you how much this feels like I'm ending a cycle, an old self. It is a spiritual death.

I am so grateful for all the countless people that read this over the years... from my eighth grade English teacher who read the first two chapters to my old friend in Sydney, Daniel Reynolds. What up! Thank you to my most recent readers in the last couple of years: Zeba Blay, David Ehrlich, Prinita Thevarajah, Lubna Hindi and Megan Williams. Y'all are some of my best friends, but also—I'm immensely grateful for your perspectives.

Thank you to Hanif, Tanaïs and Aria—and all my brilliant peers. To Monika and Eloisa, for your faith and consideration. To Unnamed Press and Mark Gottlieb.

Thank you to my father and my sister for being keepers of our familial pain. For being a sounding board, even when it wasn't easy. Thank you for being a witness to this story, thank you for trying so hard to accept me as I am. I see you trying, and I am filled with immense love. This story, in so many ways, is about all of us.

Thank you to all my closest friends and comrades who carried me through this dark as fuck life I've had. You know who you are. A special shout out to Mo Dafa and Hawa Arsala.

*

I wanted to write something about resilience. Not a lot of people believed in this book, so I owe my resilience to myself. To anybody writing a story they are being told is not sellable, keep going. Write for a purpose. Write for justice. Write to understand yourself. Write to heal. Write, and I can't exaggerate this enough, for the future. Write for the world you want.

Lastly, this book is for survivors. I believe in a world where we forgive ourselves. I believe in a world where we thrive. Thank you for surviving. You can heal. Let the pain guide you.

Onwards to global revolution, the end of patriarchy, capitalism and white inferiority. Onwards to true abolition and Black liberation. Ameen.